By the time Gracelyn had the croup tent over the crib and the steam misting the air, Emmy was burning hot. Gracelyn took her temperature as gently as she could. "Oh, my God!" she said as she traced the silver line. Emmy had never had a temperature this high. Gracelyn had to get her to the hospital in Brandon!

The soft rain had turned to sleet and before she was two miles down the Plum Creek road, it was snowing—thick wet gobs that clung to the windshield wiper. The blizzard was thickening. The Subaru was struggling through a drift when Emmy's body tightened. Gracelyn stopped the car and took the baby in her arms. Emmy's fists knotted tight and her arms began rhythmic jerking. Gracelyn felt as if the blizzard had entered her mind. When the convulsion eased, Emmy lay limp and Gracelyn was wrung out. She put the baby back on the seat and tried to push the Subaru forward. It hit the drift like a battering ram and broke through, almost running into the headlights of the vehicle on the other side.

It was Maggie's truck. Shutting off the car, Gracelyn pulled Emmy into her arms. Staggering through the snow, she went to the passenger side of her neighbor's truck.

"Josh, Maggie. We've got to get Emmy to the hospital!"

BITTER-SWEET COUNTRY

Elaine Long

ST. MARTIN'S PAPERBACKS

BITTERSWEET COUNTRY

Copyright © 1991 by Elaine Long.

Cover illustration by Charlie Gehm.

Library of Congress Catalog Card Number: 90-27507

ISBN: 0-312-92916-1

Printed in the United States of America

St. Martin's Press hardcover edition/September 1991
St. Martin's Paperbacks edition/April 1993

10 9 8 7 6 5 4 3 2 1

For Evelyn Mullenax—my first and best teacher

For Hilda Ann and Leland Brimmer

For Westy Melby

With special thanks to: Lindsay Calhoun, Cathy Conner, Mary DeLancy, Joyce Gellhorn, Susan Hellie, Pat Maslowski, Ann Nagda, and Marge Warsavage.

And with love for Arthur, from whom I stole the jokes.

Chapter One

SOMEONE had lodged a jack-o-lantern in a tree branch outside the second-floor window of the dormitory. Gracelyn Heath pulled the curtains wide and turned for her sketch book and colored charcoal pencils. Scooting the books and papers from her desk, she climbed on top for a better view of the tree, rested her feet on the radiator, and leaned the sketch book against her knees.

The early morning sun shone behind the jack-o-lantern. The triangular eyes and nose and the gap-toothed smile were dark, and the face was a dusky orange, but the rounded cap of the pumpkin had a halo of reddish light.

Sketching quickly, Gracelyn managed to suggest the shimmering light and cool shadow before the sun rose higher and the leaves around the pumpkin resumed the rusty color of late autumn and the jack-o-lantern lost its halo. She glanced up at the sky above the tree, but the Colorado blue called for a richer medium than colored charcoal.

She looked at her watch. Swinging around and off the desk, she slipped out of her nightgown and pulled on a pair of jeans and a sweater. She gave a yank to the bedclothes, picked up her sketch book, pencils, purse and a backpack full of books and hurried downstairs to the dining room.

She chose a vacant table for four and set her sketch book next to her tray. Nibbling her toast, she studied the sketch of the jack-o-lantern, adding touches to it from time to time.

"May we sit here?"

Gracelyn looked up. Three freshman girls stood next to the table. Surprised, she glanced around. There were other vacant tables. Why had they chosen to join *her*? They lived on her floor, but she knew them only slightly. The three of them, Felicia, Tara, and Julie, had their own social circle. Because she was a sophomore, Gracelyn had had first chance at one of the few single rooms in the dorm, and peaceful in her single as she had seldom been anywhere else, she was grateful not to be required to join in dormitory activities.

"That's nice," Felicia said, indicating the sketch.

"Thanks," Gracelyn said, and moving her backpack from the chair and her sketch book and pencils from the table, she made room for the three of them to join her.

The girls exchanged quick glances with each other as they made small talk with Gracelyn. Finally, Tara said to her, "Do you have morning classes?" and Julie said, "How about cutting them?"

"Yes," Gracelyn said, "I have two business classes and an art class." Turning to Julie, she added, "I might cut the business classes, but not my eleven o'clock art class." She thought of Dr. Carlson and his crisp, loaded lectures that made her feel alive—expanded—free. It was the only art class she had. She hadn't dared to make any other change in the schedule her father had worked out. She looked at the girls. "Why do you ask?"

"Would you be willing to give us a ride to Dixon?" Felicia said. "They've got a big sale on Halloween costumes at the new mall."

"Where's Mindy?" Even though Gracelyn didn't know them well, she was aware that the three of them usually rode around in a little red Honda driven by another freshman, a diminutive brunette named Arminda. She'd heard Arminda say that her mother was from Georgia, and Arminda had just a whispery husk of Southern accent. Her accent and her perfect little body and the way she opened her eyes when she talked to a male kept the guys on the brother-floor hovering. Tara and Julie and Felicia picked up Mindy's leftovers.

"Mindy's been acting weird," Tara said. "She always wants to go off by herself."

"We think she's got something going that she's not telling us," Felicia said.

"How about it?" Tara said. "If we leave now, you'll be back for your eleven o'clock." Dixon was twenty miles from Marlin Springs on the highway toward Denver. It was a pretty drive. Gracelyn shrugged. Why not? It was too gorgeous a day to sit through business classes.

The girls were friendly, including her in their conversation as she drove and later as they walked down the mall. The orange crepe-paper streamers twisting overhead turned a fiery color as the morning sun slanted through the skylight. Gracelyn was caught up in the surge of lighthearted people who tried on masks and witches' hats. She fished a pencil and sketch pad out of her purse and dropped behind to do gesture drawings.

Dr. Carlson had assigned a hundred sketches. She wished they could all be free-flowing like the gesture drawings, but he had also assigned buildings and other square things. Drawing square things made her feel suffocated. Still, Dr. Carlson talked a lot about artistic discipline, and she respected the old man and was trying to please him. She sketched the angles of a corner shop before she caught up with the other girls.

They left the mall laughing. All three freshmen had bought ridiculous costumes for the dorm party.

"Hey," Felicia said as she waited for Gracelyn to unlock the car. "Isn't that Mindy?"

They looked across the street. Mindy's Honda was parked in front of the Lazy-J Motel, and coming out of the door of the middle unit were Mindy and a man.

"Well," Tara said, "she's a long way from the brother floor."

"And he ain't no brother," Felicia said.

"Still, he's a hunk," Tara said.

Julie said, "Hunk, yeah, but he's old enough to be her father."

Gracelyn said nothing at all. She just clenched her car keys in her hand until she could feel them cutting grooves. The man coming out of the motel with his hand on Mindy's waist—the handsome hunk of a man—was *her* father.

Chapter Two

THE four of them watched as the man bent and kissed Arminda on the cheek, then got into the BMW parked nearby and pulled out onto the highway, turning south toward Denver.

As Mindy unlocked her car, Julie said, "Let's get a ride home with her and find out what's going on."

Felicia looked at Gracelyn. "Do you mind?"

Gracelyn shook her head and bent to unlock her own car door, glad for her long hair as it swung forward to shield her face, anxious to get away without having to speak.

She drove blindly for miles. She passed the turn-off to the university and swung onto old Highway 31 north of Marlin Springs, increasing her speed as she hit the straight empty road. But this time speeding didn't help.

She took her hands from the steering wheel and closed her eyes. For one moment, she thought of letting the car go where it would—anywhere, any way, to stop the picture in her mind, to stop the pain.

When she opened her eyes, she snatched her foot from the accelerator. But by the time she slammed the brake pedal down, she had already hit the dog.

The sound, my God, the sound of it. She heard the impact, heard the dog cry out even as she fought the car. It skidded toward the barrow pit and then in response to her wild turn of the wheel leaped across the highway and nosed into the bushes just off the shoulder on the southbound lane. Gracelyn grabbed for the seat belt catch, rolled out of the car, and ran toward the dog, a German shepherd.

He wouldn't let her help him. When she touched him, he growled. For ten minutes, no matter how softly she approached, nor how slowly she reached to him, he bared his teeth and snarled.

The dog lay on the gravel shoulder of the northbound lane of Colorado 31. He had run out from a clump of trees at a roadside rest stop. The blood from his mangled leg darkened the tan hair and made it ruddy. His eyes had a greasy shine. If he didn't let her do something for him soon, he was going to die.

"Oh, God, dog, I'm sorry." There was no one around to help. On a weekday afternoon, the old highway toward Cheyenne was empty. No cars were parked at the rest stop—abandoned years ago when the interstate bypassed Marlin Springs.

She moved her hand toward the dog again, but he snapped at her. Drawing deep, racking breaths, she stumbled away toward her car, pulled the blanket from the back seat, opened the hatchback, and returned to the dog.

She threw the blanket over him and before he could react, she stepped forward and rolled it around him. Half carrying, half dragging, she moved the dog toward the car. He must have weighed at least eighty pounds, and he growled and twisted inside the blanket. Despite her long arms and strong hands, he almost slipped out of the bloody bundle as she hoisted him into the back of the Subaru. As she struggled with the creature, a useless thought crossed her mind: It would have been easier to get him into the van.

She held him down with one hand and pulled the belt out of the loops on her jeans with the other. Bunching one end of the blanket, she bound it with the belt. She wound a tire chain around the other end. Though the dog still snarled, his struggles were getting weaker. She had to get him to a vet. "Thank God," she whispered as the car started. She hadn't been sure that she could even get it out of the bushes.

There was a veterinary hospital somewhere on the north side of Marlin Springs. She had zoomed past it several times. She stopped at a phone booth and looked up the address. By the time she pulled into the parking lot of the hospital and opened the hatchback, the dog had stopped struggling. She lifted him and staggered toward the door just as a pickup pulled alongside her car.

A man jumped out. "Let me help," he said, reaching for one end of the bundle. Gracelyn freed one hand to open the door. They went right through the office, the man issuing sharp commands to the girl behind the desk, who rose and followed them, answering,

"Okay, Dr. MacNair."

The doctor and Gracelyn lifted the dog onto the steel table in a treatment room. The dog struggled weakly. "Take it easy, fellow," the doctor said. "We're going to fix you up." Tears rolled down Gracelyn's cheeks as the doctor opened the blanket.

"You'd better wait outside," he said.

For the first time, Gracelyn glanced up at the man. The veterinarian was tall, at least six feet four . . . a good six inches taller than she. And lean. The skin stretched taut as canvas across the rawboned frame. Above the blue eyes and the blond brows was a curly thatch of rust-colored hair.

"You'd better wait outside," the man said again more firmly, but then as he began to waver in front of Gracelyn's eyes—the red hair blurring, the blue eyes multiplying, he said, "Whoa there," and, stepping forward, he put his arms around Gracelyn. "Don't you faint on me, girl." She heard the burr in his voice as he held her close to him for a moment.

"Get that dog ready for surgery," he said over his shoulder to the other girl, moving Gracelyn from the treatment room as he spoke and toward the drinking fountain in the hall. The splash of cold water cleared her vision. Dr. MacNair steered her toward a chair. "You wait here," he said.

She waited, hunching miserably in the chair, numb with shock, thinking first of her father, and then of the dog. An hour crept by and then another, and her head began to ache. From time to time other people entered with animals, but none were as badly hurt as the German shepherd. She swallowed a sudden rise of bitter-tasting bile and got up to drink from the fountain. What was happening to the dog? With a clarity that seemed to be her personal curse, she could see every detail of the injured creature in her mind: the leg twisted at an unnatural angle, the bone ends splintering like a worn-out brush, the blood-wet fur in sticky spikes, the wound lumpy with gravel. And along with the pictures in her mind, there was the sound . . . the thwack of the bumper against the dog and the dog's cry. She knew just how the dog felt. Seeing her father with Arminda had been like a physical blow. God, she hoped Mindy hadn't told the others his name. It was hard enough to know about this by herself. It would be unbearable to face everyone in the dormitory.

Finally, Dr. MacNair's assistant stuck her head into the waiting room. "The doctor wants to talk to you. He'll be out in a minute or two."

"Okay," Gracelyn said, her stomach tensing. She folded her arms around herself and rocked forward, staring at the tile, dreading what the doctor would say. *Please, don't let him say that I killed that poor dog.*

"Miss—"

Gracelyn looked up. The redheaded veterinarian was standing in front of her. "Your dog is going to live."

Gracelyn stood with relief. "Oh, I'm glad. But he's not my dog. I'm the one who hit him. I need to find the owner."

The doctor frowned. "He has a collar and a rabies tag, but no address. It will take awhile to find the owner. I'll have to run a check on the tag number."

"Is the dog really all right?"

The veterinarian flushed, his fair skin showing distress that wasn't evident in his crisp reply. "He's going to live, but I had to amputate his left front leg."

"Oh." Gracelyn felt the blow in the pit of her stomach, and she began to cry. It was too much. The poor creature would have to suffer the rest of his life because of her. The tears rolled from her eyes as she tried to hold back her sobs, but she could not stop, and soon she was crying hysterically.

The doctor patted her on the shoulder, and finally as she continued to wail, he pulled her toward the water fountain. He splashed water on her again with more force than seemed quite necessary. Gracelyn was so startled, she stopped crying.

The redhead grinned at her and said, "If you won't cry any more or try to faint, you can come along with me and have dinner."

Chapter Three

GRACELYN looked at her watch. Good Lord. It was six o'clock. She had cut her afternoon class. She hadn't even eaten lunch. She looked down at her clothes. Her sweater and jeans were stained with dirt and dried blood. "I suppose I should eat," she said, "but I'm a mess."

The veterinarian said, "You can borrow one of our smocks."

"My mother would be horrified." What a stupid reply. Besides, all those things that mattered to her mother wouldn't seem so important any more if she knew about Arminda. Gracelyn felt dizzy for a moment thinking of her mother and father.

The veterinarian said, "Your mother's not here." He leaned his tall frame over the front counter and pulled a blue smock from the shelf behind it. "And I won't tell her."

Gracelyn took the smock. "Thank you, Dr. MacNair."

"Alexander. Alex to my friends."

"I'm Gracelyn Heath."

When they were seated in a small café down the street from the veterinary clinic, Gracelyn felt nervous. Dinner table conversation was not her sharpest skill at the best of times and right now she could hardly think for hearing Tara's voice in her mind: *He's a hunk. He's a hunk.* Gracelyn spoke to stop the words.

"How long have you owned the clinic?"

"I don't own it. I manage it. The other two vets own it."

She was embarrassed. Now what should she say?

Before she could think of anything, the doctor added cheerfully, "And I don't want to own it. I'm saving my money to buy a sheep ranch." He dug into a mound of mashed potatoes and gravy.

"A sheep ranch?"

"Yep."

Good Lord, how was she going to keep this conversation going if he answered in monosyllables?

"Do you have to be a veterinarian to run a sheep ranch?"

He stopped eating and looked at her for a long moment. "I had to be a veterinarian to please my grandfather." His face flushed as it had when he'd told her about the dog's leg. Was he upset by her question or just nervous as she was?

Gracelyn poked at her salad with a fork. The conversation was awkward, but thinking of her own family, she had to ask Dr. MacNair another question. "*Is* he pleased?"

"He's dead."

"Oh, I'm sorry."

The doctor's face had tensed. Gracelyn wanted to say something to ease the tight set of his mouth but she didn't know whether to drop the subject or to continue. At length she said, "Do you want to tell me about him?"

"He died two years ago, the year I finished vet school. I found out then he had mortgaged his ranch to pay my school bills. The ranch was sold."

"Can you get it back?"

"I doubt it. I'll have to start with something small, buy out some old rancher who's tired of long winters and will sell for a small down payment."

She liked his face. He didn't have the smooth good looks of her father—Tara would never call *him* a hunk—but there was strength in the firm jaw, and his eyes were kind. She thought of the gentle way he had treated the dog, and remembered the brief moment his arms had been around her. And she remembered the last hug she had given her father. God, she had to talk or go crazy.

"Did you visit your grandfather's ranch a lot when you were growing up?"

"I lived there from the time I was six years old."

"How old are you now?"

The question sounded abrupt, but the redheaded doctor grinned at her, and for a moment he looked like a little boy. "I'm twenty-eight. How old are you?"

"I'm nineteen." She forced a return smile and another question. "Did your parents live on the ranch too?"

"Only my mother. My father died when I was six, and we went to Granddad's place until she could get on her feet. Then she started working in town. When I was eight, she remarried." The veterinarian took a breath. "Everyone agreed it was best for me to stay with my grandfather." The Scottish accent had returned to his voice.

"Are you Scottish?"

Dr. MacNair finished a bite of pork chop before answering. "My grandfather was. I'm just a mongrel."

"Did you *want* to stay on the ranch?" Gracelyn felt sorry for asking the question as she saw the red flush spread over his face. The poor guy blushed at everything. But his answer was matter-of-fact.

"They didn't ask me." He looked out the window and then turned back to her. "We've talked enough about the things I want. What do you want?"

Chapter Four

GRACELYN was too startled to answer right away. No one had ever asked her that question before. She thought of all the things she had wanted at the beginning of the past summer. She had wanted her three-point grade average to be good enough to please her father. She had wanted to get through the summer months without fighting with her sister or hurting her mother's feelings. She had wanted to try new things, find some sort of answer to the gnawing inside her. But now all she wanted was *not* to know about the Lazy-J Motel, not ever to know.

The veterinarian was waiting. She tried to formulate an answer that made sense. "I want something . . ." she hesitated. "I want something bigger." *Well, that certainly made a lot of sense.*

"Something bigger?" Dr. MacNair smiled at her. "Like a bigger car? You need a bigger car."

"I do?"

"Long-legged people have the right to be comfortable. You definitely need a bigger car."

For the second time in a few moments, the vet had startled her. She thought of conversations with her mother: "You'd better wear your flat shoes, Gracelyn dear. Don't fluff your hair on top that way. It makes you look too tall." In her entire life, she'd never heard one word about tall people having rights.

Annie's van had been big. Gracelyn poked at a piece of

pork chop with her fork, remembering the fuss her mother had made when she signed up for the art class. "I should think you'd spend your summer evenings in a more normal way, Gracelyn dear, having fun with other young people. Are you sure an art class is the proper place to meet friends? And at night. Will you be safe?"

"Mother, it's a community college. Hundreds of people go to night school classes."

"But you don't *need* to go to a community college. You did well at Marlin Springs last year. A class like this won't contribute anything to a business degree. Why on earth spend your evenings in some grubby downtown classroom?"

Gracelyn could not explain to her mother. Her mother had never seen anything in Gracelyn's drawings, especially not in those that held some hint of Gracelyn's feelings.

She had gone to the classes anyway, taking the bus because she didn't want to renew the discussion by borrowing either of her parents' cars. And Annie had said, that first night. "Open it up. You're tight, too tight. Put your whole body into it, Gracelyn. Don't be so proper. Expand. Expand." And expansion had led to the van.

She had been silent a long time. The veterinarian would think she was rude. She looked up from her plate and said, "I know what you mean about a bigger car. I owned a Chevy van for awhile last summer."

"What did you do with it?"

"Well, before I even owned it, I painted a mural on the side of it."

"You don't *look* like a hippie." The doctor was grinning and she knew he was teasing, but Suzanne had called Annie a hippie and Gracelyn felt defensive.

"Hippies are out of style," Gracelyn said. "My art teacher let me paint her van because she thought I needed a bigger canvas." She wished she could have explained that more clearly to her sister.

Dr. MacNair had picked up the bill, but he asked one more question, "What did you paint?"

"A thunderstorm." What fun it had been, painting after class by the overhead light in Annie's rented garage while

Annie sat on a high stool, telling stories about her travels around the country and occasionally hopping down to show Gracelyn how to use the brush to get a certain effect.

The veterinarian was searching his pockets for change, finding only a nickel and three pennies.

"Let me leave the tip," Gracelyn said. She put several quarters on the table and followed him toward the cash register.

When they returned to the vet hospital, Gracelyn slipped out of the smock and handed it to the doctor. "May I see the dog?"

The German shepherd was heavily bandaged and still groggy, but he seemed to recognize Gracelyn. When she reached out her hand to him, he licked it. She felt a prickling of tears.

The doctor said, "Don't you dare cry."

"I'd be scared to," Gracelyn said, blinking her eyes and smiling a little. "You'd throw water on me again."

The vet laughed. "Give me your phone number," he said. "I'll call you when I've located the dog's owner."

"You'd better send the bill to me at the dorm." She would *not* ask her father for the money. If she could figure out a way to avoid it, she was never going to ask her father for anything again. She wrote down her address and phone number.

Dr. MacNair walked her out to the Subaru and opened the door for her. "What happened to your van?"

"It was traded in," she said, more brusquely than was polite. It wasn't his fault, but the question made her feel drained. And she was already beat. It had been a horrible day and she still had to go back to the dorm and take the chance of running into Arminda.

She showered and went directly to her room, locking the door behind her. The four freshmen were in Felicia's room with the door open. The sound of Arminda's laughter made Gracelyn's heart pound.

She crawled under the comforter and put the pillow over her head, but she could still hear the voices down the

hall. Was Arminda telling them about her latest conquest?
Gracelyn reached for her Walkman. She put the earphones
on and turned the volume as high as it would go, blocking
out the sounds, but she could not keep out the picture of
her father's hand on Mindy's waist. She curled inward, her
hands clutching her elbows, and thought about Annie and
the van.

"You can't be serious," Gracelyn had said when Annie
suggested that she paint a mural on the van.

Annie laughed. "Why not? I always wanted to do that,
but I was afraid nobody would hire me or buy my stuff if
they thought I was too weird."

"Well, what about now?"

"I may not keep the van," Annie said.

"What if I screw it up?"

"Doesn't matter. What can be painted on can be painted
off again."

"I can't paint days. I'm working as a lifeguard."

"Then we'll paint nights."

Annie's attitude was exhilarating. With the mural and
her job, Gracelyn had finally begun to feel that she knew
where she was going. She had wanted her family to be proud
of her. But as usual, she had only embarrassed them.

Gracelyn pulled the covers more closely around her. The
rock music was giving her a headache. She put the head-
phones on the nightstand. The hall was quiet, but words
kept pouring into her mind. Mother's words about the art
class. Suzanne's words about her job. "God, Gracelyn, an
inner city pool? Do you think you're Miss Charity, dispensing happiness to the poor and miserable?"

"I'm just a lifeguard, Suzanne. I enjoy those kids. There's
a marvelous variety in that pool that we never see around
here." And then there was her father's reaction to the van.

She had finished the mural in mid-August. Every time
she looked at it, she got the same thrill. "I really did it,"
she said to Annie. "I'll miss seeing it when you leave, but
at least I know I did it."

"Would you like to buy the van?"

"You're kidding."

"No, I'm not. Craig wants to go to California. We plan to travel together, and we can't afford two cars."

"I'm not sure I can afford one car."

"I'll let you have it for whatever cash you can scrape together."

She was filled with excitement. "I'll buy it, but"—she hoped she didn't insult her friend—"I'd better do things the right way to keep my father happy."

"Whatever," Annie said.

They had taken care of the business of title and license, and then that Friday night in August after her last art class, Gracelyn had driven the van home and parked it in the driveway.

Chapter Five

"GOOD God! What is that?"

Gracelyn heard her father's voice the next morning as she stepped from the shower in her bathroom. "Gracie!" His voice was louder, and she knew he had moved to the bottom of the staircase. "Will you come down here and explain this?"

Gracelyn's chest tightened as she rehearsed the speech she had planned for her father. She slipped into jeans and a T-shirt and took a moment to control her unruly hair with a ribbon. She didn't need another lecture about grooming just now. Mother would be upset enough because Daddy was yelling.

She bent to glance in the dressing-table mirror. At least her hair was clean. Just washed, it looked closer to blond than to brown. Her eyes were always okay—a definite deep brown—and she had decent lashes. She shut her eyes briefly. There wasn't much she could do about the rest of her face. Heredity was a bummer: her father's nose and jaw and her mother's love of soft features.

"Gracelyn dear." Though her mother's voice was not loud, it was clear. They were both standing at the bottom of the stairs now.

Gracelyn went to the window and looked down at the van. The mural on the side was bright in the morning light. Her pulse quickened as her eye traced the streaks of lightning from the domineering grey clouds to the troubled greeny-grey earth below. *I could never have done that without Annie,* Gracelyn sighed to herself. *I'll probably never see her again, but I'm glad I could repay her a little by buying the van.*

"Gracie!" Her father's voice was insistent. Gracelyn took a deep breath, glanced once more at the van, and went to the top of the stairs.

Her father and mother stood in the foyer. Her father held the newspaper, still in its plastic wrapper. He was dressed in grey slacks and a blue golf shirt with short sleeves. Gracelyn stopped a moment looking at her parents—a pair of opposites, her father tall, blond, and handsome in a rugged way; her dark-haired mother tiny and elegant in her linen skirt and ivory silk blouse, every shining hair in place, even though it was early and breakfast was at least an hour away.

"Well?" her father said. Gracelyn moved slowly down the stairs. "Did you park that thing in the driveway?"

Before Gracelyn could answer, her mother said, "Let's talk in the living room and get this settled quickly. Suzanne and Steve are coming for breakfast."

Gracelyn's breath quickened again. The last thing she needed today was the presence of her perfect sister with her perfect husband.

"They always come for Sunday brunch," she said. "This is only Saturday."

Her mother smiled. "Suzanne is giving a little brunch of her own tomorrow. She wants to discuss her menu."

Gracelyn looked down at the gold-and-ivory-colored Italian tiles in the foyer as she walked slowly across them to the three carpeted stairs that led down to the living room. She couldn't remember a time when a project of hers had made her mother smile in that pleased way.

"Gracie, I asked you, did you bring home that hippie-looking pile of junk in the driveway?" Gracelyn's father had followed them into the living room. He and Gracelyn stood facing each other while her mother moved restlessly, touching the porcelain shepherdess on the mantel, straightening the magazines on the coffee table.

"Yes," Gracelyn said.

"Who does it belong to? One of those so-called artists you've been wasting your time with this summer?"

"It's mine."

"Oh, Gracelyn dear," her mother said, but Gracelyn's father ignored the interruption.

"Yours? Since when?"

"We got the title notarized yesterday."

"God, Gracie, I thought you had better sense than to get taken that way."

Gracelyn felt the color rise to her face. She swallowed and began the speech she had planned. "I took the van to your mechanic. It passed the emissions test and it runs well. He said it was worth more than I paid for it."

"You paid for it? With what?"

"The money I saved this summer—three hundred dollars."

"Oh, Gracelyn dear," her mother said. "I thought we agreed that you'd buy school clothes with your lifeguard money."

Gracelyn turned toward her mother. "I don't *need* clothes. I still have everything I started college with last year."

"Styles change, colors go out of fashion," her mother said. "I had a special reason for wanting you to spruce up your wardrobe."

Gracelyn felt a throb of apprehension. What impossible thing was her mother planning for her now? Before she could respond to her mother, her father said,

"It's not too late to get your money back. I'll just go along with you so they'll know they can't take advantage of you this time, and we'll stop this deal before it's gone too far."

"Daddy, there isn't any 'they.' The van belonged to my art teacher. She wanted to leave with her boyfriend and she needed money, so she offered me the chance to buy her van. They started yesterday for California."

"How could you just buy something like that from a stranger?" her mother said. "You don't know who's done what in that vehicle. The upholstery must be dreadful."

Gracelyn began to feel very tired. "She wasn't a stranger. She was my teacher."

"It's not suitable," Gracelyn's mother said. "And it's not safe. You'll attract the wrong element, driving a thing like that."

Gracelyn's father interrupted. "It's about time you stopped this damn art business anyhow and started planning to do something about your career. Your grades will have to be better than they were last year if you're going for an MBA."

Her mother said, "Michael, don't be hard on her about grades. Remember they said at orientation that if your freshman came home with a two-point average, you should celebrate, and Gracelyn had better than a three-point last year."

"Which will get her nowhere, Joanne, if she applies for graduate school in the East."

Gracelyn felt as if she were a ping-pong ball. The conversation bounced her wildly from one parent to the other and from one subject to the other. She tried to defend her purchase. "Daddy, I thought I could use the van to haul my stuff back to school." She attempted a smile. "At least I wouldn't be putting more scratches on your BMW."

"Well, Gracie, I'm sorry you spent your money. The bottom line is that you can't keep that goddamned eyesore. Silver Crest covenants won't even allow it to be parked in our driveway."

But I like it. It makes me feel that I can breathe. And that's my painting on the side. Gracelyn knew better than to voice any of the thoughts out loud. It wasn't going to matter whether she liked the van or not.

"I need to start breakfast, dear." Her mother was speaking to her father. "If we've got this settled, I'd better put the coffee on."

Her father sat down in his chair and slipped the newspaper from its wrapping. "I'll talk to Steve. He'll have ideas about how to get at least some of your money back."

Tears started in Gracelyn's eyes. Her father opened the paper, and her mother left the room. Gracelyn stood for a moment and then turned and climbed the stairs.

She went into her room and pulled the curtains across the windows without looking toward the van. She picked up her sketch book and a grey charcoal pencil. Gripping the pencil in her fist as if it were a paint brush, she slashed dark streaks across the paper, swirling the lines until she could feel herself being drawn into the eye of the storm she was creating on the page.

"Goodness, why is it so dark in here? It's a glorious day outside." Gracelyn's sister Suzanne had opened the door. She moved across the room and flung the drapes back from the windows. "Why are you sulking in the dark?"

"What makes you think I'm sulking?"

"Well, I know Mother and Daddy aren't going to let you keep that atrocious van. What on earth made you buy it?"

"I wanted to do a favor for a friend, and besides, I like it."

Suzanne sat down on the edge of the bed where Gracelyn had been sketching. She reached toward the sketch book, but Gracelyn flipped the cover across the drawing and stuck the pad under her pillow.

Suzanne picked up one of the pencils and turned it in her small hands. Gracelyn watched the delicate fingers without speaking. Suzanne's nails were painted a rosy shade—pale raspberry maybe. They looked pretty against her creamy skin. Suzanne was a replica of Mother. She wore her long dark hair down today, although she often twisted it into elegant swirls to show off her graceful neck and shoulders.

"Gracelyn," Suzanne said, "why do you always get the family into a turmoil? I wanted to talk to Mother about something, but she's too upset about that van. Don't you ever do anything the right way?"

Gracelyn felt the tears sting her lids. "I try to do things right. Do you think I *enjoy* having everyone upset with me?"

"Sometimes it seems like you do it on purpose."

"That's unfair. I took the car to the garage, and Daddy's own mechanic said it was worth at least twice what I was paying for it. He said it was reliable transportation."

"But it's dreadful—that awful painting on the side."

She would not cry. "I like the painting," she said through tight lips.

"You can't. Why, it would embarrass me to death to drive a thing like that. It would even embarrass me to have my little sister driving it." She stood up. "Mother says to come down and eat. Breakfast's ready."

How can anyone think I'd be hungry? Gracelyn thought, but she rose silently from the bed and followed her sister downstairs.

Chapter Six

GRACELYN'S mother had prepared a platter of fluffy-looking scrambled eggs surrounded by fingers of rolled ham filled with cream cheese. Sunshine from the window near the dining-room table sparkled on the crystal glasses filled with orange juice. Tall rust-colored candles flanked a centerpiece of late summer flowers.

As the others seated themselves, they spoke in pleasant tones. Suzanne and her mother talked about the cheese filling in the ham. Her father and Steve discussed the exhibition games that would open the college football season. No one mentioned the van, but it was all that Gracelyn could think of as she tried to eat enough to keep from calling attention to herself. There was no way that she would tell them about the painting now.

The van was comfortable. Her long legs had plenty of room. She felt in proportion as she never did in her mother's car, where she seemed gigantic as she climbed through the small door and into the bucket seat. The front seat of the van made her feel smaller. But the painting . . . The painting stretched her. She could feel her mind reaching for something, though she had no idea what it was or where to find it now that Annie was gone. She forced away thoughts of Annie and took the plate of strawberry crepes that her brother-in-law held out to her.

When the family had finished breakfast, Suzanne and her

mother went into the kitchen. Steve stepped outside to smoke his pipe on the terrace at the back of the house. Gracelyn started to go upstairs, but her father stopped her.

"You're lucky on this one, Gracie. Steve and I have worked out a way to get rid of that thing without losing your money. His law firm has a client who is a Subaru dealer. Steve called him and he's got a little hatchback wagon that will carry your stuff to school." Gracelyn's father smiled at her. "I guess it is time for you to have a car of your own, Gracie. I thought we should wait until you learned to drive more carefully, but your mother thinks that we should give you some credit for making that three-point. So this is what I'm going to do."

Gracelyn looked at her father and waited. A ray of sun rested on his arm, turning the little blond hairs to filaments of gold. He flexed his hand as he gestured toward her and the muscles in his lower arm tightened and released smoothly.

"The dealer has agreed to take the van off our hands. He'll give us five hundred dollars in trade and ship it out to Budget Auto in Denver."

It's worth six, Gracelyn thought. *The mechanic said it was worth at least six hundred dollars.* But she nodded without speaking.

"I'll put up the rest of the money for the wagon." Her father paused and looked at her. "How about that, Gracie? You'll have a better-looking car in the bargain." She nodded again, unable to speak past the lump in her throat. Her father put his hand on her shoulder. "And, hey, we'll make a day of it. You meet me at High Peaks Subaru at noon and we'll close the deal before the guy comes to his senses." He smiled at her. "Then you and I can go to the driving range and hit a bucket of balls and I'll take you to lunch at the club."

Gracelyn managed a smile. "That will be nice, Daddy." She wanted to go to lunch alone with her father, but not feeling guilty and stupid—and obligated to him for a car she didn't want. As she dressed, the tears ran down her face and she had to start over twice on her make-up. She wished that the stupid tears didn't always come so easily, and she wished just once that her father would ask her to lunch for no reason at all.

Gracelyn backed the van from the driveway and started toward the center of town, but she was suddenly engulfed by a sense of suffocation and as it grew, she swung around a corner and breathing deep gasping breaths, she headed north. Just outside of town along the highway was a collection of auto repair shops, used furniture stores, a drive-in theater, and a tree nursery. Forty miles along the road was Dixon and twenty miles beyond Dixon was Marlin Springs and the university, but she wasn't planning to go that far. She had to meet her father at noon.

When she pulled onto the highway, there was no traffic. She pushed the accelerator to the floor. As the van picked up speed, her breathing eased and she stopped gasping. The big engine moved easily to sixty, then seventy and eighty. She felt the knot in her chest release as the trees and fences blended at the side of the road, and time and space melded into a freeflowing wave that spun her feelings into a harmless foam and dissipated them in the wind. After twenty miles, she slowed the van and looked for a place to turn around, glancing only then in the mirror to see if there was traffic, or a state trooper. But the highway was empty, and she held to the speed limit as she headed back toward town.

The Subaru was small. She supposed that the dealer would call the color silver, but it was actually a muddy grey-blue.

"Now," her father said, turning briefly to her, "I thought we'd put the title in both our names. That way, we can insure it under a multi-car discount." Without waiting for her to answer, he added, "But first, let's get rid of that van."

Gracelyn handed him the title and keys to the van and sat silently as the dealer joked about hiding the van on the back lot until he could ship it out.

The day that Gracelyn had started painting the mural on the side of the van, Annie had talked about thunderstorms she had experienced, sometimes without shelter, as she moved about the country painting. "It takes everything you've got to survive a storm when you're out in it," she had said. "But, God when you do, you feel clean to the bone."

I don't have Annie's courage, Gracelyn thought. *I don't even have the guts to stand up for my own work.*

The dealer finished filling out the papers, and her father wrote a check. Then he gave Gracelyn oné set of keys, putting the other set in his pocket. Folding herself under the wheel, Gracelyn followed him to the driving range.

The power she put into her golf swing brought praise from her father and by the time they finished with the bucket of balls and went to lunch, Gracelyn was feeling less miserable.

Her father opened the massive wooden door of the club for her and seated her at a linen-covered table that looked out on the pool. While they waited for their lunch, he told her a story about a new client of his who wanted to insure a llama.

"What would you do with a llama?" Gracelyn asked, interested in spite of her mood.

"I think he plans to use it for pack trips in the high Rockies west of here."

"Are all your clients into insuring such exotic stuff?"

"Not the bulk of them. But enough of them so that challenging problems arise from time to time."

Her father was fun to be with. He knew how to tell a story and he laughed with her when she laughed, his blue eyes sparkling and warm. Now that he had solved the problem of the van, he seemed to want to make her feel better. He didn't mention the van or her grades or her art class. She was glad to focus on his stories. She listened and smiled and wondered idly how one would paint the sparkles that the sun lifted from the swimming pool.

As they rose to go, she stood beside him enjoying his size. Standing near him she always felt more comfortable about her height, even those few times that she wore high heels.

"I've got some calls to make, Gracie." Her father smiled at her. "Got to pay for that new car of yours."

"Thank you for taking me to lunch."

As she backed out of the parking space, Gracelyn took deep breaths and turned toward home instead of toward the outskirts of town.

As she opened the front door, her mother called, "Gracelyn dear." Gracelyn went to the kitchen. Her mother was seated at the table. She looked up at Gracelyn and smiled. "Would you like to help me? I'm making place cards for my bridge-club party next Wednesday, and Suzanne liked them so much that she asked me to make some for her brunch." Her mother picked up a gold card. "I'm attaching silk leaves to the cards after I print the names." Gracelyn sat down and began assembling the place cards.

"Your father called. He said that you got a nice little car." Gracelyn's mother looked at her. "You should really be very grateful to your father, dear. He canceled several important appointments to help you out this morning."

Gracelyn nodded her head, but bent it over the card she worked on, afraid of what might be showing on her face. Her mother seemed to have no idea what Gracelyn felt. For that matter, Gracelyn had no idea what her mother was feeling.

Gracelyn raised her eyes. Her mother looked like a pretty child. The pink tip of her tongue rested on her lower lip as she carefully glued a copper-colored silk leaf to the gold card which she had folded down the middle so that it would stand up and exhibit the name she had printed in silver ink. She seemed to have forgotten all about the van. Gracelyn felt a flicker of anger, but it was followed quickly by a torrent of guilt. Her mother was totally contented with the lovely life she was living, and all she wanted was for Gracelyn to enjoy it, too. *God, what's the matter with me?* Gracelyn felt the tightening in her chest and spoke to ease it.

"Those colors go well together, Mother." Then she dared

a little more. "I've learned some things about color this summer. I'm sorry the art classes are over."

Gracelyn's mother looked up and smiled. "Suzanne and I have a surprise for you."

Gracelyn took a deep breath and put her hands into her lap, clutching them tightly together to stop their trembling.

Chapter Seven

SHE looked at her mother and waited.

"Your father and I have agreed that part of this fiasco with the van is our fault. You need a chance to meet more suitable friends, and you won't meet them as a lifeguard at a public swimming pool." Her mother fingered another silk leaf.

"I'm sorry you signed up there without checking with us. Your father could have got you on at the club pool this summer, Gracelyn." She frowned slightly, "And that art class. Perhaps you do have a little talent, but it is time to set it aside as a pleasant hobby. Even good artists are seldom self-supporting."

Gracelyn's lungs seemed to be growing inside of her chest, pressing against her backbone, crawling up into her throat. Her heart beat wildly as if fighting off an intruder. *What were they planning? What would she have to do now? Dear God, why didn't Mother get to the point? Why did she always have to talk things to death?*

"Suzanne suggested, and I agree, that this year, since you're not under such pressure at school, although you could improve your grades a little—" Her mother smiled at her. "Your test scores do indicate quite a bit of intelligence."

She paused, took a breath and said, "I'm getting off the subject."

Gracelyn gritted her teeth. She hated her mother's talk

sessions. *If I ever have a child, I will not pour words all over her. It's like drowning in syrup.*

"Suzanne thinks you need the security of a sorority house. She has talked to some of her sorority sisters. They'll help you all they can, and your father has agreed to put up the extra money. We can arrange for you to go through Rush Week." Her mother finally stopped talking, but her smile lingered, along with an odd wistful look that made her seem vulnerable.

Gracelyn tried to smile, but she could not fake what she did not feel. She said, "I would never make it through."

Her mother's smile vanished. "Gracelyn, what a negative thing to say. Of course, you can make it through. Suzanne will be backing you. We'll shop carefully so that you'll look just right. All you would have to do is smile and make pleasant conversation. Now that couldn't be too hard, could it, Gracelyn, dear?"

Gracelyn closed her eyes for a moment, picturing herself on the highway with the wind rushing through the car windows, faster and faster till her feelings blurred. Her mother said, "Gracelyn?"

She opened her eyes. "Mother, I don't want to be in a sorority."

"Oh, Gracelyn, why do you drag your feet and spoil things? If you get into a sorority, you can live in the house instead of that dreadful dorm. Your social life would be so much easier. You'd have a chance to date some of the right young men—like that nice Jerry Stuart. I don't understand why you stopped seeing him."

Gracelyn winced as she thought of Jerry Stuart and put him quickly out of her mind. She returned to the subject of Rush Week. "I can't do it."

"Gracelyn, you can at least try. It's already very late to sign up, and Suzanne will have to make some plans very quickly. It would be unthinkable for you to embarrass her with her friends. The first reception is a week from Monday. You can move your things to the campus Sunday morning."

"But I have to work next Sunday." Gracelyn thought of

the van, remembering how she had turned the title over to the dealer without a word. She said again, "Mother, I can't go up to the campus next Sunday, I have to work."

"Rush Week will take up the rest of your summer, Gracelyn. You might as well submit your resignation tomorrow. We'll need to shop this coming week."

"I can't quit just like that. My boss will have to find someone to replace me."

"Oh, for goodness sakes, Gracelyn, don't make such a fuss. It's just a summer job. People don't expect students to give two weeks' notice."

Gracelyn could feel the beginning of something like terror. "Mother, I don't want to go through Rush Week."

Her mother was gathering up the place cards and the leftover silk flowers. "Suzanne is coming later to talk with you about it, Gracelyn. There is a casserole in the refrigerator. I have to dress now. Your father and I are going out to dinner."

Gracelyn's purse was still in the kitchen. When her mother closed the door to her bedroom upstairs, Gracelyn picked up the purse and went out to the driveway.

The stupid little wagon didn't have the power of the van, but she pushed it along the highway as fast as it would go until she felt calm enough to face a conversation with Suzanne, then did a quick U-turn, slowing only a little. As she pulled the car around on the other side of the highway, her fender grazed a marker post. She jolted to a stop and got out. The heavy post was undamaged. The fender was badly dented.

She called Suzanne from a phone booth at the edge of town. "I'm going to a movie," she said. "We'll have to talk later." Without waiting for Suzanne's reply, she hung up. She drove to the dilapidated old drive-in theater and sat through two inane movies about oozing creatures from space, scarcely watching the screen. She could think of no way to avoid going through Rush Week. She remembered a conversation she'd had with Annie late one night in Annie's garage.

"Why aren't you an art major?" Annie had asked.

"I wanted to be. But my parents insisted that I major in business."

"It's your life. Why don't you rebel . . . or at least resist?"

Gracelyn touched the tip of the brush to a section of cloud, darkening it, thinking about how to answer. Finally, she put the brush down.

"I do resist, Annie, but it takes an incredible amount of emotional energy. At the beginning of the summer, I fought with them about my job, and we argued about my taking this art class. It's exhausting."

"Did you fight for the art major?"

"I tried, Annie, but they were so rational about the business major; their reasons were so strong. They made sense. I didn't have any clear-cut argument to counter with. I ended up thinking that maybe I should try to change and fit their pattern. They're doing well."

"What does that mean?"

"Money, a nice home, a good marriage, sensible plans for the future."

"What about creativity? Growth? Expansion?"

Gracelyn smiled a little. Even this conversation was wearing. "Annie, even if I'd been capable of thinking of words like that, they don't stand up against words like 'career' and 'salary.' In order to fight—to have the energy to fight—you have to be *sure* you're right."

The figures faded from the movie screen. Gracelyn cruised slowly around town, thinking about dorm life and Mother and Suzanne and sororities until she was too tired to think at all. She finally pulled quietly into the driveway and parked the Subaru on the right hand side with the dented fender close to the shrubbery.

Chapter Eight

SHE rose early the next morning and left for the pool before her parents were up, stopping on a commercial street to eat breakfast at McDonald's. The children were already clustered at the gate waiting for Ellen, the pool manager, to unlock the padlock.

Gracelyn sighed as she saw The Insurgent Seven, as she and another lifeguard had christened the seven little boys earlier in the summer. They certainly knew all the rules of the pool, because they had been told them by every lifeguard at least twice a day all summer long, and they had broken them just as often. One of the boys was carrying a large-sized plastic ball.

As she joined the surge of children toward the dressing room, she said to Ellen, "I'll bet I confiscate that ball before the day is half over."

The manager laughed, "I give you until ten-thirty."

But the little boys left the ball with their towels and contented themselves with jostling at the top of the water slide and screaming wildly as they cascaded into the pool at the bottom of the slide.

Gracelyn moved her eyes constantly from one end of the pool to the other. The Sunday crowd was large. The pool scene was a wonderful mix of movement and color. It gave her the same feeling of expansion that she had felt when she looked at the mural.

One little girl with bright red hair and pale freckled skin

was digging in the sandbox on the far side of the pool, a crust of sand forming on the bottom of her wet blue suit. Gracelyn walked by the sandbox and smiled at the little girl. "Did you remember your sunscreen, honey? Your mother asked me to remind you."

The little girl glanced up. "Yep," she said and turned back to her work, jabbing the shovel into the sand with fervor.

Gracelyn swung around to check the pool. A toddler had climbed out of the shallow end and was heading unsteadily toward her mother who sat in a recliner near the fence at the deep end. Just as the toddler reached the seven-foot marker along the side of the pool, one of The Insurgents threw the plastic ball. It was meant for one of the other boys, but it was overthrown. It bounced against the fence and ricocheted into the little girl, knocking her into the deep water.

Gracelyn ran and dived even as the mother was rising from the chair. The baby was near the bottom. Gracelyn grasped the child, kicked her way to the surface, and moved quickly into more shallow water. She put the baby over her shoulder and patted her as she coughed and spit the pool water down Gracelyn's back. When the little girl stopped coughing and began to cry, Gracelyn lowered her gently into the water and held her close as she moved toward the mother who stood at the side of the pool with her arms outstretched.

Instead of handing the child to the mother, Gracelyn said, "Why don't you come into the pool with us? We don't want her to be afraid of the water." The mother slid down beside Gracelyn, and they both supported the child who stopped crying once her mother was holding her.

The other children in the pool were watching. When the baby and her mother both seemed calm, Gracelyn climbed from the pool and went toward The Insurgent Seven, who were clustered at the deep end, clinging to the pool side, wide-eyed and silent.

"Out," she said. "And head for the shallow side." Her voice left no doubt that she intended to be obeyed. The seven little boys clambered from the pool and walked meekly to the shallow end where Gracelyn lined them up. "Now, for the next hour," she said, "you're going to *help* these kids, instead of terrorizing them." Choosing carefully, she assigned each boy to a smaller child.

She kept one eye on the rest of the pool and one eye on The Seven as, under her instruction, they tried to teach their charges how to float, how to kick their feet, and how to paddle.

When the hour was up, she released the boys, who went to the refreshment stand for hot dogs, quieter than they had been all summer. Still watching the pool, she filled in the accident report, wishing that she had confiscated the ball outside the gate, but thinking, *All in all, I didn't handle things badly.* She felt a pleasant sense of being in charge of her day.

It was not until Ellen called her to the phone that she thought of her family or of Rush Week. "It's your father," Ellen said. She agreed to watch the pool while Gracelyn took the call. "That was an inspired way to handle those kids," she said as she handed Gracelyn the phone. Pleasure from the praise danced through Gracelyn's mind as she took the receiver and said cheerfully, "Hello, Daddy."

"Gracie," her father said without a greeting, "your mother asked me to remind you that you are to give notice today."

Like water rushing down a drain, Gracelyn's feeling of confidence slid away. The vise in her chest slowly tightened as she stood holding the phone, knowing that if she refused, the pressuring voices would begin: "Your mother has rearranged her week to go shopping. Suzanne has put herself out to help you. It's just a summer job."

"Gracie, are you there?"

She took a deep breath. It was pointless to fight over ten days of work, or even over Rush Week. She had survived other miserable weeks. She could survive this one. "Yes, Daddy, I'm here. Tell Mother I'll give notice, but Ellen might not be able to get a lifeguard to replace me right away."

As if the matter were totally settled, her father went on to something else. "Is your new car running okay?"

Gracelyn swallowed as she thought of the dented fender. "It runs fine," she said. The Insurgent Seven raced past the door. "Daddy, I have to go."

"Well, you be sure to do what your mother wants, Gracie."

She hung up without replying and walked slowly toward Ellen, who had stopped the little boys and was directing them to an open spot in the pool. She looked up; her eyes narrowed as she studied Gracelyn's face.

"Bad news?"

"I have to give notice, Ellen." Gracelyn swung her eyes across the pool and then toward the manager. "Can you find someone to take my place?"

"Honey, if you've got family trouble, I'll have to. You look real down. Why don't you go get a Coke?"

She was grateful that Ellen had not asked for an explanation. *What a fraud I am. I ought to tell her the truth. But I can't tell this woman who works here for a living that I'm quitting to go through Rush Week.* She shook her head.

"I'd rather stay with the kids as long as I can, Ellen." She checked the pool again. "I'm going to miss them." The telephone rang. Ellen patted her arm and hurried toward the office.

The little redheaded girl was still in the sandbox, her face showing a faint flush. "Let me put some more sunscreen on your face, Katy." The little girl tilted her head briefly, but as soon as Gracelyn's fingers left her face, she went back to work. The pit was now a yawning hole. She had dug almost to the bottom of the sandbox. Gracelyn turned back toward the pool, watching the children and thinking, *I haven't finished one thing that I started this summer, and I haven't done one thing right.* She walked slowly up and down the side of the pool, digging into her failures as deeply as the redheaded girl dug into the sand.

Chapter Nine

THE family must have had a conference about her. Now that Gracelyn was going meekly along with the plans her mother made, everyone treated her as if she were recuperating from a long illness.

When her father noticed the dent on the car, he asked, "What happened to your fender?"

"I turned too quickly and scraped a post."

"Well, take it into the shop. I'll tell the insurance company it was damaged in a parking lot."

"You don't have to do that, Daddy. It was my fault."

"We don't want to get the rates raised over some little thing like that. Take it easier until you're familiar with the car." She would have felt better if he had yelled at her.

Mother and Suzanne had made a list of clothes that Gracelyn would need. Gracelyn shopped with her mother each morning. Her dread of Rush Week was a constant weight in her chest.

She spent the evenings in her room trying to choose what to pack. Often she gave up and sat on the bed with her sketchpad, drawing the bottles on the dressing table or the tree at her window.

Suzanne came to the house Tuesday evening to discuss Rush Week procedures. "Monday morning," Suzanne said, "you'll meet the Panhellenic Rush Counselor and your Rush group. You'll get your first Date Book, which will tell you which houses you'll visit that day."

"Houses? How many places do I have to go?"

"Oh, probably twelve to fourteen."

Gracelyn closed her eyes. Fourteen different groups of strangers.

Suzanne continued with her lecture. "The first day, you'll want to dress fairly casual. You might wear that cute pants set Mother bought you or a little cotton dress. Or even your nicest walking shorts and a pretty shirt."

"I couldn't wear shorts."

"Well, then, the pants set. You won't stay any one place more than thirty minutes. You're just giving the houses a chance to look you over and get acquainted."

Gracelyn took in a deep breath, but Suzanne didn't notice. "When you get your second Date Book, probably on Tuesday morning," she said, "you'll want to wear a little better dress. You'll spend at least an hour at every house, and you'll get to tour the houses instead of just being in the living room."

Suzanne smiled at her. "That's fun. You'll see what the bedrooms are like and talk more with the girls."

Gracelyn shut her eyes again, remembering junior high school slumber parties her mother had arranged. Her jaw tightened.

"Why do I have to do this anyway?" She took her pencil and made a web of circles on the sketchpad.

Suzanne said, "You ought to be grateful to get the chance to be in a sorority. Mother never had that opportunity."

"How do you know so much about it? I don't remember Grandma and Grandpa Morton, and Mother never talks about her early life."

Suzanne reached out and halted Gracelyn's hand as she filled in the centers of the circles. "Will you stop that? You're making me nervous." She got up and went to the window. She looked toward the large maples on the other side of the street before turning back to Gracelyn.

"Mother doesn't tell me very much either, but I know that Grandpa died of cirrhosis of the liver when Mother was fifteen. He left very little. Grandma worked as a bookkeeper in a lumberyard until she died. Uncle Jimmy didn't want to go to college, so Mother got to go, but there wasn't money enough for a sorority." Suzanne walked back toward the bed.

"Mother told me about it when I went through Rush Week. She wanted me to have what she never had. She was happy that she and Daddy could afford to do it for me. I'll always be grateful." A tiny frown marred Suzanne's perfect forehead. "And you should be grateful, too," she said again.

"Even if it's something I don't want?"

Suzanne ignored Gracelyn's question and plunged back into her description of Rush Week. The more Suzanne talked, the more Gracelyn regretted her decision to go along with the plan.

"By the time you get your third Date Book," Suzanne said, "a specific girl in each house will probably have taken you under her wing. That will be Thursday. Friday you get your invitation to the preference party."

Suzanne's eyes had a dreamy look as she went on. "The parties are lovely. The girls in the house dress in matching formals. They sing some of the house songs and there's a candlelight ceremony."

"Would I have to wear a formal?"

"Not necessarily. That rust-colored silk dress with the draped skirt would be nice—and heels and hose, of course."

Gracelyn was silent. Even one-inch heels made her nearly six feet tall. She didn't want to hear any more about clothes and ceremonies right now, and she was tired of Suzanne's invading her bedroom.

"Is that all?" She sounded ungracious, but she couldn't help it. She had to be alone. She stood up and waited by the door until Suzanne left the room.

Gracelyn shopped on Wednesday for shoes and lingerie. When she returned to the house, the ladies from her mother's bridge club were just leaving.

"Come and say 'hello,' Gracelyn dear." Gracelyn carried her packages to the front sidewalk and smiled at the women who had paused there.

"Our ugly duckling is turning into a swan," Gracelyn's mother said, smiling at Gracelyn and straightening the collar of Gracelyn's blouse. "She's shopping for Rush Week."

The women smiled at her and asked her a few questions about her summer, which Gracelyn answered with polite lies. "Yes, the summer was pleasant. Yes, I'm looking forward to school. Yes, Rush Week should be lots of fun." And the rest of the day the phrase Ugly Duckling bobbed around in her mind.

To her surprise, her father seemed to sense some of her feelings. He asked her to meet him at the driving range on Saturday and he took her out to lunch again. He told pleasant stories during the meal and only once mentioned Rush Week.

"You've been a good sport this week, Gracie. I know you're not crazy about this idea of your mother's, but she does care about your future." Gracelyn nodded, too moved to speak.

When they left the restaurant, her father put his arm around her shoulder and walked with her that way to her car. He stood there for a moment that she wished could last forever, and then gave her a brief hug and let her go with a grin. "I'll miss you when you go back to school, Gracie. You manage to keep things interesting around our place."

Sunday morning, she packed the Subaru and moved her belongings to the campus at Marlin Springs.

Chapter Ten

GRACELYN clutched her Date Book and purse and allowed herself to be swept along with the froth of chattering girls like a log heading downstream on a swift current. She had chosen to wear the pants set. The other girls were wearing cotton dresses or walking shorts.

Her mother had called twice before she left the dorm. Gracelyn squared her shoulders. *Don't slouch. Walk proudly. Smile.* She tried a smile on a girl near her who looked as if she could use a little encouragement. The girl's mouth twitched into a tight grin, but she continued to look as if any moment she were going to throw up in the gutter. The rest of the girls in the group were making small talk in shrill nervous voices. *Do any of us want to be here?*

As they neared a large white colonial-style house on a street near the campus, Gracelyn's chest tightened and her breathing felt labored. She forced herself to step through the massive front door of the place, though all she wanted was to get in a car and drive until Rush Week was over.

The girls in the sorority were pleasant, but as the half-hour went by, Gracelyn became aware of a look, a critical encompassing survey, as she met each sister. In that one glance, the girl seemed to make up her mind. Gracelyn tried to match the polite conversation the girl offered, but it was harder with each introduction because she felt that it made no difference anyhow. *I don't look like I belong here,*

Gracelyn thought. *And I can't blame them for noticing that. I don't belong here. Suzanne and Mother belong here.*

Trapped in the floodtide of the Rush schedule, Gracelyn followed her Rush Group out of the first house and down the street to the next and the next and the next until the houses became blurred in her mind and the shallow conversations were a constant irritating static that eroded her self-confidence until she could make only the briefest answers. Her thoughts eluded her like a flock of frightened birds.

She had never dreaded anything as much as she did the continuation of the house visits after lunch. She sat with the girl she had smiled at on the street and tried to eat, but she could not. She drank only a cup of hot tea; that was all the other girl had touched on her tray, too. The girl asked, "Do you have a preference yet?"

Gracelyn shook her head. How could anyone have sorted out a positive response while being displayed like slaves or cattle? But she asked, "Do you?"

The girl said, "I'd like to be a Kappa." Gracelyn could see her throat move as she swallowed nervously. "Oh, God, I hope they invite me back."

I hope someone invites me back, Gracelyn thought, *or Mother will be miserable. And,* she thought with painful honesty, *I will be too. Even if I don't want to be in a sorority, I don't want to be eliminated in the first round.* She took her tray of untouched food to the counter and went to freshen her make-up for the afternoon.

The next morning was worse than the first one. As Gracelyn waited with her Rush Group to receive her second Date Book, her heart hammered against her ribs. *What if it's empty?*

But the Date Book probably wouldn't be totally empty. Suzanne's sorority would have to ask her back at least once. Suzanne had explained about sisters and daughters of sorority members. They were called "legacies," and the alumni strongly urged the chapter to consider them.

The girls in her Rush Group were quiet. Gracelyn could

feel the nervous tension as if they were all strung like beads on one taut string.

To her utter surprise, four sororities had asked her back. A rush of relief warmed her face as she thought, *I haven't failed my family yet.* But in the next moment, she had glimpsed the face of the girl who wanted to be a Kappa. It was totally without light. Even the little gleam of nervous energy was gone. The girl met her glance. Her eyes filled with tears and she turned and walked away. Gracelyn watched her cross the lawn, stumbling as she came to the sidewalk. She wanted to run after her and say, "It doesn't matter. You're still you. It doesn't matter." But of course that would be stupid. It did matter.

Two of Gracelyn's four visits were scheduled on Tuesday, two on Wednesday. Each of the houses had a theme. At the first, the theme was Circus, and the members were dressed as clowns and ringmasters and acrobats. Gracelyn trooped upstairs with several others to peer into the bedrooms and bathrooms and then, back in the living room, she drank lemonade and made small talk. She thought often of the girl who had walked away. As she went from the Circus to the next house, which was a Jungle with many female Tarzans along with the Janes, she found less and less to say.

The theme at Suzanne's house was Japanese. Each lovely kimono-clad girl approached Gracelyn with a look that said, "Is *this* our legacy?" Gracelyn's smile felt frozen on her face. Her chest was filled with cotton wads, and her throat was too tight for speech.

Wednesday evening, her mother called, and Gracelyn gave her a detailed account of her visit to every house. Then Suzanne called and she had to repeat the account. By the time she crawled into bed, Gracelyn was confused and exhausted and angry at herself. *Why am I doing this? How can I feel so miserable at the prospect of failing to get something I never wanted in the first place?*

Thursday morning, the only name in the third Date Book was that of Suzanne's sorority. Gracelyn lifted her head and smiled at the nearest girl. She would not walk away in tears.

When the other girls left, Gracelyn walked quietly back to the dorm parking lot and got into her car.

Her sketchpad and a box of colored charcoal pencils were on the front seat. She tossed her Date Book into the back seat and started the car. *I will not be someone's legacy.* She drove into the mountains, parked in a clear space on the top of a windy hill, and sketched all afternoon.

When her mother called that evening, Gracelyn let her assume that she had kept the sole date in her Date Book. Friday morning, her mother called again. "Gracelyn dear, I thought I'd come over for lunch. After you pick up your invitation to the preference party, we can talk about what you'll wear and check your accessories. I'll meet you outside the Panhellenic Office at 11:30." She hung up before Gracelyn had time to think of a way to tell her mother the truth.

Gracelyn went to the Panhellenic Office after she was sure that the others had picked up their invitations and gone. Of course, there was nothing for her.

Her mother cried. Gracelyn had never seen her mother cry before, and as they walked down the steps and across campus toward her mother's car, Gracelyn felt sick with guilt.

Her mother repaired her face before they went to the restaurant. When their meal was served, they ate in silence. Finally, her mother said, "Gracelyn, what did you *do?* Suzanne was so sure that she had everything arranged and that they would accept you as a legacy."

Even my own mother doesn't think I could have made it on my own. Gracelyn pushed her plate away. She stared out the window without answering for a moment and then said, "Mother, I didn't go to the last party."

"Why not? Oh, Gracelyn, dear, why ever not?"

"There was only one bid. And they wouldn't have asked me if it hadn't been for Suzanne. Mother, I would be miserable being someone's legacy."

Her mother said, "Wouldn't it be better than not being accepted at all?" and her eyes filled with tears once more.

Gracelyn said very gently, "No, Mother, it would not."

Gracelyn spent Friday evening alone in the dormitory, grateful that she had a private room, and even more grateful that Suzanne and Steve were out of town.

Monday morning, Suzanne called. Without even returning Gracelyn's greeting, her sister started in on her. "Gracelyn, how could you embarrass me like that after I told them how eager you were to join?"

"You shouldn't have lied for my sake, Suzanne," Gracelyn said, but Suzanne was still talking.

"As far as I'm concerned, you don't deserve one bit more help." Suzanne took a deep breath. "Why don't you just go and do what you're going to anyway and try not to humiliate all the rest of us?"

Gracelyn hung up the phone. It started ringing almost immediately, but she let it ring and ran out the door and to the parking lot.

She raced the Subaru almost to the Wyoming border before she began to breathe more easily. When she returned to the campus, Gracelyn went directly to the registrar's office, where she dropped a three-credit class called "Introduction to Financial Accounting" and picked up a three-credit class called "Basic Drawing."

Chapter Eleven

FROM the first day of fall semester, Dr. Carlson's class was a safety valve for Gracelyn. The white-haired professor looked like Santa Claus and acted like Scrooge. Class sessions were intense; Gracelyn had never concentrated so deeply, nor taken notes so quickly. Outside assignments were demanding: "You won't begin to capture the essence of an object until you've drawn it a hundred times, until you have gone beyond your awareness of lines and shadows into the meaning of the thing," he'd said.

Gracelyn enjoyed the drawing assignments. When she was concentrating on a sketch, she thought of nothing else. Time seemed to change character: it was no longer linear. It was an impenetrable space inside of which she existed only as the connection between an object and the drawing of the object.

Not once during September did she drive on the old highway. She didn't go home either. She worked—grateful to be alone in her room, but also grateful for the casual company she found in the dormitory dining room when she went down for meals.

The freshmen were like puppies or kittens, frolicking sometimes, whining and crying at other times. Free of the idea that she was expected to be in their social groups, she could talk with the boys as easily as the girls.

Once in a while, she looked around the dining room and wished that someone's face would light up as she approached, but the hurt of Rush Week lingered, and she didn't try to get close to anyone.

In mid-October, Gracelyn's father called. "I'll be in Marlin Springs today. Why don't you meet me for lunch at McQuades?"

Gracelyn dressed carefully, wearing the print that her mother had chosen for Rush Week. As usual, her father had picked a nice restaurant, and he treated Gracelyn in the courteous way he had of making one feel protected.

After dessert, her father ordered an Irish coffee for each of them. He had not said one critical thing, nor given her any advice. To her surprise, Gracelyn found herself telling him about her art class.

"I don't recall that we put that on your pre-registration list last spring," her father said, but he was smiling at her.

"I dropped Introduction to Financial Accounting."

"Three hours you'll have to make up somewhere if you're going to get a degree."

Gracelyn nodded, "I can pick it up next summer."

Her father studied her face and then said, "I don't suppose you'd like to tell me why."

He seemed ready to listen. "Daddy, I feel . . ." She hesitated, took a deep breath and went on, "I sometimes feel trapped."

"At nineteen? God, Gracelyn, you're too young." She thought she detected a faint emphasis on the *you're*, but forgot it as he went on. "And the drawing class helps?"

"Yes."

The waitress brought their bill and her father took a card case from his jacket and laid a Visa card on the tray. They were silent until the tray was returned and he had signed the slip. Then he said, "I'm glad the class is a help to you." And as he held her coat for her, he added, "But will you try not to spring any more surprises on me, Gracie? I've got a lot on my mind."

She nodded silently. He seemed discouraged. When they got to her car, she turned suddenly and gave her father a big hug. He laughed and hugged her back. As she drove away, she was happier than she'd been for weeks. School was turning into a pleasure and she had never felt so close to her father.

A door slammed in the hall. Gracelyn turned miserably in her bed, thinking of the luncheon, thinking of the Lazy-J motel. She buried her face in the pillow. It was all a big lie. *He probably didn't even come up here to see me in the first place. I was just his cover story after he screwed Arminda.*

Chapter Twelve

SHE didn't sleep at all. She finally rose at six o'clock, her stomach raw and jumpy. She dressed quickly. The one place she could be sure of avoiding Arminda was in class. She left the dorm without breakfast, an hour before her first class. Thinking of her father, she longed for a cold fast wind, but the sound of her car hitting the dog was still loud in her thoughts. She would never speed that way again. She decided to go and see the dog.

When she rang the bell in the clinic, a surly-looking young man came to the front counter.

"May I see the German shepherd whose leg was amputated?"

The young man said, "It's against the rules to let anyone in here."

"Please. I'm the one who hurt him."

The attendant shrugged and led her into the kennel area. It smelled faintly of antiseptic, strongly of dog. A row of cages lined the long wall. The dog she had hit was lying in a large cage with a plastic basket around his neck.

"Why is he wearing that awful collar?"

"So he'll leave the bandage on his stump," the attendant said, frowning at the dog. "He's been giving it hell all night."

Gracelyn went close to the cage. The dog moved the tip of his tail in greeting. "May I go in there with him?"

"If you can keep him quiet for awhile." The attendant turned away. "I've got to finish cleaning the cat cages."

Gracelyn entered the cage and sat down by the dog. The collar was definitely annoying him. She untied it and slipped it over his head. The dog licked her face, and she put her arms around him and rested her head against his, wondering what she was going to do about her life. She finally replaced the plastic collar and drove back to the campus for her eight o'clock class.

The monotonous business lectures seemed to glue her together. She took notes numbly, automatically. But Dr. Carlson's art lecture was fast-paced and exciting; it was like listening to whirling colors and, as she began to feel alive again for the first time since she'd seen her father and Arminda, she was drawn into a whirlpool of misery and anger. *It's a lie. Our whole life is a lie. I've given up things all summer long to meet his so-called standards. God, he's made fools of us.*

She left the classroom feeling dizzy. *I should eat.* She stumbled toward her car. Suddenly, she needed to go home. She needed to know that her mother was all right. She headed for Denver. But when she reached Silver Crest, she could not go to the house. She parked across the street, down three houses, and, leaning on the steering wheel, looked at her home. Her mother's car was in the driveway.

Inside the house, her mother would be tidying things because tomorrow was the day the cleaning lady came. How many Tuesdays had Gracelyn been told, "Your room's a mess. Mrs. Jordan can't even get in there."

Just an ordinary weekday. I can't talk to her. If I go in to see that she's all right, she will know that I'm not . . . and what will I tell her?

Gracelyn sat for a long time watching. After awhile, she opened her sketchpad.

Her home was wonderfully asymmetric. The center portion rose two stories and beyond that to a peaked roof, shake-shingled. The right wing was lower but still spacious enough for upstairs bedrooms and the two-car garage beneath them. The left wing was anchored by the massive chimney which drew the eye skyward.

The house had been built with used red brick mellowed to a soft rose color. Gracelyn chose a carmine red from the box of charcoal pencils and tinted the walls in the sketch, rubbing most of the color away with her finger to get the look of age.

The bricks set off the bay windows in the living room. She glanced at her own windows over the garage. They were dormer windows, but they had the same delicate diamond-shaped panes as the others. The bays and dormers made a fascinating arrangement with the varied heights and angles of the roof.

The front door opened and Gracelyn's mother came down the steps in red slacks and a red-and-white striped sweater that looked spectacular with her dark hair. She went to her car, opened the door, and slid under the wheel. The garage door lifted and the little car was driven inside. The garage door closed.

She feels safe. Gracelyn's stomach tightened. *The house is a lie, too.* She tore out the sketch and crumpled it. In a panic to leave without her mother's seeing her, she started the car, made a quick U-turn, and left the subdivision.

Dr. MacNair called that night. "I found the owners of the German shepherd," he said after a short greeting, "but they don't think they can deal with a three-legged dog. They want me to put him to sleep."

"No," Gracelyn said. "Promise me you won't." The veterinarian was silent. Desperately, Gracelyn tried to think of a solution. Finally, she said, "Couldn't you keep him there? I could work for his support and to pay for the operation."

"Maybe." The veterinarian sounded dubious.

"Your night attendant said he has too much work. I could help him."

Dr. MacNair laughed. "He's hard to get along with. I can see the two of you now. He'll growl and you'll cry." But he agreed to let Gracelyn try it.

Stepping into the foyer of her home on Thanksgiving morning, Gracelyn felt her self-control slipping away. By staying at school and seldom calling home, she had managed to fumble her way through the three weeks after Halloween, but how could she stay in this house all day acting as if nothing had changed?

"Don't leave your things here, Gracelyn dear."

Gracelyn turned, hoping that her own expression was as normal as her mother's. Before she could pick up the bag, the door opened behind her and her father stepped into the foyer, bringing with him a mixed scent of musky after-shave and a hint of cigar smoke.

"Well, Gracie," he said by way of greeting, "what did you do to your car this time?" He turned to hang his coat in the closet, and Gracelyn was glad she did not have to meet his eyes.

"I hit a dog," Gracelyn said.

"You were speeding, I imagine." His voice rose a little, "Damn it, Gracie. This will raise our insurance rates." As if that were the worst thing in the world.

She kept her voice low and even. "Don't report it. The bumper just rubs a little. I'll pay for the damage myself."

"Out of what? Your college allowance? From one pocket to the other, it's all the same pair of pants."

"From my pay. I've got a job."

"A job? Where?"

Gracelyn wished that they would at least move into the living room, but her father stood frowning, waiting for her reply.

"At the Northside Vet Clinic," she said. "I clean kennels."

"Oh, Gracelyn dear," her mother said.

Gracelyn didn't wait for her father's response. She bent and picked up the suitcase and went upstairs.

Suzanne knocked on the door of her room a few minutes later.

"We just got here. What did you do to upset Daddy?"

Gracelyn turned from the window. All the patterns of her life repeated themselves. Things were tough enough without Suzanne's input. She felt a sudden urge to rush forward and pull the combs out of the beautifully coiffured dark hair that twisted elegantly around her sister's head.

"Are you some sort of delegation?" she asked.

Suzanne moved to the desk and without invitation picked up Gracelyn's sketch book. "These are all the same," she said, as she flipped the pages.

Gracelyn took the sketch book from her sister's hand. "It's just an exercise," she said.

"Is that the dog you hit?"

Gracelyn nodded, sticking the sketch book into her purse and zipping the compartment.

"Well, Daddy and Mother are very upset about this kennel business. Why do you always have to get so carried away?"

Gracelyn wondered what Suzanne would say if she told her about Daddy and Arminda. But she wouldn't . . . because she was *never* going to tell *anybody* about Daddy and Arminda.

She felt too tired for a conversation with Suzanne, but she said, "Well, the dog's my responsibility. What would you do if you had hit a dog?"

Suzanne wrinkled her little face. "Gracelyn dear, I don't speed. And I don't plan to hit a dog. It would be too messy."

As far as Gracelyn could remember, Suzanne had never in her life done a messy thing.

"I bet you were born potty-trained," she said, "and don't call me 'Gracelyn dear' like Mother does. You'd think that Dear was my middle name."

"What should I call you? Gracie?"

"No!" Her anger exploded in the word. Gracelyn swallowed and lowered her voice. "Don't call me Gracie. Daddy calls me that. I hate it."

Her sister stepped toward the door. "I hope you aren't going to ruin Thanksgiving dinner over this dog business."

Gracelyn's anger ebbed, leaving only the fatigue. "No,

Suzanne, I didn't come home to start a family uproar." She hesitated and then said, "Suzanne?"

"Yes?"

"Do you think Daddy and Mother are really happy together?"

Suzanne turned around. "What a perfectly stupid question. They've been married twenty-eight years. Look at this house. They drive nice cars, go on trips twice a year. They have their lives in order." She moved to the mirror and smoothed her hair. "I hope Steve and I can do as well as they've done." Catching Gracelyn's eye in the mirror, she said, "What sort of mischief are you planning now?"

"For Pete's sake," Gracelyn said, "all I did was ask you a question. Why do you always think I want to start something?"

Suzanne shrugged. "I never know why you do what you do. You're so careless . . . so—so—artistic." The way she said the word was no compliment. She opened the door and said, "Let's not spoil Mother's dinner."

We've done this a thousand times before. Suzanne comes to my room and chews me out and then expects me to follow her downstairs and calmly eat a meal. Gracelyn ran a hand through her hair and followed her sister downstairs to the dining room where their father was uncorking a bottle of white wine.

The colors in the table settings were subtly blended. Gracelyn stood still for a moment to enjoy them.

"What's the matter?" her mother said, "is something missing?"

"No," said Gracelyn. "It's perfect. You're really good, Mother. You could be an interior decorator."

Her mother flushed and looked pleased. Gracelyn felt the burden of her father's secret, and her pulse jumped when her mother's expression sobered. But her mother said, "I took some design courses in college. I've thought sometimes about being an interior decorator."

"Why don't you?" Gracelyn asked. *Please, please, Mother, get something of your own, something else to be safe in.*

Her father interrupted with a laugh. "Now don't go putting wild ideas into your mother's head, Gracie. I don't want her rambling all over the city, in and out of strangers' houses."

Better than cheap motels, Gracelyn thought. She tried to push away the picture of her father and Arminda in the Lazy-J, but as she pulled her chair from her place at the table and sat down, the smell of the rich food made her feel slightly nauseated, and as she reached for the wine glass her father offered her, her hand trembled.

Could she be wrong? Could there be some other explanation for his being with Arminda? Her father seemed the same as always. He raised his glass and toasted the family with a smile.

And after dinner, when she was preparing to leave, overcoming their objections by explaining that she had to feed and water the animals, her father put his hand on her shoulder and said,

"You don't have to do that job, Gracie. I'll give you the money for car repair and to keep the damn dog, too, if you must have him."

She felt the tears start and willed them back. "No," she said, "I don't want your money. I'm the one who injured the dog."

Chapter Thirteen

DR. Carlson called her into his office right after she turned in the sketches. She stood just inside the door.

"Sit down, Miss Heath," he said, running a hand through his white hair. "This may take some time."

She sat across from him. Her one hundred sketches of the dog were spread out on his desk.

He looked down at them, fingered one of the later ones, looked at her, ran his hand through his hair again, and adjusted his glasses on his nose. "I'm damned if I know where to begin," he said. "Do you want to explain about this dog that has suddenly appeared in your portfolio instead of at least a dozen assignments that should be there?"

She shook her head slightly. He went on. "Assignments that have something to do with your passing this course. Any comment on that?"

Gracelyn shook her head again. Any explanation she could make was already there—if it was anywhere—in the sketches of the dog.

Dr. Carlson picked up one of the pictures. "I'm not saying that there isn't something here. Each time you sketched it, you came closer to the truth of the matter."

Gracelyn waited, looking down at the sketches. After a short silence, the professor asked, "Where did you get your model?"

Gracelyn said, "I created him."

"You mean you made him up?"

"No. I hit him with my car."

"Oh, I see." Dr. Carlson was silent again for a moment. "Well, you've put some good work into these. The earliest ones were rather awkward, but this one," he picked up a sketch. "I've never seen a creature so wounded."

"Wounded," Gracelyn murmured.

"You've managed to convey the idea that this dog's whole life has been changed." The approval in his tone made Gracelyn look up. Dr. Carlson went on. "And that's why I'm going to accept this group of sketches as part of your assignment. However," he pointed at Gracelyn with the hand that held the sketch, "I am still going to insist on something more to the point of my course. I know you hate to draw buildings . . ." Startled, Gracelyn met Dr. Carlson's eyes and caught the quick crinkling of the laugh wrinkles at their corners. ". . . but," the professor said, "if you want to pass this course, you had better draw some buildings."

So she drew the Lazy-J Motel in Dixon. After the family dinner at Thanksgiving, Gracelyn had tried to believe that she was mistaken, but the girls in the dorm continued to gossip about Arminda's "hunk." Gracelyn returned from the kennels one morning after Thanksgiving break in time for a late breakfast. The four girls were there, and Felicia was teasing Arminda.

"Hey, Mindy," she said. "This has been going on too long for you to keep it to yourself. You could at least tell us his name."

Gracelyn bent her head over her cereal. *Oh, God no, please don't let her say it.*

Arminda only laughed as she rose from the table and left. Julie said, "She cuts her eleven o'clock every Monday, Wednesday and Friday."

Gracelyn dumped her uneaten cereal, cut her own eleven o'clock art class, and followed Arminda to Dixon. She parked behind a trash dumpster in the mall parking lot, edging her car forward just enough to let her see the Lazy-J.

She recognized her father's BMW when he turned into

the lot. He met Arminda near her car, kissed her upturned face, and walked with her to the end unit of the motel. Gracelyn waited, making sketch after sketch of the Lazy-J.

She couldn't stay away. She cut her art class three times each week and drove to Dixon. The car was cold. Her fingers ached as she clutched the pencil and drew another picture of the building. She tried not to think of what was happening inside, but she couldn't help it. She sketched, the tears running down her face, until her father and Arminda came from the motel.

She went back to her afternoon classes with puffy eyes and a red nose. The schedule her father had assembled became increasingly alien to her. She didn't want a world like his.

But when she had time to think, she saw her father's fingers on Arminda, her father's body on Arminda, and when she forced thoughts of the motel away, thoughts of her mother rushed in. She kept going to class to keep her mind on something else, taking notes and turning in her homework assignments, all the time feeling that she stood on a crumbling dike.

Chapter Fourteen

THE only time she was reasonably sane was when she was at the clinic. Dr. MacNair, who was usually on call evenings, often stopped to talk to her. "You're pretty chipper about cleaning up this dirty place," he said one afternoon when he came upon her scooping out a kennel.

She met his glance with a smile. "There are dirtier things," she said.

When the night attendant quit his job two weeks before Christmas, Gracelyn asked Dr. MacNair if she could move into the attendant's room. (She still called him Dr. Mac-Nair even though she had given him the nickname Zandy in her mind.)

"I'll do the evening cleaning chores, then study at night near the phone. I'll fill feeders in the morning before I go back to campus."

The doctor was doubtful. "You'll be alone here."

"I've always got Pete." Dr. MacNair had named the three-legged dog Peg-Leg Pete. The dog followed Gracelyn around the clinic with his peculiar new gait, watching patiently as she worked with animals and cleaned cages, but growling if a strange human came close to her.

The doctor nodded, but said, "Are you sure you'd be all right?"

"I need the work." She was determined not to spend the money her father put into her checking account. She couldn't help it that he had already paid her tuition, but she was not going to depend on him for anything else.

"You don't owe the clinic," the doctor said. "You've worked off the surgery bill, and Pete earns his keep as watch dog."

"Still, I need the money."

"Well, we need a night attendant, and you know most of the routine already. If you think you can handle it, the job is yours."

No more questions, no advice. Zandy was unusual that way. He was the only person she knew who seemed to think that she could run her own life.

She began to spend her nights at the clinic, calling home often enough with false cheery chatter to keep her mother from calling her at the dorm. She showered and changed clothes in the dorm and greeted people in the halls, and no one seemed to be aware of her nightly absence.

Each evening, she helped Zandy on his last rounds. Working beside him, she felt calm and useful. He showed her how to give shots to the animals—matter-of-factly, as if he assumed that she had the intelligence to learn the skill.

They didn't talk of personal matters. Zandy's casual conversation was never about himself, and there was nothing she wanted to tell him about her family. She hated to lie, and she'd never tell him the truth.

She went out to dinner with him once or twice, but stopped accepting his invitations after he refused to go Dutch. "You can't afford to spend your sheep-ranch money on me night after night," she said.

"Well, anyway," he said, "you ought to eat in the dorm. Those meals are paid for."

"Scotsman," she said, intending to tease; but seeing him flush, she softened the comment by saying, "You're right, and I've got the solution. If they know I have a job, the dorm cooks will fix me a sack lunch. Why don't we eat here?"

"Because there's no place to eat," the doctor said, looking

at the desk and table tops covered with books, papers, and art supplies. He grinned at her. "Reminds me of the time the cyclone hit the chicken house."

Her clutter and the fact that she cried over every wounded animal seemed to be Zandy's only complaints. And even then his grumbling was mostly teasing.

One evening as he picked her charcoal pencils off a chair and sat down, he said, "Is this how your mama taught you to keep house?"

Her mother's pristine living room flashed across her mind. "Heavens, no. She has never let me touch her house. She agrees with you. I'm too messy. My sister calls me 'artistic,' but she means the same thing."

"Don't you like order?"

"It's not important to me—it makes me feel restless. Order is . . . order is boring." Gracelyn explored the thought for a moment, surprised by the truth she found in it. She smiled at him. "But I'm sorry if my clutter upsets you, Zandy."

"Zandy?"

"That's my nickname for you, Alexander. Zandy."

He looked pleased, but all he said was, "Beats Peg-Leg Pete. Shall we do the rounds?"

One evening, Suzanne dropped in at the clinic. Gracelyn glanced toward the door of the tiny room where she slept. She didn't want Suzanne telling Mother that she lived here. She planned to wait until Christmas break to tell her parents about the night job. She steered her sister into the kennel area.

Just then, Zandy came through the back door, returning from a large-animal call. He was wearing boots and jeans, a brown wool stockman's coat, and his Stetson. He brought in a clean smell of hay and fresh air, and his face had a shining scrubbed look from the cold. Gracelyn introduced him to Suzanne.

Zandy took off his hat and said, "Glad to meet you." He added, "Your sister has been a lot of help to us."

Gracelyn said, "There's a lady with a sick cat waiting out front, but that's all beside the late rounds."

"Thanks," he said and went out the door to the office.

"Well, your boss is a real country bumpkin, isn't he?"

"Just because he wears cowboy clothes? God, Suzanne, you're a snob."

"Oh, his clothes are kind of cute. No, I meant his bashful ways. I thought for a minute there, when he took his hat off and blushed, that he'd say 'Aw shucks, Ma'am.' "

"He can't help it if he's a redhead and his fair skin shows his emotions." Gracelyn could feel her own face flush. "And he's not a country bumpkin. He's intelligent and he has a good sense of humor. And he's great with animals."

"Why, Gracelyn dear, I think you've got a crush on your boss."

"Don't be stupid, Suzanne." She wasn't about to tell her sister about the nights she and Zandy shared dinner, nor about the peaceful feeling she had working beside him. "I don't have to have a crush on someone to be able to see his value as a human being. And I'm grateful to him for letting me keep Pete here."

She turned to the dog. "Here boy, come meet my sister. And bite her if she calls *you* a country bumpkin." She was glad when Suzanne glanced at her watch and said,

"Heavens, I told Steve we'd have a late supper because I was shopping at the mall, but I don't think he expects me to be this late."

"Thanks for dropping by."

"I promised Mother I'd check on you."

"Oh." Gracelyn walked her sister to the front door and, feeling a little self-conscious, went to help Zandy check the animals.

She turned in one hundred and ninety-nine sketches of the Lazy-J Motel to Dr. Carlson. She had done two hundred, but she held one back and took it to a framing studio where she chose a complementary mat and an expensive frame. The young man who waited on her glanced at her picture. "Evil-looking place," he said as he rang up the money.

She wrapped the picture in silver foil, topped it with a

red ribbon, and, when she arrived home Christmas Eve, put it under the tree with the rest of her gifts to the family.

Suzanne and her husband Steve joined them for brunch and eggnog on Christmas morning before they opened their gifts.

They chatted amiably as they passed the packages around, refilling their eggnog cups from the crystal punch bowl her mother had set on the coffee table.

"Well, this is a pretty package, Gracie," her father said as he removed the silver paper. And then he looked at the picture and all the color drained from his face. She had wanted him to know that she knew, she had wanted that much honesty, but for a moment she felt as if she had hit him the way she had hit the dog.

He raised his eyes to Gracelyn's. Although it took all her nerve, she met his look.

Her mother was gathering up the discarded wrappings. She glanced at the picture as she bent for the silver paper. "That's nice, dear."

Standing, she turned to Gracelyn's father. "Michael," she said, "aren't you going to give the Christmas toast? We're done with the packages."

Gracelyn's father stood still for a moment, a rush of red now darkening his tan. He laid the picture face down on the coffee table.

Taking the cup his wife had filled, he raised it. "To our family," he said, repeating the familiar words of the toast, "to our wonderful, happy family." They all lifted the cups to their lips, but neither he nor Gracelyn drank. Gracelyn returned to the clinic as soon as she could get away.

Chapter Fifteen

SHE was on her hands and knees in front of a kennel on the day after Christmas when Zandy came into the room, his red hair on end, his face flushed.

"What's the matter?" she asked.

"I've got good news," he said.

"Your face doesn't show it," she said, rocking back on her knees to study him.

"Well, it's only good news if you'll marry me."

"Marry you!" Gracelyn sat flat on the floor.

He squatted beside her. "Marry me, Gracelyn, and go to Montana with me. I've got my ranch." Then he looked at Gracelyn sitting beside the pile of dirty newspapers from the kennel, the wet scrub cloth dripping on her jeans. His face flushed even redder and he said abruptly, "Your mother called. She said to tell you to be home in time to dress. You've got company for dinner." He maneuvered his tall frame upward and practically ran from the room.

Zandy is going away. Gracelyn looked around the animal room, which was suddenly just cold cement floors and barred cages. With her heart hammering in her chest, she put the wet cloth back in the bucket and went in search of him.

When she found him he was checking the stitches on a cat he had neutered earlier that day. He didn't respond when she spoke his name the first time. She said, "Zandy! Would you like to tell me what's going on?"

He looked up. His face was bright red.

"Did you just ask me to marry you?"

"I didn't mean to," he said, and then he groaned. "Good God, I've done it again." He put the cat back in the cage and shut the door. He stood up and took Gracelyn's hands. "I've found my ranch. That's what I meant to tell you when I came into the kennel."

"And you don't want to marry me," Gracelyn said, trying to smile, but giving it up when she realized that there wasn't a smile in her. She tried to pull her hands away, but Zandy would not release her.

"I must have a case of foot-in-mouth disease." Zandy tried a lopsided grin, but Gracelyn simply waited and Zandy's face took on a worried look. "I am going to start all over. Gracelyn, I do want to marry you. Will you let me take you out to dinner?"

Gracelyn smiled then, and said, "You just told me that my mother said I had to go home for dinner."

But she didn't go home for dinner. She went with Zandy. He suggested McQuades, but remembering her last luncheon there with her father, she said, "No, I'd rather go to the café where we ate the first time I met you."

He didn't seem to know how to start the conversation. They ate their salads silently. Gracelyn was too nervous to think of anything to say. Finally, Zandy said, "You *will* go with me to the ranch, won't you?"

The blunt question startled her, and she answered it almost as bluntly. "I don't know anything about sheep ranching."

"You have a knack for calming frightened creatures." *Except you*, she thought. But Zandy was still talking. "And you understand that the animals' needs have to be met first." He smiled. "The other vets will probably threaten to horsewhip me. They say you're the most dependable night 'man' they've ever had."

The conversation was totally unromantic. Zandy didn't say he loved her, and Gracelyn felt a sense of loss, a flat lonely feeling that made her think for a moment of going out and getting into her car and driving away. But Zandy kept looking at her and something in his eyes held her there.

And sometime during the evening as Zandy talked of sheep and land and working together, the question was settled. They would get married, he would buy the ranch and Gracelyn would help him make a go of it. She would be earning her own way. Gracelyn was suddenly peaceful. Marrying Zandy solved so many of her problems.

But most important, Zandy would not be leaving her behind. The one clear feeling she had had all day was her terror when Zandy had said that he was leaving and that he hadn't meant to propose.

They drove back to the clinic. Zandy stood beside her in the office, gazing down at her. The look in his eyes made her heart beat faster. As he bent toward her, she lifted her face to his. His kiss surprised her. There was no shyness in it. His lips were demanding and his arms were strong around her. She felt the desire in his long body as he held her close to him, and her own body responded. The embrace reassured Gracelyn. Maybe words didn't matter. Zandy kissed her again just as Peg-Leg Pete came padding into the room and pushed his way between them.

Zandy laughed and let her go. "Don't worry, old boy, I won't take her away without you." He turned to Gracelyn. "Your folks are going to wonder why you didn't show up for dinner. Shall we go and tell them?"

Gracelyn thought of the van, and her job, and Rush Week. She didn't dare to tell her parents about Zandy until she was already married to him. She didn't want to fight with them and take the chance of losing again.

Gracelyn said, "If we tell them first, Mother will want a big formal wedding." She grinned at Zandy. "You have no idea how many friends and relatives would have to be invited, and we'd have to send invitations to your family, and wait for replies. It would all take months. I insist that we elope and then tell my family."

She went to see Dr. Carlson before they left Marlin Springs. The business professors didn't matter. She hadn't cut their classes, and she didn't care about them anyway, but she owed *him* an explanation.

Since the college was closed, she asked Zandy to drive her to the professor's house. His wife showed them into Dr. Carlson's study. He swung away from his desk, looked at Gracelyn, and scowled. "Well, this is a surprise. You cut classes for three weeks and then show up during vacation."

Gracelyn said, "I need to tell you something." Her heart was beating fast, and it pounded even harder when Dr. Carlson turned to Zandy and said,

"I'd like to talk to this young lady alone. Would you wait outside?"

Zandy went out of the room, and before Gracelyn could put together the words to tell Dr. Carlson that she and Zandy had been married that morning, he was berating her in angry tones.

"I don't appreciate the joke you tried to play with your building sketches. You're too damned arrogant. Certainly you have talent, more than I've seen around here for a long time, but you don't respect it. You owe it some discipline, some self-control. Good God, you owe it a major. Why are you a business major?"

Gracelyn felt the tears start, but Dr. Carlson went right on. "Talent is like a wolf. You'll never really tame it, but you can control it with training and at least keep it from eating you alive. And that's all we're trying to do in these art classes—help you to discipline the damn thing until you're old enough to respect it. If you won't take it seriously, you might as well . . ." Dr. Carlson stopped.

Gracelyn was sobbing. Dr. Carlson's words had touched something inside her that no one had ever come near, and she suddenly felt the same sort of terror at giving up the art class as she had felt when she had thought of Zandy's going away without her.

She tried to talk, fished in her purse for a tissue, blew her nose, hiccoughed a couple of times and then said,

"I've quit school. Zandy and I were married this morning. I'm going to help him run a sheep ranch."

"Good God!" the teacher exclaimed and was silent. Gracelyn wished she had never come here. Dr. Carlson wasn't helping any. He just wanted her to do what *he* thought was right, like everybody else in her life.

Finally, Dr. Carlson said, "I suspect there's something you haven't told me." He studied Gracelyn's face. "Did you withdraw from your classes?"

"No, I just quit."

Dr. Carlson made an exasperated sound and reached for a piece of paper. "Tell me what they are. I'll make sure that you don't flunk fifteen hours by default. You'd never make it up if you wanted to return."

Gracelyn gave him the information and then said, "But I'm through with school. I don't belong here."

"And you think you're going to belong on a sheep ranch?" The professor snorted and dismissed her with an outflung hand. But before she reached the door, he said, "Miss Heath . . . Gracelyn," and she turned back.

"Perhaps this isn't such a bad step for you as an artist."

"I'm not really an artist," she said.

"You're not a trained artist, but you see like an artist and you think like an artist." The doctor sighed, and then said, "and unless you keep improving your skills, I can tell you that you're going to end up crazy as Van Gogh." He stood and turned toward his bookshelves. "No, leaving here won't hurt you, but you can't stop studying. You'll need some materials to take with you."

"I won't have time to study. We don't have any ranch hands but ourselves."

"God help you. Here," he said, piling books into her arms, "These will give you a start." He opened the door. "Good luck. Drop me a line or sketch from time to time."

Outside, Zandy said to her as he took the books from her arms, "What did you do? Step on his corns? I could hear him bellering through the door."

Gracelyn sighed and said, "He's just mad because he can't control my life."

Zandy grinned. "Stallion instinct. Hates to see a filly stray from the bunch."

Gracelyn said, "Well, *his* reaction doesn't make it any easier to tell my parents."

Chapter Sixteen

"A sheep ranch!" Her mother's nose wrinkled as she spoke the words.

Gracelyn felt the insult to Zandy and answered, "Zandy's going to start a large-animal practice in Montana, and he's always wanted to have a sheep ranch, and he just got the chance to buy one, and he has to leave right away because there is no one to care for the sheep." She was babbling. She had expected her mother to be upset about her sudden marriage, not to focus on the ranch.

Her father, who had been silent since she had introduced Zandy, spoke now. "Where did you say you were married?"

He doesn't believe us, Gracelyn thought, a rush of anger spreading heat into her cheeks. But before she could speak, Zandy answered her father.

"I know this all seems pretty sudden, sir." He smiled at Gracelyn's father and then turned to speak to her mother, "and I hadn't planned to snatch Gracelyn away from you so quickly. I'm sure it's a shock. But I have to be in Montana by Wednesday noon to sign the papers at the bank. Once I take over the ranch, I won't be able to get away to come for Gracelyn." He smiled at Gracelyn this time. "And so we rushed things a bit. We were married at the county courthouse this morning."

Gracelyn smiled back at him. He did a much better job of explaining their marriage than he had of proposing to her.

"Well, surely, you're not leaving tonight," Gracelyn's mother said. "It's late to start such a long trip. And the weather is terrible."

"No, Zandy has to go back to the clinic tonight. I'll stay here and meet him in the morning."

Zandy had insisted that Gracelyn should stay at home overnight to talk alone with her parents and pack up her belongings.

She couldn't tell him that she dreaded being with her family, so Gracelyn had said lightly, "It isn't my idea of the perfect wedding night, but it's better than the kennels."

Zandy grinned and said, "I'll make it up to you. We'll have a honeymoon in the best room in the best motel on Interstate 25." Zandy's eyes were twinkling, as they had been every time he had looked at her since the night he had proposed.

After Zandy left, Gracelyn's father poured himself a drink. He never met Gracelyn's eyes, not even when she took a deep breath and looked straight at him. Her mother tidied the living room, emptying the ash tray of the few ashes Zandy's pipe had left, giving Gracelyn sideways looks. The silence was unbearable, and Gracelyn fled upstairs.

She was packing when Suzanne opened her door.

"This time you've really done it! Gracelyn, are you crazy?" Gracelyn bit her lip and went on folding sweaters. "You have been so weird ever since Thanksgiving. What's happened to you?"

Gracelyn looked up at Suzanne. "My room already reeks of your lectures. I'm going for a walk. If you want to talk to me, you'll have to get your coat."

Suzanne did just that. She put her coat on and followed Gracelyn right out the door. Before Suzanne could start asking questions, Gracelyn said, "Suzanne, I am leaving here in the morning, and I hate to go away feeling angry at you, so don't start on me. I can't see why you feel that you're responsible for my actions. Who gave you the job?"

Suzanne stopped in the middle of the sidewalk and looked at Gracelyn. Tears welled in her eyes. Then she started walking slowly along. Gracelyn kept pace silently. Finally

Suzanne said, "They always told me to take care of my little sister. And it was so hard. You had this kind of scary undirected energy. I could never be sure you'd come out all right."

Gracelyn bent and scooped up a handful of snow and began forming it into a ball. "Suzanne," she said, "you can't ever be sure of things for somebody else, but I appreciate your caring enough to try."

The tears spilled down Suzanne's cheeks. "I just don't understand you. Why did you marry that cowboy?"

Gracelyn threw the snowball at a bush and said, "I just had to get away."

"Get away!" Suzanne turned and stared at her. "Gracelyn, when people want to get away, they go skiing for the weekend, they don't quit school, get married, and start raising sheep."

Gracelyn laughed and gave her sister a sudden hug. "At least you won't have to be in charge of me any more. Be grateful for that."

When they returned to the house, Gracelyn's father called her into the living room. He was standing by her mother, next to the couch. "Your car insurance is paid up for a year," he said. "If your husband . . ." he stumbled on the word and said it again, "if your husband wants to put you on his policy after that, it would make sense. Insurance will be cheaper in Montana away from the populated areas."

He reached out a hand to touch her shoulder, but the ghostly little form of Arminda floated into the room, hovering between her father and mother, and Gracelyn's stomach tightened. She backed away.

That night, Gracelyn's mother surprised her by coming into her room after Gracelyn was in bed. She smoothed the covers over Gracelyn and bent to kiss her cheek. She murmured, "This is not what I would have chosen for you, Gracelyn, dear, but try to be happy."

Touched, Gracelyn said, "You, too, Mother. You try to be happy."

Chapter Seventeen

GRACELYN stood by the loaded Subaru, shivering in the cold wind.

"God, I hope you know what you're doing," her father said. Gracelyn was silent. There was nothing she could say to him.

She turned to her mother, who murmured, "You've thrown so much away."

Suzanne held onto Steve's arm, just staring at Gracelyn. The sky was thick with little feathers of snow.

Gracelyn said, "I've got to go." As she backed from the driveway, her family turned toward the house.

When she parked at the clinic, Zandy came out with Peg-Leg Pete at his heels. She slipped from under the wheel and turned to survey her car, which was filled with boxes and suitcases, her easel, and the books Dr. Carlson had given her. The back of Zandy's pickup was loaded and tarped down. The cab was crammed with groceries and veterinary supplies. The dog would have to ride with her.

Zandy said, "I've got a present for you." He stepped inside and returned to place a scraggly black-and-white cat into her arms.

Gracelyn looked from the cat to her car to Peg-Leg Pete, who was sniffing at the bedraggled creature. She said, "I don't have room for Pete, let alone a cat-carrier."

Zandy flushed. "She came in yesterday. There's nothing wrong with her that a little loving care wouldn't cure.

But she's a stray, and if we leave her, they'll euthanize her."

Before Gracelyn could reply, Pete stuck his nose against the cat's rear; the cat jumped from Gracelyn's arms into the front seat of the car. Pete followed. Scrambling through Gracelyn's belongings, Pete pursued the kitten to a back corner where the easel blocked him. The cat crouched below the rear window. Gracelyn climbed into the car, grabbed Pete's collar, and dragged him to the front seat.

"Well, I guess the cat's found a safe spot," she said, smiling at Zandy. She felt like a stray herself, and she was glad he believed in loving care.

"*Now* there's plenty of room for Pete," he said, laughing as he got in his pickup. Gracelyn settled the dog in the front seat, started her car, and followed the blue truck into the storm.

The snow-covered roads were polished to a dangerous sheen by the constant wind. The canvas tarpaulin over the load in the back of Zandy's truck billowed like a sail. Gracelyn fought the wheel mile after mile, steering to counteract the force of the wind, squinting to see through the ground blizzards that obscured the road and Zandy's truck.

From its spot beneath the rear window, the cat meowed steadily. "It's all right, kitty," Gracelyn said over her shoulder, "at least you're alive to yowl."

When the snow whirled around the car and Zandy was out of sight, Gracelyn felt lost from the world and as scared as the cat. The Subaru crept steadily toward Montana as her thoughts ranged backward toward the unbearable situation she'd left behind, and forward again toward the unknowable situation she'd promised to stick with, for better or for worse.

The car was hit by a sudden gust of wind, and she turned the wheel to get back to the proper lane. Pete licked her face. She curved her hand around his neck and pulled his furry jaw close to her cheek for a moment.

The wind died down, the snow eddied to the ground, and she could see a long stretch of snow-covered highway and Zandy's truck moving steadily along. She snapped the radio on and tried a quick turn up and down the dial, but there was too much static for her to hear anything clearly, so she shut it off.

Ahead, Zandy was signaling a right-hand turn. She followed his pickup into the truck stop. They let Pete out for a few moments and then gave water to him and to the cat before entering the café.

When they had been served coffee and a heated sweet roll with butter melting across it, Zandy grinned at her and said, "Well, we're about through the Cheyenne wind belt."

"Some belt. It must be eighty miles wide."

"It'll let up a little now."

"I'm glad. Maybe the kitty will calm down. She's a real crybaby."

Zandy reached out and touched her cheek with one finger. "Are you doing okay? This turned out to be a rotten driving day."

Gracelyn said, "I'm fine." And it was true. The moment she was with him again, her memories receded, the future looked easier, and she felt more sure of herself.

"Then we better get going. We've still got a long six hours' drive ahead of us." Gracelyn shivered a little as she got into her car. She didn't want to spend six hours alone just thinking, but she started the engine and followed the blue truck.

The kitten continued to cry, and Pete moved restlessly in the seat. She wondered if Zandy had thought about the animals when he spoke of honeymooning in a motel.

After two monotonous hours, Zandy's pickup slowed, and they entered the outskirts of a town. He pulled into a diner at the right side of the road.

Over lunch, Gracelyn said, "I know you promised me a motel tonight, but I don't think Pete and that crybaby cat will be happy if they have to stay in the car. Maybe we ought to go straight to the ranch."

Zandy flushed. "Are you sure? It would be a lot easier that way. Mr. Radson called this morning. He's staying in town tonight and heading out for Florida right after he signs the papers tomorrow."

Gracelyn wondered for a moment if Zandy had meant to stop at a motel at all, but she didn't interrupt him. "A temporary hand they call Old Daniel is at the ranch," Zandy said, "but Radson couldn't guarantee he'd hang around."

A scared feeling fluttered in Gracelyn's stomach as they left the café. She gave Pete a napkin full of bread scraps, tossed a scrap of meat to the cat, and pulled out of the lot behind Zandy once more. This seemed like the longest drive in the world. Maybe she was as crazy as Suzanne had said she was.

Chapter Eighteen

A S the day wore slowly away, the outside temperature began to drop and the pavement iced up. The highway northeast was a long, straight scratch across the snow-covered land. Gracelyn had to concentrate on her driving, but she was aware of the vast empty spaces, and she felt a ripple of excitement whenever she glanced across the plains. No buildings, few trees, just the slight rise and fall of land; land stretching endlessly. A rocky knob, a fence line, a gully provided brief focus, but each time she looked away from the road, it was the empty land that held her gaze until she was forced to return her attention to her driving.

At last, Zandy's pickup turned off the highway on a gravel road, patches of which showed red where the wind had scraped it clean. The snow drifts were as high as the Subaru on each side.

Every mile they came to a fence with an opening in it that allowed passage over an odd grating, made up of metal bars and open spaces. Zandy's pickup went right through each narrow gap without slowing and Gracelyn followed, the car rattling as it crossed the bars.

The road curved around small reservoirs, frozen and snow-covered. On one curve, there stood a lonely-looking windmill. "Turning, of course," Gracelyn said aloud to Pete. "This must be the *Montana* wind belt."

She didn't see any sheep, but a few red cows lifted their heads as she passed. Her shoulders were tight after the long hours of driving; a knot of pain had settled at the base of her skull.

Gracelyn had followed Zandy for eight miles along the gravel road when they topped a long hill. A valley stretched out in front of them.

To her left, rocky bluffs loomed above the valley like stern faces, whiskered with grey-green cedars and showing a nose or cheek of red rock. Below the escarpment, a few stands of evergreen trees marked the snowy slopes.

On the valley floor the vast expanse of snow was broken occasionally by pale grey sagebrush. Huge cottonwoods indicated the line of the creek in the center of the valley, their bare branches etched into the silver sky.

At the bottom of the hill, Gracelyn could see a red barn and a handsome, two-story white house protected by large spruce trees. The road ended there. Beyond it were snow, hills, and sky. Gracelyn slowed the car, feeling the power of the land. The blue pickup moved steadily down the hill.

"You can stop your fussing," Gracelyn said to the cat, "We're here." But the blue pickup didn't turn in at the gate to the ranch. Gracelyn blinked, but there was no time to give in to disappointment. Zandy's pickup plunged into the drifts at the end of the road. She gripped the wheel and followed the pickup's trail.

The snowbanks towered above the car. The track curved and fell and rose again, once dipping to meet an aging, narrow bridge across a deep gully. For three miles, Gracelyn struggled to keep the wheels of her car in the pickup's track. At last, they rounded one more curve and climbed a final hill.

Across the creek on a snowy plateau was a small brown house partly sheltered by a thin strand of trees. The road went between the house and a garage.

The creek reversed itself just beyond the garage and curved to the right, separating the house and garage from a weathered brown barn and a long, low shed that looked as if it had squatted on that hillock forever.

Gracelyn had slowed almost to a stop at the sight of the

ugly buildings, but Zandy didn't hesitate. He crossed the
creek and pulled up in front of the little house.

"Well, Pete," Gracelyn said. "There's no way we could
turn around in this snow, so it looks like we're going to
have to follow him."

She dipped down to cross the creek, drove up to the
house, and parked behind the pickup. For a moment, even
the cat was quiet. The silence in the valley was immense.

Zandy got out of his pickup and came toward the Subaru,
grinning. Pete scrambled across Gracelyn to the door. She
opened it and let him out.

"Not such a bad trip, was it?" Zandy said cheerfully,
giving her a hand as she got out of the car feeling stiff and
tired. Pete made wide circles in the snow.

"Did you look at this place before you bought it?"
Gracelyn asked, hoping the question didn't sound as discouraged as she felt.

Zandy said, "Just once. We drove over the pastures and
hay land. I checked out that garage for a vet shop and
walked around the lambing sheds and the barn."

"What about the house?"

Zandy flushed. "I guess it needs a few things. I didn't look
it over too closely. I figured you'd want to make your own
changes."

Gracelyn gave up her feeling of aggravation to laugh out
loud. "What if I hadn't agreed to marry you?"

"Then I'd have hired you," Zandy said with a grin. "I
can't run this place without a lamb-licker."

"A lamb-licker? What does that mean?"

"You don't want to know," Zandy said, "at least until
you've had a hot meal." He turned toward her. "The house
isn't very convenient right now. But we'll have a wool
check in the spring, and we'll get the plumbing hooked up
then."

"The plumbing's not hooked up?" Gracelyn repeated the
words without fully understanding them.

"Mr. Radson said he started fixing up the place so he
could sell it easier, and he bought the sinks and shower and
stool with last year's wool check. But the market price

wasn't right for his lambs last fall, so he didn't finish bringing the pipes from the well."

Gracelyn looked around, partly to keep Zandy from seeing her face. She didn't want him to know how much she wanted a hot shower. "What do we use for a bathroom?" she asked.

Zandy pointed. "There's an outhouse on the creek bank behind the garage." She went toward the garage.

The door to the outhouse had blown open, and the snow had drifted onto the seat. She brushed away a clear space and turned to close the door, but it was anchored firmly in a hard-iced bank of snow. She shrugged, then sat down on the cold seat and gazed out at the cottonwoods that leaned above the frozen creek.

Peg-Leg Pete came back from one of his circle tours, galloping toward her with his funny three-legged gait. Gracelyn reached a hand to restrain the wild rush, then patted his head. "I'm sorry about your leg, fellow," she said.

Thoughts of the accident brought thoughts of home. Gracelyn closed her eyes tight and swallowed to hold back tears. After all those years of pride and toasting, what had her family given her to remember? And what was her mother going to do if she found out about Arminda?

Gracelyn wiped her face and blew her nose with toilet paper from a damp roll that rested in the drift of snow on the floor. She didn't want Zandy to think she was crying about the ranch and that odd house. She came around the garage again and hesitated, looking at the house, which was made up of two sections pushed together haphazardly, much as a careless child might place a couple of blocks.

Zandy had opened the hatchback and picked up the cat. When Gracelyn came near, he handed the cat to her. "Have you chosen a name for her?"

"I've been calling her Crybaby. It didn't shut her up, but it didn't seem to make her yowling any worse." Gracelyn glanced at the house again.

"Kinda looks like two freight cars passing on a narrow road bed, doesn't it?" Zandy said.

Gracelyn cuddled the cat as she followed Zandy inside,

but she said nothing. The house was so different from her parents' home. Zandy kept talking. Gracelyn had seldom heard him say so much at one time.

"As you can see, this was not a planned house. As far as I can figure, they started off by shoving a one-room granary and a two-room granary together where the doors met. They must have added that little room onto the one-room granary later. Its floors don't sag quite so much."

Zandy stopped talking and looked at her, his face red, his hair standing upright where he'd run a hand through it. "Do you think you can live here, Gracelyn? I know it's not what you're used to."

Gracelyn put the kitten on the floor. She had no idea what she was going to do with this house, but she said, "I didn't expect your sheep ranch to be in the middle of a city, Zandy."

Zandy stepped forward and put his arms around her. The cold shock she had felt when she first saw the shabby ranch began to ease. Zandy's poor little dream ranch. She raised her eyes to his.

"I didn't see any sheep. How can I be Bo-Peep without any sheep?"

Zandy held her for a moment longer. "They're just over the hill with Old Daniel, I hope. After we warm this place up and eat something, we'll go find them."

It was late afternoon, and the winter dusk was cold. They began to unload their vehicles. Zandy set the groceries on a counter that stretched along one side of the kitchen.

The space above the counter was divided. Half of the wall was covered by a tall cupboard painted yellow. Gracelyn grasped the porcelain knob and opened the door to look inside. The shelf papers were so grimy that it was hard to see the pattern of green leaves that swirled along the edges.

"How long has Mr. Radson been a widower?" she asked when Zandy brought her easel and art supplies into the kitchen.

Zandy's eyebrows lifted. "How did you know he was a widower?"

"Well, no man would have put these shelf papers on the shelves, and no woman would have let them get this dirty."

Zandy grinned, but all he said was, "There are some more shelves in that room off the kitchen. We'll be sleeping there because the other bedroom is full of plumbing supplies, but I think there's room for your art boxes."

He went for another load. Gracelyn looked out the low windows that filled the rest of the space above the counter. She could see the dark shapes of the trees down the slope by the bridge.

She was thinking of the black silhouettes of the trees against the dusky sky as she picked up the box of art supplies and pushed open the door at the end of the kitchen to put them away. I'd use black charcoal and grey paper. Then she stopped, entirely forgetting the scene she wanted to sketch.

The small room was almost filled by a huge iron bed frame with wooden slats supporting old-fashioned springs. There wasn't any mattress. Gracelyn hugged the box to her chest and shivered as she stared at her honeymoon bed.

Chapter Nineteen

ZANDY came in with more boxes. Gracelyn turned toward him. "There isn't any mattress on the bed."

Zandy stuck his head into the other room. "Well now, what did that old bastard do with the one that was here? It didn't look great, and it smelled kinda mousey, but it would have done us until we got a new one."

Gracelyn stood for a moment, remembering the firm boxsprings and clean mattress she'd slept on the night before in her bedroom at Silver Crest.

Zandy said, "We'd better unload the rest of the stuff. We've still got to bring in coal and water and check on the sheep. Then we'll find a place to bunk."

Gracelyn backed away from the dismal bedroom, too discouraged to speak. Zandy was watching her. His mouth was tight and his eyes had lost their sparkle.

She wanted him to smile. She tried a joke. "Shall I order a pizza for supper?" She was rewarded with a laugh.

Then Zandy said, "The kitchen stove runs on bottle gas. Could you fix us something to eat while I unload the rest of our stuff?"

Gracelyn found a package of bacon and a dozen eggs amongst the groceries. The stove shared the wall at the end of the kitchen with a porcelain sink, which had faucets and a drain, but no pipes underneath it. A five-gallon bucket stood below the drain. An iron skillet hung on a nail behind the stove. She reached for the skillet and set it over the burner.

While the skillet heated, she unpacked the groceries, storing the milk, butter, and salad materials in the refrigerator . . . a real antique with the motor mounted on the top.

It was almost dark outside. Gracelyn snapped on the overhead light as Zandy came back in the door with a bucket full of coal and an armload of kindling.

Gracelyn said, "I'd make coffee, but I don't know where to get water."

Zandy nodded toward a bucket which sat on the counter near the sink. "There's a pump behind the house. Just hang the bucket on the spout and start pumping. I don't think you'll need to prime it, but if you do, give a holler. I've got a five-gallon jug of water in the truck."

As she stood in the dusky light, shoving the iron pump handle up and down, she felt renewed excitement about the land. The earth and sky were shrouded with heavy clouds. The air around her was multi-dimensional, a cold dark blue, but shading into a feathery grey mist that seemed to envelop floating rooms and ghostly shapes. She gazed into the swirling mist entranced. When water finally gushed from the pump, and she lugged the heavy bucket back inside, the house seemed even smaller than before.

After she made the coffee, Gracelyn improvised a litter box, gave the cat a dish of milk, and put a pillow on the floor by the bed. Then she shut the cat in the bedroom, so that Pete wouldn't terrify her.

Because the kitchen was cold, they ate in the living room next to the huge brown-enameled stove in which Zandy had built a fire. The room had no windows, but a second door led to a back room. Gracelyn liked the glints of fire that showed through the slits in the stove door, but that was *all* that she liked about the living room.

She couldn't identify the color of the smoke-darkened walls. A lumpy cot served as a couch, and a scarred end table held a lamp made from a plaster-of-Paris cowboy boot.

On the outside end of the room was a big vinyl recliner, the back cushion split around the edges.

Zandy said, "This is a pretty good supper. I wasn't sure you could cook." His eyes were twinkling again, but Gracelyn didn't smile. She had not imagined that everything would be so difficult. She couldn't really cook. Her mother had never liked to have her in the kitchen: "Why don't you let Suzanne do it, Gracelyn dear. She's so much tidier."

Gracelyn said, "You're seeing most of my recipe collection right here. How often can you eat omelets and salad?"

"Until you learn how to make biscuits and gravy, I guess." Zandy was still grinning. "My recipe collection is thinner than yours."

"Good Lord," Gracelyn said. "We'll have to live on eggs."

"That's okay," Zandy said, "Mr. Radson threw in fourteen hens and a rooster on this deal."

"You're kidding! I don't know anything about raising chickens."

"You'll learn. You'll be wanting to buy art supplies with your butter and egg money."

"Butter doesn't come from chickens," Gracelyn said. "I think that a cow has to be involved."

"See, you're not such a city girl after all," he said, grinning. "Let's go check the sheep. You'll find out about the milk cows soon enough."

Gracelyn followed him out the door, acutely aware of how often Zandy turned to jokes instead of discussing a situation. She swallowed nervously and looked up. Though the stars were still obscured, the clouds had lifted and the sky stretched black and immense for mile after silent mile. Annie had said, "Expand, Gracelyn. Put your whole self into it." She swallowed, thinking of her marriage as much as her artwork, and climbed into the truck.

Chapter Twenty

THEY took the pickup as far as the barn, crossing the creek on a plank bridge. "That thing's more of a raft than a bridge," Zandy said as they clattered across.

The barn was tall with a sloped roof, the paint the same brown color as the house and the sheep shed. Zandy got out of the truck and went to the corral. Gracelyn followed, but stopped as she saw the huge dark shapes inside the fence.

"It's just the milk cows," Zandy said. "That old hand of Radson's must have done the chores, or the cows would still be out in the pasture."

He stepped to the barn, slid back the door, and reached inside to snap on the lights. "Yep," he said, "the milk buckets are here. He probably fed the milk to the chickens."

It was warm inside the barn, even though the floor was icy and snow had sifted in under the door. The air smelled of hay and cow manure. Zandy took a flashlight from the tool shelf. He stepped behind the milking stalls and went to a small door at the back of the barn. "Come see your chickens," he said.

Gracelyn peered around Zandy into the fenced yard outside the little door. A small shed filled one corner of the pen. The door hung open. Zandy frowned. "Damn. He forgot to shut the chicken house. Just lucky that something hasn't gotten in."

"What something?" Gracelyn asked as she went with him

to the shed. The reddish-brown hens slept on slender poles that were fixed to the walls at varying heights like bleachers in a stadium. The chickens shifted when the flashlight beam hit them; one of them made a little clucking sound; and then they settled down again, their scrawny claws clutching the poles.

"Fox, coyote, skunk," Zandy said, putting the tongue of the latch over the ring and snapping the hook through it. Then he walked to the back of the hen yard and opened a small gate.

"We'll walk up to the sheep," he said, reaching back for Gracelyn's hand. Glove in glove they trudged along a track in the snow which took them up the slope and onto a rise. The flashlight reflected off the snow, giving plenty of light to the trail. As they topped the small rise, another fence barred their way until Zandy dragged the long gate backward and let them into a second pasture. Here, the snow was disturbed and rough.

"They've been milling around," Zandy said.

But the sheep were quiet now. They had gathered together toward the center of the pasture and bedded down on a flat area near a small wagon with a rounded top.

Zandy stepped up on the front of the wagon near the tongue and looked inside. Then he jumped down again. "Want to see inside?"

"Won't Old Daniel mind?"

"He'll never know."

Zandy handed her the light, and Gracelyn climbed up on the wagon tongue and peeped through the canvas curtains at the end of the wagon. The inside of the wagon was surprisingly neat.

Cooking utensils and a few dishes sat on a shelf above the little stove. A yellow slicker and a set of grey coveralls hung on the wall opposite the bed. The bed itself was just a wooden shelf supported by two-by-fours at each corner.

An old man with brown-toned skin lay on top of a bed roll that had been thrown on the shelf. Fully clothed in another set of grey coveralls, he had his socks on, but his muddy boots sat on a paper just inside the door. He never moved as Gracelyn flicked the light across his face. His head was back, his chin up, and he snored in loud, gurgling tones.

Gracelyn stepped down and handed the light to Zandy, and they made a slow circle of the herd.

"I don't expect predators this close to the barn, but with all the snow we've had, you never know what might be getting hungry out there," Zandy said. "Damn coyotes have increased threefold since the Sierra Club got the government excited about poison. A fellow I talked to lost so many lambs it put him out of business."

Zandy put his arm across Gracelyn's back and rested his gloved hand on her shoulder as they returned to the barn through the crisp air. She leaned her head against him, grateful for his silence. She wished that they could walk along like this all night and not go back to the house and the naked bedsprings.

Aside from joking about the honeymoon motel, they had never gotten near the subject of sex in the week between Zandy's proposal and their marriage. She wished she knew more about real sex. Mother had never discussed sex, nor Suzanne, but she knew from stories in the dorm that there had to be more to it than her first and only experience.

Zandy stepped away from her to open the gate, and she walked along slowly, remembering how awkward she had felt in the backseat of Jerry Stuart's car. That nice Jerry Stuart, her mother had called him.

There wasn't room for her legs, and Jerry had been impatient. Even now she could hear the exasperation in his voice as he said, "Can't you prop your leg on the back of the seat somehow?" She had wanted then to push him away and get out of the car, but she was afraid to stop him, and so she had spread her legs the best she could while he forced his way quickly inside her. He finished while she was still feeling the pain of his entry.

Zandy went through the chicken yard into the barn, picked up the milk buckets and went out to the truck.

When they got to the house, Zandy said, "Let's put Pete in the back room and leave the cat in the bedroom; we'll sleep in here on the floor by the living room stove."

Gracelyn called Pete through the door at the end of the living room and flipped the light switch. The back room was fair-sized, but at the moment it was cluttered with the sink, stool, shower stall, hot water heater, lengths of copper tubing, and rolls of black plastic pipe.

Zandy had set most of their household boxes in that room as well. She was surprised to see her easel standing near the large, curtainless window on the north side. Zandy stepped into the room while she was looking at it. "I thought you'd get the best light from that window," he said, "when you want to paint."

He was nice. Gracelyn smiled at him and helped him as he carried blankets and pillows to the living room. They gave Pete a pan of water and shut him in the back room where he scratched at the door and whined. Finally, when they continued to ignore him, he flopped down on the other side of the door and was quiet.

Zandy heated water in the teakettle. "It's kinda cold to try for a bath in a tin tub tonight. Can you make do with just the washpan?"

Gracelyn went into the kitchen, grateful that he gave her a few moments of privacy. She had chosen the best nightgown she owned, a sleeveless, striped cotton, which she slipped into after she washed.

Then she stepped into the living room where Zandy had spread the blankets and pillows on the floor in front of the stove. When he looked at her in her nightgown, his face turned quite red, and he went quickly past her to the kitchen.

Gracelyn sat down on top of the blankets, her nervousness easing because Zandy seemed nervous, too. After a moment, she began to shiver, so she opened the blankets and crawled into the makeshift bed, which was chilly on the cold floor. Zandy turned out the lights before he joined her inside the covers.

Zandy was different in the dark. He no longer seemed shy.

He reached for her and pulled her into a strong embrace. He kissed her and began to caress her slowly.

His hands were gentle, but not tentative. Gracelyn felt her body respond as he ran his fingers across her breasts and across her stomach and then slowly, slowly up and down the insides of her thighs. He touched her as if he cherished her, not rushing her, not asking anything of her. Her body felt warm and alive and deep inside her something began to melt. She snuggled closer to him and tipped her head to reach his mouth. When he kissed her, he let his tongue linger for a moment just inside her lips.

Gracelyn ran her hand across his face. He wrapped his hand around hers and kissed the tips of her fingers. "This isn't such a bad honeymoon hotel, is it?" he said. "It's not the Best Western that I promised you, but it's a lot classier than that old Lazy-J Motel that you spent all of November and half of December drawing."

In that instant, Gracelyn became ice cold. Confused images of her father and Arminda and her mother collided in her mind. The shock of the memories made her ears ring. She didn't hear Zandy's next words. When her head cleared, she found that she had pulled away from his arms.

"What's the matter?" Zandy asked. She could hear the concern in his voice, but she could not tell him, could no longer respond even with words.

Zandy was silent too, waiting. Finally he said in a flat voice, "We'd better try to get some sleep. We have to be up at four-thirty." He turned on his side with his back to her.

Gracelyn lay silently, heavy as stone. *Daddy, how could you have done this to me? If you ever loved me at all, how could you have made sex seem so cheap and dirty?* Feeling ashamed, knowing she had cheated Zandy, she clenched her fists and stared into the dark, thinking, *Damn you, damn you and Arminda.*

Chapter Twenty-One

"GRACELYN, it's five-thirty."

She sat up, clutching the blankets around her, confused. Five-thirty? No wonder she was groggy. The last time she had looked at her watch, it said three-thirty.

"We've overslept an hour," Zandy said, pulling his pants up and zipping them.

"It's dark outside."

"It will still be dark at seven. We're pretty far north." He turned on the lamp in the plaster-of-Paris boot.

Gracelyn didn't say any more. She had just remembered why she had not been able to sleep. She looked at Zandy. He was watching her.

She should tell him right now about Daddy and Arminda so he'd know that last night wasn't his fault. They shouldn't start out their marriage with such a thing between them. But what would he think of her family if she told him?

Before she could get up the nerve to speak, Zandy smiled at her and said, "Why don't you stay under the covers until I get a fire going. And since you're still a tenderfoot, I'll milk all the cows this morning." He was so damned nice. She couldn't spoil his sweet gesture by reminding him of last night.

Zandy bent to stir the coals in the big stove. He started with kindling. When the fire blazed up, he added more wood.

"I can at least get breakfast," she said.

He smiled. "I bet we're going to have eggs."

She stuck her tongue out at him. Zandy grinned and let Pete out of the back room, then laughed while Pete kissed Gracelyn's face with a wet tongue and great enthusiasm as Gracelyn tried to hide under the covers. Finally Zandy went outside with the dog, taking the milk buckets with him. She could hear him pumping water. They hadn't washed the buckets last night, or the dishes either, for that matter.

Gracelyn got up and went to the small room off the kitchen. She scooped Crybaby into her arms and took her back to bed, snuggling under the covers until the stove began to send a few breaths of warm air her way.

She was just taking up the bacon when Zandy came back from the barn. He carried the milk bucket brimming with foamy milk into the kitchen and set it on the counter.

"There you are," he said briskly. He smelled of fresh air and hay. A faint scent of cow manure rose from his boots.

"What do I do with that?" Gracelyn asked.

Zandy smiled at her. He hung his coat and hat on hooks near the door. "Oh, a lot of things," he said. He filled the grey enamel washpan with hot water from the teakettle. As he soaped his hands, he continued. "First you take the straining cloth that Mr. Radson left with those gallon jars under the counter and strain the milk into the jars."

Gracelyn followed his instructions and poured the milk through the cloth. She was shocked at the dirt on the strainer.

"What's next?"

"Cover it for now. I'll show you how to separate after breakfast."

"Separate what?" Gracelyn said, as she fried eggs in the bacon grease.

"The milk from the cream."

Gracelyn dished up the eggs and Zandy sat down at the table. "When we're done with the milk, I'm going to need your help feeding sheep. Old Daniel apparently figured he'd done his duty by us. He took off."

"I didn't see a car."

"He had an old green pickup parked at the far end of the barn. It's gone now."

After they ate, Gracelyn put the breakfast dishes in the sink and followed Zandy to the back room off the living room, where he pulled away the sheet that covered up the separator, a small blue machine mounted on a sawhorse.

Gracelyn laughed. "Its handle hangs down like a monkey's tail."

"Well, I hope you'll make a pet of this monkey. You'll be twisting his tail twice a day." Zandy lifted the large tin bowl that was fitted into the top of the machine. It was full of odd-shaped parts. "Separator lesson coming up," he said, carrying the bowl to the kitchen. Gracelyn followed, feeling hopeful for the first time that morning. Her happiest times in the clinic had been those when Zandy was teaching her something new.

"The big bowl is called the tank," Zandy began. "This cone-shaped piece is called the bowl."

"Wait a minute," Gracelyn said. "Why isn't the bowl-shaped piece called the bowl?"

"Because the bowl-shaped piece is called the tank."

"That's not a reasonable reason."

"Why do you have to have reasonable reasons?"

"Because I can't understand things unless I can make pictures in my mind. Why don't they call the bowl a bowl and that cone-shaped thing a cone?"

Zandy grinned at her. "Because the West got set up before you came along to make pictures." He picked up the bowl. "Now quit asking unreasonable questions and concentrate."

"Yes, sir!" she said, returning his smile.

"First put the rubber gasket in the groove around the bottom of the bowl. Then you put these twelve cone-shaped discs over the spindle on the bowl . . . like this. Then this top piece that is heavier than the other discs and then the cover for the bowl."

"For the cone," Gracelyn murmured, but Zandy ignored her.

"Fit the bottom edge of the cover into the groove on top

of the gasket and screw the nut down tight with this special wrench. Any questions yet?"

"Reasonable or unreasonable?"

"Ask me the question, and I'll tell you what kind it is."

"Will you put the whole thing together again?"

Zandy laughed and unscrewed the nut, removed the cover, dumped the discs into the tank, and picked the rubber ring out of the groove. "Here," he said, "you do it."

Gracelyn fitted the notched discs over the spindle, replaced the lid and started to screw the nut tight.

"Wait," Zandy said. "You left out the rubber ring."

"What would happen if I didn't put it in?"

"The milk would run out on the floor."

Gracelyn took the bowl apart again and put the ring in. Zandy picked up the tank with the rest of the parts and took it back to the machine. "Set the bowl over the center pin in the machine, fit the spouts over the bowl . . . milk spout on bottom, cream spout on top . . . set this section on top of the spouts and place this metal float inside it. Then set the tank on top of that and fit the spigot into the center hole, so that the milk won't run out until you're ready. Any questions about that?"

"Are you sure this is what sheep ranchers do?"

Zandy grinned at her and said, "Stop changing the subject and bring those milk jars in here."

When Gracelyn brought the jars to the back room, Zandy said, "Shut the spigot on the tank and pour in the milk."

Pointing to the handle, he said, "Your monkey's tail turns the bowl. When you're turning it fast enough, this little button on the end of the handle goes in and out. When that happens, let the milk in."

He stepped into the kitchen for the milk bucket and set it under the lower spout. One of the jars went under the upper spout. Gracelyn watched everything he did, blurry-eyed from lack of sleep, but determined to be helpful. She had come here to earn her own way. "Now turn," Zandy said.

"What if I don't turn fast enough?"

"The cream will be thin as water."

"What if I turn too fast?"

"The cream will be thick as paste. Don't worry, you'll soon be able to tell by the sound if you're going the right speed."

"What do I do with it when the milk is gone?" Gracelyn asked over the hum of the machine.

"You take it apart and wash it so you can put it back together and separate again after we milk the cows tonight."

"I was afraid of that," Gracelyn said.

"Do you want me to tell you how to make cottage cheese and butter now?"

"Haven't you got something to do in the barn?"

Zandy laughed and reached for his hat and coat. "You don't seem very sociable. I guess I'll go load the pickup so we can feed sheep when you're done here."

Chapter Twenty-Two

ZANDY left, and Gracelyn was alone with the separator and a feeling of unreality. *We joke as if there were nothing else on our minds, as if last night had never happened.* She turned the handle faster and faster until the little button moved, and then she opened the spigot in the tank.

As she kept turning, she was astonished to see the bottom spout fill with skim milk and the stream of skim milk pour into the bucket; it had an anemic cast, different from the whole milk and in real contrast to the thick, ivory-colored cream that came more slowly from the top spout into the glass jar. *I feel like that,* Gracelyn thought . . . *two separate, unrelated streams, neither of them whole, one too thin, the other too rich. I wish I could turn the handle backward and put everything together. But I'd have to go so far back. When was I ever whole and honest with anyone?*

The machine hummed as she turned, and phrases floated in her mind. *Cream of the crop, cream of society.* And suddenly another phrase became very real: *Cat who's into the cream.*

Crybaby had found the lovely ivory stream from the upper spout and had raised her head to capture it with her tongue. Cream spattered all over the cat's face, her whiskers dripped cream, and small puddles were gathering on the floor.

Gracelyn didn't dare stop turning the handle. She held the cat away with her free hand, until the milk was gone from the tank, and the spouts stopped pouring. Then

Gracelyn let go of the handle, which moved a short way by itself, slowed, and stopped. She scooped up the cat.

"Damn it, Crybaby, Zandy will expect me to be ready to go with him. You'll have to stay outside until I get this mess cleaned up." She hurried to the front door and set the cat out into the snowy yard. Pete had gone with Zandy, thank goodness.

She put the jar of cream into the refrigerator and then looked around desperately for something to mop up the cream in the other room, but she couldn't find the box with the dish cloths in it, and there weren't any paper towels. She finally used a face cloth that was draped over the wash-pan.

The cream was sticky. She went back to get the cloth wet, but the teakettle was empty, and the little bit of water in the bucket was cold. The cold water congealed the fat in the cream, making it harder to scrub away the spots.

When most of the mess was cleaned up, she took the bucket of skim milk to the kitchen, filled two gallon jars and opened the refrigerator to store the milk. As she stood for a moment in front of the open door, she thought of the orderly shelves in her mother's refrigerator: Milk in plastic bottles, neatly labeled "2% milk fat," cardboard cartons of Half 'n Half, butter in smooth sticks in its own compart-ment, cottage cheese in a plastic container. *I never once wondered about the origins of all that stuff.*

She shook her head. She had scarcely slept last night. She was too tired to think about anything but the work. *I'd better wash the milk buckets for tonight,* she thought. She poured the rest of the water from the bucket into the teaket-tle, but it didn't even come to the halfway mark. *I'll have to get more water.*

When Gracelyn opened the door, Crybaby scooted into the house. Gracelyn hurried around to the pump. The storm had cleared. To the north she could see the broad, snow-covered pasture, pristine, gleaming in the sun, stretching up the slope toward the blunt hills crowned with stubby evergreens. She took a deep breath of icy air and looked at the sky, high, remote, pale as skim milk. Everything was so big. She pumped the bucket full and took it back into the kitchen. While the teakettle was heating, she went to take the separator apart.

"Oh, damn it, Crybaby!" The cat had jumped upon the sawhorse and was licking the cream spout. Gracelyn shooed the cat away, then lifted the big tank from the other parts on the machine and held it in one arm.

A few drops of milk leaked from around the spigot and ran down the front of her blouse, mingling with the sticky cream spots and the cat hair that Crybaby had left on her front.

She put the other parts into the tank, took everything to the kitchen sink, and looked around for a dish pan. There was nothing above the sink. As she bent to look under the sink, the acrid scent of the slop bucket met her nostrils. The bucket was full to the brim with blue-grey slop water.

"That bucket's not sanitary," Gracelyn said to the cat, who had hopped up on the kitchen counter to lick her whiskers again. "I'd better dump it before I start washing the separator."

She reached under the sink, grunting with effort as she hauled the bucket out and stood up. The handle was slightly greasy and there were bits of garbage floating around on the water. She lugged the bucket to the kitchen door and stepped outside.

Just then Zandy pulled up in front of the house with a pickup load of hay. As Zandy opened the pickup door, Peg-Leg Pete jumped out and ran toward Gracelyn, barking his joy.

He lunged at her and hit the slop bucket. It tipped. The rim hit Gracelyn's shin bone and slop poured down the front of her legs. The rancid water froze to her socks, and a piece of wilted lettuce slid inside her shoe.

Tears started in her eyes, and she looked toward Zandy, only to realize that he was doubled over laughing, one hand on top of the gate, one hand at his mouth. Pete hopped around on three legs until he spotted Crybaby just inside the open door and chased her into the house.

Zandy came toward Gracelyn grinning. "I think it might be better, dear, if you dumped the slop bucket over the bank behind the shed."

Gracelyn stood still, sniffing back her tears, trying to force a smile. But the odor that rose from her clothes won out over her sense of humor, and she turned and stalked into the house.

Zandy followed saying, "I'm glad you're just finishing up with your work. I need you . . ." Gracelyn turned. Zandy had stopped talking and was looking at the sink full of dishes and separator parts and the teakettle boiling over onto the gas stove.

Chapter
Twenty-Three

GRACELYN watched Zandy's face, her throat tightening the way it had when her mother scolded her for her messy bedroom.

"I had some problems," she said.

Zandy didn't say anything. He just stepped to the stove and turned the heat off under the teakettle. Then he turned and grinned at her. "You'd better put on some dry clothes," he said. "I don't want that slop water thawing out in my truck."

Gracelyn exhaled with relief. She stripped quickly, washed her arms, hands, and legs, and dressed in clean clothes. Meanwhile, Zandy rinsed the milk buckets with hot water and turned them upside down on the counter. He poured the rest of the water over the pieces in the separator tank.

"You'll have to start over this afternoon. You can get caught up while I'm in town."

"Oh, that's right. You have to go sign the papers."

Zandy nodded. "Are you gonna stay on as ranch help?"

Gracelyn smiled. The day wasn't ruined. "Well, I'm going to stay on the ranch. Time will tell whether I'm any help or not."

"Where did you get the hay?" Gracelyn asked as she and Pete and Zandy headed toward the barn in the pickup.

"Mr. Radson baled a good batch last summer. He stacked it over in that big meadow north of the creek. I may move the sheep down there where it's easier to feed, but for now, we'll have to haul it to 'em."

"Is that all they get? Just the hay?"

"No, we'll supplement with cake."

Gracelyn burst out laughing. "You're kidding." A ridiculous picture flashed through her mind: sheep feeding at a large angel food cake with candles.

Zandy turned his head and looked at her. "What's funny about cake?"

Gracelyn said, "I don't think we speak the same language. What *is* cake?"

"Oh," Zandy said. "It's dried, compressed grain; comes in little pieces about two inches square and an inch thick. We scatter it on the ground before we feed the hay."

They circled the barn and drove up the hill they had climbed on foot the night before. Gracelyn opened the gate and then shut it after the pickup pulled through. The pasture was large and fairly level near the sheep wagon, sloping upward to a flat-topped ridge. A windmill and water tank stood near the fence.

The sheep obviously knew that the truck meant food. They followed it to the rise at the far side of the pasture and crowded around the pickup as soon as Zandy stopped.

"There's where you get your wool suit and your lamb chops," he said. "What do you think of them?"

Gracelyn studied the bleating, shoving herd of sheep. "I think there's a long distance between your sheep and my Evan Picone suit, and the whole span is probably filled with work."

"Well, as far as I can tell, you like work."

"When I know what I'm doing. I was no great success with the house chores this morning."

"Too much, too soon. You'll get the hang of it." Zandy looked around. "Old Daniel's been feeding them on this ridge," he said. "So, we will too, although there's more shelter down near the wagon."

"What do you want me to do?"

"Just drive along slowly, keeping a steady speed, while I

scatter cake and again while I break the bales and spread hay."

Gracelyn forced her door open against the crowding sheep and started around to the driver's side.

The sheep milled, making sounds and pushing their long faces against her. One of them stepped on the toe of her snow boot.

She took off a glove and touched the back of the sheep. The wool was thick. She poked her finger down into it. The inner parts of the fibers were cleaner, more ivory-colored than the greyed surface.

The sheep crowded her close to the pickup; some of them put their front feet on the bumper. Others jumped up and put their front feet on the backs of other sheep. They all kept up the crying sounds.

In the back of the pickup were bales of hay and five-gallon buckets full of the little cubes of feed Zandy had described.

Zandy had stepped down from the driver's seat. He held the door for Gracelyn, pushing back an inquisitive ewe who stuck her head in toward Pete. Pete was barking, but Gracelyn shoved him away from the steering wheel and climbed in.

Gracelyn looked at Zandy. "They don't say Baa like the sheep in nursery rhymes. It's more like Buuhhh."

Zandy grinned. "And lambs don't say Baa either. You'll hear 'em this spring. They holler Maaa."

"Do you think Pete could be trained to move sheep?"

"He sure wants to try. But keep him in there for now, and just drive slowly along the ridge. Give me a chance to scatter the cake pretty good, so they won't bunch up." Zandy climbed into the back of the pickup.

Gracelyn put the pickup in gear and pulled forward. The sheep continued to mill around the truck as it moved. Some of them even moved in front of the pickup. Gracelyn looked in the rear view mirror. Zandy was holding a bucket over the tailgate.

She looked to the front again just as one sheep leaped

over another and right into her path. She hit the brake sharply and caught her breath. Oh, Lord. She'd probably thrown Zandy out of the pickup.

But she caught a glimpse of him, hanging onto the stack of bales. She turned her full attention to her driving, determined not to fail at anything else today.

The sheep spread out to eat the cake Zandy was scattering, and by the time she turned around at the end of the feeding area, they had cleaned up most of it. She glanced in the mirror. Zandy was breaking bales and tossing chunks of hay over the tailgate. She could see his breath in the air.

When he finished the last bale, Zandy knocked on the back window and she stopped. He climbed over the tailgate and came to the driver's window. "Pick me up at the windmill. Sheep will lick snow if they need to, but since we're out here, I may as well break the ice in the tank. And I want to walk through this bunch and see what I've got."

Gracelyn waited for him at the windmill. When he climbed in the passenger side, he said, "We'll stop and feed the chickens and break the ice in their water, too." Gracelyn had never driven with a man in her car. The men she had known just naturally assumed the driver's position. Zandy didn't pay any attention to her driving. He was looking out over the pastures.

The milk cows were still in the corral in front of the barn. "I didn't let them out," Zandy said. "There's not much out there to eat, and I didn't want to chase them to hell and gone when I get back tonight."

"Are you going to do anything else besides go to the bank?"

"Well, we can't sleep on the floor all the time. I'll have to find us a mattress." Zandy's face was flushed. Gracelyn was sure he was thinking of the night before.

When they got back to the house, Zandy stoked the fire in the living room and then left for town. Gracelyn watched his pickup through the kitchen windows until she could no longer see the blue dot in the snow.

Chapter Twenty-Four

SILENCE settled around the house. The dark, angled branches of the bare trees along the creek emphasized the vast reaches of snowy field. The sun was only a pale luminescence in the milky sky. There was a faint blue cast to the scene. She stood for a moment thinking how she might paint it. Watercolors, definitely. Oil was too heavy.

There wasn't time to think of sketching, let alone planning a painting. "Come on, Pete. We'd better get the sink cleaned out. Zandy's gonna make a joke if this dumb machine isn't ready at milking time." She patted his head and he wandered away to investigate Crybaby's warm spot behind the living room stove, but Crybaby hissed at him, and he drew back and flopped down on the floor near the front of the stove.

Gracelyn had found the sink stopper, so she heated water and filled the sink with hot soap suds and started in on the separator. The milk had made the parts slimy. The odor was faintly animal and a little sour. The water cooled quickly and the suds went flat, leaving a scum on the water.

She had to refill the water bucket and the teakettle before she finished, but by noon, she had the sink empty and the slop bucket full again.

As she opened the door, Pete was ready to follow. "Oh, no you don't," she said. Shutting the door firmly behind her, she lugged the bucket out of the yard and across to the creek bank behind the garage. She dumped the water into the deep snow.

As she turned to go back to the house, her eye caught a movement at the edge of the garage. She stood still. A rabbit was poking around a clump of dried grass on the south side of the building. She waited and studied him. He seemed brown, but his fur was really made up of grey, black, and brown hairs. He stood on his hind legs to nibble at the top of the grass. His underside was lighter. She had never been this close to a wild creature. She watched until she began to shiver.

The fire had died down. She re-stoked it and started to work. The quiet moments with the rabbit had given her a feeling of comfort. Pete and Crybaby were dozing by the stove again. It was a relief not to have any people around to worry about. Mother, Daddy, Suzanne, Dr. Carlson . . . even Zandy. She could tell already that she wasn't going to be able to totally please him.

She unloaded the canned goods onto the kitchen counter and cut the grocery sacks to fit the cupboard shelves. After she washed the shelves, she relined them with the brown paper.

When she opened the cabinets under the kitchen windows, a musty smell pervaded the room. Crybaby came into the kitchen and crawled into the far corner of the cabinet nearest the bedroom.

"I hope you're a good mouser," Gracelyn said. "You might as well earn your keep." Crybaby ignored her and crouched in the corner motionlessly, only moving when Gracelyn slid the shelf paper under her. Gracelyn stopped for lunch, which was frosted flakes with fresh cream and an apple. Cooking was easy, too, when one was alone.

Thinking of cooking made Gracelyn uneasy, but when she stored the canned goods under the counter, she noted with relief that there were several big cans of stew. She kept one out to heat up for supper. She unloaded the boxes of cooking utensils and appliances and all the rest of the dishes onto the counter. She put the dishes in the lower shelves of the upper cabinet and hung the pots and pans on the hooks by the iron skillet.

She was trying to decide where to put the big knives and the cooking spoons when Pete whined to go out. She opened the door for him and stepped outside.

The afternoon was drawing to a close, and to the west where the trees followed the creek up the valley, the dark branches now stood out sharply against an orange smear of setting sun.

Gracelyn hurried back inside, scrabbled in the art supply box until she found a big sketchpad and her colored charcoal pencils, slipped into her coat and went out again. The light would fade quickly. Kneeling in the snow, Gracelyn sketched as fast as she could. The first sketch didn't capture the depth of the sky. She flipped the page and began again. She finished as the orange light was draining away, and the sky was closing down with the grey of early evening.

While she was studying the picture, she heard a noise. Oh, Lord, it was an engine noise. Zandy was coming back, and she hadn't finished the kitchen counters.

She ran inside, tossed the sketchpad and pencils into the corner of the dish cupboard, and started grabbing the rest of the utensils.

By the time Zandy pulled up in front of the house, the kitchen counters were cleaned off and all the cupboard doors were closed, but she realized that the house was cold.

She'd let the fire go out. She stepped into the living room and saw the tumbled blankets on the floor. *Oh, hell. I forgot about the bed.*

It was too late anyway. Zandy was stamping his feet outside the kitchen door. He stepped in and smiled. "Hi, you wanna come help me with this mattress?"

Gracelyn was still wearing her coat. She followed him out the door. Zandy said, "It could snow again any minute. Let's get this into the house before we do chores."

They wrestled the mattress through the narrow door and leaned it against the kitchen counter. "I've got ideas about rearranging this place," Zandy said. "We'll just leave it here for now." He reached for the milk buckets, without mentioning the clean sink or the tidy kitchen.

On the way to the barn, Zandy said, "You didn't happen to feed the chickens, did you?"

"No," Gracelyn said. She wasn't about to tell him that she'd forgotten all about the chickens.

"Well, I'll show you how, and then you can take care of them morning and night from now on." But the chickens had already gone to roost. "Just get the eggs," Zandy said. "You can feed in the morning." He handed her an empty feed can, and Gracelyn went wearily into the hen house. It seemed like three days since she'd gotten up this morning.

She looked around in the dusky light of the shed. Fastened to the wall opposite the roost was a row of boxes with a board nailed across the lower third of the front. She reached gingerly into the first box and found two cold eggs. She tried the next and the next. When she finished searching the last nest, she had eleven eggs and she felt less tired.

"It's like a treasure hunt," she said to Zandy. "I got almost a whole dozen eggs."

He smiled at her and fastened the chicken house door. "Yeah, eleven's a pretty good count for fourteen hens, but wait until spring and the mothering instinct comes out in them. They'll never go near those boxes. You'll have a real treasure hunt when they hide out to hatch their chicks. Did you get pecked?"

"The nests were empty. The hens were all on those poles."

Zandy laughed. "Well, you've got some experiences ahead of you." They walked into the barn, and he dipped oats from a bin behind the milking stall and dumped them into the long boxes at the front of each stall. Then he said, "If you're ready for a milking lesson, you can go out and start those cows this way."

Chapter Twenty-Five

GRACELYN went to the corral. The ground was rough, frozen into ridges around the prints of the cows' hooves. She sidled along the barn until she was behind the three cows. One was honey colored, one was black and white, and the third one was a rich tan with smoky-colored tail and face hair.

The cows moved a little as she approached, but they didn't go toward the barn. What was she supposed to say? She felt like a fool saying "shoo," and her voice wouldn't come out loud enough to say "Hy-yah" as they did in cowboy movies. She finally clapped her hands. The cows ambled toward the barn.

Zandy stepped to the door. "Slap 'em on the fanny. If we're going to move furniture tonight, we'd better hurry with the chores."

Gracelyn reached out and patted the honey-colored cow on the flat place near the ridge of spine just above her tail. The hair was coarse, but surprisingly smooth. Full bag swaying from side to side, the cow clattered across the cement door sill and nosed into one of the stalls. The black-and-white cow followed the first cow into the same stall.

Zandy stepped in between them, grabbed the black-and-white cow's head and backed her into the open area. Then he smacked her on the rump, and she entered the next stall.

"I'd be scared to do that," Gracelyn said.

"I'll give you a week," Zandy said, "and you'll be exasperated enough to whack this old holstein with a milking stool. She tried that same business this morning."

The tan cow with the smoky face had stepped quietly into another milking stall. Zandy nodded toward her, "Put the neck rope on the Brown Swiss, will you? Be careful, though. She flings her head backwards."

Gracelyn slid along the stall divider toward the manger at the front. The cow's side bulged. She could scarcely get past her.

"This cow is awfully fat," she said.

"A bonus for us," Zandy said. "That cow is with calf."

After Gracelyn had secured the cow to the post, Zandy said, "Come and milk the guernsey. She lets her milk down easier than the other two. Get in here on the right side."

"Why the right side?"

"For the same reason you get on a horse from the left side."

Gracelyn laughed. "Your explanations are things of wonder. They always leave me wondering."

Zandy offered her a one-legged stool. "If you learn too much, I'll have to raise your pay." The laugh wrinkles around his eyes deepened for a moment. "Here," he said. "Squat down and put the seat of the stool under you."

Gracelyn tried, but her knees ended up under her chin. "My legs are too long."

"Just back up a little and lean into the cow."

Gracelyn managed to make a wobbly three-legged stance. "Now what?"

Zandy handed her a milk bucket. "Hold this between your knees at an angle toward the udder."

"Why can't I just set it under the cow?"

" 'Cause she can kick faster than you can grab, and if she doesn't kick it over, she may end up with her foot in the bucket. Enough stuff gets into the milk without letting the cow wash her foot in it."

Gracelyn swallowed. "I noticed the strainer," she said. "I'm not sure I'll ever drink another glass of milk."

Zandy laughed. "Well, you're supposed to dust off the udder before you start . . . or scrape it, depending on the weather."

"What with?"

"Your hand. Go ahead. Clean off the extras and then grab a couple of teats, or as the Victorian ladies called them, a couple of quarters."

"Thanks for that bit of trivia," Gracelyn said and reached a hand to the bag. It had the feel and texture of a warm, hairy waterbed. As she brushed the udder, it swayed with the weight of the milk. When the bag was free of dust and hay particles, Gracelyn curved her hands around two of the teats.

"Now what?"

"The point is to coax the milk from the bag by way of the teat into the bucket, so kinda squeeze from the top down, one teat and then the other."

Gracelyn squeezed the teat in her right hand. Her large hands made it fairly easy, but she got a surprise when the milk reached the end of the teat. The opening in the teat was off side, and she sprayed milk all over her jeans.

Zandy laughed. "Too bad you didn't bring Crybaby. If you're not going to spray into the bucket, you might as well feed the cat."

There was no point in getting mad at him. He was going to tease about everything. Gracelyn tried the other teat. The spray went into the galvanized bucket with a ringing sound.

"You've got it," Zandy said. "Just keep a steady rhythm. In no time, you'll be doing all three cows."

He took another stool and sat down by the black-and-white cow. Gracelyn leaned against the warm side of her cow, pulling one teat and then the other. They milked in silence while the cows munched the oats.

Gracelyn's wrists began to tire, and the cow was sweating where Gracelyn had her cheek against the belly, but the milk was pooling in the bucket, and now she heard a satisfying swish every time she pulled and aimed.

The cows had finished their grain and were beginning to get restless. Zandy grumbled, "Damn it, stand still," After another moment, he said, "If you switch that tail into my face one more time, I swear I'm going to hack it off."

Gracelyn's cow swung her head around and rolled out a long tongue to scratch at her shoulder. Her belly jiggled so much that Gracelyn had to stop and re-position the milking stool. Meanwhile, Zandy continued to scold his cow. "Stand still. Move that damn foot."

Gracelyn said, "You just told her to stand still."

Zandy ignored her. "Come on, you stubborn black-and-white . . . move that foot back." Suddenly Zandy jumped up, holding the bucket high as he backed away from the stall. The cow arched her body, hoisted her tail, and let go with a full stream of hot, smelly pee.

"Oh, for God's sake," Zandy yelled. "You had all day to do that."

Gracelyn was trying not to let Zandy hear her laughing. She put her face in the cow's side and sputtered with giggles.

Zandy poked his head around the end of her cow. "What do you find so funny?"

Gracelyn lifted her face. "Why, the very same thing you found funny when Pete knocked slop water down my front."

Zandy grinned at her before he returned to his stall. They milked quietly for a few moments more, then Gracelyn said "I think my cow is empty."

"Did you strip her?" Zandy asked, but before Gracelyn could answer, he groaned. "I've just gone and made another of those pictures in your mind. Don't answer. Just take your thumb and finger and go down each teat with a fairly tight, sliding grip. When the teat stays limp, you've stripped her dry for now."

"Do you want me to milk the other cow?"

"I want you to milk *all* the cows *all* the time. I hate milking."

By the time Gracelyn had milked the Brown Swiss, her bucket was brimming. Zandy had finished the holstein. He hung his bucket on a nail above the tool bench and took some hay out to the corral. Gracelyn could hear him breaking the ice in the water tank. He hollered to her, "If you're finished, let 'em loose and send 'em out here."

Gracelyn eyed the restless cows. She chose the guernsey first, trying to step as confidently as Zandy had. She shoved on the cow's rump, and the cow moved over peaceably.

After she released the cows and sent them out of the barn, she looked down at her leather, fur-lined snow boots. They were smeared with a mixture of olive green manure and bits of hay. The cows had churned up the floor of the barn just as they had churned up the corral.

"They sure make a mess," she said to Zandy as she wiped her boots in a snowbank near the gate.

"Yeah, cows will do that. Not like sheep. Sheep pack it down hard and smooth." He went for the milk, then handed Gracelyn the buckets so that he could snap off the lights and close the door. She was tired, but triumphant. *I actually milked a cow. Zandy didn't have to help me, and I did twice as many as he did.*

"Go ahead and strain the milk," Zandy said, "but we'll wait until we're done moving furniture to separate it."

"What's wrong with the furniture the way it is now?"

"It's not arranged right." Zandy frowned as he looked into the bedroom. "The separator and my vet supplies ought to be in this room off the kitchen. And this bed should be in the big room off the living room. It bugs the hell out of me when people arrange stuff illogically."

Gracelyn strained the milk silently, feeling criticized even though it was Mr. Radson's fault the bed was in the wrong room. She didn't want to think about the bed anyway.

It took them an hour and a half to get the rooms set up the way Zandy wanted them. They opened the linen box, and Gracelyn made the bed.

"You can store the rest of the bedstuff and towels on those shelves in the corner."

"Now?" Gracelyn asked. "What about supper?"

"Might as well do it now and get rid of one messy box."

Gracelyn was tired and hungry, and she smelled like cow

sweat, but she transferred the linens to the shelf and took the box out to Zandy, who tore it up and burned it in the stove.

At least he had gone ahead with the separating. The dirty separator tank and the other parts were in the sink again, and the clean milk buckets were upside down on the counter.

When Gracelyn started to open the can of stew, Zandy said, "I was sort of thinking we'd keep the canned stuff for emergencies. There's some fresh hamburger in the meat drawer."

Thoroughly tired of being bossed around, Gracelyn fried hamburgers silently and served the patties on bread with slices of onion. Zandy drank milk, but Gracelyn made herself a cup of tea. As she sat down at the table, she said, "Since you can't cook, why did you assume I could?"

Zandy opened his sandwich and smothered the hamburger patty with catsup. "I never knew a girl who couldn't cook."

"Male chauvinist. Whom have you been dating? Home Ec majors?"

Zandy grinned at her and took a big bite of his sandwich. When he had chewed enough so that he could speak, he said, "When I was a kid on that ranch up north, before my dad died, and even after that, until Mom re-married and moved to Oregon, all the women I knew lived on ranches." He licked catsup from the corner of his mouth and continued, "The girls learned to cook about the same time that they learned to milk cows and feed chickens. Girls on ranches still learn to cook pretty young. There are some big crews to feed."

Gracelyn was enjoying her own hamburger. Frosted flakes didn't go very far when you worked as hard as she had today.

"Well, I'm glad that I only have to cook for the two of us. Pete and Crybaby can eat up my mistakes."

Zandy's face turned very red.

"What's the matter?" Gracelyn asked. "Did I say something wrong?"

Zandy ran his hand through his red hair, increasing his distressed look. "No, but I've got to tell you something."

"Tell me what?"

"I contracted with a guy to shear sheep about mid-April, and I told him you'd feed his shearing crew."

Chapter Twenty-Six

GRACELYN nearly choked on her hamburger. "Good Lord, Zandy, don't you think you might have asked me first?" She pushed her plate away and got up and began washing dishes with quick angry motions. What made him think she could cook for a crew of strange men?

Zandy attempted a couple of jokes, but she was too upset to respond. She ignored him, and he lapsed into silence until she finished the dishes. Then he carried the slop bucket out, and she washed herself and went to bed. When Zandy joined her on the new mattress, she pretended to be asleep, and he turned on his side. They slept stiffly apart on the second night of their honeymoon.

Gracelyn was still upset the next morning. She didn't respond to Zandy's early morning banter, just milked the cows and helped to feed sheep without a word, thinking and worrying all the while, *How will I ever be able to cook for a shearing crew?*

After they finished feeding, Zandy said, "I've got to go back to town and talk to the local vet." Gracelyn unpacked all morning, and when Zandy returned, he brought a CB radio and Annie's first letter.

Dear Gracelyn,

Help! I've become respectable. I'm Artist in Residence at a little college here in Southern California, and I'm married. On our trip cross-country, Craig and I found out that we could stand each other for twenty-four hours at a time, so we made it legal. But I need a wild kindred spirit as a safety valve.

How are you doing? Have you gone on to painting bigger things, like the side of a greyhound bus?

Write to me.

Love, Annie.

Gracelyn was so happy to have the letter that she had to share her joy with someone and, since her husband was the only other person on the ranch, she read the letter to him. He took time to listen to the letter and then said with a grin, "You're at least *reading* to me. Saved by Annie . . . she can put her boots under our table any time."

Gracelyn said, "If I learn to cook," but she managed a grin, and they were on speaking terms again.

Zandy installed his new CB radio at the end of the kitchen counter. "I've got a radio in my truck, but this is a base station," he said. "Its range is somewhere between twenty and thirty miles. Not all the ranchers can reach me, but I've made a deal with the fellows at The Silos to relay names and numbers and Maggie Norman will let me use her phone to return clients' calls."

"Who's Maggie Norman?"

"She owns that ranch with the big white house and red barn just three miles back on the Plum Creek road," Zandy said. Gracelyn remembered the house. She had thought it was her new home.

"Why can't we just have the phone company put in a phone of our own?" she asked.

"Because the phone company charges an arm and a leg for every pole and every foot of line, and the greedy bastards sometimes measure the distance from their central switching station instead of from the nearest pole. We'll have to make do with the CB until we've got the place running good. We need every spare penny to get the stock through the winter."

From the first moment the CB was installed, Gracelyn

found the constant chatter and static annoying, but she couldn't turn the radio off. Zandy said their budget depended on his getting calls for veterinary service. He had posted notices at the feed stores and in the cafés. The other veterinarian in town was middle-aged and extremely busy. He was glad to take Zandy's name as a back-up vet.

Once satisfied that his plan was well set up, Zandy concentrated on the sheep and the ranch buildings. He and Gracelyn settled into a daily routine.

During the first two months, before increasing calls on the CB began to change things, they fed sheep together each morning. Zandy loaded hay while Gracelyn milked the cows and fixed breakfast. Then they drove along the snowy track to the ridge, and, taking turns driving, they scattered cake and tossed hay to the sheep, working in a pleasant rhythm that reminded Gracelyn of their days in the clinic. They never mentioned their first night or any of the troubled nights that followed. Gracelyn ached to find a way to solve their sexual problems, but when he wasn't joking, Zandy spoke only of the animals, the land, and the work, and she didn't know how to begin.

On the ridge, fighting the wind and ground blizzards, Gracelyn learned to handle the truck's low gears and use the four-wheel drive to keep the pickup moving. When she spelled Zandy in back, she learned how to spread the cake to keep the sheep from bunching and became skilled at tossing hay downwind from the sheep, away from their backs.

Her lungs burned in the cold air, her arms ached from carrying the buckets and bales, but she would not have missed a morning. Often when Zandy came to the tailgate ready to take his turn, he lifted her down and warmed her close to his body. Standing in the shelter of the truck in Zandy's embrace, joking or silent, Gracelyn could forget the nights and her continuing struggle in the house and the other hungers that were never satisfied.

On mornings when the sun sparkled on the snow and the carmine bluffs stood out against the blue of the sky, Gracelyn and Zandy leaned against the pickup bed, resting side by side, enjoying the beauty of the country, alive with the hope brought by the fattening ewes and the first hints of the coming spring.

Back at the barn, they went to their separate jobs. If there were no calls on the CB, Zandy worked all day long on the old sheep buildings. After he repaired the shearing platform, he started re-roofing the lambing shed.

Gracelyn fed the chickens and then started the never-ending house chores, always feeling inept and often feeling angry with her mother. *What good was it to give me tennis lessons and skiing lessons and golf lessons and swimming lessons? Why didn't you teach me to cook, to learn some sort of housekeeping habits? Everyone needs to be able to take care of the space around her. Why didn't you teach me something useful?*

She tried to plan complete meals, gritting her teeth as she thought of Zandy's promise to the shearing crew, but she didn't have time to read recipes. She had the milk to care for, and cheese and butter to make, and eggs to gather and store, and ashes to take out, and clothes to wash. She wished she had time to drive in to Brandon to the laundromat, but the town was forty miles away, and anyway, at home she could do three things at once, heating the wash water in the tin tub while she separated milk and set her milk and cream to sour. She took time one morning to answer Annie's letter.

Dear Annie,

Your cry for a kindred spirit was forwarded to me, and just knowing I can write to you makes me happy.

I'm married, too. (When I finally rebelled, I didn't even bother about arguing with my folks. We eloped.) His name is Zandy and we raise sheep. And I milk cows, Annie. Every morning and every night, I bring home two buckets brimming with warm foamy milk. Sometimes I think I'm going to drown in milk.

We won't have bum lambs until spring, the chickens are practically floating, and the dog runs at the sight of the bucket.

So I let my milk sour and put it to use. City milk never seemed to clabber. As far as I can remember, it spoiled before it soured. I like the acrid smell of country clabber, but I never thought anyone could spend so much thought on one little gallon of curds and whey.

I'm snowed in, forty miles from the mailbox and three miles from the nearest neighbor and a telephone, but I don't have time to get lonesome. I'm getting my degree in cheese-making by the guess-and-by-golly method, as Zandy calls it. I never get it off the fire at the right moment. Too soon, and the cheese isn't completely separated from the whey. Too late, and the cheese is like rubber.

I have to learn to do it right. We need the protein and we need to save our cash where we can. We eat cottage cheese with canned peaches, cottage cheese with radishes and onions (on grocery day when we have fresh vegetables) and cottage cheese with cream and sugar.

Did you know that modern ranch women still do all this stuff? I make butter, too.

One day, I set the electric mixer in the sour cream to agitate it and separate the butter fat. I went outside for a quick moment of sketching, which turned into half an hour. When I returned, the cream had doubled and run over the side of the bowl and down the front of the counter, but it wouldn't turn to butter because the beaters went too fast.

After that, Zandy bought me an old-fashioned daisy wheel churn with manual handle and paddles, and I'm stuck in the house because if I don't turn the handle, the paddles don't make butter.

Her correspondence with Annie provided a few pleasant breaks in the steady grind of ranch chores. Otherwise, with constant inside and outside work to do, Gracelyn was too busy to think of anything but her next task and an occasional quick addition to her sketch book. From what Zandy told her, their neighbor was just as busy. It was not until early March that Gracelyn finally met Maggie Norman and heard Josh Franklin's name for the first time.

Chapter
Twenty-Seven

ZANDY was gone. The radio had called for Doc, which was Zandy's "handle," just before evening chores. Gracelyn had taken the call and gone to find Zandy at the lambing shed. He gathered his vet supplies and left for Maggie Norman's ranch to use the phone.

After he left, Gracelyn walked to the barn again, grateful for the company of Peg-Leg Pete. As she fastened the cows in their stalls, Pete flopped down outside the barn door. Gracelyn was just stripping the guernsey when Pete started barking. She heard a pickup stop at the corral gate.

"Hello the barn!" a woman's voice called. "Gracelyn, are you there?"

Gracelyn carried her bucket and the milkstool to the door. "Down, Pete," she commanded as a woman opened the gate. She was a small woman about the age of Gracelyn's mother, dressed in jeans, boots and a Levi's jacket. Kinky strands of blond-red hair escaped from under the blue polka-dotted scarf she had tied around her head.

She came right into the barn and looked around. "I'm Maggie Norman. Alex said you'd be up here milking. Finished yet?"

Of course Zandy had introduced himself as Alex. Gracelyn looked down at the milk bucket and milk stool. "I was just about to start the second cow."

"Well, give me the other bucket, and I'll do the third cow. Then we can go have a cup of coffee and talk."

"My husband didn't send you out here to help with the milking, did he?"

Maggie Norman laughed. "No, Alex wasn't hiring any new hands today. He sent me up here with a message. How stupid of me not to tell you right off."

Gracelyn smiled at the woman. It would have been impossible not to smile at her. Her leathery face was creased with wrinkles, and most of them seemed to be laugh wrinkles. Her blue eyes sparkled, even in the dim light from the overhead bulb.

"What did Zandy—Alex—want you to tell me?"

"He won't be home tonight. He's got a real problem with Harry Courtney's mare."

Gracelyn swallowed. Zandy had been late a couple of times since they'd been on the ranch, but he had never stayed away overnight. She didn't know if she was ready to spend a whole night alone.

But she didn't want Maggie Norman to know she was scared, so she said, "Thanks for coming up. I'd have worried."

When they had finished the milking, Gracelyn ran to shut the chicken coop and then rode with Maggie to the house, thinking of the mess she'd left in the kitchen and hoping that Maggie didn't expect some kind of pie or something with her coffee.

But Maggie sat down at the kitchen table, pushed back the lunch dishes, and reached for an ash tray. "I've been meaning to come up," she said, "but I'm short-handed at the ranch, and Josh's gone rambling again."

Gracelyn turned from straining the milk to ask, "Your husband?"

"My brother. Josh Franklin. He's a roamer. Shoulda been born in a different century so he could have trailed herds up from Texas."

"Do you run the ranch together?" Gracelyn put the milk in the refrigerator and stepped to the sink to rinse the coffee pot.

"No, it's my place. I ran it with my husband until he died. Josh's supposed to be my foreman."

"Do you have sheep?"

"Not as many as we used to. It's too damned hard to get help for lambing season." Maggie bent her head to light a cigarette. "If city people didn't gobble up so much fuel, the oil companies wouldn't be stealing our hired hands."

Gracelyn was silent, thinking of the gasoline her family wasted. They almost never used the bus line that served Silver Crest. She put the pot over the burner and, taking the dirty dishes from the table, stacked them in the sink. There wasn't room on the counter. She had set a basket of clothes there when she had brought it in from the line.

Maggie grinned, "No offense meant to city people."

Gracelyn laughed. She had felt defensive for a moment, but she couldn't be cross when Maggie was grinning at her. "None taken," she said. "Anyway, I'm no longer city people."

Maggie nodded at the basket. "Are you washing on the board?"

Gracelyn glanced down at her roughened hands. "Only until we get the wool check," she said. "Then we're going modern."

"Ah, the wool check," Maggie said. "That's the pot of gold at the end of the rainbow. If your ranch is anything like mine, there are ten places that each year's wool check should go."

Gracelyn smiled. She liked this brusque, honest lady. "Well, I'm glad we'll only be nine years behind by spring."

Maggie laughed. "Alex tells me that you're not too happy about feeding the shearing crew."

Gracelyn turned toward the cupboard. Was Zandy complaining about her to the neighbors? She busied herself with cups and spoons until she could answer lightly.

"It's the shearing crew that's not going to be happy, I'm afraid. Did my husband tell you that he's been living on eggs and cottage cheese?"

"No, he didn't mention that. He just said you were worried about how to cook for so many."

Gracelyn relaxed a little. Maybe Zandy was only trying to help. She set a cup of coffee in front of Maggie Norman and met her neighbor's eyes. They were friendly, not critical.

Gracelyn sat down at the table, put her hands around the warm coffee cup, and said, "Maggie, I'll tell you the truth. I not only don't know how much to feed a bunch of men, I don't know *what* to feed them. And if I have to help tie or toss fleeces to cut costs, I can't see how I can be in here cooking dinner at the same time."

Maggie Norman lit another cigarette and stretched back in her chair. "Well, let's see. Best thing to do is get an entire rump roast." She squinted at the oven. "Will that thing run on a low heat, like 300 or 325?"

"I think so." Gracelyn had done nothing with the oven but heat a pizza that Zandy had brought from town one day.

"Well, you put your roast on in the morning before you go to the barn. Salt and pepper it, and rub a garlic clove over the top if you're feeling fancy, and then let it cook along slow until noon."

"Wait," Gracelyn rose and picked up a sketchpad that was on the counter by the clothes basket. "I want to write this all down." She started to flip forward to a clean page, but Maggie said, "Let me see."

Gracelyn handed her the sketchpad, which was partly filled. She had done hasty sketches of that first sunset, the trees along the creek, Peg-Leg Pete, Crybaby, a couple of chickens, and an old sheep.

"These aren't bad," Maggie said.

"They're okay," Gracelyn said, "but I never really get what I see onto paper." The sketches *weren't* okay. There wasn't one she would send to Dr. Carlson. He suggested one hundred sketches of a subject. She seldom had time to do more than one. Maggie was waiting. Gracelyn sighed, and taking the sketchpad, she flipped to a clean page.

"Rump roast. How many pounds will a whole one weigh?"

"Oh, nine or ten pounds."

"Ten pounds of meat for one meal?"

"Wait until you see the way a shearing crew eats. Besides, you'll want leftovers for supper and maybe for stew the next day. You'll be feeding those guys at noon for several days. You go ahead and cook the whole roast."

"Okay, I'll take your word for it." Gracelyn continued writing, then asked, "What next?"

"You said you had cottage cheese?"

"Yes, but I can't be sure it will be fit to serve to company. I can't seem to get the cooking time right."

"That's easy. You cook it on a low heat and take it off just at the moment when the curds begin to separate from the whey."

Gracelyn smiled at Maggie. She did make it sound easy.

Maggie smiled back and said, "A week or so before shearing, make extra cheese every day. Hang it up in its drain cloth until it's real dry. Store it in your refrigerator. Then when those starving males are due, drag it out, dump it in a big bowl, and stir in gobs of fresh cream."

"Okay, that's meat and cottage cheese. What else?"

"Green beans are easy. Fry several slices of bacon in a big pot, add two or three big cans of green beans and cook 'em low and slow the night before. Then just heat 'em up while you're making the gravy."

Gracelyn put the pencil down with a groan. "Gravy! Maggie, do I have to have gravy?"

"Well, those men are going to want potatoes, and potatoes mean gravy."

Gracelyn sighed again and picked up the pencil. "Tell me how to make gravy." Maggie dictated the steps for gravy-making and then said,

"You tell Alex that you'll have to quit working with the fleeces an hour before they expect dinner. Even if you peel your potatoes in the morning, they're going to need an hour to cook."

Gracelyn was silent. How was she going to get the milk chores done, do dishes, peel potatoes, put in a roast, and ever get to the barn to help with shearing?

"Tell you what," Maggie said, draining her coffee and rising from her chair. "You and Alex come up to my place about eleven on Sunday, and I'll help you cook a dinner. It's a lot easier to show you than tell you."

"But you're so busy," Gracelyn said.

"I'm glad to have another woman on Plum Creek. It'll be fun to show you around the kitchen."

Tears started in Gracelyn's eyes. *Why couldn't my mother have been more like Maggie?* "Do you have to go? There's more coffee."

Maggie grinned. "I didn't do my lunch dishes either. And Old Daniel's coming. I need to get him lined out for fixing fence tomorrow. I'll see you on Sunday."

Gracelyn walked to the door with Maggie and watched her drive away in the red-and-white Ford pickup. When Maggie was out of sight, Gracelyn felt a sense of loss. Pete jumped up against her, and she caught him around his upper half in a hug.

"You're my buddy, aren't you, Pete? You won't let the boogey-man get me tonight."

Chapter Twenty-Eight

GRACELYN went back inside, cheered by the thought of Maggie's dirty lunch dishes. She washed her own dishes and the separator and the milk buckets. She folded the clothes and put the basket away. The CB was quiet. Gracelyn looked around the house and sighed. It certainly wasn't as clean as her mother's house; it would *never* be that clean. She put a record on her stereo, but the music made her nervous. The rock music she had enjoyed in the dorm seemed too loud for a house on Plum Creek. She switched to the radio and caught a weather forecast.

At least they weren't predicting snow. She wouldn't be isolated by a storm. She picked up her purse and looked inside for the letter her mother had sent. It wasn't there, so she went to the bedroom and stirred around in the pile of stuff on top of the dresser. No letter. No point in writing unless she could answer the questions her mother had asked. It would be difficult whenever she wrote. Her mother hadn't a clue to ranch life. Gracelyn had to give answers if she was going to say anything at all. She couldn't ask questions: *Do you know yet, Mother? Do you know about Arminda?*

She opened her sketchpad and studied the menu she had copied down. Bless Zandy for sending Maggie. Gracelyn picked up a pencil and began to sketch the milk buckets and their reflection in the many small panes of the windows. The first sketch didn't catch the depth of the night behind the windows. She turned the page and began again. Exasperated with her crude perspective, she turned the page again and worked more carefully, and even then the awkwardness of her lines was apparent. She worked until she was cold.

"Damn," she said to Pete, who rose from the floor the moment she moved. "I wish this place had a thermostat . . . or we had enough money for another load of coal. I'm tired of trying to burn cottonwood and sticks."

She went outside for wood. There was no moon, the stars were remote, and the darkness was immense, bigger than daylight could ever be. She heard the cry of a coyote in the bluffs. *I ought to check the sheep.*

She built up the fire and put in a large chunk of wood to hold the heat in the house for a while. Then, whistling to Pete, she climbed into the Subaru and drove up the road and over the plank bridge to the barn. The track to the near pasture was rutted, and she was afraid she'd high center if she took her car up there. Annie's higher-wheeled van would have made it. For a moment, she thought of the picture she had painted on the van. Where was it now?

She went into the corral, comfortable with the dark shapes of the milk cows in the corner. She smiled, remembering how afraid she had been to slap the guernsey on the rump. Now, since the milking was her regular chore, she poked, prodded, pried, smacked—anything to get the cows to go where she wanted them.

She took the flashlight from the tool bench and looked around for a stick. She spotted the sheep hooks that hung along a rafter at the back of the barn. Zandy had said she'd learn all about them come lambing season. She lifted one down, balanced it in one hand and went out through the back door.

Pete bounded forward. "Come back, Pete." The dog obeyed and she patted his head when he reached her side.

Blown into waves by the wind, the old snow had refrozen in hard crusts. With every step, she broke through the crusts into the softer snow underneath. Pete floundered along a trail of his own making. The wires in the gate had contracted in the cold and were stretched tight. She leaned her

whole body against the upright pole on the gate and finally
got enough slack in the wires to allow her to lift the loop
over the post.

"I'd better shut the darn thing," she said to Pete, struggling with the gate again. "I don't want to be chasing sheep
all the way to Maggie's place."

As she and Pete moved slowly around the sleeping animals, the flashlight beam glanced off the bony part of the
sheep's faces and caught the shine of their eyes. Their wool
coats were so thick that the sheep looked as if they were
hiding in the fleeces instead of wearing them. When they
tucked their skinny legs under to lie down, they were certainly cozy enough. Zandy had said, "The cold air isn't
going to hurt them, but watch out when a sheep gets wet.
Then you've got trouble."

The sheep hook made a clumsy walking stick because the
pole was so tall, more than six feet, maybe eight. The hook
on the end was the same shape as Little Bo Peep's. She
remembered her father reading nursery rhymes to her when
she was little. She could not think of him now without
thinking of Arminda. She stopped walking and shut off the
flashlight.

The darkness spread for miles and miles. There had to
be a way to convey the multiple facets of darkness, to draw
its depth and the various qualities of light, to show how
every object had its own texture and shadow. *Dr. Carlson
said that I see like an artist.* She did not want to think about
the rest of his words.

She flicked the light on again and struggled with the
gate, opening and closing it. Then she walked down to the
barn, stopping to check the chicken house lock. She wasn't
very fond of the smelly fowl, but she certainly needed the
eggs until she learned to cook something else. She slid a
beam of light across Pete's nose. "A real artist could paint
the smell of chicken manure and cow pee and sheep."

The dog seemed to enjoy her talking to him. He looked
up, his tail wagging slightly. Gracelyn replaced the sheep
hook and shut out the barn lights. As she opened the car

door, she looked again at the sleeping milk cows. *At the moment I'm a real ranch hand. Until Zandy comes back, I am absolutely necessary here.* She had never before been absolutely necessary anywhere. But the thought didn't ease the miseries that lay like stagnant swamp water in her mind. *It isn't enough. I'm a real ranch hand, but I'm not an artist. And I'm not a real wife.*

By the time she re-fueled the fire and stacked wood behind the stove for morning, it was eleven o'clock. They were usually in bed by ten-thirty, since Zandy liked to be up by four-thirty. "I want to get the chores done early and get to the feeding," he had explained, "so I can have the rest of the day to work."

"Chores and feeding don't count as work?"

"Nah. They're just a necessary nuisance. Work is something that stays done."

"Then I haven't done a bit of work since we moved up here."

"You're just warming up."

Zandy was amazing. He worked every bit as hard as she did, and when he was exhausted, he still joked.

She hated to go into the bedroom. *Every* night she hated to go into the bedroom. Zandy might turn to her, but she knew that no matter how gently he caressed her, where he touched her, how much time he took, she was going to end up disappointing him.

Zandy never mentioned their lovemaking, but he had to be aware of the tension that never left her body. She tried to block from her mind the picture that had invaded their wedding night. But, when Zandy touched her, Arminda and her father were there, and sometimes her mother.

The scenes that spun through her mind were more and more confused. She forced her body to respond, trying to forget her family, trying to focus on Zandy. She attempted to bring back the warm feeling of working together on the ridge with the sheep. But she was tormented by pictures of her mother making the bed in the Lazy-J Motel, of her father on top of Arminda on her mother's living-room

couch. The harder she tried to stop them, the worse the
pictures became and she stayed hard and cold inside. Zandy
finally went ahead and climaxed, but she never could.

Gracelyn stepped into the bedroom and snatched her
nightgown from the hook in the closet. She took the blanket from the bed and went back to the living room. She
was such a mess, she didn't blame Zandy for staying away
all night.

Good God! What was she thinking? Zandy was trying to
save Harry Courtney's mare. She couldn't possibly suspect
Zandy of anything. Damn her father. Gracelyn paced the
room, trying to think of other things. Thinking of Zandy,
thinking of Maggie, thinking of Annie. She picked up the
letter pad and a pencil.

Dear Annie,

I once told Zandy I wanted something bigger. I had
no idea then what I meant. I'd just painted the storm
on your van and my mind was stretching—reaching
out somewhere. Now, oh Annie, *now* I think I've
found what I needed, and it's bittersweet.

This country expands me. From the everchanging
bluffs above us on the south to the purple-shaded
hills to the north, the land is magnificent. The sky,
especially the night sky, demands that I pay attention
to subtle textures, to the intricacies of darkness, to
the shades of light and shadow.

Annie, it is as if a part of me has gone into that
sky, and I must draw it back with brush or pen, but I
don't know how, and I haven't any spare time to find
out.

God, when I think of the hours I wasted in Silver
Crest. I had no chores—no work at all. (I can hardly
believe that I did no work.) All that time to sketch,
to study technique, to experiment. My mouth waters
just thinking about it. Here, I've done twelve sketches
. . . twelve sketches since January!

Dr. Carlson, the professor of the art class I took

after you left, once told me I had talent and it would eat me alive. Well, tonight for the first time, I begin to know what he meant. Something is gnawing at me, Annie, and I am so afraid.

She was crying, and she didn't have time for it. She had to be up early for chores if Zandy didn't get back to help. She left the letter unfinished and, picking up Crybaby, lay down on the living room cot.

Chapter Twenty-Nine

"I am so excited, you'd think we were going to New York to visit art galleries," Gracelyn said to Zandy as they got ready to leave for Maggie Norman's ranch on Sunday.

"I didn't know you wanted to go to New York."

Gracelyn grinned at him. "I thought I'd use the wool check."

"That must be the six-thousandth thing we've put on the list. After spending the night in Harry Courtney's horse stall, I'm planning to buy a camper with a decent bed."

"We're probably going to be in hock for the rump roast Maggie insists I'll need for the shearing crew. The thought still scares me."

"They won't be here until April. You've still got a month to practice."

When they turned in at Maggie's gate, Gracelyn remembered the excited moments on her first day in Montana when she had thought this place was her new home. Maggie's house wasn't odd-shaped like theirs. It was a rectangular, two-story building with white siding and a red roof. A circle of big spruce trees curved around the house like a loving arm. Beyond the house at the end of a graveled area were corral fences, round silver-colored grain storage units, and the big red barn. Maggie's lambing shed sat on a rise beyond the barn. Made of steel, it resembled an airplane hangar.

"Our place is going to look this way some day," Zandy

said as he knocked on Maggie's door. The wistfulness in his voice was painful to hear. They were so far from having a ranch like this.

Gracelyn turned impulsively and kissed him, murmuring, "Even better."

"Well, look who's necking on my doorstep." Maggie stood in the open doorway grinning at them. Zandy was red-faced as they entered Maggie's living room.

Gracelyn gazed around with pleasure. "If ever a room could make one feel at home, this is it," she exclaimed.

She turned in time to catch Maggie blushing. The woman met Gracelyn's eyes and then looked down. She hasn't had a compliment in a long time, Gracelyn thought. She looked around the room again.

The pillowed couch was done in gorgeous warm colors vermilion and cadmium orange and Indian yellow. A tall pottery vase filled with an arrangement of native grasses stood on a low table made of burled wood. The wide floor boards were waxed and polished. On the mantel above the fireplace was a collection of carved wooden miniatures. The fireplace itself was made of the same reddish stone as the bluffs that rose above the valley. It wasn't carmine when the sun wasn't shining on it. Burnt sienna. That was the closest color, but redder than that.

The room was more inviting than her mother's living room. Gracelyn moved toward the fire holding out her arms. A person could live and breathe in this room.

She turned toward Maggie. "You'd better take me to the kitchen before this room captures me for good."

"I just started the roast a little while ago," Maggie said. "I didn't figure we needed a whole rump roast." Her eyes twinkling, she bent to open the oven door. The kitchen was pleasant too. *But no more pleasant than ours*, Gracelyn thought. *She doesn't have our long low windows and the view of the creek.* She turned her attention to Maggie's instructions, concentrating harder than she had ever concentrated in any college class.

Just as Gracelyn and Maggie were setting dinner on the large, wooden kitchen table, they heard someone stomping his boots on the back porch. In a moment the door crashed open, and a man in boots, hat, and Levi's jacket grabbed Maggie from behind and swung her around the kitchen.

"Damn it, Josh, put me down. I'm not one of those rodeo fillies that you do-si-do at the fair. Where in the hell have you been this time?"

The man set Maggie down and said with a flash of white teeth, "Ridin' the trail, Sis, just ridin' the trail. And I'm hungry. Put another plate on the table."

Maggie introduced her brother, who was as dark as she was fair. He was two or three inches shorter than Zandy and heavier muscled. He took off his Stetson, revealing brown, almost black, hair. His face was deeply tanned. His brown eyes were serious and sincere for the few moments of introduction, but in another moment he was regaling them with stories of the broncs and bulls he had ridden in small-town rodeos from Texas to the Canadian border.

Josh entertained them all the way through dinner. Gracelyn and Zandy laughed, but left most of the spoken response to Maggie, who tried to get her brother to talk about ranch work and lambing season, with little success. He wanted to talk about rodeos.

"Damn it, Josh. If I hadn't raised you myself, I'd say you were spoiled rotten."

Josh reached over and tugged a lock of Maggie's strawberry blond hair. "You did okay, Pinkie, considering that you're not all that much older than I am."

"Ten years is a lot of years, and stop with the Pinkie bit, or you don't get any pie."

Gracelyn had not helped make the pie. She was glad that Maggie had baked it earlier. Her head was swimming with the cooking advice she had received. And with Josh there, she didn't have time to think it all through again. He wouldn't let them settle down.

As soon as they had left the dinner table, he said, "Let's have some music."

"Nope," Maggie said. "Not until we clean up the kitchen. You go talk to Alex while Gracelyn and I get the dishes done."

"There's one thing in your kitchen that I envy you," Gracelyn said as she dried the plates. "And that's your hot water faucet. I never seem to have enough hot water for the milk buckets and separator."

"Yeah, milk and cream get purely slimy in cold water."

Gracelyn was impressed by the speed with which Maggie cleaned up the kitchen. Maggie told her where to put the dishes and utensils and didn't offer any warnings, as her mother often did, about how they must be shelved.

"Okay, Josh," Maggie called into the living room as she wiped out the sink, "you can get out that squeeze box now."

Josh Franklin played the accordion well. Maggie backed him up with her guitar. Gracelyn, who had seldom danced in public, found that it wasn't hard to learn to polka with the insistent rhythm from the accordion bouncing off the walls and Zandy counting, "ONE two three, hop, ONE two three, hop" into her ear. They polkaed until they were breathless and laughing, and then Josh said, "I get to teach Gracelyn how to waltz. Play us a waltz, Maggie."

Zandy took a harmonica from his pocket, ran up and down the scale and said, "Play something I know, Maggie, and play it in D."

Gracelyn stared at Zandy. She had never heard him play the harmonica. She hadn't even known that he owned one. He winked at her and put the harp to his mouth as Maggie started to play and sing a song about a dark-haired girl named Evelina. Josh followed Zandy's example and counted out the waltz step, saying, "RIGHT two three, LEFT two three," until Gracelyn fell into the proper pattern and responded to the beat in the music. Then Josh sang along with Maggie, "Evelina, my sweet Evelina, my love for you will never, never die."

They had more pie and coffee before heading up the road to do evening chores. Gracelyn moved closer to Zandy in the truck and said, "I can't remember ever having so much fun on a Sunday afternoon. Why didn't you tell me that you could play the harmonica?"

"You never asked."

"Can you play a zither or a balalaika, or a mandolin?"

"Nope."

"Well, don't say I never asked."

"What do you think of Josh?" Zandy said.

"He's nice enough, but he doesn't help seem to help Maggie very much on the ranch, and he should. She works awfully hard." Gracelyn paused, thinking of the way Josh skirted the subject of ranch work. She let it go and said, "I really like Maggie, though, and I'm crazy about her living room."

It turned out that Maggie's living room was the cause of their first real fight.

Chapter Thirty

During the two weeks following their outing at Maggie's, Gracelyn cooked three small roasts for Zandy. Each turned out different: one was too rare, one too well done, one tasted too much of garlic.

Zandy didn't comment on the food. He rushed through his meals and left to answer a vet call or to work at the lambing sheds. Once when Gracelyn asked him about the meat, he gave her a hurried unfocused look and said, "It's fine . . . fine. Don't make such a big deal out of cooking for the shearing crew. They'll eat what you put in front of them."

Gracelyn turned so that Zandy wouldn't see the tears in her eyes. If he didn't have time to evaluate her cooking efforts, he certainly wouldn't want to talk about the living room. Gracelyn wanted a room like Maggie's almost as much as she wanted that damn roast to turn out right.

She knew Zandy was too busy, but she was *trying* to help. The day of their fight, she slipped from the bed at 4:30, taking her barn clothes with her to the living room. Zandy had been out on a vet call most of the night, crawling into bed shortly after three. She shut the bedroom door and built up a fire as quietly as she could.

She took the pickup to the barn, hoping to be back before Zandy was awake, but when she entered the kitchen with two buckets of milk, he was sitting at the table clutching a cup of coffee. He looked up with a frown.

"We're late. Why didn't you wake me?"

"You needed the sleep."

"I need to finish the holding pen for the shearing crew."

Gracelyn strained the milk and set it into the refrigerator. She'd better feed him his breakfast. She could separate later. "You've still got two weeks."

"Unless that squawk box pulls me away."

Gracelyn didn't answer. She fried bacon and eggs and made toast. "Thanks for making the coffee."

"I don't see how you can do the milking before you have coffee." He sounded less grouchy.

Gracelyn changed the subject. "I want to have the living room fixed up before the shearers get here, or at least before lambing season. Can I send my cream and a shopping list to town with you?"

Zandy grinned at her. He said, "You could earn more money if you made butter out of that cream."

"No way am I going to churn butter for sale." The conversation was beginning to irritate her.

Zandy picked up his fork and attacked his breakfast. "Well then, how about making some cottage cheese for sale. Yours scarcely bounces now."

She knew he was just teasing, but she didn't laugh. "Maggie told me how to time it right."

"Darn. What will we have to talk about if we can't discuss your cottage cheese?"

That's true enough, she thought. *If we don't joke or talk about ranch work, we're silent.* She sighed, thinking of the things she had never told him and of how seldom he voiced an emotion himself.

She had to leave the breakfast dishes in order to feed sheep with him. It was snowing. The wind on the ridge was icy. Gracelyn stood in the pickup bed tossing hay until her chest hurt from breathing. They had used up the baled hay and were now loading from an old haystack of loose hay. She forked hay over the side, legs spread wide to balance herself, her arms trembling as she tried not to fork the hay onto the backs of the sheep. "Keep the wool as clean as you can," Zandy had said. "We'll get more money for the fleeces."

Zandy stopped the truck and got out. Gracelyn rested for a moment and gazed out over the flock of sheep. No two were the same. Gracelyn could even recognize some of them by the sound of their bleating.

"Soon as you can tell these sheep apart by smell as well as by sound," Zandy said, "you'll be a professional lamb licker."

"*When* are you going to explain that term?"

"It can't be explained. To define it, you have to see it." He smiled, but he sounded tired. "I guess it's my turn to pitch hay." He nodded toward the truck. "You want to drive for awhile?"

Gracelyn crawled in and drove slowly along the hill, thinking about the living room. Their room was not as big as Maggie's. She'd have to take that into account and work around the stove, too. Zandy had already said there wasn't money for new furniture. *I'll start with the walls—paint and pictures. The furniture can be disguised some way.*

Back at the house, Gracelyn put the separator together, still planning the living room. She wound the handle up to the proper speed and let in the milk. When the milk reached the bowl, it leaked out all sides.

"Oh, damn," Gracelyn said out loud, grabbing for the shut-off key. She lifted the tank from the base and stepped into the kitchen where she set it dripping onto the kitchen counter. "I must have forgotten the blasted ring."

Sure enough, the rubber ring was in the sink. Gracelyn took the separator apart and put it together properly. By the time she had the milk mopped up, it was time to peel potatoes for lunch. She did that quickly and went back to her separating. As the handle went around and around, her mind returned to the living room. When the tank was empty, she left the spouts to finish dripping and went into their bedroom.

From under the bed, she dragged the box that held the spread and pillows and some other decorative items she had used at college. She spread the contents out on the unmade bed. The plaid throw in blues and greens might make a chair cover. Her mother had chosen the colors for her dorm room. They were adjacent cool colors—decorator colors—and she preferred warmer ones, but the material was nearly new. She spent some time experimenting with various combinations.

"Hey, what's burning?"

Gracelyn dropped the pillow she was holding and ran to the kitchen. Zandy was standing by the stove.

"I forgot about the potatoes," she said, grabbing the pan and shoving it into the sink, burning her fingers.

"Well, didn't you smell the pan scorching?"

"No," Gracelyn said. Tears welled in her eyes. His tone caused as much pain as the hot pan handle.

"Damn it to hell, Gracelyn, it seems like a man could come in here just once without finding a god-awful mess. Surely your mother taught you something about organization."

Gracelyn whirled to face him. "You know damn well what my mother taught me."

"And you know how much I like order. That ought to count for something. You could at least try."

Gracelyn thought of her morning-long efforts to do something with their impossible house. She burst into tears, ran to the bedroom, and threw herself in the middle of the pillows. Her sobs escalated into wails. She buried her face in a pillow and cried until Zandy sat down on the edge of the bed.

He just sat there. Gracelyn choked off her sobs, but left her face in the pillow. Finally, Zandy said in a mild voice, "Is this really serious enough to cry about?"

Gracelyn lifted her face an inch. "If nothing about me suits you, why did you marry me in the first place?"

"Because you reminded me of my first horse."

Chapter Thirty-One

GRACELYN dropped her head again, murmuring into the bedclothes, "A horse! Oh, Zandy."

But he didn't hear her. He went on talking. "God, she was beautiful. Long-limbed and graceful with a full flowing mane. She was smart and sure-footed. And she had spirit. When I saw you struggling with that bloody dog, I thought of her. I'd put her at some tough climb or kick her into a gallop after a stray calf, and she never hesitated. She put her whole heart into the job, no matter what it was."

Gracelyn rolled over and stared at Zandy. He was gazing off toward the north window as if he could see that mare in the meadow beyond. She put her hand out and touched him.

"I try, Zandy."

He looked down at her. "I know you do, Gracelyn. I just can't figure out how you can put everything exactly right in one of your pictures and leave such a mess in the house."

"I'm sorry, Zandy."

He covered her hand with his. "I didn't mean to yell at you. But when I'm so damn tired, I hate to come in here and find the place cold and piles of stuff everywhere."

"Not to mention the aroma of burned potatoes," Gracelyn said, grateful for his hand on hers.

Zandy grinned at her. "Was our lunch in that pot?"

Gracelyn felt herself flush. "I was thinking about fixing

up the living room. I'm not sure what we're having for lunch."

Zandy stood up, pulling her with him. "We'd better find something. I have to get back to work."

Later, after they finished the canned soup she had heated, Zandy said, "Maybe you shouldn't plan on redecorating the living room until after shearing. You'll be plenty busy tying fleeces."

Gracelyn was bone tired. Her hands hurt where the twine scraped, and her back ached from bending over. She grabbed the fleece that the man running the clippers had shoved under the fence. Taking a paper string from the line of strings the crew boss had counted out on the fence before the shearing had begun that morning, she quickly tied the fleece. Then she tossed it into the mouth of the metal tube that was fitted around the burlap wool-sack. The wool-sack extended eight feet along the ground. Zandy was running the tromper, a hydraulic cylinder that pushed the fleeces through the metal tube and into the sack and packed them tight.

Gracelyn put her hand to the small of her back and rubbed hard before reaching for the next fleece. All around her, sheep were bleating. The ones that had just been shorn were milling about in the small corral behind the lambing shed, which was a shearing shed at the moment.

Zandy had built a temporary runway in the lambing shed by wiring together wooden panels. The runway stretched nearly the length of the shed, maybe thirty feet. It ended at the shearing platform, which held a small pen.

Zandy kept the runway filled with unshorn sheep from the big corral. As the shearers started on the last two sheep in the little pen on the platform, their helper opened the gate and pushed in several more. Zandy hurried around to drive more sheep into the runway and then rushed back to tromp the fleeces Gracelyn had tossed into the tube.

"They're a ragtag bunch," Zandy had said of the shearing crew he'd hired. "But I can't afford the big crews with their chutes and cookhouses. There's just gonna be two shearers and a helper."

Gracelyn had scarcely finished separating that morning when the crew roared across the bridge in an ancient Dodge pickup that looked as if it had rolled off the bluff at least once. A huge, rusted dent marred the driver's door, and the fenders were rusted through above the rear wheels. The topper on the back of the truck was painted in swirling designs with wild colors, their brilliance in sharp contrast to the faded beige paint on the pickup.

"Now don't you scare these fellows," Zandy said, peering out of the window. "They seem a little shy."

Gracelyn laughed, but her heart was beating faster. "Are these crews willing to work with a woman?"

"They're getting used to it," Zandy said. "The oil companies hired away so many men, help is scarce. A lot of crews will carry a woman to tie fleeces and run the wool tromper."

"Won't they let a woman shear?"

"It's a matter of money. Guys who follow the shearing crew can make more money if they shear. Say they're charging a dollar-sixty-five a head, the shearer will get a dollar-thirty of that. And the only thing he has to provide is his own hand piece. The guy who runs the crew provides the motor."

Before Gracelyn could reply, Zandy picked up his hat. "I'd better go get 'em set up. You come along as soon as you can. Once they get going, we'll need you."

Gracelyn glanced up at the shearers as she slid another fleece from under the fence rail where it had been shoved the moment it came clear of the sheep.

The head of the crew was probably about Zandy's age. He wore a flat-crowned, wide-brimmed black hat. She couldn't tell what color his hair was, but his eyebrows were thick and black and his eyes were greyish-green. He wore Levi's with a big hand-tooled leather belt and a wide buckle. Despite the fact that it had been spitting snow all morning, he worked in shirt sleeves, with just a leather, fleece-lined vest.

As he wrestled with a sheep, he kept up a steady stream of curses, "Come on around here, you son-of-bitchin' old sow, goddamn you, hold your head still . . ." and on and on. And all the while, he was steadily running the clipper.

The crew had hung up a big mechanical arm about four and a half feet long with a two-foot extension on the end. "It has an electric gear-driven motor," Zandy had told her, "and the arm hangs on a bevel so it can move." The hand-piece, which was plugged into the end of the mechanical arm, moved easily wherever the shearer pulled it.

The other shearer was short and dressed in coveralls. He had taken off his brimmed cap a couple of times and run the back of his hand across his blond hair, but he didn't stop to talk or to rest. He worked quickly, his clipper laying back the fleece smoothly, and with fewer nicks, less blood, than the other man. He seemed to like the sheep. He reassured the animal he was clipping, crooning the same soft words over and over as he worked. "There you go, that's a baby, easy does it."

Gracelyn sympathized with the frightened sheep. They struggled and rolled their eyes and then submitted, as if the noise of the motor, or the crooning and cursing, had hypnotized them. When the shearer finished, he had to push that sheep aside to reach for another one.

"I hate the way they look," Gracelyn said to Zandy, who had stepped to the platform to check the runway. "Naked and blood-spotted that way, they seem so vulnerable. And those ratty-looking patches the shearers missed are awful."

Zandy glanced at the growing crowd of shorn ewes in the small corral. "Yeah, they're sorry-looking."

"They must get cold. Isn't it dangerous to shear them this close to lambing?"

"Some say you should back off a bit, but one thing about it, you take off a ewe's long pajamas, she hunts a place out of the wind." Zandy smiled and added, "She finds shelter, and that's good for the lamb." He was always patient with her when she asked questions.

Zandy went around to push more sheep into the runway.

Gracelyn smiled at the young man who was filling the shearing pen. He blushed from his collar to his hat and turned away.

Gracelyn glanced at her watch as she tied another fleece. In an hour, she'd have to quit to go cook dinner. Her stomach was nervous. If they didn't like her cooking, would they come back tomorrow? The crew chief was pretty cocky. She had disliked him from the moment his eyes raked up and down her body as Zandy was introducing them. She didn't like the way he talked to her sheep, either.

Gracelyn sighed. Tying fleeces was boring. She didn't want to think about the roast; she couldn't do anything about it now. She thought briefly of Zandy's comparing her to his horse, taking some comfort from the words "beautiful, full of spirit." Her mind turned to Zandy himself. He was working too hard.

He had been to town practically every day since their fight. The CB squawked and off he went, to come home late and tired.

"What in hell did they do for a vet before I came along?" he grumbled as he came to bed one night long after Gracelyn had done the chores and checked the sheep and put supper away in the refrigerator.

He didn't mention the house, although Gracelyn had spent most of the evenings he was gone trying to create the sort of order he wanted.

Creating order was not as easy as Zandy made it seem. They had very little storage space and most of the shelves in the separator room were taken up by Zandy's veterinary supplies.

Gracelyn had discovered a resistance in herself to the rigid straight lines of cleared dressers and tidied tables. There was interesting texture and depth to a pile of something. She enjoyed looking at the folds of an abandoned shirt and longed to explore the artistic possibilities of the shadows deep inside the folds.

"We're not at all alike," she said to Zandy one morning at breakfast.

"No," he said. "We're not. Me, Tarzan. You, Jane."

She smiled, but pursued her thought. "You are a symmetrical person and I am an asymmetrical person."

"Interesting," Zandy said. The CB interrupted them. He rose from the table, saying, "Do you want me to leave the laundry off in town?"

"Now there's an offer I can't refuse."

Gracelyn hated washday. Washing on the board was hard miserable work, especially when it was snowing. Mr. Radson had left behind a big round tin tub and an old washboard. Gracelyn had to heat the water on the gas stove, propping the tub on bricks to keep it from smothering the gas flame. She pumped and carried water, heated it, scrubbed their clothes, and then carried the water back outside to dump it. The moment she hung the clothes on the line, they froze. She made jokes to herself about getting knocked out by a pair of frozen Levi's, but she didn't talk about the washing with Zandy.

She hated it too much, and she was afraid her joking would sound bitter. Sometimes her knuckles bled when she was scrubbing. And her back ached and her hair got stringy and fell in her eyes.

Suzanne and Mother wouldn't believe her new life, even though she tried to describe it when she had time to answer their letters.

Suzanne wrote that she had been studying the map.

"I've found Brandon, the city where your post office is located. How far is that from your ranch?"

Gracelyn was touched. It was sweet of Suzanne to try to be interested. But Gracelyn laughed out loud when she read the rest of Suzanne's questions:

"Do you shop in a mall at Brandon? How many good restaurants are in the city? Do four-star films play the local movie houses?" She wished she could see Suzanne's face when the answer to her questions arrived.

"Dear Suzanne, I haven't any idea. I've never been to Brandon."

Gracelyn reached for another piece of twine and another fleece.

It was true. Gracelyn had never been to Brandon, which was forty miles from the ranch. Zandy's vet practice had taken off so quickly that he often passed through Brandon on his way to one ranch or another. He picked up mail and groceries when he came back. He took Gracelyn's cream and eggs to sell in town and brought her whatever she put on her shopping list. But since Zandy also stayed late frequently, Gracelyn was needed at home to do chores. She had taken a lot of things for granted before she had married Zandy: the library, art galleries, long leisurely evenings, hot baths.

She had been off the ranch twice: once to have dinner at Maggie's place, and the other time, she had gone with Zandy thirteen miles to the end of the Plum Creek road.

There, where the gravel road crossed to the east under the interstate highway, was the settlement called The Silos. A greasy little gas station with two old-fashioned pumps sat in the weeds in front of four huge grain silos that loomed above the railroad spur, dwarfing the scale house and the trailer house at their feet. Gracelyn had stepped inside out of the snow while Zandy gased up the pickup. He had his own gasoline tank on stilts at the ranch, but the gas tanker that refilled it had been delayed by the storm. On the gas station shelves, next to quart cans of oil, fan belts, and flyspecked plastic cards holding fuses, were a few loaves of bread, a box of candy bars, and several cans of pork and beans. Zandy paid the bored-looking young Mexican behind the counter and then they went back out the Plum Creek road.

Mother's questions were well intentioned too. "Do you need clothes? Cosmetics? Books?" She even asked if Gracelyn needed art supplies. Gracelyn read the rest of the letter with tears in her eyes. Mother was being very sweet. She would answer, "Thank you, Mother. Yes, I need cosmetics, specifically about a gallon of hand lotion. I don't need art supplies at the moment." (Will I ever get to use up what I brought with me?) "And I don't need books or clothes." Gracelyn still hadn't unpacked her books.

The next fleece she grabbed wasn't clean. She wiped her

hands on her pants before tying it, glad her mother couldn't see her wardrobe.

Until Zandy's last shopping trip, she had needed blue jeans, but she wouldn't have asked her mother to buy them. Mother would send designer jeans. Zandy had bought some tough old Levi's, murder to wash and hard to wear when they were new, but they resisted the guck in the barn and protected her legs when she climbed in and out of the truck.

Back in mid-February, Zandy had brought her something else her mother would never have thought to buy. "Here," he'd said, holding out a bulky package. "Happy Valentine's Day."

Inside the big box was a pair of knee-high insulated rubber boots. Gracelyn had laughed and given him a quick hug. "Only someone who wades in cow manure morning and evening can know what a truly romantic gift this is."

Gracelyn had slowed down. The clipper was three fleeces ahead of her. She pulled the fleece toward her, eyeing it critically. When Zandy had first told her she'd be tying fleeces, she'd said, "Good. My hands will get nice and soft from the lanolin in the wool."

"That's not all that's going to be on the wool. You'll get first smell of everything on those fleeces when they come your way."

Gracelyn wrinkled her nose at the odor and tried to concentrate only on the fleece. She didn't want to think about the only letter she had received from her father. Inside the bulky business envelope, along with the title to her car and the insurance policy, was a terse note. "Gracelyn, I'm enclosing some papers that should be kept in your safety deposit box."

She hated her father's cold business letter, even if he *had* enclosed a clear title to her car. But the part of the note that sent her weeping to do evening chores was just one word. Gracelyn. Never in all her life had her father called her anything but Gracie.

Chapter Thirty-Two

GRACELYN left the shearing shed at eleven. When she stepped into the house, her heart started to pound. The odor of overcooked meat was strong. She washed her hands and arms and face, but there wasn't time to change clothes. She took the roast from the oven. The outside of it was dark and dry. With trembling hands, she took a knife and sawed off one end of the roast. The inside was done, but it wasn't burnt. A little juice ran down the face of the cut section. She could have wept with relief. She peeled the potatoes quickly and got out the green beans she'd cooked the night before. Crybaby jumped up on the counter and meowed.

"I know, kitty cat. I've been gone all morning." The cat arched its back and rubbed against Gracelyn. The sleek, cream-fed pussy was nothing like the scared ball of ratty fur that had yowled for four hundred miles on the way to Montana. Gracelyn scooped her off the counter and hugged her.

"I'd better put you in the back room. You know how Zandy is about your joining us at the table." She filled the kitty's dish with fresh cream and shut her into the separator room. Then she hurried to set the table, aware that she smelled like sheep.

"Oh, well, they'll never notice. We all smell like sheep."

By the time the shearing crew and Zandy pulled up in front, the teakettle was steaming. She had remembered that they would need water to wash. Everything was ready but the gravy. Her hands trembled again as she strained the thickening into the beef broth. She was exhausted. God, what she wouldn't give for a long hot soak in a real bathtub.

Zandy and the shearing crew came in, stomping snow from their boots. They hung their hats and coats on the hooks by the door. Zandy showed them to the wash pan and then went to the refrigerator for beer.

"Come on in here and sit until dinner's on the table," he said. He handed each man a can of beer, scarcely giving Gracelyn a glance. The men had nodded at Gracelyn when they came in, but they trooped into the living room without speaking to her. They sat down and began to talk about sheep with Zandy.

The business talk continued through dinner. Gracelyn passed the food and re-filled the potato dish, feeling invisible. When the men had finished the fruit and cookies Gracelyn served for dessert, they pushed their chairs back and returned to the living room.

Zandy stoked the fire and tipped back in his recliner while the shearers sprawled on the cot. The man with the fancy belt buckle put his head back. In a moment, he was asleep with his mouth open, snoring loudly. The young member of the crew sat down on the floor by the stove and scratched Pete's belly.

Gracelyn cleared the table, determined not to cry. Of course she didn't expect any help from the shearing crew, but Zandy hadn't even asked if she needed help. She put the food away and stacked the dishes on the counter. She heated more water and washed the separator first. At least that would be ready at chore time. She washed and drained the dishes, every minute hating the man who snored. Her body ached with the need to lie down on that cot herself.

She poured the last of the coffee into a cup and sat down at the kitchen table just as the four men in the living room stirred and came looking for their hats.

"You want to ride over to the barn with me?" Zandy asked.

Gracelyn was suddenly furious. How dare they all take it

for granted that she was ready to start tying fleeces again. Of course, she didn't get tired cooking. Cooking was non-work. The important stuff was what they were doing.

Gracelyn glanced up at her husband and said with a smile, "No, you go on. I have a few things to do, yet. I'll be over in about twenty minutes." The tone of her voice was sickeningly sweet.

Zandy looked at her and cocked one eyebrow. He hesitated for a minute. The other men were starting out the door. "You mad at me about something?" he asked.

"Should I be?" she said in the same sweet tone.

Zandy stared at her for another long moment and then turned to leave.

"Zandy?"

He turned back.

"Why didn't you offer me a beer and a chance to sit down with the rest of the crew?"

His face reddened and he was silent for a second. Then he said, "Well, Gracelyn, I know you have to work with those rowdies, but I didn't think you'd want to *socialize* with them." And she couldn't tell for the life of her, whether he was joking or serious. He said, "You sure you don't want a ride?"

"I'm not ready yet," she said. Zandy patted her shoulder, put on his hat, and left.

Gracelyn set the stove timer for twenty minutes, picked the decorative throw off the recliner, rolled it around herself, and lay down on the cot.

Chapter Thirty-Three

"WELL," Maggie Norman said, "I hear you made it through shearing all right." Maggie was sitting in Gracelyn's kitchen.

Gracelyn smiled. "The crew probably got sick of roast beef, but they never complained."

"Alex said they finished up in good time for a cut-rate crew."

"Tying fleeces is dull work. I'm glad my first shearing season is over," Gracelyn said.

"And now lambing season is about on us," Maggie said. "That's why I came up today. I want to make a trade with you, and once lambing starts, we'll all be too busy for visiting."

"What do you need? Milk? Eggs?"

"No," Maggie said. "This is something I don't really need. It's something I want." She picked up a package that she had carried in with her purse. Opening it, she shook out a crib-size quilt that had a sunbonnet girl motif in the same warm colors that brightened the living room at her ranch. The background squares were cadmium yellow and each little sunbonnet girl was done in two colors. In one square the bonnet was cadmium orange and the dress was vermillion and in the next square, the colors of dress and bonnet were reversed.

"How beautiful," Gracelyn said. "You can't mean that you want to trade that?"

"I've made at least a dozen of these. I can make more."

Suddenly Gracelyn had a tentative idea for her living room. "Do other ranch women make quilts?"

"Quilts, afghans, woven wall hangings, knitted stuff."

"If I had that quilt, I'd hang *it* on the wall. But I don't have anything to trade."

"Yes, you do. I came to talk you out of a couple of those sketches you showed me."

"You're kidding. They're too rough."

"They may be rough, but they're real. Will you let me have the ones of the sheep and the trees along the creek?"

"For this beautiful quilt? You'd be cheated."

"That's for me to say. I'll get Josh to mat and frame those sketches. You just sign 'em."

Gracelyn felt a rush of shame. She picked up the sketchbook and flipped through it. The sketches should be better. She thought of the hours of art classes she had cut.

Taking up a pen, she signed each of the sketches. "I've sprayed these with a fixative already. They won't smear. How much would Josh charge to frame the quilt?"

Maggie smiled at her. "Don't worry about it. I'll get Josh to make you a frame."

"The living room is dreadful now," Gracelyn said, "but I'm going to paint the walls a light color and use them for background for the gorgeous shades in the quilt." She rose to fill their coffee cups and sat back down. "I wouldn't think of hanging your quilt until I paint those walls. I just hope the ewes will hold off until I finish."

Maggie laughed. "You've just doomed yourself to an early lambing season."

"Oh, don't say that. It's too cold and wet for lambs yet. Zandy doesn't want to lamb in April. He's hoping for mid-May and warmer sunshine."

"Old Man Radson always lambed early. He liked to get some age on the lambs before the mosquitoes started. I'll bet you'll be lambing before the first of May."

Gracelyn sighed. "Well, if you think we'll be lambing, I'd better not plan to paint right now. Still, I'd like to get the quilt ready."

Maggie smiled as she stood to leave. "I'll get Josh right on that frame."

Maggie was true to her word. Josh Franklin dropped by a few days later with the quilt frame.

"You've sure made Maggie proud with your plan to hang her quilt," he said. "And she likes your sketches." He met Gracelyn's eye and continued, "You know, if you really worked at it, you'd be good."

Gracelyn could feel herself flush. She had known when Maggie took the sketches that they were little better than exercises, but it hurt nonetheless to have someone else point that out. She made herself meet Josh's eyes, but she couldn't answer his comment. She looked away and picked up the frame, which was smoothly sanded and finished with a satiny varnish.

Josh said, "I hope the color is right."

Gracelyn smiled at the cowboy. She said, "The frame is beautiful. I hope you'll be around when I'm ready to do some more wall hangings."

"Oh, I come and go. You'll have to catch me on the near swing."

"Do you think we can barter for the frames?"

Josh Franklin looked at Gracelyn. "I'm sure you've got something I want." His look made her intensely uncomfortable. She walked to the window and looked toward the barn. Zandy was building jugs, but he ought to be down for lunch soon. Crybaby, who had been restless all morning, yowled at the front door.

"Must be a tomcat around," Josh said.

Gracelyn opened the kitchen door and stepped outside with Crybaby. Josh followed and stood beside her. She wished he would go home. She looked toward the barn again and saw with relief that Zandy's pickup was just dipping down to cross the funny little bridge on Plum Creek.

"I don't see why we even need a bridge here," Gracelyn had said soon after they had moved to the ranch. "There's hardly enough water to wet the undersides of the boards."

"Look at those meadows," Zandy had answered. "See

those piles of branches and tree trunks? That's flood debris. You can be sure that springtime will bring high water."

Zandy pulled up in front of the house and stepped out of the pickup with a grin, followed by Pete, who immediately scared Crybaby up the skinny little tree by the gate.

"We've just had a little lamb." Zandy's face was full of light. Gracelyn stepped forward, but Josh spoke before she could.

"Oh, oh," he said, "sounds like the work is going to start around here. I'll be shoving off."

"Thank you for the frame," Gracelyn said. She and Zandy watched him get into his pickup, then turned toward each other.

"Put on your barn clothes and boots," Zandy said.

"I've never even *seen* anything born. Do you really think I can deliver lambs?"

Zandy grinned at her. "Sure you can. You'll be a champion lamb-licker."

Chapter Thirty-Four

A light rain was falling as she followed Zandy up the hill to the long, low shed south of the barn. It was old, but sturdy. Thick uprights served as studs for the rough plank walls, which were painted brown on the outside, but were an aging natural grey inside.

Zandy had dismantled the long runway as soon as the shearing crew had rattled their truck down the road. He had immediately begun erecting the small pens that he called jugs.

"No matter how I re-arrange those damn panels," he said a day or two after he had started the job, "I still can't come up with enough jugs. I need a couple of large spaces in there, but if I leave room for shuffling the sheep around when I need to, I sacrifice jugs. I'll have to put some jugs outside."

When Gracelyn had gone to see the shed again, it looked like a honeycomb inside, with row upon row of little pens four-by-five feet wide. She had helped Zandy shovel sawdust into the jugs for clean flooring.

"You won't be as willing to shovel this out," Zandy said while they rested their backs. "Those sheep will change its character." He grinned at her. "Do you have that shade in your palette?"

"Sure. Ripe sheep dung. Just next to raw umber."

Zandy laughed. "You ready to move the drop bunch?"

"Which bunch is that?"

"Well, at the moment, it's the whole damn herd, except the rams. We have, I hope, about 400 head of pregnant ewes ready to drop their lambs."

She and Pete had helped move the drop bunch the next day. Pete moved back and forth behind the herd, urging strays along.

"He's getting the hang of this," Zandy said. "He doesn't rile 'em by racing around and barking."

The sheep didn't need any riling. They stirred themselves up, bleating constantly as they moved down the hill, bunching together behind a leader, only to turn back and go up the hill again if the leader was spooked by a sage brush, a rock, the sheep wagon, or her imagination.

Gracelyn was puffing and cussing by the time she turned one sizeable group. "Sheep are just dumb," she said, as she came within talking distance of Zandy.

"Be glad this isn't a turkey ranch," he said. "Turkeys are dumber."

Gracelyn liked some of the ewes. They had sweet faces and their large eyes looked out at the world in a contemplative way that made her feel peaceful. When the drop bunch was finally in the big corral, they began to settle, some lying down, others picking at the hay that Zandy had forked into the long feeders along the far edge of the corral.

"Well, that's our maternity ward," Zandy had said as they watched the ewes. "Old Man Radson's rams did a good job." There was an odd tone to his voice. Gracelyn glanced at him. He looked soberly back at her. He was probably thinking about their rotten sex life, but it wasn't all her fault. Zandy came home late so many nights, too exhausted even to eat supper, that they had not even attempted sex for two weeks.

But Zandy surprised her by saying, "I'm afraid lambing is going to be too hard for you."

He wasn't criticizing her in his mind, he was worrying about her! Gracelyn smiled at him. "Lambing will be interesting."

And now the first lamb had been born. Inside the shed, in a jug near the south wall, was the ewe with her little knobby-kneed baby.

"She's a good mother," Zandy said. "She cleaned him right up and got him up to suckle. He'll thrive." Gracelyn would like to have sketched the wobbly baby, or at least taken a minute to study him, but Zandy went right on through the shed and began to walk slowly around the drop bunch. She followed him.

"Look for a string of bloody afterbirth on the rear of a sheep," he said, "and watch the ewe to see if she claims her lamb." In a moment, Zandy had spotted a lamb lying on the ground. A bedraggled ewe circled away from them as they approached.

"We should have brought a sheep hook," Zandy said, "but we'll take this one in without it. Pick him up by one back leg. Be sure it's a back leg. Never pick a lamb up by just one front leg. You'll dislocate his shoulder."

Gracelyn grasped the hind leg of the lamb with her bare hand. The wool was slicked down with the moisture from the water sac and sticky with mucus.

She looked at Zandy. "Shall I take him to the shed?"

"Not without his mama. See if you can get her to follow you."

The ewe came nearer, but instead of following when Gracelyn took a few steps, she jerked around and ran up the hill, panicking the whole flock.

Gracelyn started to chase her, carrying the lamb.

"Put the lamb down on the rise where she can see him," Zandy said, "and bring the ewes back to the lamb."

Gracelyn laid the lamb in the dirt and hurried up the hill looking for the bloody ewe. The baby would be getting cold, even if the rain was light. She brought the flock slowly back toward the lamb. The mother finally went over and sniffed it.

"She's checking to be sure it's hers," Zandy said. "Now pick it up again and move slowly toward the shed."

Gracelyn was sweating with nervousness as she picked up

the lamb. The ewe made a little sound and stuck her nose toward the baby. She followed warily as Gracelyn held the lamb upside down, its nose just off the ground. Zandy had found another lamb and was leading another ewe toward the shed in similar fashion. Gracelyn could hear him making a soft bleating sound, "meh, meh, meh," as he coaxed the ewe down the hill. The ewes shied at the gate, but didn't rush back up the hill.

Slowly, with their eyes on the lambs and the skittery mothers, Zandy and Gracelyn lured the animals into the holding pen in the lambing shed. They put each mother and baby into a jug.

Zandy went to the cabinet at the north end of the shed and came back with a brown plastic bottle with a spray nozzle on it.

"Here," he said. "Spray the end of the umbilical cord where it tore away from the mother."

Gracelyn bent over the first jug and turned the lamb belly-up. She pulled the umbilical cord out straight and aimed the nozzle at the end of it. A stream of brownish-yellow liquid went all over the end of the cord and covered the palm of her hand as well.

"Yuk," she said. "What is that? I thought I was just going to wash the dirt off the cord."

Zandy was laughing. "It's iodine to prevent infection."

Gracelyn looked around for something to wipe her hands on and then shrugged and wiped them on her pants.

Zandy had brought sheep hooks from the barn. Back in the drop bunch, they spotted two lambs in the dirt.

"Twins," Zandy said. He thrust the sheep hook he carried into Gracelyn's hand and hurried toward the farthest lamb, whose face was still obscured by the milky membrane of the sac. He tore the membrane quickly and peeled it away from the lamb's nose and head. Lifting the lamb with his hands cupped under its chest, he said, "Breathe. Come on now, come on now."

Gracelyn held her own breath, waiting for the lamb. Finally, he let out a weak little "maa."

Zandy took the sheep hook and slid it under the lamb's

belly just in front of the rear legs. "Get the other one on your hook," he said, "and we'll try to get the mama down the hill. Try your best not to spook her. She's a two-year-old, and this is her first lambing season."

Gracelyn extended the long pole and hooked it under the other lamb's belly. Her arms quivered when she lifted the lamb. Hanging out there head-down at the end of the sheep hook, the lamb was heavy. A coating of dirt darkened the creamy yellow substance that covered the surface of the wool. The ewe side-stepped away from Gracelyn as she offered the baby to its mother. Gracelyn reached out farther with her arms, adding length to the hook. The ewe finally moved forward and sniffed the baby. Slowly, one careful step at a time, Gracelyn enticed the ewe toward the lambing shed.

When they put the ewe and her twins in the jug, the mama sniffed and nuzzled the larger one, but paid no attention to the baby Zandy had brought in. He felt her udder.

"She's not going to have enough milk for both of these babies, and besides, she doesn't want to claim the other twin." Zandy took the small lamb from the pen and handed it to Gracelyn. "Here, hold him a minute while I get a bum pen set up."

The lamb was nothing but bones covered with a wet nubbly material that did not even look like wool. He lay limply in her arms. She held him closer to try to warm him. As she waited for Zandy, she looked over at the jugs where they had put the first two lambs. Both ewes were cleaning the babies' hides with their tongues.

Zandy stepped up beside her. She turned to him and said, "I quit."

He looked startled. "Was it something I said?"

"Yes . . . lamb-licker . . . about ten times without explanation. Now I see why."

Zandy followed her glance toward the two ewes who were busily licking their lambs. He grinned. "If I'd told you about that, I'd never have been able to get you to leave Colorado." He handed her a clean burlap sack. "Here, you can use this on *your* baby."

Gracelyn rubbed and dried the lamb and put him in the pen under the heat lamp Zandy had wired to the panel. Zandy took a tin cup and, cornering one of the old ewes in her jug, milked about two ounces into the cup. He poured the milk into a long-necked bottle and attached a thin black nipple to the bottle. He climbed into the pen and cradled the lamb in one arm. Inserting the nipple in the baby's mouth, he held the bottle up with his left hand. With his right, he rubbed the baby's rump lightly.

"I want him to think his mama is urging him to eat," he said. "Now, you try it. You're going to be mama to all the bums."

Gracelyn stuck her finger into the lamb's mouth as she tried to insert the nipple. "He's already sucking," she said. "He didn't seem well enough to suck."

"He's just fine," Zandy said. "Later tonight he'll be hollering 'maw' at you, every time you come near the pen."

Zandy left Gracelyn with the lamb and went to carry hay and water to the ewes and lambs in the jugs. When the bottle was empty, Gracelyn snuggled the lamb for a moment. Then she put it in its warm spot under the lamp and joined Zandy.

"Can you check the drop bunch again?" he asked. "This young ewe doesn't want to let the baby suckle. He's got to have a few drops of mother's milk real quick here, and then his mama's got to eat. She's pretty tired. She'll be a better mama if she gets some food in her."

"We forgot the iodine."

Zandy, who was bending to hold the lamb's head to the ewe's udder, glanced up at her with a smile. "You catch on quick. If you start thinking on your own like this, I'll have to deed the place over to you and see if you'll hire *me* as lamb-licker."

It wasn't the same sort of praise as he'd given his horse, but Gracelyn was pleased. She smiled and went for the iodine bottle.

By the time Gracelyn had treated the babies' umbilical cords, it was dark outside. She took a sheep hook and the flashlight and stepped out of the shed.

It had stopped raining, but the clouds hung low, covering stars and moon. Gracelyn paused briefly to enjoy the eerie quality of the scene. Ground fog obscured the fences at the back of the corral. Her flashlight penetrated only a few feet in the mist. The drop bunch was restless. The sheep milled; several of them bleated nervously.

Gracelyn flicked the light back and forth and caught sight of a lamb standing on wobbly legs, crying lustily. She started toward the lamb only to realize that behind it was another one and a few feet from those two was another, on the ground yet, but struggling to rise.

Now *how* was she to tell which lamb belonged to which mama? She moved all the sheep toward the first lambs, hoping the mothers would pair up with their babies. Only one ewe approached.

When the ewe sniffed one of the lambs, Gracelyn started forward, but the ewe butted that lamb away and stepped to the next one. Apparently satisfied with the scent of the second lamb, she nuzzled it and licked its rump. Gracelyn reached out with the hook and captured the lamb.

Zandy went back up the hill with her after she delivered the mother and lamb she had just paired up. There were at least three more lambs standing, besides the two she had spotted.

Zandy moved on around the herd. Gracelyn's light caught the small white sac-covered bundle on the ground at the same moment his light flicked across it.

Zandy cleared the mucus from the lamb's nose, but it was too late. The lamb would not take a breath. Finally Zandy lifted it and laid it outside the corral fence.

Gracelyn began to cry. "I didn't even come to the top of the rise," she sobbed. "If I'd been here sooner, I could have saved the lamb."

Zandy put his arm across her shoulders and hugged her to him for a brief moment.

"You can't let it get you," he said. "There are five cold babies waiting for us in the fog. We've got to take care of the live ones."

Gracelyn choked back her sobs and walked along with

him, dragging her sheep hook. By the time they reached the other lambs, she had managed to stop crying and was only sniffling.

"That's better," Zandy said. "If you're crying 'maa' too loud, the mamas will think they have to come find you."

"How can you joke at a time like this?" Gracelyn asked.

"How can you not?" Zandy said, as he hooked another lamb and turned immediately back to business. "We'll have to put this whole bunch in that big pen for a little bit until they sort themselves into mama-baby combinations."

Gracelyn's arms trembled as she lifted another lamb and held it out on the long hook. No mother responded. She sighed and put the lamb down. She was so damned tired. She hoped that she wouldn't have to chase the ewes up the hill too many times before she found the mamas that went with the lambs. By midnight they had eleven combinations of ewe-and-lamb in jugs. Zandy brought in some large cardboard boxes. As he dropped them into the jugs, Gracelyn filled them with hay.

"Feed first," Zandy said. "Let 'em get good and thirsty, and then we'll give them as much water as they'll take."

"They don't eat it all," Gracelyn said.

"No, sheep are that way. They'll leave the stems. Damn, I hate that too. There's a lot of nutrition in the stems. Some of the more modern ranchers are grinding the hay."

"How?"

"With a machine made specifically for grinding hay. You can mix some oats with it and get a good nutritious combination. They don't waste nearly so much, either."

"Is it expensive?"

"Well, not when you consider that the savings in hay is fifty percent. A grinder will pay for itself within two or three years."

Gracelyn silently said goodbye to her new living-room furniture. She'd be lucky to get a washer and dryer. "I take it you've seen one of these machines in action?"

Zandy flushed. "I've been looking at a tractor and a grinder. It's a good deal. I could get them both used from a guy for just what the grinder would cost new."

"Is that what you want to do with our share of the wool check?" Gracelyn was tired and hungry. It was a stupid time to be having this conversation, but she didn't even have the energy to feel angry about it.

"Well, if we buy equipment that saves money, we'll come out ahead in the long run. I gave the guy a little earnest money, but I was thinking of waiting until fall, to be sure we get a good lamb crop."

Gracelyn leaned over the side of a jug to pick up an empty water bucket. She couldn't very well insist on a couch or anything in the house when a grinder would save fifty percent on the cost of the hay.

She filled the bucket and set it in the next jug. "What do you think?" Zandy asked.

Why did he ask her after he'd already made up his mind? She didn't know what to say. She filled another bucket. Her lower back ached as she bent over the jug to set it near the ewe who stuck her nose in and drank with long slurping swallows.

Gracelyn finally let it go. There was no rational objection she could make. She turned and said, "I think I'm hungry." The relief on Zandy's face told her that he had no idea how many meanings there could be to that phrase.

Chapter Thirty-Five

THE days and nights of lambing blurred together. Gracelyn cooked a large stew before she went to the lambing shed on the second day. They ate it for breakfast, lunch, and dinner until it was gone, and then she put on a pot of pinto beans and ham.

By the fourth day of lambing, the jugs in the shed were full, and Gracelyn had four bums to bottle feed four or five times each day. She fed two at once, holding onto the nipples where they fit over the mouth of the bottle. The lambs grabbed hold and sucked rapidly, their tails bouncing up and down.

"I don't know how I'm going to feed any more of these greedy little guys. The ones that have already eaten keep bumping their heads into the ones I'm trying to feed."

"We'll set up a bottle board. You can feed ten at once with that."

Zandy kept a close eye on the new mothers and their babies. "If we get in there with an antibiotic right away, when they show signs of pneumonia or anything else, we can pull them through." He showed her how to give the shots. "If the lamb's mouth is cold, he's probably already sick, but this will help."

"I'm worried about the littlest bum," Gracelyn said. "He isn't gaining the strength to fight his way through the crowd. I've been feeding him separately but he seems too weak."

Zandy gave the lamb a shot, and Gracelyn warmed him and fed him carefully. The lamb sucked until the bottle was empty and curled up under the lamp with the other bums, but when Gracelyn came to feed the bums at midnight, she found him dead in the pen. He was cold and stiff. She stayed there, numbed by the death in her hands, while the other lambs, vigorous with life, butted her exuberantly.

Zandy found her sitting flat in the dirty sawdust of the bum pen, holding the dead lamb, the tears running down her face.

"Gracelyn, you can't cry over every dead lamb." He took the little corpse and threw it over the corral fence. He had carried the body of the suffocated lamb they'd found the first day to a place he called *the bone pile*. "There's always a certain percentage of loss."

"I feel so useless," Gracelyn said. "Mother Nature doesn't give a damn what I do. They just live or die according to some huge plan of hers."

"That's part of the challenge," Zandy said. "Ranchers are bigger gamblers than anyone you'd meet in Las Vegas."

The fifth morning of lambing, Zandy got an early call on the CB. Gracelyn stepped outside with him as he loaded his supplies on the pickup. A silvery mist hung over the valley, lightly veiling the rust-colored bluffs. The pines and cedars near the crest of the hills were dark. The slopes showed the new green of spring.

"We can turn the milk cows out, now that the snow is melting in the cow pasture," Zandy said. "It'll save some hay."

"Will they come back on their own?"

"No, we'll probably have to go get 'em more than half the time."

"On foot?"

"When I'm here, we'll use the pickup."

"You don't mean to turn them out this morning, do you?"

"No, if I don't get back, you'll have enough to do. We'll wait until we're done lambing." Zandy looked at the sky, which was beginning to clear. "God, I hope this weather holds."

Gracelyn shivered at the thought of more snow. It had snowed right after the shearing crew left. She and Zandy had moved the naked sheep from the open pasture and urged them toward the shelter of the trees in the meadows along the creek. They and the animals had been miserable together as they struggled to feed in the storm.

Zandy snapped the lid to his supply box and turned. "Do what you can up at the shed, and I'll be back as soon as I find out if this is really an emergency. I branded ten pairs of ewes and lambs and emptied their jugs, but I didn't have time to dock, so leave that group in the large pen." He startled Gracelyn with a kiss on her cheek. "We need the vet money, or I wouldn't leave you." She walked around to the driver's side with him.

"Don't look so scared," he said. "I'm only leaving you alone with my entire fortune and my prospects for future wealth."

"It's a good thing you never saw me balance my check book," she said.

Zandy grinned and, gunning the engine, took off down the road.

As soon as Gracelyn finished milking the cows and separating the milk, she took her bucket of bottles and the skim milk and headed for the lambing shed.

She made a quick trip through the drop bunch. The first sign of birthing was a small, white sac like a skinny balloon or a fat plastic string filled with fluid. Gracelyn had found that if she brought a ewe with just that beginning sign of birthing into the large pen in the shed, she lambed quickly after that, and Gracelyn could give her food and water. Giving birth was so exhausting to the sheep that even the best mothers were worn out and needed nourishment immediately. But the first ewe she spotted was already in labor.

The ewe stood with her head back and her neck stretched forward. After the first contractions, she flung her head nervously toward her rear, and then stood again with her neck stretched forward, straining her whole body as the membrane-covered head and hooves slowly emerged from the uterus. The ewe lay down.

Gracelyn circled slowly, keeping an eye on the laboring ewe. There was one new lamb with an attentive mother already nudging it toward the bag. Gracelyn decided to let that lamb suckle before she jugged the pair. She spotted another ewe with the telltale balloon. Using the long sheep hook as a guide and as a device for separating the ewe from the herd, she took the sheep down the hill and put her in the empty large pen.

The other large pen was filled with twenty mamas and babies. Brightly painted numbers showed clearly on each ewe's back near her tail; matching red numbers were painted on her lamb's right side. Everyone was hungry. Gracelyn took a moment to watch the two-day-old lambs leaping around. They and their mothers made a constant voice check. The mother would cry a low-pitched "baa," and the baby would answer with a high-pitched "maa." They kept it up until they found each other in the group. Reassured, a lamb would bounce away, lose his mother, and the crying would start all over again. "I'll feed you guys pretty soon," Gracelyn said, and went back out on the hill to check on the laboring ewe.

The ewe had pushed the lamb most of the way out. She struggled up and moved about with the lamb hanging behind her, the membrane tight around its head. Gracelyn was reminded of a television picture she had seen of a hold-up man caught in the act. The nylon stocking over his face flattened his features. The lamb's face had the same obliterated look.

The ewe strained one more time and then swung her rear end sharply around as the final contraction gave the baby a push. Her whirling motion broke the membrane, freeing the baby's face. The lamb fell into the dirt with a rush of fluid. Gracelyn waited but didn't go too near.

The ewe stood with head down for a moment, breathing heavily. Then she turned and stretched her nose to the baby and began to lick away the sac. "You're a good mama," Gracelyn said. "You get him cleaned up, and I'll be back to jug you in a little bit."

She jugged the other pair from the drop bunch and went back for the lamb she had watched being born. By the time she jugged it and its mama, the ewe in the large pen was going into labor. Gracelyn used the iodine spray on the new lambs and then made another quick trip through the flock. The drop bunch was quiet, so Gracelyn held the bottles for the lively little bums who shoved and jostled for position at the nipple. When the bums had sucked every bottle dry, she wiped their drool from her hands and set the bucket of bottles on the counter near the door.

She had just begun to take hay and water to the jugs and the noisy crowd in the large pen when she noticed that the laboring ewe in the other pen was down and having trouble. Gracelyn could see only one leg thrusting from her rear. "Oh, damn, damn," she said, her heart beginning to beat hard and her breath coming fast and short.

She ran to the north door of the lambing shed and searched the road to the house and beyond as far as she could see. Not a sign of Zandy's truck. Rushing back to the supply cabinet to grab a bar of soap, she rolled up her sleeves and scrubbed her hands and arms, shivering at the touch of the cold water. She forced herself to breathe slowly and deeply, and then she went to the laboring ewe.

Chapter Thirty-Six

SHE knelt behind the sheep and studied the position of the leg. The head and legs were supposed to come out together. Something was twisting the lamb and projecting this leg unevenly.

She pushed gently on the leg. It moved backwards, but the ewe bore down again and the contraction shoved the leg forward once more. Gracelyn waited until the contraction had eased and then pushed the leg back inside the stretched opening, following it with her hand.

As quickly as she could in the cramped space, she moved her fingers around to find the head. It was turned to the side. The ewe began another contraction. Gracelyn cried out in pain as the strong muscle squeezed down on her arm. Her hand was trapped hard against the skull of the lamb. She bit her lip and waited, her hand turning numb.

When the contraction ended, she willed all of her strength into the hand that lay on the lamb's head. Her fingers tightened and pulled. The head moved straight; the legs went into the right position. With the next contraction, Gracelyn's hand was expelled and the lamb's head and front legs followed.

Gracelyn grasped the legs and held on until the ewe bore down again, and then pulled steadily until the lamb was free. She cleaned the mucus from its nose and face and put the baby near the mother's head.

Her arm ached from the squeezing and her hands burned

from the acid of the afterbirth, but Gracelyn didn't care. She sat on her heels and cried for joy, and then she cried some more as she fetched the iodine bottle and treated the baby's navel. She was glad to be able to cry alone.

When she was cried out, she fed and watered the ewe, who was tired and droopy, but on her feet. The ewe drank deeply and ate half a box of hay before returning to the lamb. She began to lick away the gold-colored slime from the lamb's body.

"Do a good job," Gracelyn said. "That stuff turns a yucky brown color when it's dry." Gracelyn finished the first hay-and-water rounds and checked the drop bunch. She was grateful to discover that the two new lambs on the hill belonged to concerned mothers. As soon as Gracelyn picked each lamb up with the hook, the mother moved forward anxiously, her eyes focused on the moving lamb. It was easy to put those two pairs into jugs.

"Thank you, you old dear," Gracelyn said, dropping a kiss on the head of the last ewe she'd brought in. "At the moment I'm not up to doing twenty laps of the corral, chasing some dumb two-year-old who took off without a backward look." The wool was beginning to grow again on the ewe's head. It had a soft, knotty feel.

"I'm glad now that they sheared you before lambing," Gracelyn continued aloud, eyeing the bloody string of afterbirth that hung down from the ewe's rump. "If you had all your wool, you'd be a mess."

The old ewe's lamb was suckling happily, its tail flopping up and down as it shoved its face greedily into the udder, sucking faster than it could swallow. The ewe looked at Gracelyn with a calm eye, and then turned her head slowly to look around the shed. Gracelyn followed her gaze.

Now that the sheep were eating, they were calming down. The bums slept under their light. Even the group in the large pen was quiet. The lambs rested near their mothers. An occasional soft "buh" had taken the place of the loud bleating.

Pete came pattering in from the north door. He kept his

distance when Gracelyn said, "Stay." She wanted to enjoy the quiet moment while it lasted.

"You just can't get good help these days. I turn my back for a moment, and you quit work to stand around leaning on your shovel."

Gracelyn turned. Zandy had come in through the large door that faced the corral. She protested, "I beg your pardon. I'm a lamb-licker and I was leaning on my *sheep hook.*"

Zandy grinned. "I checked the drop bunch," he said. "They're calm at the moment. Do you have any problems in here?"

"Not now. But I had to pull that lamb. His head was turned sideways." Gracelyn pointed to the lamb she had rescued.

Zandy leaned over the jug to inspect the ewe and the lamb. He stood up. "I take back what I said about good help. I couldn't have done better myself."

Gracelyn warmed with pleasure, but she said only, "I was lucky that the head turned easily."

Zandy joined her near the fence to the large pen. "I'd better get these little guys docked, castrated, and earmarked so that we can put them out in the corral. Do you want to learn how?"

"Not if it means cutting. I don't think I can cut a lamb."

"I only cut the ears, but I use a knife and it is kinda bloody." Gracelyn shuddered.

"Well, I just use rubber bands for the rest of it." Zandy picked up a strange-looking pair of pliers and handed them to Gracelyn. There were metal pegs around the head. "These are docking pliers, used to put the bands on the tails and for castration. I castrate with rubbers when I can catch a lamb young enough. Want to learn to use the docking pliers?"

"No thanks."

Zandy grinned at her. "Well, I know you can use paint. Maybe you can brand instead of cutting and docking."

"I'll do *anything* else."

Zandy showed Gracelyn how to dip the branding markers into the paint and stamp them on the sheep. The markers were just numbers made from heavy wire with a length of wire extending upward as a handle.

"I branded ten of them, so you start with number eleven. I'm using red for a ewe with one lamb, black for a ewe with twins, and if we get any triplets, we'll put a big T on the mama's rump."

Gracelyn picked up the paint can, but paused to watch as Zandy took the docking pliers and wrapped a rubber band around the pegs. He chose a male lamb, turned it upside down, and opened the pliers, thereby stretching the band, which he slid around the testicles. He released the band from the pliers and it tightened on the lamb.

"Ouch," Gracelyn said.

Zandy fitted another rubber band to the pliers and snapped it around the lamb's tail.

"Why do you dock the tail?"

Zandy grinned at her. "So they look like proper lambs. You never saw a long-tailed sheep in a nursery rhyme."

"Seriously."

"For cleanliness. Their tails get damn dirty. They attract flies and mosquitoes. Also, docking's done for easier breeding of the ewes."

"It makes me sad to think of these babies ending up as leg-of-lamb in a fancy city restaurant."

"Only the wethers. We'll keep the ewes, and I won't even cut the ewe lambs' ears. I'll just tag them." Zandy opened a pocket knife with a blade so sharp it gleamed along the honed edge. He cut a notch in the ear of a wether lamb. The blood ran down, and Gracelyn turned away.

It was past noon when they finished. "I brought the mail out," Zandy said as they stepped into the house. "And I brought Kentucky Fried Chicken."

"Well, I was going to say that I'm hungry enough to eat a horse, but I'll settle for chicken. As long as it's not one of my hens."

"I thought you didn't like those fowl creatures."

"Well, they're still family. I don't eat family."

Zandy laughed and took the teakettle from the living room stove. "I knew you'd want hot water first thing."

Gracelyn washed her face, arms, and hands, wishing that

she could dunk her hair in the water, too, but the bums would be hungry again before her hair dried. There wasn't time to get really clean.

Zandy handed her a letter from Annie and three envelopes the size of greeting cards. "What's the occasion?" he asked as she opened the first card.

"It's a birthday card from Suzanne."

"A birthday card! Gracelyn, is this your birthday?"

"I don't know. What day is it?"

Zandy stepped into the separator room, where he'd hung a large calendar for keeping track of sheep data.

"We started lambing April 27. This must be May first."

"Then it's not my birthday. I turned twenty on April 28."

Zandy flushed. "I'd forgotten that you even had a birthday coming. I'm sorry."

Gracelyn grinned. "That's okay. I forgot it myself. The days have been kind of running together this past month."

"Well, we can still celebrate." He looked around. "Dinner is keeping warm in the oven, and there are two donuts left over from the half dozen I bought to eat between vet calls."

"You're getting popular."

"It's a damn good thing they needed a large-animal vet up here. I've discovered, as they say in business, that I'm under-capitalized. We'd be in trouble without those vet calls."

Gracelyn frowned. "I didn't know we were so poor."

Zandy touched her hand. "I said we're under-capitalized, not down and out." He smiled at her. "But back to the subject of your birthday. We've got dinner and a birthday donut. What would you like for a present?"

Gracelyn considered, then said, "I'd like two hours off. I'd like to scrub the sheep smell out of my hair, and while it dries, I'd like to paint those cottonwoods along the creek."

Zandy looked toward the window where she pointed. Gracelyn said, "The trunks and branches are rough and twisted. The new leaves make them look awkward. They're like gnarled old bag ladies wearing Easter bonnets. I can just see their snaggle-toothed grins through the veil." She sighed.

"Something the matter?"

"Well, I wouldn't want you to take this the wrong way, but

sometimes I wish I hadn't quit school. I don't know enough technique. I can see the picture in my mind, but I don't know all the strokes necessary to putting it on paper."

"Didn't that old prof of yours give you some art books?"

"They're still in boxes under the bed, and I never have enough time to drag the boxes out and read and paint, too."

"Well, take the time you need today." Zandy filled the teakettle and set it on the burner. "Your hair water will be hot by the time we finish eating. I'll feed the bums and monitor the drop bunch."

Gracelyn put Annie's letter in her pocket to read later, but she opened the other birthday cards. One was signed by her mother, with a note saying, "a package is on the way." The third card was from her grandmother. Nothing from her father. He was probably too busy at the Lazy-J Motel.

"Bad news?" Zandy asked, watching her.

She shook her head. Her father ruined their nights; she was damned if he'd ruin their days. She smiled at Zandy. "I'm just starving to death."

She read Annie's letter after lunch, when she had finished washing her hair.

Dear Gracelyn,

I enjoyed your letter about the cottage cheese . . . after I got over being surprised at your marriage. Boy, kid, when you finally rebel, you do it with all you've got. (I might have suggested art school in Chicago, instead.)

Your second letter, speaking of your need to draw, reminded me of the years I wandered those empty western spaces and lived through the storms. It doesn't surprise me that you respond to the land.

The most painful . . . and the most glorious . . . event in one's life is to discover what is most important. Painful because so much else will have to be excluded, glorious because it almost doesn't matter.

It's easier for men to have one thing they care about exclusively and, lucky dogs that they are, it's usually their work. (I'm not exactly saying the honeymoon is over, but I notice that Craig can paint for hours and never think of having dinner ready when I get home from the college.)

Gracelyn, there has to be *some* time in the ranch schedule that is entirely under your control. Out of that time, you'll have to salvage moments for sketching and studying.

I'm beginning to sound like a preacher. But I'm just a teacher, really. I hate to see my students get tangled up in things that keep them from using their abilities.

End of lecture. Write to me again. I love the details about ranch life . . . and thanks for the sketch of the separator.

The letter was more frightening than comforting. As she took her paint box to the meadow, Gracelyn thought, *Nobody ever suggested before that it's all up to me.*

Chapter Thirty-Seven

BY the time her hair was dry, she had done three sketches and a watercolor. She wasn't satisfied with any of them, but she felt calmer than she had when she'd read Annie's letter and more centered than she'd been in weeks. Time had such a marvelous unbroken quality when she was sketching. Gracelyn looked at her watch and sighed. Her birthday present was used up. The two hours had turned into two and a half.

She rested for a moment longer against a big cottonwood tree. *Twenty seems old. When you're no longer in your teens, thirty is much closer. I haven't accomplished a whole hell of a lot in twenty years. Will I have done any better by the time I'm thirty?* She thought of Annie, and then Maggie Norman's quilt. *Maggie is an artist, too. But talk about multiple priorities! Maggie loves her ranch, her house, her quilts, her brother.* Gracelyn rose and picked up her painting supplies. The chickens and cows and bum lambs were waiting.

Zandy and Gracelyn worked the sixth day of lambing together under a delicate blue sky. The old snow was melting quickly.

"The air is delicious," Gracelyn said. "I can taste spring."

They put the branded and docked lambs into the large corral with their mothers. The corral slanted upward toward the far fence. After the lambs had suckled, they were full of energy and high spirits. While their mothers rested, the lambs played. One lamb wheeled and raced toward the fence and all the others followed. When they reached the fence, they turned in unison and ran down the slope again.

Zandy said, "I think they look like rushing water when they run that way." It was true. Clean white wool gave their backs the look of foam.

"A waterfall of lambs," Gracelyn said.

When the lambs were tired, they cried "maa," and their patient mothers answered until the lambs found them. Then the ewes lay down, and the lambs stretched themselves across their mothers' front legs and snuggled under their mothers' heads.

"Nature can be so brutal in birth," Gracelyn said, "and then turn around and be like that." But Zandy didn't respond to her comment in a philosophical way. He was thinking of profit and loss.

"She's been bountiful today," Zandy said. "Look at the twins we've jugged. Puts us right back into the 100-percent bracket."

"How much will a lamb bring at market?"

"Depends on the market, but somewhere around seventy dollars these days."

"If we have four hundred lambs, that's twenty-eight thousand dollars!"

"Well, we won't sell all the ewe lambs. We'll definitely need to replace the six-year-old ewes, maybe some of the five-year-olds."

"Seems a shame. Those old ones are the nicest mamas."

"Yes, they are, but when their teeth get gappy, they can't eat, and they don't thrive."

"How much of the twenty-eight thousand dollars does Mr. Radson get?"

"He gets a third of the gross."

"That's quite a chunk."

"Best deal I could get. Just three years out of vet school and no practice of my own to sell, I didn't have a down payment."

"You mean he just let you take over on shares?" Gracelyn

reached up and turned Zandy's face down to hers and, holding onto his chin, stared at him intensely.

"What are you doing?"

"Trying to see what he saw in your face that made him trust you with a whole ranch."

"What he saw in my face was a chance for him to get out of the sheep-ranching business and get to Florida before he had to go through another lambing season on his own."

"That's right," Gracelyn said. "He didn't have a woman to milk cows and feed the bums."

Zandy smacked her lightly on the rear. "Don't forget the chickens, eggs, cream, butter, and . . ."

Gracelyn joined in with him: *"Cottage cheese."*

By May eleventh, over half the ewes had lambed. Gracelyn was feeding thirteen bums. She had saved a twin by spotting it quickly and cleaning the membrane from its nose. Another lamb had died because its mother lay down on it.

"That's another reason we shear early," Zandy said. "With a full load of wool more ewes would lie down on their lambs and suffocate them without even knowing they were there."

There were several little lambs with black faces and stockings. One of the ewes had a black face and silvery-grey wool. "I like that ewe," Gracelyn said. "I'm eager to paint her."

"How would you like to own her and all the lambs that have black faces?"

"Are you serious?"

"Why not? I'm not particularly anxious to have a 'black sheep' in my flock. You can start your own herd. We'll tag all the off-color lambs and the ones with odd wool with some number that shows that they belong personally to you."

"I'd like to have a whole flock of odd ones. They're interesting."

The next day another lamb was added to Gracelyn's Odd Bunch.

"Look at this," Zandy said. "If I hadn't delivered the ewe myself, I'd say that this fellow belonged to a Pomeranian pooch."

"Oh, the poor thing," Gracelyn said, kneeling beside the strangest lamb she had ever seen. The tiny creature had no wool. Instead it was covered with silky hair, the color of pale taffy.

"You little beauty," she said aloud, petting the lamb, "you are just what I wanted."

"Are you going to start a freak show?" Zandy asked.

"Now you stop that. You are *not* to tell this lamb that he is anything but gorgeous." For a moment she was back in Silver Crest and her mother was straightening her collar. *This is our ugly duckling.*

Gracelyn was bending over the bottle-board for the bum lambs when Zandy brought a ewe into the large pen. "I'm going to need your help here."

Gracelyn looked up. An immense bulb of bloody membrane hung from the ewe's rear. "Oh, my God, what's the matter with her?"

"Prolapsed uterus. She turned herself inside out when she gave birth. I've got to put her uterus back. I need you to hold her legs."

As soon as the bums had sucked the bottles dry, Gracelyn went to the large pen. Zandy had gathered some supplies: a bucket of water, a "uterine bolus," which was a large antibiotic pill, and a needle and suturing thread.

"Grab her rear legs and pull them toward you. Keep her from kicking me and try to hold her still. She's not going to like this."

Gracelyn gripped the legs and pulled back, slightly elevating the ewe's rump. As she positioned herself in a half-squat, Gracelyn could feel the pull on the quadriceps along the fronts of her thighs. The ewe rolled her head back along Gracelyn's arm. Her eyes were wide and slightly bulged, but she never made a sound. Zandy was pulling the afterbirth connectors away from the wall of the uterus, a slow job because it had to be done without tearing the uterus. The ewe remained silent.

"Why doesn't she bleat? It has to hurt."

"I don't know," Zandy said. "They don't bleat during labor either. Maybe it's nature's way of protecting them, not calling attention to them when they're down."

When Zandy had finished cleaning the afterbirth from the uterus, he began slowly inverting the bulge, pushing it into the cavity. Occasional spasms inside the ewe worked against him. But Zandy kept at it, carefully, patiently working the uterus back into the sheep. Gracelyn had to admire him. He didn't joke, but he didn't complain. He simply did the job, and Gracelyn did her job, although her legs ached, and there were knots gathering in her shoulders, and she wanted to weep over the poor creature suffering in her arms.

At last the bloody flesh was back inside the sheep. Zandy placed the bolus deep inside and then, picking up the bucket of water, he poured the uterus full. "The water pushes it back into place and holds it there," Zandy explained, as he sewed up the opening.

"You can let go of her," he said as he finished, swinging back on his heels out of the way of the ewe's sharp hooves as Gracelyn released the sheep's legs. The ewe regained her feet slowly and then went to the corner of the pen and stood with her head drooping.

"She'll live, but we'll mark her for sale," Zandy said. "She's liable to throw it again next year. Damn, I hate to lose a mature ewe."

They were behind with feeding and watering. Gracelyn staggered a little as she picked up a bunch of hay, and Zandy was limping as he went from jug to jug with the water buckets. "Just like a couple of drunks," he said.

"You got a bottle stashed out here?" Gracelyn asked.

"Don't I wish. Would you settle for a piece of chocolate?" Zandy kept bags of Hershey's Chocolate Kisses in the cabinet by the door. He stepped out of the pen.

Just at that moment, a wild young ewe in a jug near Gracelyn reared against the panel. The wire latch gave way, and the ewe burst out followed by twin lambs. Gracelyn ran behind them and aimed the trio back into the pen. The ewe went around the jug walls like a ball in a pinball machine and ricocheted into Gracelyn, knocking her down and running right over her.

When Gracelyn got to her feet, Zandy said, "When I want to see a ewe's belly, I just turn her upside down."

Gracelyn didn't feel like joking. She wanted to cry, but she didn't because Zandy had climbed the fence and was beside her, offering her a chocolate kiss. And anyway, she was too tired to cry, too numbed by the constant extremes of lambing.

"I can't stop thinking about that poor prolapsed ewe," she said. "I don't think nature has done a very good job designing the birth method."

"I'm glad you don't go on vet calls with me," Zandy said. "They never phone a vet until it's almost too late, and then they expect miracles."

"Well, you *do* miracles," Gracelyn said.

"Any old farmer could put back a prolapsed uterus," Zandy said, but he had flushed, and she knew he was pleased.

"Well, I'm not any old farmer," she said, "and I'm impressed."

Zandy put his hand on her shoulder for just a second. "You're prettier than most old farmers."

Despite the off-hand nature of the compliment, Gracelyn went back to feeding the sheep with renewed energy.

The next morning, the CB radio called Zandy away again. The drop bunch was restless. Lambs arrived faster than Gracelyn could jug them. By midday, she had to stop and brand ewes and lambs and release them into the big pen to make room for the new pairs. And by late afternoon, the inside jugs were full. She put three new pairs in the outside jugs, although the fine rain that had started falling after lunch had not let up. Her arms ached from carrying lambs on the hook. She fed and watered whenever the drop bunch was quiet and held the bottle-board for the bums as close to schedule as she could. The greedy little bums were always hungry. It seemed that she had just washed the bottles when she had to fill them again.

It was almost time to milk the cows when a two-year-old

ewe went into labor and could not give birth. She fled from Gracelyn into the flock each time that Gracelyn approached with the hook. The flock milled and bunched and milled and ran. Gracelyn finally made a driving catch, hooking the ewe's rear leg, but falling flat as she caught the sheep. She lay in the damp dirt for a moment. When she got her breath, she struggled up, holding onto the sheep with the hook.

Slowly Gracelyn pulled the ewe backwards toward the large pen. One hoof and a skinny leg protruded from the ewe's rear. There was no pen to put her in, so Gracelyn left her in the runway between the shed and the outside jugs. After she washed her hands and arms, she returned to the sheep and found her down, which was just as well. Gracelyn was too tired to put her down.

She positioned herself behind the sheep as she had before and slowly pushed the leg back. The opening was so small that Gracelyn could hardly get her hand inside. This was not going to be easy. God, she wished Zandy were here. She pushed her hand inside the ewe and felt for the head of the lamb, waiting out the pain of a contraction. "You poor thing. If this hurts me, think what it's doing to you."

The head of the lamb was turned backwards and the other leg was bent. It would be necessary to try to reposition the lamb. How? Should she push on the leg, pull on the head? Gracelyn withdrew her hand to rest it while she considered. The ewe was so small. It would seem that if the legs were straight, the head could then be turned. The ewe lay on the ground, not even trying to rise. "Don't die. Please don't die."

Gracelyn pushed her hand inside the hot, crowded cavity again. It was almost impossible to find space to move the bent leg. She moved the lamb backward a little, but before she could change the position of the leg, the ewe bore down and the contraction shoved the lamb forward, squeezing Gracelyn's arm against a bone. She gasped with pain, but she had hold of the bent leg, and she waited out the vise-like grip of the strong muscle. Then she pushed the lamb back a bit and tried to change the position of the leg.

There was just no room for movement. The ewe went into contraction once more. The pain brought tears to Gracelyn's eyes, but she was too busy to wipe them away, and they ran down her cheeks unchecked.

Finally, she had to rest her arm. She withdrew it and sat back on her heels for a moment. The sheep stretched her neck forward and rolled her head as another contraction wrung its way down her body. When she relaxed, Gracelyn reached inside the ewe once more. She tried every movement she could manage, but the leg could not be straightened in the small space.

Gracelyn was sobbing with the effort. It was raining harder now, and she and the ewe were both getting wet. But she kept trying.

She did not know how much time had passed when someone touched her, and a strange male voice said, "Let me."

Chapter Thirty-Eight

GRACELYN turned. Old Daniel was kneeling beside her in the mud. "The doc sent me."

"Is he coming?"

"No."

Gracelyn pulled her aching arm away from the sheep and tried to stand, but stumbled against the fence. She stood wiping away the tears as Old Daniel took over the job she had failed at. She had seen the old man only once before, asleep in the sheep wagon. He wore grey coveralls, as he had that night, and a dark blue knit cap rolled up at the edges. When he knelt behind the sheep, Gracelyn could see his heavy work boots, the soles thatched with mud.

As Old Daniel forced his hand inside the ewe, she began to thrash around. Gracelyn stepped forward and held the rear legs as she had held the other ewe's legs for Zandy. "There, there, there," she murmured to the sheep. The ewe's eyes were unfocused. "Why you should trust me, I can't tell you, but we are trying to help you." Old Daniel worked silently for several minutes.

Then he said, "Lamb's dead."

Gracelyn bit her lip and looked away. Another dead lamb to her account. Old Daniel seemed to know what she was thinking. He said, "Nobody could have pulled it. Ewe's too small."

Gracelyn turned. He met her eyes for a moment and then looked down at the lamb's leg. Gracelyn watched in horror as he took a knife from his pocket and cut the protruding leg off at the joint. He tossed the bloody leg aside and went back to working inside the ewe. Gracelyn took several deep breaths and finally got her nausea under control. She had felt the small cavity. The lamb was dead. They had to save the ewe. She hoped that cutting off the joint would give Old Daniel enough room to turn the lamb's head.

But it was no use. Old Daniel worked as she had worked, waiting out the contractions, trying again and again. Finally, he withdrew his arm. He looked at Gracelyn and shook his head. The ewe was very quiet now. Gracelyn could almost feel the life slipping out of the animal's body. She put the sheep's legs down into the mud.

Old Daniel got up and went around the side of the lambing shed. In a moment, Gracelyn heard his pickup. She opened the gate to the runway and Old Daniel backed the truck up to the ewe. Gracelyn could see the rifle in the rack across the rear window. He got out, and she bent to help him lift the ewe. The poor thing was so small. *I bet she's not even a two-year-old.* Gracelyn was suddenly furious at Mr. Radson. *How could he have bred the poor thing so young?*

The ewe rolled her eyes and struggled as they hoisted her into the pickup. *If Zandy were here, he could do a cesarean.* But Zandy wasn't here, and she was furious with him, too. Such arrogance, such cruelty in all of these males, to put a female through so much torture for their gain. But then she saw Old Daniel's brown hand move to the head of the ewe and caress it again and again.

Tears blinded Gracelyn and she turned away. She stumbled through the large sheep pen and climbed into a jug and out of it again on the other side and ran through the bleating sheep in the other large pen and grabbed up her milk buckets and ran down the slope to the barn.

She cried as she milked the cows, but crying didn't change the fact that Old Daniel was slowly pulling his truck up the hill to the bone pile. She heard the shot on her way to the house.

By the time she had finished separating, she was so tired

she could hardly lift the buckets, but she filled the bum bottles and carried them out to her car.

When she had finished feeding the bums, she branded enough pairs to open up several jugs. Then she moved the pairs from the jugs that were out in the open. The lambs and their mothers were wet. She rubbed them down with burlap sacks and fed them. She was about to start up the hill to check the drop bunch when Old Daniel came out of the dusk with a lamb on his hook and the mother following his soft, "Beh, now, beh, now."

"Drop bunch is all right now," he said.

Gracelyn began to feed and water silently. She would have been grateful just for the old man's company, but he went right to work too. He docked and castrated and earmarked the two-day-old lambs and then moved them into a large pen, freeing more jugs.

It was well after dark before they finished feeding and watering. Gracelyn went up into the drop bunch with her hook and the flashlight. The rain had stopped, but a slight fog remained, silvered by the moon, which had just risen over the top of the near hill, silhouetting the dark pines at the top.

Gracelyn stood still. The beauty confused her. How could the same force that let that pitiful ewe suffer so uselessly offer a scene of such delicate beauty that Gracelyn could hardly breathe, just looking at the gauzy mist looping in and out of light and shadow?

She brought twins down, one in each hand with the mother following, just as Zandy's truck pulled up to the shed. Old Daniel stepped out to speak to Zandy. Gracelyn sprayed the new lambs' navels and jugged the three of them, then went back for her hook and found another lamb.

Zandy met her at the runway. He took the hook from her and jugged the new pair. Then he set the hook against the fence and turned and took her in his arms.

"I should have been here," he said.

She began to cry as she leaned against him. "I tried to pull the lamb," she sobbed.

"I know. Old Daniel told me." Zandy was patting her

back. "Nothing could have saved it but a cesarean. I should have been here."

Gracelyn tried to look at the living sheep and find some comfort as they walked back through the shed, but she could think only of the poor young ewe who had suffered all afternoon for nothing, and then died for her efforts.

Supper was late and cold and silent. Old Daniel had gone up to the sheep wagon.

"How many still in the drop bunch?" Zandy asked her as they rose from the table.

"About a hundred twenty-five, I think."

"I'll go check 'em. You better get good and warm and then get a bath and some sleep."

Zandy had not made one joke since he had met Old Daniel at the lambing shed door. He said nothing now as he left to go back to the sheep.

When he returned, his face was pale and drawn. Gracelyn was lying on the cot. She followed him mutely to bed, not knowing how to comfort him for so much loss in one day.

She was too tired to sleep well. Aching awareness of her tired arms alternated with nightmares in which the sheep bleated and begged for her help. She left the bed quietly just before dawn. Pete followed her to the kitchen and asked to go out. When Gracelyn opened the screen door, a gust of wind pulled it away from her and banged it against the wall.

The noise didn't matter. She would have to awaken Zandy immediately anyway. It was snowing.

Chapter Thirty-Nine

IT snowed all day and all night. The wind blew. The drifts piled up in the corrals and in the large door of the lambing shed. On the hill where the drop bunch huddled, the snow was already a foot deep by the time she and Zandy reached the sheep at dawn.

By dark, it was so deep that Gracelyn could not lift her feet above the drifts. She kicked her way through them toward the ewes in labor. And still it snowed, and the drifts got deeper. Finally she just fell forward and wallowed across the snow on hands and knees. Picking up whatever soggy lamb she could reach, she flailed her way back to the lambing shed, trying to make a path for the mother if she was lucky enough to know which wet, bedraggled ewe *was* the mother.

Coming down the hill, she met Zandy on his way back up, his hat pulled low to shield his face.

"All we can do is try to get them to shelter," he yelled above the wind. "I'm double-jugging and we'll double up in the large pens, too, but we'll have to watch for crowding. They'll suffocate themselves even faster than they'll die of exposure."

Gracelyn nodded and Zandy went on into the blowing snow. She jugged the pair she had brought down. Somehow, she had to find time to milk the cows. The numbers of bums had doubled and then tripled as the ewes lost track of their babies in the storm. She was out of milk for the bottles, and besides, the cows would be suffering.

Zandy would have to try to get through to the hay. If they could feed, they might save the sheep in the shed and the ones in the large corral with the older lambs.

Zandy staggered in with a new lamb under each arm. He set them in the large pen. "Can you come help me bring in ewes? I'm just going to hook all the ewes that look like they've lambed and haul them down here to shelter. Maybe they'll remember something about these little ones. God, I hope they don't *all* bum their lambs."

Gracelyn felt a wave of affection for the ewes who did manage to find their own lambs and suckle them. It was miraculous in all the wind and wetness that they could still remember the smell of their own babies. Zandy rested beside her for a moment, warming his hands inside his jacket.

"We better eat something," he said. "Sure wish we had some more of your birthday chicken."

Gracelyn thought of her two-hour holiday and the picture she had painted in cadmium yellow and May green and raw umber, the colors of spring. She stood up and moved her neck and shoulders around. Zandy reached out and massaged her shoulder muscles for a moment.

"Thanks," she said. "I'll milk the cows, and then I'll go down and fix us something to eat. Will you come to the house, or shall I bring you a sandwich?"

Zandy peered through the storm toward the drop bunch and then turned to her. His eyes were bloodshot, his face was red from the cold, and he looked dreadfully tired. "I'd better stay here. Bring what you can. Meantime, I'll grab a couple of kisses."

He grinned briefly and bent and kissed her on the mouth. She was glad that he could joke, even a little, and his affection cheered her as much as anything could.

Sometime during the next day, Old Daniel showed up. Zandy said, "I'm damned glad to see you, but I thought you were working with Josh and Maggie."

The old man just shrugged and reached up to the rafter for a sheep hook. It was still snowing, and the wind was blowing the snow in thick curtains. Old Daniel was out of sight in the blizzard almost as soon as he left the lambing shed.

Gracelyn looked around. She hadn't slept, and she couldn't focus. She had to force her mind to register the tasks ahead of her. Feed the bums, so many bums now. She had to separate them in groups of ten and feed each group from the bottle board, then fill the bottles and start again. When the bums were satisfied, she carried hay and water to the rest of the animals. The surging crowd in the lambing shed was never satisfied, never quiet.

Zandy was pitching hay into the north door, stacking it near the cabinets. Old Daniel brought in another lamb, wet, cold, motherless. Gracelyn only glanced at it. She could almost tell by looking that it wasn't going to live. Her business was with the living.

But Zandy never gave up when there was even the tiniest spark of life. He took the lamb from the sheep herder, wiped it down, sprayed its navel, gave it a shot, forced milk down its throat, and set it under the heat lamp in a box. The lamb dropped limply to the bottom of the box.

Gracelyn said, "If he lives, I'm going to call him Lazarus." Zandy grinned at her, but said nothing. He just pitched the last of the hay out of the pickup and headed back for more. Gracelyn attacked the stack he'd left behind, portioning it out in the odd assortment of boxes and barrels they'd gathered together for feeding.

When Zandy came back, Old Daniel was waiting for him. "Let's put the rest of the drop bunch in the corral near the cow barn." Those were the most words Gracelyn had ever heard Old Daniel speak at one time.

"How in hell are we going to get them through that snow?" Zandy asked.

"Drive the trucks; break trail. Got to get them to shelter. They're wet. If it clears tonight, it'll turn cold."

Zandy said, "It might be the way to save what's left."

Gracelyn turned back to her work. She refused to consider the loss. She wanted nothing to do with dead things. The sheep in the shed were her responsibility. She would not allow them to die. She moved constantly, checking the jugs, checking the pairs in the larger pens. If a ewe wouldn't let a lamb suckle, Gracelyn climbed in the jug and, pinning the ewe against the panel, forced her to stand still.

"You old sow, you're going to let that baby eat." The ewe struggled and reared, but Gracelyn flung a long arm around its neck and forced it down. "You are alive, and you are damn well going to help this baby live." Not until the lamb's stomach was full and the baby had stopped its miserable bleating would Gracelyn release the ewe. Again and again, the same ewes refused to suckle their lambs.

When Zandy came into the shed, he stood for a moment watching her as she wrestled with a balky ewe, cussing while she struggled. He said, "I *told* your mama I'd help you to grow up to be a lady."

Gracelyn stuck her tongue out at him. He stepped over to her, reaching for one of the Hershey's Kisses in his pocket. He peeled the silver wrapping away and said, "Stick your tongue out again."

Gracelyn welcomed the sweet candy. They must have consumed five pounds of it in the last three days. Nobody stopped for meals. Whenever she took milk to the house, she brought back food. At some point yesterday she had remembered to take a roast from the freezer. She had put it in the oven when it was still dark this morning, and around noon, they had dropped by the house on their way back from the meadows with a pickup load of hay. They had eaten huge hot chunks of meat, sopping up the juice with bread and downing it with several cups of hot coffee. Her mouth watered now just thinking of it.

She left the jug when the lamb finishing suckling and stepped to the north door. She looked east along the creek, hoping to catch sight of the older lambs and their mothers. She and Zandy had moved them toward the shelter of the trees the first morning of the storm. She couldn't see through the swirling snow. It was pointless to stand there and worry. She moved back to the jugs.

Zandy said, "We're ready to move the drop bunch. If you and Pete can drive from the rear, Old Daniel and I will work the sides, heading them down through the corrals to the barn."

The men had used their four-wheel-drive pickups to make a discernible trail, but the snow was drifting into it already. Gracelyn buttoned her coat up around her neck, pulled her hat down around her ears, and started up the trail to the drop bunch.

How could they go anywhere? Some of the sheep couldn't even move. Gracelyn forced her way to one ewe who stood in a drift, head down. Gracelyn kicked the snow away until the ewe was out of the drift and then pushed her onto the trail.

The men were rescuing other sheep in the same way. The freed animals began to mill about, helping to tramp the snow, and little by little, despite the storm, Gracelyn and Zandy and Old Daniel managed to gather the flock.

When a sizeable number of the ninety ewes left in the drop bunch were grouped together, Gracelyn whistled to Pete, who was in the back of Zandy's truck. He leaped into the snow and made his way to Gracelyn. The two of them began to move up on the stragglers and force them to join the flock. It took so much effort to move through the drifts that Gracelyn was sweating in the heavy clothes she wore. Forward motion was slow.

Zandy said, "Don't rush them. We don't want a ewe to go down and get trampled."

So Gracelyn kept Pete back. He watched her and paced himself to her motion. "I'm kinda glad I ran over you," she said once as he swung near enough for a pat on the head, "or you wouldn't be my dog now."

The snow seemed to be lessening. The wind had died down a little. The flock moved as it could. And slowly the big barn came into view. Gracelyn could see that the north and south fences of the large corral on the front side of the barn had been reinforced with snow fence material. The milk cows had been moved to the little corral north of the barn.

When Zandy dropped back near her, Gracelyn said, "I see you've decided to do the milking in the family."

Zandy looked puzzled. Gracelyn pointed to the cows out in the storm. "I'm a city girl. I can't milk cows without a nice warm stall."

Zandy grinned. "Yeah, it's been bugging me these past couple of days how you shirk your chores the moment a little bit of wind blows."

Zandy had set up feeding troughs around the corral. The tired sheep crowded toward the food.

Gracelyn rested, watching the rear ends of the flock as they nosed into the hay. Suddenly, she spotted the telltale balloon of fluid on one of the ewes.

"Zandy," she called. He turned, and she pointed. He went into the barn and came back with a sheep hook. Together they moved the ewe inside the barn where Zandy had set up some temporary pens.

Gracelyn went out to the nearest trough and brought back hay for the ewe. "Now don't you bum your lamb," she said.

Zandy looked at her, and she said, "I've already got enough bums to fill up half the day all summer long. I can't believe I have to bottle feed them until August."

"They won't all survive." Zandy's face was sober.

Gracelyn was afraid to think about the dead sheep. She knew that Zandy had been putting the dead lambs over the fence near the big pasture by the lambing shed, but she had never looked at them. She didn't want to know.

Zandy said, "I'm sorry I brought you into such a mess. This isn't the way it was supposed to be."

"Well, it won't get any worse than this, will it?"

"God, I hope not."

Old Daniel was moving quietly through the drop bunch, hook in hand. Gracelyn said, "I'm sure glad he came back to help. I wonder if Maggie sent him."

"He's not here because of Maggie; he's here because of you."

"Me? We haven't exchanged three full sentences."

"When he showed up after it snowed, I told him I couldn't offer full wages and he said, 'I wasn't askin' pay. I come to help the girl.'"

Gracelyn remembered the young ewe and the old brown hand caressing the head. Tears came to her eyes as she looked at the patient old man silently working his way through the sheep.

Zandy was looking at him too. He said, "He knows that we're liable to have a bunch of new babies all at once after stirring them up like that."

Their respite was short. Gracelyn milked the cows. Then it was back to the lambing shed, where she started the unending rounds again. About two o'clock in the morning, Zandy came in and took the water bucket from her hand. "Come on, we're both dead on our feet. We've got to get some sleep."

"What about the drop bunch?"

"Old Daniel's sleeping in the barn. He'll look after them."

The next morning, it was over. The storm had blown itself out. The sun on the snow was blinding, and already the snow was beginning to melt. All the eaves dripped. The approach to the lambing shed would soon be a mud wallow.

Zandy and Gracelyn fed and watered everything in the shed. Gracelyn went with Zandy to spread cake and hay for the sheep in the meadows. They took a head count as the sheep spread out over the feeding area. Five ewes and seven lambs were missing.

"Shall we search along the creek bottom?"

Zandy shook his head and pointed. Gracelyn's throat tightened as she saw the mounds in the snow.

Silently they went back to the lambing shed. Zandy drove the pickup to the corral fence and began to lift dead lambs into the back of it. Gracelyn wanted to run to the house, but she could not let him do that job alone.

She turned and looked into the lambing shed at Lazarus, who was so tiny that she could not put him with the bums for fear they would squash him. He was bleating for a bottle again although it wasn't time. She had not believed he would live, and she had been ready to abandon him. But Zandy would not, as long as there was life.

Gracelyn climbed over the corral fence and began to lift the cold stiff lambs into the truck. She rode with Zandy to the bone pile and helped him to throw the dead animals onto the awful mound and then to clean out the truck.

When it was done, she stood and looked around her at the spring day. The hills were so beautiful that it hurt her to look at them. The wind had cleared patches of ground on the slopes. The grass was washed clean, and the green color glowed in the sunlight. The sky was so high, so blue. She tipped her head back and was drawn into its depth.

Zandy came and stood beside her. She turned to him, but said nothing. "Thank you, Gracelyn," he said quietly. Why didn't he scream or cry or curse? Seventy lambs and eight ewes had died in the storm.

But he said nothing else. Gracelyn turned and climbed into the truck. When she got out at the lambing shed, Zandy went off for a load of hay. And then she could cry. She leaned against the gate post and sobbed. She stopped only when she became aware of the din made by the hungry sheep. She blew her nose and wiped her eyes and started feeding the sheep in the jugs on the south wall.

All day long, Zandy was silent. He didn't cuss at the ewes who refused to suckle their lambs. He didn't offer her chocolate. He gave shots to the weakened animals, docked and castrated the stronger ones, hauled hay and cake, fed and watered, and made regular trips to the barn to check the dwindling drop bunch. Each time Gracelyn saw him, the lines in his face were etched deeper. For the first time she was truly aware of the nine-year difference in their ages.

She thought of the first days after she had seen her father with Arminda. The pain had made her feel old and lonely. Zandy looked old. She didn't know what to say to him. *I'm sorry* was such a feeble phrase. And since he didn't joke, she didn't dare to joke, even to comfort him.

They ate supper, finished the evening chores, and finally around midnight they went to bed. But Zandy didn't sleep. He lay stiff and silent. Gracelyn held her breath, listening for a long, long time, and still he lay there, awake and rigid in the darkness. She knew that he was seeing the bone pile, as she was, and tossing the dead lambs over and over again.

At last she could stand it no longer. Gracelyn turned on her side and put her hand on him. Thinking of the caresses he had given her so many times, she began to copy them. She stroked his face and chest. When he still lay stiff and silent, she thought, *Was this how I seemed to him?*

But though she had failed him every time, he had always been gentle, always tried again. Their unhappiness in bed had certainly not been his fault. The thought of his patience made Gracelyn continue to touch him. She leaned to kiss his cheek. She snuggled close to him to offer her warmth to his body. She caressed his chest and his neck and his face.

Finally, she moved her hand slowly downward, gently moving her fingers on his body. She ran her fingertips along his thighs. Feeling timid, she slowly put her hand over his penis and held it there, feeling it warm in her palm and finally begin to harden. She continued to stroke him until suddenly Zandy took a deep breath and turned and took her in his arms.

She lifted her face to his kiss and touched his lips with her tongue. Zandy ran his own tongue deep into her mouth, and then he moved on top of her and entered her.

Gracelyn was so glad to feel him move, to hear his groans and bear the weight of his thrusts, she pressed her hands on his buttocks and urged him deeper and deeper.

Her own climax took her entirely by surprise. She gasped and cried out as she felt her body gather together and then dispense as if she were part of a fountain, laced with colored lights. She cried out again and Zandy's voice joined hers and he climaxed and fell on top of her.

Zandy rolled over and lay there until his breath came slower. After a few moments, he leaned over and kissed her on the mouth and then dropped back to the bed. Gracelyn whispered, "I love you," but if Zandy heard her, he made no reply. He turned on his side and began to snore.

Chapter Forty

THE next morning, Gracelyn waited for Zandy to mention their lovemaking, even with a joke. But he said nothing . . . just dressed as usual, smiled at her and went to the lambing pens to check the sheep.

She had allowed herself to believe that if the nights were better, Zandy would speak of love, and she would feel that their marriage was more than the business arrangement it had seemed on the day he proposed.

Climaxing had left her vulnerable. She knew that she loved Zandy and she wanted her marriage, but sex was strange and troubling, even when it was fulfilling—especially when it was fulfilling—because it was not enough.

It was terrifying to discover that despite the beauty and release in her climax, she had hungers deeper than sexual needs: hungers she had no words for, needs tied in with leaving school too soon, giving up just when she had started her art training.

Her confusion intensified when she realized that now her feelings about the sheep were just as strong. No way would she leave her ewes and lambs solely to the care of the men.

She started the milking, thinking of the frightened two-year-old ewes who had lived, but didn't know what to do with their babies. She pictured the small-boned ewe who had died with her dead lamb inside her. *Damn the males who bred her too soon.*

And suddenly, for the first time, Gracelyn was thinking

of Arminda as a person—a small-boned girl, probably frightened by her attraction to Gracelyn's hunk of a father. She wasn't even eighteen. Arminda's college years will never be what they could have been if my father had not gone rambling. As she stripped the third cow, Gracelyn thought, *God, how men rule our lives even when we think we're making our own choices.*

She let the cows out into the pasture and took the milk to the house, where she found a note from Zandy. He had gone on an early call. When he came back, later that morning, he brought Josh with him to start plumbing the bathroom.

"I didn't know we could afford a cabinetmaker," Gracelyn said, with a smile for Josh as she thought of the smooth frame he had made for her quilt.

"I traded Maggie some vet work for Josh," Zandy said.

Josh laughed. "I'm just another ranch commodity."

The shelves in the separator room off the kitchen were shortened to make space for the shower stall, sink, and stool. Zandy's vet supplies were crowded together; Gracelyn's art supplies joined her books under the bed in their bedroom. Sawdust covered everything in the house.

For several days, it seemed that Josh was always there, requiring conversation and attention; and of course, he expected lunch and dinner too, if he worked late. There was no time for private conversation with Zandy.

"I had to buy a used washing machine," Zandy said, the day he brought the machine home, "and I'm afraid we can't afford to put in the two-twenty line for a dryer."

"That's okay," Gracelyn said, "I can wait until winter for the dryer. I enjoy hanging clothes in the spring sun."

It was true. Each moment, the land seemed to change. The cottonwood trees were fully leafed, the early green ripening into a rich deep shine. Two baby bunnies had emerged from a hole in the creek bank to play in the grass around the outhouse. The sage on the slopes was feathery green instead of the harsh steel grey of the winter stalks. She could hear a killdeer crying in the meadows.

Gracelyn came back from feeding her bums at eleven-thirty one morning to start lunch and Josh said, "I've been waiting to give you the honor of the first faucet load." He watched her with a smile as she turned the faucet, and cold water rushed into the sink. She returned his smile and made appropriate noises of praise and appreciation, but she was conscious at the same time of a sense of loss: She had enjoyed pumping water, connected to the depths of the earth by the pump handle and the long steel rod, and with her own effort bringing up sweet water untouched by man and, because of that, not needing to be treated and chlorinated.

"I'll have the hot water heater installed in a day or two," Josh said.

"Fantastic," Gracelyn said. But, Lord, the house was a mess. Bits of wood and pipe and wallboard littered the floor of the separator room and drifted into the kitchen. Ashes from the living room stove dulled the living room and bedroom floors. Table tops and dresser tops were cluttered.

Gracelyn turned her back on the chaos of her house and went to the animals. She had a new one to deal with now.

Zandy had come in from town one day, with a wide grin on his face. "Come and see the present I've brought you." He pulled her out to the barn where he had unloaded a black horse.

"Meet Silkworth's Sooty Satin."

"Where on earth did you get him?"

"Harry Courtney gave him to me to pay that big vet bill he built up last winter."

"What am I supposed to do with him?"

"You can ride, can't you?"

"Stable horses."

Zandy snorted. "Well, he's better than any old stable horse. You can ride him out after the cows."

"Why does he have so many names?"

"He's a registered quarterhorse."

"Aren't you a little suspicious that somebody would just give you such a valuable animal?"

"Hell, no. I saved Courtney a damn valuable mare and colt and stayed all night to do it."

Zandy had saddled the horse for her the first few times, and to her surprise, the black horse was much easier to ride than the plodding stable horses she'd ridden at Estes Park in the summer at home. But he had some quirks.

Dear Annie,

I'm really a country girl now. I have a horse . . . an ornery little devil who Zandy swears is a registered quarterhorse by the name of Silkworth's Sooty Satin, but whom I call Soot when I'm not cussing him.

The first time I saddled Soot by myself, he puffed up his belly immediately. Zandy had warned me about that, so I punched him in the belly and tightened the cinch as tight as I could make it.

But I didn't get it tight enough. The moment my weight hit the stirrup, the saddle slid toward me. I jumped. The saddle slid under Soot's belly and hung there. Soot snorted and bucked. Each time he moved, the saddle hit him in the belly again and that put him into a panic. He bucked all over that corral.

After I finally caught him and dragged the saddle off his back, Soot lowered his head and backed away from me and wouldn't let me re-saddle him. So I went after the milk cows on foot that night.

But I've finally figured out how to saddle Soot before he can puff up, and I've convinced him I'm the boss.

I'm still thinking about your last letter. I don't see where I can get the extra time you mentioned, and I'm still scared by the idea that somehow it's all up to me.

I did do a quick motion drawing of Soot, which I enclose. I would have done more, but I had to save time to write this letter. Write to me soon.

Gracelyn discovered that she loved to ride. Galloping across the pasture gave her the same sense of freedom that speeding along Highway 31 had given her; her sorrows whipped away in the wind as she went in search of the cows. Of course, she couldn't gallop back because she wouldn't make the cows run, but the leisurely trip home behind the cows, who plopped along the dusty track they had worn and always used, gave her time to study the colors of the grass and to rest in the beauty of the sky. In June it stretched clean and blue into infinity, pulling Gracelyn's mind along with it and easing the grief of lambing season.

They had moved the ewes and lambs to the summer pasture in mid-June. Zandy checked on them as often as he could, but he was extremely busy in the hay fields. He had bought a used tractor and had borrowed a baler.

Gracelyn spent part of every day helping Zandy cut and rake the natural hay on the meadows near the creek. They used the tractor and baler to bale the hay, but they had only the pickup for hauling. Stacking hay was a hard, tiring job made worse by the heat as they moved into summer.

Gracelyn looked forward to her daily ride on Soot. She was just saddling him to go after cows on the July evening that Suzanne drove into the yard.

Chapter Forty-One

GRACELYN didn't realize it was Suzanne's car at first, but so few cars ended up in front of their house, any car was cause for excitement. Pete ran back and forth from the corral to the bridge, barking.

She gave Soot a whack in the belly and fastened the cinch strap before he could re-inflate. The next moment, she was in the saddle. She reined Soot in and leaned down to slide back the bar latch and open the gate.

She put Soot into a gallop, and off they went downslope to the creek, clattering across the bridge, and flying up the opposite side. Pete tried to keep up, but the horse's four legs outdid Pete's three legs, and he fell behind panting, as Gracelyn and Soot made a fast run along the road and a quick stop in front of the car.

"Suzanne!" Gracelyn was off the horse in a flash. She tied the reins to the fence and turned to hug her sister. She could tell by the wrinkling of Suzanne's nose that she smelled of horse and sheep and cow and other things of which Suzanne was not tolerant. Gracelyn laughed and backed away.

"You don't need to tell me. I smell like the corrals." Before Suzanne could respond to that, Gracelyn said, "But I can't believe it's you. What are you doing here?"

Suzanne looked around. "Could we sit down or something?"

Gracelyn felt herself flush. "Oh, I didn't mean to keep

you standing out in front of the house. Come on in. There might even be some bottom-of-the-pot coffee on the stove."

Gracelyn opened the gate and went ahead of her sister, trying to remember what state the house was in. Zandy was driving the tractor and he had asked her to take some salt blocks up to the summer pasture. After that, she had gone back for a pickup load of bales. She had parked the pickup near the new stacks to be unloaded later and had walked to the barn to start chores without even checking in at the house.

The house was a mess, even by Gracelyn's standards. By Suzanne's standards, it was a disaster. Suzanne stood in the kitchen doorway and stared. Crybaby was on the counter licking the cream spout, which had not been washed after its morning's use. Gracelyn scooped her up and shut her in the bedroom. She gathered the dishes from the table and dumped them and the separator pieces into the sink and picked up the dish cloth.

Wiping the table clean, she said, "Sit down. I'll fix you a brand new pot of coffee."

"I—I need to go to the bathroom," Suzanne said.

Gracelyn breathed a silent prayer of thanks to Zandy and Josh for having the bathroom finished before Suzanne arrived. She handed her sister a clean towel from the new closet outside the bathroom door. A laundry nook opposite the separator now held the washer. Gracelyn had done a sketch of her washboard and tub and banished them to the shop.

Suzanne came out and sat down at the table.

"I still can't believe you're here," Gracelyn said. "That's the longest drive in the world."

Suzanne nodded. Her face was drawn. She looked around the kitchen silently.

Gracelyn felt uneasy. Silence was not Suzanne's favorite sport. She was probably criticizing the housekeeping. Gracelyn felt her mouth tighten. She was damned if she would apologize for the house. It was *her* house. She wasn't accountable to Mother, even Mother in the form of Suzanne.

But Suzanne didn't mention the clutter on the counter. She said, "I didn't know you could ride a horse that way."

"After hunting milk cows every day for weeks, up the hill and down the gully on Soot's back, I know what that horse is going to do before he does."

"You're different."

"You probably mean that I need a shower. But I have to bring the cows in, milk them, and feed my bums before I get a shower."

"No, I didn't mean that you need a shower . . ." Suzanne smiled a tiny smile, "Although I'm not fond of your perfume."

Suzanne was different, too, but Gracelyn didn't mention it. The conversation was making her nervous. She said, "How's Steve?"

"Oh, Steve's fine. He sends his love." Suzanne looked out the windows toward the creek.

That in itself was strange. Steve had never before sent her even a greeting, let alone his love. Gracelyn glanced at the clock. It seemed that Suzanne was not ready to explain her visit any time soon.

"Well," Gracelyn said, "would you like to put on a pair of pants and ride out with me to get the milk cows?"

"Ride? On what?"

"We can double up on Soot."

Suzanne picked up her coffee and took a long swallow. She set the cup down abruptly and said, "I guess so. I don't want to keep you from doing your work."

Gracelyn caught the glance Suzanne threw toward the sink full of dishes. She rose and said, "I'll get your suitcase."

The pastures were lovely in early evening. When the heat of the day eased, a breath of cool air came from the shady places along the creek. A light haze tempered the blue of the sky toward the east, and the clouds were a translucent cadmium orange.

"You okay?" she said over her shoulder to Suzanne, who sat behind the saddle and hung on around Gracelyn's waist.

"It's a little bumpy."

"I won't let him gallop . . . or trot . . . trotting's worst."

They met the guernsey and the holstein stepping along, full udders swaying. The Brown Swiss was nowhere in sight, but Gracelyn had watched the direction the cow had gone that morning, so she swung the horse to the right toward a rocky slope.

"What are your cows' names?" Suzanne asked.

"The only names I ever call them are not ladylike."

"I thought you were on a sheep ranch, anyway. I haven't seen any sheep."

"You'll only see my bum lambs around here and maybe the rams. The ewes and their babies are in summer pasture. If Zandy can spare the pickup, I'll take you up there tomorrow. You *are* going to stay a few days, aren't you?" Gracelyn turned to look for the cow.

"I don't know. I guess so."

Was Suzanne so uncertain just because she was out of her own territory? Gracelyn pulled the horse to a stop at the edge of a steep-walled gully. She pointed toward a grassy space in the bottom.

"See. There she is."

"She looks so pretty: the brown of her coat against the green grass."

Gracelyn laughed. "Suzanne, you'd better be careful. You're becoming artistic." She slid from the horse and offered her sister a hand.

"Let's rest here for a little bit before we start after her. It's a tough ride into the gully."

Gracelyn tied the horse to a bush, and she and Suzanne sat down in a grassy spot. Gracelyn pulled a long blade of grass and chewed on it for a moment before tossing it away and turning to Suzanne.

"Well," she said, "are you about ready to divulge the secret of this visit? Did Mother and Daddy send you up here to check us out?"

Suzanne's eyes widened and a deep flush spread over her face. "No," she said, "Mother and Daddy don't even know I came."

Suzanne said nothing more. Gracelyn didn't know how

to continue. She waited through a few moments of awkward silence and then scrambled up and went to the edge of the gully. Shadows were gathering in the bottom where the Brown Swiss grazed. She sighed.

It wasn't that she was unhappy to see Suzanne, but company complicated things. Zandy would be tired and uncommunicative if he was even home for supper. Since they'd had such a large loss of lambs, he was taking every vet job that came over the CB.

Suzanne said, "Mother and Daddy are getting a divorce."

Gracelyn whirled to face her sister. "A divorce!"

Suzanne nodded. Gracelyn sat down beside her. "So, she found out."

"Yes," Suzanne said with an odd note in her voice. "She found out."

Gracelyn was silent as the pictures of her father and Arminda flooded her mind. It still hurt. But a divorce? She hadn't let herself consider that. She felt as if Suzanne had punched her in the stomach.

Suzanne said, "It was all a lie. Our whole pretty life. I hate Mother."

"*Mother?*" Gracelyn said. "Why do you hate Mother? Daddy's the one who acted like a fool."

"She always made everything perfect. She should have done something."

"Oh, for God's sake, Suzanne, how can you blame Mother?" Gracelyn picked up a stick and jabbed it viciously in the dirt. "He's the one who got hot pants for his little Georgia beauty. He's the one who threw it all away."

"You've known all along about her. That's why you got so weird."

Gracelyn nodded. "I saw them at a motel in Dixon."

"Why didn't you tell me?"

"I tried to once. We haven't always been on the same wavelength, you know."

Suzanne nodded and began to cry. "What am I going to do? I patterned my whole life after her. Now there's nothing left."

Gracelyn glanced sharply at her. She'd never had such a rambling conversation with Suzanne. "Nothing left? What are you talking about?"

"They're selling the house. Daddy doesn't want to sell it—he doesn't even want the divorce. But Mother is strange. You never saw her the way she is now. She's absolutely determined to divorce Daddy." Suzanne was sobbing now. "It's all my fault."

"First you blame Mother, and now you're blaming yourself. Why is it *your* fault?"

Suzanne sniffed back her tears, wiped the back of her hand across her nose, and looked at Gracelyn. "I told Mother about that girl."

Gracelyn stared at her sister. She couldn't speak. It was unthinkable that Suzanne would do such a thing. Finally, she had to ask, "Why?"

Suzanne was sobbing again, and it was hard to understand her as the words tumbled out. "I was shopping in Dixon at the mall, and I saw the motel you painted. Daddy's got that picture hung over his desk, but I had no idea that it was a real place." She stopped to blow her nose. Gracelyn felt a lump in her throat. Why would her father have hung that damned picture?

"Anyway," Suzanne continued, "I was just standing there looking at the motel when I saw Daddy come out with a little dark-haired girl." The tears were flowing again.

"Her name is Arminda," Gracelyn said.

Suzanne wailed, "I don't care what her name is. She's young enough to be . . . she's younger than I am."

Gracelyn said, "Our father is a goddamned fool, but why did you tell Mother about it? It might have blown over after a while. He might have come to his senses."

"I didn't mean to tell Mother. But you know that Mother and I talk several times a day, and I couldn't hide the fact that there was something wrong. I stopped calling so often, and I made every excuse I could think of to hang up when she called. One day, she just marched into my kitchen and sat me down at the table."

"So you told her." Gracelyn winced for the careful, lovely woman who was her mother.

"I had decided by then that if she knew, she could talk to Daddy and set things straight."

"But she didn't do that?"

"She moved out of the house and got a lawyer. She won't talk to Daddy at all."

Gracelyn stood up and walked away, thinking, *It won't work, Mother. You can run away, ignore his letters, put him out of your mind, but he'll be there, tormenting whatever new life you think you can make.* Gracelyn's anger was like acetylene fire. She turned to Suzanne, picking up on her sister's earlier declaration.

"How dare you hate her! What did she ever do but try to make him a beautiful home? What's *his* part of the bargain? To cheat and lie and sleep with whatever little tramp turns him on? Did he ever think of her, of us?"

She had not known, until just now, when Suzanne had told her that it was to be sold, how much she loved the beautiful house she had grown up in. Maybe she had learned to love it more since she had tried to create something pretty in that miserable ranch house. She was suddenly exhausted.

"Let's go get the cow," she said.

Chapter Forty-Two

EVEN though he looked tired, Zandy was charming all through dinner. Suzanne had asked Gracelyn not to tell him about the divorce. "Mother doesn't want him to know."

Suzanne asked Zandy about his vet practice, and he told her several stories. Then Suzanne said, "It's all so much work. It's so hard; what makes you do it?"

Zandy smiled at Gracelyn's sister. "Have you ever been in rush hour traffic in Denver on Friday afternoon, breathing carbon monoxide, looking toward the mountains, but not seeing them because of that brown cloud?"

Suzanne looked puzzled, "Well, yes, but I don't see what you're getting at."

"Every poor so-and-so in that traffic mess is there because he's dependent upon somebody else for his job; somebody else is making his decisions."

Gracelyn listened with interest as Zandy hesitated, glanced at Suzanne, and then went on.

"A rancher is both labor and management. Of course it's hard work when you're on both sides of the board, but I have more freedom, more choices, than the average guy working in Denver."

Suzanne said, "What about Gracelyn?"

Zandy looked at his wife and smiled. "Gracelyn is labor and management, too. She's learned more here in six months than most people are offered the chance to learn in a lifetime." He raised his eyebrows and tilted his head toward Gracelyn as if waiting for her response.

Gracelyn was inundated with confused feelings. It was uncomfortable to be in the middle of such a conversation. She knew what Suzanne was really saying with her questions. "It's ugly, smelly, dirty, lonely. How can you stand it?" She could see the ranch through her sister's eyes, and sometimes she agreed with Suzanne's view, but Zandy was right, she had already learned a lot. They had plenty of problems, but she was damned if she'd give Suzanne the satisfaction of looking down on her.

"I do more interesting and important things in one day here than I did in a month at home," she said, with a glance at Zandy. His pleased flush was her reward.

"Of course, as we go along, the operation will become profitable," he said, and Gracelyn had the feeling he was talking as much to her as to Suzanne. Maybe *he* was seeing things through Suzanne's eyes too.

"How long will it take before your ranch is what you call profitable?"

"Depends on the weather and the market, but we ought to be showing some progress in four or five years."

Gracelyn almost choked on a swallow of coffee. Zandy had never shared that dismal timetable with her.

"Could you run cattle on this ranch as well as sheep?" was Suzanne's next question.

"Yes, it's possible. And it would be good insurance. When I can afford it, I'll probably pick up a few heifers."

Gracelyn was suddenly back in the dining room of her parents' house, listening to her mother as she asked about her father's day, eliciting facts. It was as if Suzanne had learned a lesson from Mother's Book, Chapter Five: How to Show Interest in Your Husband's Job.

It was working. Zandy had told Suzanne things he hadn't shared with her. During their days in the vet hospital in Marlin Springs, Zandy had talked of his dream of owning a sheep ranch. Actually *owning* the ranch kept them too busy to talk about it. Zandy hadn't told her it would take five years to show a profit. Maybe she should get Suzanne to ask about their love life. Maybe Zandy would say, "Gracelyn has learned more about responding in bed in the last six weeks than she learned in the twenty years before. We will have a profitable sex life if we ever manage to talk to each other."

Her attention switched back to the table when she heard her own name. Zandy was saying, "Gracelyn's a good lamb-licker."

Suzanne wrinkled her nose slightly and laughed with him as Gracelyn got up to serve dessert.

"He's nice," Suzanne said after supper as she helped Gracelyn with the dishes. Zandy had driven down to Maggie's to phone a rancher who had called in on the CB, which was, as usual, too static-filled for a clear conversation.

"Yes, he is," Gracelyn said. It was true. Zandy had always been nice—from the first day he'd helped her to lug Pete into the clinic.

She took a pork roast out of the freezer and set it on the counter along with a frozen loaf of Maggie's bread.

"Now, we can sit in the living room and visit for awhile," she said, trying to ignore the fact that the living room was a dismal place now that summer was here and there was no cheery fire in the stove. She wondered what else there was for them to say, anyway.

Suzanne sat in Zandy's recliner, but she was so short that her feet dangled above the floor. She scooted forward and sat awkwardly on the front of the vinyl-covered seat. Gracelyn sat down on the lumpy cot that served as a couch, but it was so low that her knees humped upwards. When she swung her legs up on the cot and bent them under her, she couldn't look directly at Suzanne.

She said abruptly, "This is no place for a tête-à-tête. It's a gorgeous night. Let's go for a walk."

The outdoors more than made up for the shortcomings of the house. The moon had risen above the pines. If she were painting the sky, she'd use ultramarine deep instead of indigo because the moon seemed to thread its light through the air, giving a glow of day to the night sky. The air was balmy. Along the creek a breeze teased the leaves on the cottonwoods. They whispered and shimmered in the moonlight.

Beside her, Gracelyn felt Suzanne shiver. "It's so lonely," she said. "How can you stand it?"

Gracelyn was startled. She considered her answer and then said slowly, "Since we came up here last winter, I've been cold and tired and wet and mad and unhappy and frustrated at one time or another, but I haven't been lonely."

"But it seems like Zandy is gone a lot. Isn't it hard to stay here then?"

"When Zandy is gone, Suzanne, I am so vital to all the ranch creatures that it is exhilarating. There's no place on earth that I am truly necessary except when I'm alone here."

"Well, it's a funny marriage. He's gone all the time. You work in the barn and neglect the house. Mother would just die. She thinks you're wasting your education anyhow."

"What education?" Gracelyn said. "I'm not educated for anything. Not to earn a living. Not to run a business."

"What about your art?"

Gracelyn was silent. The question stung when Suzanne asked it. "I do a little sketching." She didn't say how little nor add that she tore up half of what she sketched and cried over the rest.

The luster had gone out of the evening. It was not pleasant to think of Suzanne and Mother discussing her. She knew that she was helping Zandy to reach his dream, but Old Daniel could do as much as she did and do it better. Maybe she was kidding herself about being necessary.

A coyote on the ridge called out, and another answered. Soon there were several of them yipping. Suzanne said, "What is that awful sound?"

"Just coyotes welcoming the moon."

"I don't like it. Let's go inside."

They sat at the kitchen table. Suzanne didn't mention the divorce again. She seemed to have regained her poise and her big-sister arrogance. She wasn't interested in all the things that Gracelyn did with the milk and cream.

When Gracelyn tried to tell her about lambing, she said, "Oh, yuk!" The only time she showed real interest was when Gracelyn unfolded Maggie's quilt.

"Oh this is beautiful! And expensive! I've seen some not near as nice as this at the Country Boutique for two hundred dollars. Steve won't let me spend that much on an 'old-fashioned blanket' as he calls it. How much did you pay for it?"

"I traded Maggie some of my sketches."

Suzanne's eyes glittered. "How much would you take for it?"

"It's not for sale. I'm hoping to collect more of them."

"What will you do with them?" Suzanne glanced toward the living room. "You haven't any decent place to put them."

Gracelyn felt her jaw tighten. She was saved from snapping at Suzanne by the sound of Zandy's truck. He came in and joined them at the table, accepting a cup of coffee and a piece of pie.

Suzanne said, "Do you carry a CB in your truck, too?"

"Well, yes, I do, but I'm not always *in* my truck, and sometimes I'm way the hell and gone up some ranch road where I get lousy reception. Having the CB here at home base where there's fair reception gives me a chance to pick up more calls."

"Was it anything serious this time?" Suzanne asked, just as Gracelyn was framing the same question.

"A guy wanted to talk about ticks on his sheep."

"Are ticks a problem?" Gracelyn noted that Suzanne didn't say, "Oh, yuk."

"The ticks are there all winter, laying eggs in the wool, next to the body. If you don't treat the sheep in the fall and again at shearing time, the eggs hatch out when the weather warms up and drive the sheep crazy."

"Are they dangerous?"

"When the ticks start moving, the ewes start itching. If they can't find anything to rub against, they'll lie down scratching. If they happen to get on their backs and can't roll over, they'll die."

"How sad."

"Have you ever seen a tick, Suzanne?" Gracelyn asked.

"A wood tick attached itself behind Steve's knee one time. It was horrid. Daddy made it back out of Steve's leg by holding a match to it."

"Well, sheep ticks are about three times that big," Gracelyn said. "They're grey and they get bloated with sheep's blood." Gracelyn was enjoying herself. She continued breezily. "We missed pre-treating one ewe, and she ended up with so many ticks, she looked like a freckle-faced kid. Zandy and I pulled the ticks off by hand."

Gracelyn relished the expression on Suzanne's face. She asks all the right questions, Gracelyn thought, but she doesn't really want to hear the answers.

She rose to get more coffee, a little ashamed of herself. No wonder Suzanne is scared. She copied herself after Mother. If Mother couldn't hold on to Daddy, Suzanne's probably terrified about hanging on to Steve. Gracelyn felt sorry for her sister.

Turning to Zandy, she asked, "Where do you think Suzanne would be most comfortable? On the cot with something extra to even out the lumps or on the floor?"

"Why don't you two take the bed, and I'll bunk on the cot."

Gracelyn bent and kissed him on top of his head. "Suzanne says you're nice, and I agree." He flushed, and the smile he gave her was warm.

Suzanne stayed for three days. After she had watched Gracelyn feed the bums and milk the cows one time, she said, "Why don't I stay in the house and be of some help there? I don't see how you can get everything done."

It was like being a child again. Gracelyn came into the house at noon, after making a run to the summer pasture to check the ewes, just as Zandy came in from the hayfield. The table was set and a delicious odor came from the oven.

"Oh Suzanne, what is that heavenly smell? It can't be Mother's angel food cake."

Suzanne turned from the counter where she was dishing up potatoes. "You have so many eggs."

Gracelyn grinned at Zandy as she said, "I usually just fry them. When we first came here, Zandy threatened to take me back to Colorado if I didn't figure out some other way to cook them."

Suzanne had also tidied the cot, made the bed, and washed the dishes.

"I would have washed the separator," she said, "but I couldn't figure out how to take it apart."

"There's a special tool," Gracelyn said, "but for heaven's sake, don't apologize. You've done miracles in one morning."

Lunch was festive. Suzanne had picked some yellow cactus blossoms and put them in a sauce dish with several yellow and brown cone flowers for a centerpiece.

"I've just found out what I want," Gracelyn said as they finished up the meal with fresh angel food cake topped with thick whipped cream.

"How can you want anything else?" Zandy said, with a groan. "I'm too full."

"I want a ranch wife," Gracelyn said, smiling at Suzanne. Suzanne's return smile brought a moment of pleasant unity to their relationship, which had been mostly tense and uncomfortable for as long as Gracelyn could remember.

Gracelyn drove Suzanne up to the summer pasture the last evening she was at the ranch. As they sat in the pickup watching the lambs cavorting in the late sunshine, Suzanne said, "Steve has been wanting children for quite a while. I think when I go back, I'll go off the pill."

Gracelyn felt renewed pity. Suzanne's self-esteem was at an all-time low. "Don't have kids until you really want them," she said. "Steve loves you. He wouldn't want you to get pregnant if you're not ready."

"I feel so sorry for Daddy. Maybe grandchildren would bring Mother and Daddy back together."

"That's a terrible reason for getting pregnant," Gracelyn said, but she thought, *What you mean is, maybe children will guarantee that Steve and you will stay together.*

"Oh, I really do want kids. Don't you?"

For a moment, Gracelyn was back in lambing season, remembering the ewe who had labored and died and the others who slept with their lambs tucked under their chins.

She started the pickup and turned toward the ranch road. "I don't know," she said, "I'm still having a debate with Mother Nature over the whole question of motherhood."

When Suzanne left the next morning, she gave Gracelyn an unexpected hug. "I'm glad I came. I wouldn't be a rancher; it's too lonesome. But I'm going to tell Mother that you're learning a lot of things, and Zandy couldn't run this place without you."

Gracelyn watched her sister leave through a mist of tears. Here was something else that would never have happened if her father had not been unfaithful. The strange list was growing. I wouldn't have Zandy or Pete or Crybaby . . . or this ranch. And Suzanne would never have spoken to me as an equal. On the other hand, I'd have finished Dr. Carlson's class. She sighed and turned back to the ranch house, which was unusually tidy . . . and unusually lonely.

She sat down at the table and picked up a pencil, sketching idly as she thought of her family and of Suzanne's visit. When she was finished, she looked at her sketch and tears started in her eyes again. She had drawn four people standing in a circle with their backs to one another. The picture answered a question about loneliness, but it wasn't the question Suzanne had asked. She wiped her eyes and closed the sketch book. It was time to feed the bum lambs.

The third night after Suzanne had gone back to Colorado, Zandy had an unexpected evening at home. They did chores together and ate a leisurely supper. Zandy sat and talked with her while she finished up the dishes. Then he smiled and said, "Let's head for bed before that damn CB starts squawking."

When Zandy put Pete outside and locked Crybaby in the separator room, Gracelyn's pulse jumped. It was exciting to know, even though he didn't say anything, that Zandy was thinking of sex.

When they were in bed, Gracelyn turned to Zandy, welcoming his caresses and the rising tide of excitement in herself.

But she could not climax. When she was almost there, her mind betrayed her, and all the old pictures of her father and Arminda came tumbling in, along with a new picture of her mother's house. She could see it standing empty, tumbleweeds piled up on the porch, and her mother, like one of Wyeth's women, staring with haunted eyes.

She faked the orgasm, hating herself as she did it, but not wanting Zandy to stay awake. If she was going to cry, she wanted to be alone.

When Zandy was fast asleep and snoring, she rose from the bed, dressed, and slipped out the door. Pete got up from his place near the gate and followed as she started across the pasture north of the house, feeling lower, emptier, than she had ever felt in her life.

Chapter Forty-Three

CRYING didn't make her feel any better. She went back to bed and didn't sleep. She could hardly drag herself out of bed the next morning, and though she worked all day, she couldn't sleep that night either.

Zandy was haying. She should have stayed home to help, but when Old Daniel showed up the next day and offered to drive the tractor, Gracelyn said, "Zandy, I need to run down to Maggie's for a while."

"Ask her about that trucking company we talked about, will you? I've been meaning to get back to her about shipping our lambs together."

Maggie was on her way to the barn. She turned and smiled. "Well, Gracelyn, what a surprise!"

"I've run away from home, Maggie."

"You just caught me. I was going to ride out and fix fence." Maggie hesitated, studying her. "Do you want to use the phone?"

"No, I just wanted to talk." Gracelyn was sorry she had come. Maggie had work to do.

Maggie said, "Well, if you've got a little time, why don't I saddle two horses, and you can ride fences with me. I'd be glad of the company."

Gracelyn followed Maggie to the barn. "Wouldn't it be easier to drive?"

Maggie laughed. "There are places in my pastures where even a jeep can't go."

"Where's Josh?"

"He's like every other cowboy. He hates to fix fence. It's more work nagging him than doing it myself."

Gracelyn mounted the little palomino that Maggie saddled for her and followed Maggie out into the large meadow behind the huge lambing shed.

Maggie rode slowly along the fence, stopping now and again to replace a staple or tighten a wire. When they were ready to cross into another pasture, Maggie showed Gracelyn a "let-down."

"See this. To save building so many gates in a fence, ranchers purposely leave the wire loose in some spots so that it can be unfastened and lowered to the ground." She dismounted and unfastened the wires.

"Take it easy," she said. "Goldie's afraid of barbed wire."

Maggie stood close to the post and held the wires down with her foot. Gracelyn rode Goldie to the wire. The horse refused to cross. She brought her around again and gave her a good kick as she turned.

Goldie crossed the wire with a wild lurch, almost unseating Gracelyn. She clutched the reins and the saddle horn, too, as the horse raced up the hill. When Goldie slowed down, Gracelyn got her under control and rode back to Maggie, who was laughing.

Gracelyn dismounted to hold the wire down so that Maggie could take Big Red across the let-down. The big horse shied, too, but Maggie had him firmly under control.

After they re-fastened the wire, Gracelyn said, "Lose your sense of humor for one moment, and this ranch country finds a way to shake you up. It simply won't let you feel sorry for yourself."

Maggie gave her a sharp glance, but said nothing. They crossed gullies and climbed hills, always alongside the fences, checking for broken wires. As they rode down one hill, Maggie suddenly stopped Big Red. "Look!" She pointed to the fence.

The skeleton of an antelope or a deer was hanging from the fence. The poor creature had attempted to jump the fence, but one hind foot had caught between the two top wires. The leg bone was still caught in the wire. The skeleton hung down. The skull was resting on the ground.

"Oh," Gracelyn said. She looked out across the miles and miles of rolling plains to the purple-tinted mountains on the far horizon. "What a lonely way to die."

"A terrible way to die," Maggie said as she released the foot and set the skeleton free. They rode silently and steadily for a while before making a broad turn and heading back to Maggie's ranch.

"Now," said Maggie as they walked toward her house after unsaddling the horses and giving them oats. "What did you want to talk about?"

Gracelyn had decided on the ride home that she didn't want to tell Maggie about her parents. It didn't help to think about them; it wouldn't help to talk about them.

But there was something else. "I want to ask you a question," she said.

"Oh?"

"How do you keep your house so tidy and still get the outdoor work done?"

Maggie smiled at her. "Been seeing your house through your sister's eyes?"

Gracelyn could feel herself flush. "How did you know?"

"Honey, I've got a city sister-in-law of my own. Come on in. I want to show you something."

It was cool inside Maggie's ranch house. The drapes in the living room were drawn against the sun. Maggie took a couple of Cokes from the refrigerator, opened them, handed one to Gracelyn and walked through the living room to her bedroom door.

"Come and look."

Gracelyn looked into the room. It was tidy to the point of being bare. There was nothing on the dresser tops, nothing draped over the back of the lone chair. The bed was covered by a quilt. The pillows were hidden inside pillows shams that matched the quilt. A clothes basket sat in one corner.

Maggie said, "My husband was raised by a woman who could spot a speck of dust at a hundred paces. His big sister grew up just like his mother, and both of them used to show up here pretty regular when I was a young bride, their noses turned up over every unmade bed . . . even if I was busting my ass to feed bum lambs and haul hay."

"How could you stand it?"

"Well, Howard didn't marry a mouse. I just damned well decided I'd fix this house so they couldn't sniff at it. I wanted one real pretty room, so I worked on the living room."

"I dream of a room like your living room."

"I didn't do it all at once. We were just starting out like you and Alex. But I decided that I couldn't keep up if I had to deal with piles of this and that. So I made a few rules for myself."

Gracelyn leaned against the door casing. "Maybe I should take notes."

"No need to. It's simple. Look at that bedroom. I can make the bed in sixty seconds flat. I can dust the dresser tops in another thirty seconds. Nothing . . . absolutely nothing . . . gets dumped down. Howard was used to being picked up after, but it didn't take him long to get the drift after I threw out everything that wasn't in that basket."

Gracelyn laughed.

Maggie moved into the living room. "Everything in here is something I love. I like to clean this room. I rest myself by dusting my pretty things."

She moved on to the kitchen and Gracelyn followed. Maggie pointed to a wicker basket on the table. "The mail is piled in this basket once a week or whenever we get to town to get it, but I never let the sun go down on a new batch. I dream over the junk mail for a few minutes and then into the stove it goes."

"What about the important stuff?"

Maggie opened a kitchen cabinet and showed Gracelyn two boxes on the first shelf. One was marked "Letters to Answer" and the other "Letters to Save."

"When either box gets full, I take a morning and deal with it. In the meantime, it's out of the way. I have a tin box up there," she pointed to the top shelf of the same cupboard, "where I save longterm important papers. You'd be amazed how few there are."

She turned around and spread out her hands palm up. "That's it, Gracelyn. As soon as I got the table tops and dressers cleaned off, I could keep them clean. One good swipe with the dust rag, a few swirls with the dust mop, and my sister-in-law couldn't find anything to sniff about." She grinned. "Of course, once in awhile, I had to stash the dirty dishes inside the washing machine until she went home."

Gracelyn laughed. Then she said, "It's a good system, but I'd have to have some place to keep my art supplies."

"Well, you might need an extra cabinet in the bedroom. I've got one dresser that holds quilt scraps and all my sewing stuff. But the secret is: Nothing on top."

"I also need a room to love," Gracelyn said. "That living room embarrasses me. There wasn't even a chair Suzanne could sit on."

"It will come in time. Get some order first and then try for beauty."

"We never seem to have any extra money for the house," Gracelyn said.

"That will come in time, too. Remember what they say, 'Support the barn, and the barn will eventually support the house, but it doesn't work the other way around.' Give it a chance." Maggie's smile was warm.

"Thanks, Maggie." Gracelyn moved toward the door. "I've got to go, I'll be half a day behind." She turned back to give Maggie an impulsive hug. "You're a comfort," she said.

Chapter Forty-Four

SHE was home in time to feed her bums and fix lunch. Old Daniel didn't stay to eat with them. "Where does he go?" Gracelyn asked.

"Oh, he rambles around the country, working for this rancher and that." Zandy tipped his chair back against the kitchen wall and sipped his coffee. "I wish I could afford to hire him as a summer herder."

"Do we need a herder? The sheep seem to be doing all right up there."

"The damned coyotes are beginning to worry me. Ever since the Sierra Club got up on its high horse, it's been illegal to poison coyotes."

"Well, how do you control them?"

"We're not. It's a damn shame when eagles get to the coyote bait, but I hear more and more scare stories of coyotes getting to the sheep, and I've patched up a few sheep for other ranchers already this summer." Zandy drained his cup. "When the law was pushed through, the government promised that trappers would control the coyotes, but they didn't fund their promise. There's one overworked trapper for the whole southeast corner of the state."

Zandy frowned as he set his cup on the table. "A couple of ranchers I know never could get the government trapper, and their lamb losses put them clear out of business."

Gracelyn felt a flutter of worry, but Zandy tipped his

chair down and asked, "What did Maggie say about shipping?"

"Oh," Gracelyn's hand flew to her mouth. "I forgot all about shipping. I never asked her."

Zandy shrugged. "I'll ask her next time I see her. But what was so important for you two to gab about all morning?"

Gracelyn was silent for a moment. "I went down there to tell her something, but I didn't tell her." Gracelyn's eyes filled with tears.

Zandy had started to get up, but he sat back down and looked at her. She said, "I think I should tell *you*. Do you have time to talk?"

Zandy's face turned red, but he said, "You better tell me what's on your mind. That tractor won't go anywhere without me."

"Suzanne said Mother didn't want you to know . . ." Gracelyn hesitated, swallowed and then said, "Mother and Daddy are getting a divorce."

And then she was sobbing. She didn't tell Zandy about Arminda. She just wept until he said, "Don't you think their problems will blow over?"

She choked back her sobs, and when she could talk clearly, she said, "They've already filed; the house is up for sale."

Zandy patted her shoulder and said, "I'm sorry, Gracelyn. And surprised. They seemed to have things pretty well in hand."

Gracelyn washed her face. After that, she dumped the dishes into the sink and put them to soak. The CB called for Zandy. She put on her straw hat and gloves and went to drive the tractor for him so that he could go to town. He came back with a letter from Annie.

Dear Gracelyn,

Loved the story about Soot. (Want to trade him for Craig?) I get a real charge out of your ranch reports.

I'm returning your sketch with a few suggestions.

Forgive the red pencil. I've been grading test papers.
I'll write a real letter soon. Thought you might like
to get the drawing critique back right away.

Gracelyn wrote back,

Dear Annie,

Thanks for the discussion of my sketch of Soot. I
can see how shading the lines would give a better
sense of motion. Your suggestions help a lot.

I am glad that my ranch reports provide you so
much amusement. You would have had a good time
watching me the first day I drove the tractor.

Zandy was plowing. He wants to raise some of his
own grain. I rode Soot over to tell Zandy that he was
wanted as a vet and he talked me into running the
tractor and plow while he was gone. "You're crazy,"
I said. "I've never even been on a tractor." "Nothing
to it," he said. "You just go round in circles."

He showed me how to start and stop the tractor
and how to run the hydraulic lift that raises the plow
out of the ground. I climbed on the machine, sprad-
dled my legs to reach the foot pedals, and in that
immodest position, started off around the field.

As I took off, Zandy said, "When you reach the
corner of the field, use the lever to raise the plow,
then turn the tractor, line it up, and put the plow
down again without leaving too much unplowed
ground." How easy he made it seem.

I never could get into sync with those levers on the
hydraulic lift. If you want to raise the plow, you push
the lever down; to lower the plow, the lever is supposed to come up. My mind simply refused to direct
such a backwards process, so each time I made two
false starts. By the time I got the plow down again, I
had to lift it and back up so I could plow half a
mile of ground left unplowed by my uncoordinated
cornering.

Zandy got on Soot and followed me around the field during my first trip, but when I looked back and caught him laughing, I waved him away.

I plowed every minute of three hours. I finally learned how to cut my cornering gaps down, but mostly I learned that the noise of the diesel is deafening, the dust fills your nose and gets in your mouth, and above all: Plowing is BORING.

Zandy tells me of modern tractors with air-conditioned cabs and AM/FM radios, but there are no such machines in our horoscopes. Equipment takes money.

Gracelyn put down her pen. She had awakened a few minutes early and had decided to use the time to answer Annie's letter, but she didn't want to complain. She just wished she had a little cash to spend on the house. Maggie's ideas about housekeeping were great, if you had some place to store your stuff so that table tops and dressers *could* be bare. She heard Zandy stirring in the bedroom. She put the unfinished letter away.

Zandy came into the kitchen. He smiled at her and said, "I was going to run up and check the ewes and lambs before we start the day. You wanna ride along?"

"What about the bums and the milking?"

"We'll be back before the sun's full up."

Gracelyn grabbed a couple of apples and a pint jar of cottage cheese from the refrigerator. "Come on, Pete," she said, adding two spoons to the collection in her coat pocket.

A sliver of moon glimmered above the trees. Zandy turned on the pickup lights and caught a flicker of white as a cottontail scooted into a clump of sage.

"Night and day, this land is busy," Gracelyn said.

"All of us just trying to make a living."

Gracelyn ate half of the cottage cheese while Zandy ate an apple, then she passed him the jar and a spoon. "What do you think about while you're plowing?" she asked.

Zandy glanced at her, the laugh wrinkles around his eyes deepening as he smiled. "I think about crop yield and high interest rates and the national deficit and how in hell to get better equipment without putting us into jeopardy. What do you think about?"

Gracelyn said, "How grateful I am that you're not a Kansas wheat farmer."

Zandy laughed, then said, "I could use a cup of coffee."

"We might stop at the sheep wagon and brew a pot." They had moved the wagon to the summer pasture to store vet supplies, fencing materials, and salt.

"Your bums won't like waiting for their breakfast."

"Those bums run the whole show." The bottle-fed lambs were bigger than Pete. "They're so enormous and rambunctious I ought to wear a full suit of armor when I feed them."

"Don't knock it, girl. We're selling by the pound."

Gracelyn swallowed. "I don't want to think about selling them. I know every one by character and disposition, if not by name."

Zandy stopped so that Gracelyn could open the pasture gate, drove through, and waited until she closed it and got back in the truck. He started toward the windmill. "We'll fill the tank . . . Oh, my God!" He jammed on the brakes and was out of the truck and running before Gracelyn could respond.

"Stay here, Pete." She shut the door behind her and followed Zandy. In a moment, he was kneeling beside a lamb which had just taken a drink from the tank.

"Don't look," he said as Gracelyn came near, but it was too late.

The lamb's throat had been chewed open. It was ragged-edged and bloody. The water that the lamb had drunk was leaking from the torn esophagus and running down the white wool on its chest.

Gracelyn's stomach churned. "What happened?"

"Coyote." Zandy reached in his pocket for his knife. Gracelyn knew he had to finish the job. There was no way to save the lamb. She walked away and leaned against the truck to throw up the breakfast she had just eaten.

When Zandy rejoined her, he said, "I wish the damned Sierra Club had been here to see that."

They drove slowly, silently around the herd, which was

nervous. The ewes split away singly and in small groups; lambs bleated; the flock merged again and rushed up the slope only to turn and rush back down.

"Damn," Zandy said. "I wish I could afford to hire Old Daniel, or somebody, as night herder."

Gracelyn had an idea, but she looked out across the big pasture, considering for a moment before she said, "Could I do it?"

Zandy pulled the pickup to a stop at the top of the rise and looked at her. "I don't know. Do you think you could?"

"What's required?"

"Nothing except awareness of the flock. You'd have a shotgun, but you'd only want it for the noise. Coyotes come in just before daybreak. You couldn't see to kill anything."

"If I had Pete with me, he'd alert me to anything that came near."

"True. But the hard part of this job is being alone up here. Could you handle that?"

Gracelyn thought of the many nights that Zandy was gone now. The sheep wagon wouldn't be any emptier than the house.

"Let's go do the chores and talk about it. How would I get up here?"

"I could drop you off."

"But then I wouldn't have transportation if I needed it."

"Would you want to ride Soot?"

"I don't know if I'd have that much extra time. It's nearly dark some nights by the time I milk and feed the bums."

"I could take your Subaru. Most of the time I'm on good enough roads."

"But then you wouldn't have the CB."

They circled the flock again, before going back to the barn, where they continued talking. Zandy spoke of coyotes and storms and other things that might spook the sheep.

He took time to help her milk and feed the lambs. They didn't have much milk left over these days. The Brown Swiss had calved, and they had to let her bucket-baby have some of the milk. Before they went to the house, Zandy showed Gracelyn how to load and shoot the shotgun.

They were just pouring their long-delayed coffee when Josh drove up. He accepted a cup too and sat down at the table.

"Maggie sent me," he said, "to drag you workaholics away from your place."

"You can't tell me Maggie is having a party at seven o'clock in the morning."

"No," Josh said, "Maggie doesn't practice what she preaches. She says *she* has to work today, so she sent me to the rescue here."

"What's the bait?" Zandy asked.

"A country auction."

"Who's selling out?"

"Aubrey Tyler over on the Larkspur cutoff. His wife died last winter, and his health isn't too good, so he's going to move down near Gillette to his daughter's place."

Zandy stirred his coffee for a moment and then asked, "So he's selling everything?"

"Well, his son-in-law is taking the big equipment."

"Oh." Zandy looked at Gracelyn. "I don't think I can take the day off, but why don't you go? I'll feed your bums again at noon."

Gracelyn glanced at Josh. She wasn't sure she wanted to take a trip alone with him. Zandy reached in his shirt pocket and took out his wallet. "Here," he said, handing Gracelyn a worn twenty. "Maybe you can put this with your egg money and find a bargain on a couch."

That put a new light on the whole thing. Gracelyn took the money. "Tell me about a country auction. What can I find there?"

"Well," Josh said, "a country auction is held on a farm or ranch, usually when they want to sell out. No telling what you'll find there. The flyer says that everything on Tyler's place is up for sale . . . furniture, dishes, luggage, bedding, equipment, stock, and the place itself."

"Furniture," Gracelyn said. "Okay. I'll go. What should I wear?"

"Clean jeans, comfortable shoes, and a big hat. The sale is right out in the sun."

Gracelyn turned to Zandy, "You don't mind feeding my bums and getting your own lunch?"

"Nope. You haven't been away from this place since we got here. You deserve a day off, especially if you're going to man the sheep wagon at night."

"I'll need some sort of bedroll in the wagon, and I guess tonight, you could just drop me off up there and keep your truck." Zandy nodded, and she headed for the bedroom. She changed clothes quickly, scooped her egg money out of the dresser drawer, and stuck a sketchpad and pencils into her purse.

"I'll take Pete to the hay fields. I plan to haul bales again."

"I ought to stay and help you stack them."

"Come on," Josh said. "Can't cure you this way. All you're doing now is talking about more work. Besides, we've got a hundred and thirteen miles to go."

"You're kidding. Will many people go that far?"

"It's an occasion for a real get-together."

Zandy gave Gracelyn a hand up as she climbed into Josh's truck. "Have fun," he said.

"Thanks for the money," she said and waved as Josh swung the truck around and headed back toward Maggie's place and the main road.

Chapter Forty-Five

"LARKSPUR'S east and north," Josh said, "in some pretty rough country—dry, rocky."

"I bet the old man loves it anyway."

"Maybe. If the hard work killed off his woman, he might hate every bony ridge."

They turned north at The Silos on an old road that angled across open country. The narrow highway was paved, but rough in places. On each side, the plains stretched away to forbidding hills and rocky bluffs that made Gracelyn's fingers itch for a pencil. From time to time, they passed deserted ranch buildings. Broken windows stared vacantly across the prairie. Barns and outbuildings leaned in the wind.

"Why did so many people leave?"

"They didn't leave," Josh said. "They moved back into the hills to find better shelter from the wind." He pointed out a sign by a gravel road attesting to the presence of several ranches ten, thirty, even fifty miles off the paved highway.

"Are there any towns between here and Larkspur?"

"Nope, not even a general store," Josh said. He nodded to the side of the road. "Look there."

A group of antelope were grazing in the pasture with a herd of sheep. They raised their heads as the pickup passed and then turned together and ran away. As they leaped gracefully across the sage, their big white tails bounced.

"They look like French can-can girls flipping their skirts," Josh said.

"Have you been to France?"

"No, just to a lot of old French movies."

"Around *here?*—"

"In college."

"I didn't know you went to college."

Josh changed the subject. "Did I hear Zandy say that you're going to sleep in the sheep wagon?"

"Yes. The coyotes got a lamb this morning."

"Damn environmental do-gooders who don't see the whole picture . . . they ought to have to live out here awhile. How do you feel about herding at night?"

"I don't know. Zandy asked me the same thing."

Josh took his eyes from the road and studied Gracelyn. His scrutiny embarrassed her. She looked out the window. He said, "You're a different sort of woman."

"Yeah," she said lightly, "odd one out."

"Hey, I wasn't criticizing you. Most females your age would act real stupid about sleeping alone in a sheep wagon on some mountain. You don't know how you'll feel, so you're willing to give it a try."

"I don't often know how I feel. Or at least I can't put it into words."

Josh said, "Ever try to put it into pictures?"

Gracelyn moved slightly away from him toward the door of the truck. His knowledge of her made her uncomfortable. He was waiting for an answer.

"Sometimes. But no one ever reads them right. Well, that's not quite true. I had a professor at college who came close."

"Sorry you left college?"

"I just told you I don't know how I feel." She wished he would change the subject.

But Josh continued probing. "You never get off the ranch. Wouldn't you like to go dancing or to a movie or somewhere?"

"I'm going to a country auction."

"That doesn't count. I practically kidnapped you. So tell me why you don't go out on the town."

Gracelyn laughed. "Town is forty miles away. I get up before dawn, work all day; if I had any spare time, I'd draw."

"See. That's my answer. You *are* sorry you left college and came up here."

"Stop putting words in my mouth," Gracelyn said.

Josh gave it up for the moment and pointed to the road once more. An eagle was tearing at a dead rabbit with his beak. He had a proud, clean look.

"He's wonderful," Gracelyn said. "The eagles in the zoo always look miserable."

When the pickup came near, the eagle rose slowly with lazy, unconcerned power. Gracelyn looked back as they passed. The eagle immediately circled to land on its unfinished meal. She thought of the lamb that the coyote had attacked. Would she trade the eagle for the lamb?

Josh pushed the pickup along at eighty and ninety miles an hour. He inserted a cassette of Hank Williams' songs into the tape player. "There's coffee in the thermos," he said. "Want to share a cup?"

"Sure." Gracelyn filled the cup, enjoying the hot steam that carried the scent to her nose. She sipped the coffee and looked out the window at the fence posts that zipped by quickly and regularly, enjoying the mournful sound of the singer's voice. When the cup was half empty, she turned and offered it to Josh.

"You don't waste any time getting places, do you?" she said. "I was counting those fence posts, and we're doing more than a mile a minute." Zandy's kind of humor.

Josh grinned and took the cup. Gracelyn was glad that the music kept them from talking. It was luscious just to sit and do nothing, responding to no creature, animal or man.

The Tyler ranch was one of the nearer ones; it was ten miles off the paved road, only thirty-eight miles from Larkspur.

As they pulled into the ranch yard, Gracelyn said, "Look at all the pickups. There must be a crowd here."

"Sure. I told you. Whole families will be coming to this sale. They make it a holiday."

As Gracelyn got out of the truck, she could hear people calling greetings to each other. Children grouped together and started noisy games around the barn. "I've got to do a couple of sketches," she said. "Do you mind?"

"I'll go get a cup of coffee."

Gracelyn sketched furiously, settling for the quickest lines she could draw, flipping pages to get many sketches in a hurry. She stopped reluctantly after several minutes. Josh would be waiting.

She walked toward the house. A sign at the table said, "Larkspur Methodist Auxiliary . . . Lunch and coffee, $2.50." The women clustered together, chatting and drinking coffee. The men made the rounds, looking at piles of tools and pieces of small equipment.

Gracelyn felt suddenly shy. What would she do if Josh joined the men? She hesitated and looked around, but Josh said, "Come on. Let's go check out the bargains."

Gracelyn followed him toward the barn and the oddest collections she'd ever seen: old hub caps full of rusty nuts and bolts, tin cans full of bent nails, a hay wagon without wheels, a chipped enamel chamber pot holding copper rivets. Behind the barn was a graveyard of rusted machinery.

They circled the barn, looking into the pig pens, where a black-and-white sow shared a heap of dirty straw with several young pigs.

"You want to raise your own pork chops?" Josh asked.

"Not me. I can't even kill our chickens. I don't need to tend another pet that eats but can't be eaten."

Back at the house, they stopped for coffee and hot dogs. "I want to look at the furniture," Gracelyn said.

"Okay, but don't bid on anything. You just pick out what you want and let me do the bidding."

Gracelyn passed a table loaded with cheap necklaces and shiny earrings. *You could probably buy the whole collection for a quarter,* she thought.

She smiled at the woman manning the coffee pot, and

was startled when the woman spoke to her. "I'm Bertha Liggen. I haven't seen you around Larkspur."

"I'm Gracelyn MacNair. We're on a ranch southeast of Brandon."

"Sheep?"

"Yes."

"How was lambing this year? Did you get caught in the big storm?"

It was easy after that to carry on the conversation. Gracelyn and the woman spoke for several minutes before Gracelyn moved on into the house to look at furniture. *Maybe I was born to the wrong family,* she thought as she pictured her mother's reaction to the big-boned, blowsy woman clad in a bright plaid cowboy shirt and Levi's. *She seems less a stranger to me than the women in Mother's bridge club.*

Gracelyn continued to think about the conversation as she fingered the towels on the counter in the dead ranch woman's kitchen. *It wasn't just small talk. She cared about our lambs, and I felt like weeping over the loss of her prized ewe.*

Gracelyn moved into the bedroom. Her eye was caught immediately by an embroidered cloth in a barnwood frame. The stitches were almost invisible and the picture of sky, bluffs, and valley was breathtaking. Josh must bid on the picture. This was not a stenciled design; someone had created an original.

Gracelyn looked around the rest of the house. No running water. A pitcher pump on the counter, a slop bucket underneath the counter. How did the woman ever find the time to do her embroidery? Gracelyn leaned against a door jamb, thinking of the yearning that had been growing inside of her all summer. Josh was right. She *was* sorry she had left college. Dr. Carlson was right, too. She needed training and practice to get good enough. Annie had implied that it was up to her. If she didn't improve, she was going to be increasingly miserable, but she had no idea what to do about it. Grow old and die like this woman had, with one framed piece to cherish?

"Are you thinking of buying that bookcase?"

Gracelyn moved, startled. She looked at the woman who had spoken and then into the living room beyond. She had been staring at a bookcase, but she hadn't even seen it. "No," Gracelyn started to say, and then she really saw the bookcase. "Oh, yes, yes, I am."

The bookcase was magnificent. Made of fine old wood, it was at least eight feet long and shoulder high. Every one of her books would go into it. It would just fit across one end of her narrow living room. And it would do for that room what Maggie's mantel did for Maggie's living room. The top edge of the bookcase had a carved molding. Gracelyn's heart began to hammer. "Were you thinking of buying it?"

"No, I haven't got room in my TV room. That bookcase would cover up half the window."

For the first time, Gracelyn was grateful for her dark little room with no windows. So many wonderful walls to put things on.

Did she have enough money to bid on the bookcase? She moved around, scarcely daring to look at it. There was a couch for sale in the living room, too, but it sagged worse than the cot they had.

She wandered into a second bedroom. Odds and ends of a lifetime were piled on the dresser. Between the dresser and the end of the double bed was a rollaway bed, folded up. It looked new. The mattress was firm. It would make a nice daybed and serve as a guest bed, too. She saw only two other things for Josh to bid on: a pair of straight-backed chairs with decent varnish.

She went outside to find Josh, and just as she spotted him, there was a stir in the crowd. The auctioneer was beginning his spiel. The men gathered in a circle around the auctioneer. The women didn't enter into the bidding for tools and equipment, but Gracelyn stepped to the circle of men to join Josh and watch the auctioneer at work.

Aside from his sing-song voice, there was no sound. The weathered, denim-clad, booted males, young and old alike, stood in a uniform slouch, eyes on the auctioneer, who was almost hypnotic. His voice kept up a melodious chant which urged, wheedled, and commanded in happy rhythm.

Gracelyn whispered to Josh, "I begin to see why he sounds so happy. The money this sale is going to rake in would make a city dealer lick his lips."

"Shh," Josh said, "and be careful what you do, or you'll bid on something you don't want."

When a rancher wanted to bid, he would nod his head or raise a finger. The auctioneer was quick to catch this motion, so quick that Gracelyn was afraid to move her head. She put her hands firmly in her pockets.

Everything was selling well. The chamber pot full of rivets brought $11.50. A pair of rusted fencing pliers was bid up to seven dollars. Gracelyn began to worry about the price of the bookcase.

After the auctioneer had sold the last piece of cracked leather harness and the last rusty bucket from the barn, he entered the house.

The women were noisier and more ferocious bidders than the men. They bid avidly on chipped dishes, kettles with no lids, lids with no kettles, pieces of silverware that didn't match, and the flotsam and jetsam of years of housekeeping. The collection of junk jewelry went for nine dollars.

The auctioneer controlled the crowd. He sang out the bid and urged the next bidder to action. He smiled at one lady, nodded to another, and called out the bids as they rose higher and higher.

Gracelyn's hands were cold. She was so nervous about the bookcase that she hardly noticed when Josh won the bidding for the rollaway bed, and she didn't care when he lost out on the chairs.

Since Josh had paid sixteen dollars for the rollaway bed, Gracelyn had only a little over twenty dollars left to spend. This sale was a gold mine for the seller. But maybe people were bidding high on purpose. It was a form of charity that left Mr. Tyler some dignity.

At last the auctioneer turned to the bookcase. The early bidders didn't last long. Finally, it was down to Josh and a woman Gracelyn hadn't noticed before. She was dressed in a good-looking pantsuit. Her hair and face had not been victims of the weather. She kept raising the bid. *Damn her,* thought Gracelyn, *she's antique shopping. She probably doesn't even need a bookcase.*

Chapter Forty-Six

THE bidding on the bookcase went up to fifty, then sixty dollars. What was Josh doing? Gracelyn didn't have sixty dollars. He finally let the bookcase go to the woman when her bid reached seventy. Before Gracelyn could even take a deep breath, the same woman began bidding on the only other thing at the sale that Gracelyn wanted—the embroidered picture from the bedroom.

The antique dealer took the bid to thirty-five dollars before she quit and let Josh bid in the picture. Gracelyn knew that Josh didn't have thirty-five dollars of her money, but it didn't matter. She'd pay him back. That picture belonged in a ranch house with a woman who knew the *real* cost.

"Thank you," she said to Josh. "I'll pay you back as soon as we get home."

"No, you won't," Josh said. "That damned woman doesn't care about that picture. It shouldn't belong to her."

Gracelyn was tired now . . . and disappointed about the bookcase.

"Wait here," Josh said. "I'll get the truck, and we'll load the bed."

Gracelyn stood outside of the house near the refreshment table, watching the people load up their treasures. Two women were packing away the rest of the food and the coffee pot and cups.

"Where's your husband today?" one of the women asked. "You and Jacob usually come to these shindigs together."

"He's in Washington, D.C."

"More soil conservation work?"

"No, he's trying to get the IRS to change a ruling."

"You're kidding. Even God can't get the IRS to do that."

"Jacob might be angrier than God."

"What ruling is it?"

"They told him that I cannot be declared a business partner on the ranch because I didn't invest any money in it. My work and my time have no value."

"Oh, Bertha, Jacob would have lost the ranch if you hadn't done your share."

"I know that."

Gracelyn had to sneak a look at the women. They sounded so calm. Bertha was the same big woman she had talked with about lambing season and the storm. Bertha said to the other woman, "He isn't going to win, but he had to try."

"Doesn't it make you feel useless and kind of desperate when they say we have no value because we have no money?"

Bertha laughed. "The IRS can say anything it wants. All that matters to me is what Jacob believes." Gracelyn, looking at her face, thought she had never seen a woman so beautiful. *I want my marriage to be like that. I want Zandy to value me.*

Josh backed the pickup close to the door. He and a cowboy loaded the bed. Gracelyn took the picture and climbed into the truck.

When Josh turned north and east again on the main road, Gracelyn said, "Hey, aren't we heading the wrong way? We're going toward Larkspur."

"We're headed that way, but we're not going that far."

"Well what are we doing then?"

"I'm ready for a drink and some dinner. Hot dogs aren't my idea of real food."

"I can't go out to dinner. We won't be back to the ranch by chore time if I do."

Josh flashed her a grin. "You've got no choice. You're my prisoner."

"What will Zandy think?"

"It serves him right. He's kept you to himself all winter and half the summer."

Gracelyn turned the picture around in her hands. She knew Josh was just kidding, but she was silent until he pulled into the parking lot of a bar and café that sat at the junction of the Larkspur cutoff and a larger highway.

Josh dropped down from the truck and came around to open the door for her. As they walked toward the building, he put his arm around her shoulders. Gracelyn stopped.

"Don't do that," she said, pushing his arm away.

Josh shrugged and stepped forward to the door of the café. Inside, he raised a hand in greeting to the man behind the bar and led the way to a booth in the back.

The bartender brought two glasses of water. "Hey, Josh," he said with a grin, "did you finally win one of them bronc-riding contests? Your rodeo girls are getting better-looking."

Gracelyn felt the blood rise to her face. Josh said, "No, I'm not that lucky. I'm just trying to steal my neighbor's wife. Bert Randolph, this is Gracelyn. She's married to Doc MacNair."

Bert stuck out a big hand and shook with Gracelyn. "Hey, your old man's a good vet. He sure fixed up my cutting horse. Welcome to Bert's Place."

Josh said, "I always told him he ought to call it something more fancy like 'Cow Pie Parlor,' but he's real stuck on putting his own brand on things."

Gracelyn smiled at both of them. She felt safe inside the shelter of Zandy's name. Safe enough to make a joke. "When I open up *my* café," she said, "I'm going to call it 'The Lamb Licker.'"

Bert roared with laughter, and Josh looked proud. He said, "Give us a couple of Coors and two of Bert's Best." He looked at Gracelyn. "Maybe I should ask. Will a sheep rancher eat steak?"

Gracelyn smiled at him and said, "Sure. Then I can be certain I didn't raise it."

When their dinner was served, Gracelyn discovered that she was very hungry. They attacked the steaks and ate steadily. When they began to slow down a little, the way her bums did when their bellies were getting full, Gracelyn decided to try out Suzanne's method of conversation on Josh.

"I think it's interesting that you went to college. Where did you go?"

"The University of Colorado at Boulder."

"What was your major?" Gracelyn almost made a face as she asked that question. It was the one she had hated most on her few dates in college.

"I wanted to be an architect."

"That's why the frames you make are so nice. You have a real eye." Josh flushed, but said nothing. Gracelyn said, "What happened?"

Josh raised two fingers to Bert for more beer. "Rodeoing was always in my blood. I made pretty good money during the summers." Bert set two bottles of beer in front of them. Josh waited until he went back to the bar and then continued. "Maggie and Howard were having a tough time paying my way through school, and I figured if I dropped out for a year and followed the rodeo circuit full time, I could save up enough money for the next year."

"Did you do it?"

Josh smiled. "I was the luckiest damn rider you ever saw." His eyes seemed to look inward for a moment. "Yeah, the first year, I hit some big ones, won a silver belt-buckle for All Around Rookie Cowboy and paid my way at Boulder for my sophomore year."

"That's exciting."

"It was too damned exciting. I got the bighead and decided that I could make some real money while I was young. So I put architecture off until later."

Gracelyn sipped the beer, feeling a little uneasy about the direction the conversation was taking. "You didn't go back and finish?"

"No," Josh said. "I made good money the first two or three years, but it's damned expensive to follow the rodeo circuit. If you don't put something away to tide you over your losing times, you're always hocking your silver belt buckles or your saddle and that doesn't pay tuition."

He paused and Gracelyn waited. After a long silence, Josh said, "And when you start losing more often than you win, you get desperate and careless, even reckless."

"You got hurt," Gracelyn said.

His eyes sparked with emotion, but all he said was, "I thought I could be a bull rider. Busted most of my ribs, my leg, and my right arm one summer."

"But you ride now."

He chugalugged his beer and said, "Old bronc riders are a dime a dozen; we can't quit. We follow the circuits, but every year or so, we spiral downwards. Finally we're back to riding the minor rodeos, competing for skinny purses that scarcely buy the whiskey it takes to keep our bones from hurting."

"You talk like an old man."

"All athletes are old men at thirty-five, but especially rodeo riders." Josh looked at her and said, "Well, that's my life story. Let's talk about you."

Gracelyn smiled. "I'm not much of a talker. It takes me forever to get together the words I need to get a point across."

Josh said, "I've got a confession to make."

"Oh?"

"Maggie ordered me to find out what's really upsetting you."

"I told her."

Josh looked at Gracelyn for a moment, and she could feel the heat of the lie rise from her neck to her forehead. "Okay, I didn't tell her."

"You want to tell me?"

Gracelyn picked up her napkin and rolled it around her fingers. "I shouldn't have gone down to Maggie's. But I was upset about something, and my sister told me not to tell Zandy."

"Sisters-in-law have no business meddling in marriages. Maggie and Howard would have been a helluva lot happier if Annadean had butted out."

"Was Annadean the one who was so snooty about Maggie's house?"

"Her house and almost everything else."

Gracelyn said, "Well, I finally did tell Zandy part of it. Suzanne said Mother would be upset if he knew, but I needed to tell him. My parents are getting a divorce." Her eyes filled with tears. "And they're selling the house I grew up in." She was still twisting the napkin. Josh waited silently. Gracelyn looked up at him and said, "There's no place to go back to."

Josh reached out and put his hand over her two hands, stilling them on the table. "Gracelyn," he said, "were you thinking of going back?"

Chapter Forty-Seven

JOSH tightened his hand on her hands and said again, "Are you thinking of going back?"

She pulled her hands away and put them in her lap, wishing she'd never told him anything. "You know that's not what I meant," she said at last, "but all of us like to think that we can go home again."

"I think you *should* go back," Josh said, "while you still can."

"What are you talking about?"

"Go back to school. Study art. Give yourself a chance."

"You don't think I have a chance here?"

"You don't have time. You and Alex do nothing but work. He uses you like any ranch hand."

Gracelyn didn't know how to answer. Who was Josh to criticize Zandy? He didn't seem to have any goals of his own. Finally she said, "Zandy has always dreamed of his own place and I want to help him. Of course we work hard. We couldn't get anywhere if we didn't."

"I didn't say you weren't helping him. He's lucky that you came along, but are you willing to settle for a second-hand dream?"

"I can learn on my own. It will take more time, maybe, but I'll refine my technique. I'll get better."

"There. You won't say it. You're *not* willing to settle."

"I don't think I have to. Other artists have gone off alone

and done all right." She picked the first painter she thought of. "Van Gogh went to Arles and produced tons of work."

"Van Gogh didn't have to milk the cows, feed the bums, and drive a tractor."

Gracelyn said, "Well, true, but Van Gogh was insane and I'm not. That ought to count for something."

Josh would not lighten up. "You come from a cultured background. I can tell by the way you talk that you've already got a start on a good education. Can you bear a lifetime of talking about the weather and the sheep?"

"I love this land, Josh. It gives me more inspiration for drawing than anything I ever saw in the city. And it's important to know about the weather out here. I care about my sheep."

"You're kidding yourself. You'd hate to end up like that old ranch woman who died out on the Larkspur cutoff."

"Why couldn't I end up like Maggie? She does wonderful quilt work."

"You wouldn't want Maggie's life either, Gracelyn. Howard and all his kin made it hell for her sometimes. As far as the quilt work goes, that's only how she relaxes. Maggie's dream is the same as your husband's. She wants to ranch, and by God, she does it." Josh brought his hand down flat on the table.

"It didn't matter who tried to take over when Howard died. Maggie was one ferocious tiger about that ranch. She won out, but she wouldn't have if the place had only been her second-best dream. The fight was too bitter."

Gracelyn was glad to have Josh focus on Maggie for awhile. He had stirred up all her uneasy feelings, and they swarmed like mosquitoes.

But Josh was not done with her. He looked at her, and his eyes were stormy. "God, Gracelyn, can't I make you listen to me? You could go back and start over. You're still just a kid."

"Nobody who has been through a lambing season like I've just been through is still just a kid."

"Well, then, you can see what it's going to be like from

now on. Go back before your life gets complicated with children."

"You seem to forget that my life is complicated, as you put it, with a husband."

"Maybe it shouldn't be. How did you ever wind up on a sheep ranch anyway, Gracelyn MacNair? Why in hell would a twenty-year-old city girl with looks and talent throw it all away on a sheepherder?"

She was annoyed. "Zandy's a lot more than a sheepherder and you know it."

"But are *you* ever going to get a chance to be more than a sheepherder? If you've made a mistake in getting married, you should correct it right away."

"Josh, how dare you say I've made a mistake in marriage? This conversation is crazy anyway. I just told you how I feel about my parents getting a divorce. Are you actually telling me to divorce Zandy?"

Josh wiped a hand across his forehead and then looked down at the table. "No, I suppose not really. Alex is a nice guy, for a workaholic. And he's a helluva good vet."

Josh lapsed into silence. One finger traced the lines of the Montana map that was printed on the place mat. When he looked up, his face was haggard.

"But one day," he said, "you're going to wake up hollow and dry as a yucca pod; you'll have nothing left but the weather and the sage brush and the sheep. Your goddamned talent will have chewed out your guts, sucked up your blood, and gone."

Gracelyn knew that he wasn't talking about her at all, but the conversation had shaken her deeply. They rose and left Bert's Place. Josh put Hank Williams back into the tape deck, and they listened to his mournful wail for a hundred and thirteen miles.

Chapter Forty-Eight

ZANDY'S truck was gone when Gracelyn and Josh got back from the auction. Josh pulled up in front of the house and turned to Gracelyn. "Admit it. You're nervous about staying up in the hills all alone tonight."

Gracelyn looked at her neighbor. She was a lot more upset by the things he had said earlier than she was about spending the night on the mountain. "I'll have Pete," she said. She opened the door and got out of Josh's truck. Josh shut off the truck and followed her into the house.

Zandy had left a note on the kitchen table. "Got a call. Your bed roll and supplies are in the sheep wagon. Evening chores are done. Bums are fed. I left Pete in the house so he wouldn't follow me. I'll try to be back before dark."

Pete pushed his nose into her hand and Gracelyn scratched his head. Josh was watching her. Thinking of his criticism of Zandy, she was not about to let Josh know that she was irritated with her husband.

She glanced at the CB radio on the counter. She had told Zandy she could ride Soot to the summer pasture, but if she took the horse, it would be dark before they got there. Besides, she had wanted Zandy to take her to the wagon for her first night on the mountain. Damn that CB. Every time she really needed Zandy, he got a call on the radio and off he went. She stepped to the door to let Pete out, then turned to Josh.

"Would you have time to run me up to the summer pasture?"

Josh frowned at her. "I do, but I don't approve of your going."

Gracelyn laughed. "I don't need your approval, I need your pickup." She scrawled a reply on the bottom of Zandy's note. "Josh will drop me off. Please come get me in the morning."

She whistled to Pete, who jumped into the cab and sat with his head against her shoulder as Josh drove along the trail to the summer pasture in the higher hills several miles beyond the main ranch.

Gracelyn opened the gate to the big pasture and closed it after the pickup went through. When she got back into the truck, Josh said, "Didn't Zandy at least provide you with a shotgun?"

Gracelyn swallowed. "The gun makes me nervous," she said, "but, yes, he said he'd leave it in the wagon."

They drove up the slope to the level spot where the little sheep wagon stood. It looked like a covered wagon from a Western movie except that the rounded top was made of wood. The wagon had been painted green at some time, and along the bed bright green patches were still visible. The rest of it had weathered to a satiny grey. The narrow tires on the big wheels were settled into a grassy spot. The wagon tongue pointed away from the steps toward the rocky bluffs and the sheep who were still grazing the upper slopes beneath the bluffs.

Josh shut the engine off and got down from the truck. "You don't need to stay," Gracelyn said. "I'm sure Maggie has something for you to do, since you played hookey all day."

"My sister is a slave driver, same as your husband. The work will wait. And I'm worried about you."

Gracelyn felt a flicker of annoyance as Josh climbed up on the wagon step and looked around inside the wagon. She said, "Josh, get off my front porch. I don't need a babysitter."

Josh jumped down and turned to grin at her. His eyes

met hers and lingered. She remembered his crack to Bert Randolph about stealing his neighbor's wife.

"Go on home, Josh, and tell Maggie how that city slicker got away with our auction treasures." She was getting as good as Zandy at joking to hide her emotion.

Gracelyn stepped up onto the sheep-wagon step. Her dog moved in front of her and turned slightly, facing Josh and growling deep in his throat.

Josh laughed. "I've just quit worrying about you," he said. "Thanks for going to the auction with me. It was a good day."

Now that he was going, Gracelyn could relax. "Thanks for bidding on the picture."

Josh waved as he drove away.

Relieved, Gracelyn turned to check out her new house. The narrow bunk was smoothly made. Coffee, canned food, and boxed snacks were lined up on the shelves. She glanced at the wide low shelf that served as a table; a flashlight, wash cloth, soap, towels, and clean underthings were neatly placed there. And next to them, Zandy had set one of her sketch books and a box of colored charcoal pencils. Touched, she said to the dog, "Come on, Pete, our boss is treating us like top hands. Let's go do our job."

She and Pete walked slowly through the flock of sheep. The animals had moved closer to the wagon, but they were still grazing. The last rays of the sun fanned out over the bluffs above her. She turned slowly, checking the ewes and lambs. Behind the wagon and down the slope a little was the big stock watering tank, the graceful windmill beside it, the sun glinting off the blades.

The sheep were not afraid of her. At one time or another in the past six months, she had wrestled them, fed them, doctored them, and consoled them. She stood idly, touching the nubbly back of an old ewe, thinking of all that she had learned since she had married Zandy. Denver and Marlin Springs and the campus seemed more than four hundred miles away. The distance between Montana and her old life was immeasurable. But Josh had suggested that she go back.

Suddenly, one lamb saw Pete, jumped all four feet in the air, lit, bucked a little, and then side-stepped to the group of lambs and butted heads with another male.

"Hey, little guy," Gracelyn said. "Don't you remember being castrated? You can't be king of the mountain."

As if in answer, the lamb jumped stiff-legged into the air again, and when he landed, he spooked the whole flock. Gracelyn watched them flow up the hill. The ewes were much prettier now that their wool was coming in again.

"That's my kind of cash crop," she said to Pete. "One that grows right back." The sheep stopped running and began to graze again, moving slowly back toward the wagon. Gracelyn and Pete walked downhill to check the water tank, which was full and overflowing. The water's silvery surface reflected the sky, which was now shading to pink.

The July evening was still warm. The water looked wonderful. There was no one around for miles. Gracelyn ran to the sheep wagon for a towel, and then undressed and stepped into the big tank.

The bottom of the tank was slimy with algae, but she could swim on top in the cool, clean water and never touch bottom. She side-stroked slowly across the tank and floated back again, watching the horsetail clouds turn salmon, then deepen to rusty red. As the sun slid farther behind the hill, the colors seeped out of the clouds, leaving them smoky. The opalescent sky floated on the water with Gracelyn.

She stretched, enjoying the water's slide across her body. If you want to get on a horse, she thought, long legs are a real asset. If you want to hang onto a bale of hay, you need long arms. She stretched again, liking her body as she never had in Silver Crest. Pete paced around the tank, then stuck his nose in for a drink.

The sheep were bunching now. She could scarcely see them as they settled down on the meadow near the sheep wagon, but she could hear them as mothers called to lambs, and the young ones answered. She dogpaddled across the tank and climbed out. The air against her wet skin made her shiver. She hurried to the wagon and dressed, then sat on the step toweling her hair.

After Gracelyn combed her hair, she held a match to the gas burner in the little stove, heated water, and returned to the door step with a cup of hot cocoa and a box of crackers. She snacked and listened to the night, occasionally tossing Pete a cracker. The sheep chewed their cuds. An owl, hunting for its supper, called to another, which answered from the direction of the cottonwood trees down in the valley along Plum Creek.

If she had not gone out to dinner with Josh Franklin, she would have been able to enjoy the rest of this evening. But Josh's questions were dumped on top of a precarious heap of questions that Gracelyn herself had already piled up. The whole structure threatened to topple: "How did you ever wind up on a sheep ranch, Gracelyn MacNair?" "Why in hell would a twenty-year-old city girl with looks and talent throw it all away on a sheepherder?" "How did the two of you get together in the first place?" Josh's questions . . . which she had struggled to answer. Her own unanswerable question: *Are Zandy and I really together?*

Gracelyn looked at the sky. A cream-colored moon had risen. She got up from the step. Pete lifted his head, then rose and followed her. The moonlight changed the looks of the pasture. Trees that were lighted blended with the grassy hill, trees that were silhouetted looked huge. Dark pockets of shadow deepened under the scrubby bushes.

The night was peaceful, but she could not match the mood. She moved around the resting sheep and went slowly up the moonlit slope. Suddenly from behind and above them a coyote began to yip. Another coyote answered from a distance. *I'd better get back to the sheep, and to the gun.*

A few of the sheep on the outer edge of the flock rose as she and Pete hurried by, but they didn't seem upset by the coyotes' singing, and they soon lowered themselves to the ground, the ewes speaking in familiar voices to their lambs.

Gracelyn recognized the deep "baa" of a dependable old ewe who had mothered twins. Thinking of some of the flighty young ewes who caused so much trouble, Gracelyn felt a surge of affection for the old one. "Goodnight, Old Dear," she said softly as she passed by the sheep.

She climbed into the wagon and lit the lantern. The shotgun in its leather case was lying underneath the shelf that served as her bunk. She set the case on the bed and opened it to remove the gun. The shotgun was heavy. She stepped to the door and lifted it, aiming at the sky as Zandy had instructed her, searching for a balance point along its stock to give her more control. She didn't pump a shell into the chamber, nor did she release either of the safety devices. She would not shoot the gun as long as the coyotes were still up on the bluff. The sound would spook the sheep as much as it spooked an intruder. "To be real honest," she said to Pete, "I'm not yearning to be kicked in the shoulder again by this thing."

She lowered the gun and turning, set it on its stock and leaned the barrel into the corner of the wagon near the door. As with most of what she did on the ranch, handling the gun had been easier when Zandy was there, calmly giving instructions and patiently answering her questions. Zandy was not a slave driver, no matter what Josh said. Zandy was a good boss and they worked well together. She felt renewed annoyance with Josh. *Why couldn't he leave things alone?* His persistent probing made her nervous. Her problems with Zandy had nothing to do with work. *God, if they didn't share the work. . . .* She let the thought go. It was too painful and she was tired. Zandy would be here just after dawn.

She slipped out of her boots and jeans and shirt and crawled into bed, leaving the wagon door open. She heard Pete flop down and heave a big sigh. The coyotes were silent for a moment. "Night, Pete," she said.

But she couldn't sleep. When the coyotes were yipping, she lay tensely, trying to estimate the distance between them and the sheep camp. When the coyotes were silent, she pictured them moving in toward the flock. *I've got to sleep. Zandy needs me in the field tomorrow.* She moved restlessly on the hard bunk. The sheep were settling. Pete will let me know if the coyotes move closer. She was drifting toward sleep, when Pete suddenly rose from his spot by the wagon tongue, a loud growl issuing from his throat. Gracelyn jerked upward on the bunk in the sheep wagon, and at that moment the peaceful night was torn apart by a scream.

Chapter Forty-Nine

THE sheep were up, bleating and milling. Gracelyn's heart beat so quickly that she could hardly catch her breath. What was it? It had sounded like a woman's scream, but there wasn't a ranch within miles. *Why would a woman be up here in the middle of the night?* Gracelyn fumbled in the dark for her jeans and boots and slipped into them as quickly as her trembling hands would allow. She found the flashlight on the wide shelf and turned it on. She could feel the wagon rocking as the sheep churned around it.

Picking up the gun, she released the safety on the pump and loaded a shell into the chamber. She left the safety on the trigger as she stepped down from the wagon, holding the light in her left hand and balancing the shotgun in her right. Before she could adjust her eyes to the night, another scream rent the air.

The shrill cry terrified the sheep. They came together in a surging mass. She had to lift the gun high as they rocked against her. It didn't seem human this time, but it could not be a coyote. She had never heard a coyote make such a sound.

What if the cry had been from a sheep? She shuddered. She had to see if something was attacking the lambs.

Pete was ahead of her, growling. She flicked the light toward him. The hair on his neck had risen in a thick ruff. Moving after the dog, she edged her way through the flock, her heart pounding, the shotgun wobbling in her hand.

She aimed the barrel toward the sky. She could not take the chance of discharging the gun into the sheep. Until she knew what was happening, she didn't dare discharge it at all. Scattered, the sheep were easier prey than when bunched.

Could it have been a wolf? She didn't think it was a wolf. There was no howl to the sound. It had definitely been a scream.

"Come back here, Pete," she said in a low voice. The dog slowed and she caught up with him. A breeze stirred the leaves on the bushes and trees, and their shadows moved on the ground. Other shapes moved on the pasture at the edge of the herd, but the moonlight made things look so strange, she couldn't tell what was real and what was shadow.

Slowly, with Pete at her side, she moved outside of the sheep, talking aloud to the dog to give herself courage. "Maybe the sound of my voice will scare it away," she said, "maybe your fine doggy smell will spook the intruder." Her voice shook. "Oh, my God, Pete, I wish you could talk. I wish you'd tell me that scream came from an animal who is just as scared as I am."

She flashed the light under the trees and bushes. Nothing there. The hair on Pete's neck began to flatten. Gracelyn took a deep breath and moved faster. The breeze rustled through the bushes with the sound of stealthy footsteps. Gracelyn whirled to light the grass behind her, but saw only the gentle ripple caused by the wind. She wished that she had her shirt on. The wind chilled her bare skin. She shivered. It was too quiet. She had to make some sort of noise.

She spoke in soothing tones, talking to the sheep. "I'm here, lambkins. Nothing's going to attack you while a human walks with a gun. Settle, now. Take it easy." The words gave her more confidence. She continued talking aloud as she reached the far edge of the flock near the upper slope and rounded it to cross the pasture.

If the sound had come from an animal, her voice would discourage the creature from coming closer. If the sound had been human, perhaps the mention of the gun would make a difference. If the sound had an inhuman source, there was nothing to do anyway but keep walking.

"Stop that, Gracelyn," she said. "There is some logical explanation, and you'd better keep telling yourself that, because it's a long time till dawn." She flicked the light over her wrist watch. Nearly midnight. At least four and a half hours until sunrise, longer before Zandy would come to get her.

She kept moving on the hill, finally curving back toward the wagon. The sheep were beginning to settle. Pete moved easily on his three legs, relaxing into a gentle gait. Gracelyn directed the light along the meadow and under the trees and deep into the bushes. She caught no gleam of eye. Her hands had stopped trembling and her breath came easier.

But even though she had seen nothing by the time she reached the wagon, Gracelyn knew that she would not sleep. She set the gun carefully in the corner. She pulled on her shirt and, taking a blanket from the bed, she sat down on the step and wrapped the blanket around her. She shut off the flashlight and let her eyes become adjusted to the light of the moon.

The scream was not repeated. The sheep gathered close and lay down again. Pete dropped by the wagon tongue. Gracelyn stared out over the moon-dappled pasture. Nothing moved. The silence lengthened. And finally, relaxing her vigilance a little, though still wide awake, Gracelyn began to feel calmer. As long as Pete slept on the ground beneath her, she was safe. But how was she going to get enough sleep to do her work at the ranch if the wild animals kept her stirred up like this every night all summer?

The night air was sweet. She took in several deep breaths. Josh made it sound so damned easy when he suggested that she just pick up and leave the ranch. He had no idea how much of herself was invested in the land and the sheep. But he was right about her artwork. She would have to do something. She huddled in the blanket thinking until the darkness became shallow.

The sun was coming up. Gracelyn rose gratefully, letting go of her nightlong thoughts as she stretched in the doorway. A lemony light washed the sheep, who spread across the meadow to graze. She yawned. Pete got up and padded over to a shrub to raise his leg. He looked around for a minute and then trotted down the hill toward the water tank. Nothing in the brightening morning explained the screams that had kept her from sleeping. Her muscles ached with fatigue.

She was turning back inside to make a cup of coffee when she saw Zandy's pickup jolting across the pasture. He stopped near the wagon and stepped easily down from the truck. He was lean and tanned. His blue-and-white striped cowboy shirt picked up the blue in his eyes. Gracelyn had never been so glad to see anyone. She hopped off the step and went toward him.

"You're early."

He said, "I was worrying about my sheep." But he wasn't looking at the sheep. He pushed back his Stetson and smiled at her, the laugh lines crinkling around his eyes. "How's my night herder? Did you have any problems? Any predators?"

She said, "I'm not sure. The coyotes stayed up in the bluffs, but something else was close. It screamed just like a woman."

"The hell you say."

"It was horrible. I couldn't spot anything and the sound only came twice, but it was really a scream."

Zandy put his hand on her shoulder. "Sounds like a mountain lion came through. God, that must have been a shock. I never thought to warn you about mountain lions."

"I couldn't sleep after it screamed."

"What a helluva initiation into night herding." He patted her shoulder and said, "Let's go see if we can find some sign."

They walked slowly in the direction from which the second scream had come. There was nothing near the herd. Zandy went farther up the hill. When he called to her,

Gracelyn joined him in a clear space on the slope to stare down at the marks in the soft dirt. The track looked just like Crybaby's paw print, but it was much larger, maybe three and a half inches in diameter. Gracelyn shivered.

"See how the cat put its foot straight down?" Zandy said. "A coyote or other animal will slide his foot into place. The cat steps down." That wasn't what Gracelyn cared about at the moment.

"Would it have attacked the sheep? Or Pete? Or me?"

"The sheep maybe if you hadn't been here. I doubt that you were in any danger. The cat was probably more scared than you were. Did you fire the gun?"

"No. I was afraid of driving the sheep right into the jaws of the prowler."

"Did you get *any* sleep?"

"No."

"Well, things look pretty good up here. Let's go home for breakfast, and you can rest." Zandy seemed so much the same as usual that Gracelyn climbed in the truck feeling suddenly irritable. *How could he be so damned calm about everything?* Didn't he have any idea what it was like for her to hear that scream in the dark and then spend the whole night awake, scared and unsure of herself?

Gracelyn used the bathroom while Zandy put the coffee pot on. As she stepped back into the separator room, she glanced at the shelves full of veterinary supplies. She stood still, studying them.

"Coffee's ready," Zandy said. "I need to get to the chores."

Gracelyn entered the kitchen and took the cup Zandy offered, but she didn't sit down at the table. She leaned against the counter and looked at her husband. "I want to know something."

"What's that?" Zandy said.

"You have a whole barn, a lambing shed, and a shop to keep your stuff in. How come you have to use the shelves in the separator room, too?"

Zandy grinned at her and started to speak, but she interrupted him before he could answer. "Don't make a joke. I'm serious. I want those shelves."

Zandy studied her face. She didn't smile. It was hard enough to stand her ground without trying to make it a sociable occasion. "Okay," he said finally. "As soon as I get some time, I'll clean out the shop and make room for my stuff out there."

Gracelyn reached out and turned the milk buckets upside down on the counter. Then she sat down on the floor in front of the cabinet and folded her arms in front of her chest.

"What are you doing?" Zandy asked.

"I'm going on strike." She grinned at him, beginning to enjoy herself. "I'm not milking another cow until those shelves are bare and every bit of your junk is out of that room. I can't clean up this place if I don't have some storage space."

Zandy was slow to return her smile, but he finally grinned and said, "God, it makes you grouchy to have a mountain lion scream at you. Okay. I'll have those shelves cleaned off by the time breakfast is ready."

It was that easy. Maybe Annie was right. Some things were in her control.

Gracelyn was too keyed up to rest. After Zandy had cleaned off the shelves and they'd finished breakfast, he said, "Get some sleep. I'll manage in the fields alone." But as soon as he drove over the hill, she dragged her art supplies and books out from under the bed and arranged them on the shelves in the separator room. They looked so much more available there, she felt a rising excitement which gave her energy, and she attacked the bedroom with Maggie's rules in mind.

She stripped the bed and then re-made it carefully, tucking the blankets in tightly so that they'd stay tidy longer. She rearranged the dresser drawers, making space for most of what had been on top. Those things that would not fit went into a box that she stored in the separator room. She set another box in the corner of the bedroom for dirty clothes.

When she started on the living room, she saw that the rollaway bed had been leaned in the corner near the old cot. She dismantled the cot and dragged it out the front door. Leaving it by the gate, she went back into the house and set up the rollaway. "I am going to paint this place, *this* week," she muttered as she spread a dark brown blanket over the bed.

The brown would look nice with pale yellow walls. And pale yellow would be a perfect background for Maggie's quilt and the picture she and Josh had bought at the auction. The vinyl floor covering was Indian red. It wouldn't look bad with the other colors. She thought longingly of the big bookcase and then shrugged and let it go. Her books and supplies were within easy reach.

Gracelyn had to leave the house to feed her bums, but by the time Zandy's truck pulled up at lunchtime, every surface in the house was bare and dust-free. She had made space on the shelves in the separator room for storing the separator parts and milk buckets. She had labeled three boxes to serve for mail and storage files. The kitchen table and counters were clear of everything except Crybaby, who sat in front of the window cleaning her fur. Gracelyn looked around—all squares and angles and flat surfaces.

"It's boring and absolutely unartistic," she said to the cat, "but it's simple to clean and at the moment, that's all that matters to me."

Zandy stepped in and stared. "I thought you were sleeping." He looked around and whistled. "You haven't even been resting. It's great . . . I really like a house this way . . . but you didn't have to do this after the night you had."

"I didn't do this for you, Zandy. I did it for *me*." Zandy looked at her without his usual grin. She continued. "I did a lot of thinking last night after that lion screamed—while I waited for morning to come." He was actually listening to her. His gaze never moved from her face. "The only ranch time that is under my control is the time I spend on housework, so I'm giving myself some of that time every day for sketching and studying.

"I've figured out that if I can do the bedroom in a minute and a half and the living room in two minutes and the kitchen in fifteen, even with a minimum of one hour allotted to housework, I've saved forty-one minutes."

Zandy laughed then. "Forty-one minutes. Can't you be more exact?"

She said, "Exactly forty-one minutes. And I intend to use every minute on studying or drawing." She added, "But I'm not quite done with the house. I want you to pick up some pale yellow paint for me on your next trip to town." She added a belated, "Please."

Zandy grinned and touched a finger to Gracelyn's chin. "Sure, boss. Pale yellow it is."

Gracelyn smiled and served his lunch. As tired as she was, she'd never felt so good. She'd show that damn Josh that she wasn't a kid, wasn't a failure, and wasn't going to end up like any old yucca pod.

Chapter Fifty

THE summer days flew by. Each morning after she fed her bums, Gracelyn set the clock where she could see it and took exactly forty-one minutes for herself no matter how much milk and cream and baled hay awaited her.

The days were crowded, but she did her routine work without even thinking about it. Her mind was filled with the interesting things she was reading and the exercises she set for herself.

She whacked the cows to make them move over and milked them while thinking of perspective or the use of lighting. She laughed at the antics of the bums and ran back to the house, the bottle bucket swinging.

She and Zandy had breakfast together, spoke briefly of the day's work, and parted. Sometimes he was home for lunch; often he was away for dinner. If he didn't give her a ride to the sheep camp, she saddled Soot.

It was easiest to be alone. She didn't want to see Josh. His comments at Bert's Place had scraped her mind, leaving sore spots. And Zandy was acting oddly.

He sometimes hung around after breakfast, pouring an extra cup of coffee, telling her stories about vet problems at various ranches, as if he had no work in the fields. Or he would pick up her sketchpad and study the pictures silently.

She caught him looking at her several times when she

glanced his way. Finally, she said, "Why do you stare at me like that?"

Zandy blushed, but of course his answer was a joke. "You've been such a whirlwind lately, I'm keeping one eye on you and one eye on the cyclone cellar." She couldn't tell if it was a complaint or a compliment, and it made her uneasy.

Damn it, why didn't the man say what was really on his mind or get on with his day? She was eager to get to her special time. Little by little she was making progress.

Dear Annie,

I did it! I found time for sketching and studying. Each morning I spend twenty minutes reading and twenty minutes sketching. And I sneak in a little more reading by propping an art book in front of me when I churn.

I work more carefully than I ever have, doing the same sketch at least three times, approaching the scene first as a draftsman seeking dimensions, the second time as a camera seeking details, the third as a lover seeking . . . something different . . . something of my own. It took me a week to do one set of sketches.

The summer flies by. One of my hens hid out with her eggs and brought me seven little chicks. Zandy helped me devise a brooderhouse for them. I still help in the fields and sleep at the summer pasture.

Thanks for your nice notes. Until you've lived forty miles from the mailbox, you can't appreciate mail.

Gracelyn was writing in the sheep wagon by lantern light. Annie's were the only letters she got these days. She had heard nothing from her parents or Suzanne since her sister's unsettling visit a month ago. How could they just shut her out of a family problem like this? She couldn't shut *them* out. Nights as she lay on the bunk listening to the sounds on the mountain, she pictured her mother packing up all her pretty things. *Was Daddy there to help? Did they even talk to each other? Had he moved to the Lazy-J Motel?*

Gracelyn pushed that thought away and picked up her sketch book. In a glass on the shelf was a stalk with several yucca pods attached. She turned it so that the lantern shone on a large empty pod. In the silky lining, the black and silver stripes alternated, the light falling into the black, only to rise from the silver.

She worked until midnight, though she shouldn't have. She and Pete had to rise before dawn to patrol the flock. In the early murky light, the coyotes were most dangerous. The mother coyotes were teaching their growing young to hunt for their own food.

Gracelyn was studying the sketch of the yucca with a pleasant sense of the improvement in her work, when Pete began to bark.

She slipped into her shoes and stepped out of the wagon. Headlights reflected on the meadow. Her heart began to beat faster as she reached back inside the wagon for the shotgun. She preferred animal prowlers to human ones.

When the lights got closer, Pete stopped barking and began to wag his tail.

"Zandy! What are you doing out here in the middle of the night? Is something wrong?"

Her husband reached into the truck for a large grocery sack and stepped up into the wagon. He set the sack on the bed and turned to her, grinning. "It all started with the cheese," he said. He took the shotgun from her hands and set it in the corner. "I wouldn't want you to shoot me over Brie cheese."

"I can see that you're going to tell this in your own way," Gracelyn said. "I might as well get comfortable." She kicked off her shoes and sat cross-legged on the floor of the wagon by the door. Zandy sat down on the bed.

"I had a late vet call way past Brandon, so I stuck your grocery list in my pocket just in case."

"There wasn't any Brie on my shopping list."

"Pretty dull shopping list."

"I don't think you've ever tasted Brie."

"Who's telling this story?"

Gracelyn laughed, rubbed her eyes, and yawned. "If I shut up, will you tell it straight through?"

Zandy grinned and tousled her hair. "I was in this big old all-night market in Brandon and a lady in high heels and a fancy suit came up to me with a tray." Zandy wrinkled his nose. "She said, 'Would you like to sample our Brie?'

"I said, 'What's Brie?'

"She said, 'Oh, it's a nice party cheese.' And before I could say anything else, she picked up one end of this toothpick and stuck a piece of soggy cheese in my mouth."

Gracelyn hugged her legs. She was beginning to enjoy the story.

Zandy wiped his mouth with the back of his hand. "I swallowed and said, 'Something else must go with it to make the party.' And before I could back up and run, she had a box of fancy crackers, a jar of huge Greek olives, and a half pound of that cheese on top of my staples. 'Now put a nice wine with that,' she said, 'and you've got a party.'"

Zandy reached in the bag and took out a bottle of white wine, crackers, butter, the olives and the cheese. "I figured I could eat the crackers and butter, and you'd appreciate the rest of it."

"Well, I'll be damned," said Gracelyn. "The hardworking Dr. MacNair is courting a sheepherder."

Zandy flushed, and Gracelyn felt sorry that she had been so flip. This was the most romantic gesture Zandy had ever made. She appreciated it, but she wished that one time in her life, someone would simply put his arms around her and say "I love you." She yearned briefly and intensely for the words she'd never heard. Zandy was looking worried.

Gracelyn got up. "It's still warm outside. Let's take the lantern and the bedroll out on the meadow and have a picnic."

They settled on the bedroll and chatted as they sipped their wine and snacked on the cheese. Zandy was thinking of ways to make more cash crops.

"I think I'll try to put in more grain next year." He

grinned. "Of course, I'll have to teach you to plow a little straighter." He fished an olive out of the jar. "I can use the cash from the wheat to buy cake for supplement in the winter. And after harvest, we can turn the ewes into the stubble. Fat ewes breed better." Zandy spat the olive seed out toward the meadow.

So much for romance, Gracelyn thought, but she answered in the same vein. "I've decided that I don't want to sell my dark wool ewes. I saw an article in the *American Wool Growers* paper about a weaver who wants to buy natural grey and brown wools. She offered more per pound than we got for our wool."

Zandy said, "I think I could pick up a dark ram pretty cheap." He grinned at her. "But you'd have to keep him out of my flock."

Gracelyn shuddered at the thought of uncontrolled rams in a flock. Maggie had told her of the year her rams broke through into the ewe pasture four months too early: "I was lambing in mid-January with snow up to my ass."

Zandy was talking about grain again. "If I put in wheat, I'd have to rent a combine or hire a harvest crew. I don't think you and I could get it all done."

"Lordy," Gracelyn said, "I thought we'd never get the first cutting of hay put up."

"Second cutting won't be quite so heavy. We might get to the baling and hauling before time to ship the lambs."

"Did you and Maggie get the trucking set up?"

"Yep." Zandy poured more wine into their coffee cups. Gracelyn spread another cracker with Brie. He said, "Do you really like that stuff?"

Gracelyn looked at the hors d'oeuvre. "It has its place at a cocktail party, but I don't think it would keep me alive in the lambing shed." She looked up. Zandy had set the wine bottle aside and moved closer to her. He bent and kissed her, cradling her head in his big hand. Gracelyn's pulse skipped. Zandy's touch was not shy.

He blew out the lantern and pulled her down on the bedroll. He held her close to him silently, circling one thumb on her breast. The night sky was beginning to lighten a little, but the sheep were still lying down. Zandy continued to caress her. She was relaxed from the wine. When he turned to her, Gracelyn opened her clothes and welcomed him. She climaxed with her eyes open, looking at the stars. A coyote was singing high up on the bluffs. She did not say, "I love you." It would hurt too much if Zandy didn't answer this time.

She had enjoyed the wine and cheese, and it was nice to make love without thinking of the Lazy-J. Zandy had fallen asleep. She snuggled closer to him, enjoying his warmth in the cool air. They slept for a few hours and then patrolled the flock together at dawn.

Gracelyn missed her period in August. She didn't realize she'd missed it until she missed her September period. She had just finished her forty-one minutes and had stepped into the separator room to put her materials back on the shelf when it occurred to her that her period was late. She moved to the calendar and counted the days. And then she sat down on the floor, holding the sketch book to her chest, and cried.

Chapter Fifty-One

THEY were getting ready to move the sheep down from the summer pasture for shipping. Old Daniel hadn't been around for awhile, and nobody they talked to had seen him in the Brandon area.

"I guess it's just you and me, a black horse and a three-legged dog," Zandy said. "You and Pete can take the rear. I'll ride Soot and be ready to turn the point in a hurry if the bellwether gets any funny ideas."

When they got the herd bunched and headed toward the home pasture, Gracelyn and Pete dropped back to move slowly along the rear edge of the flock, from one side to the other.

As Gracelyn watched for stragglers or strays in the flock of ewes and lambs, she picked out some of the young ewes who had been such flighty mothers. She was beginning to understand them better. *I don't know if I want a baby.*

The thought brought a torrent of feelings. There wasn't enough of anything to give to a baby. Money. Time. Love. She hadn't told Zandy about the baby yet. She needed to get over her feelings of loss first. A baby would certainly take away her forty-one minutes.

How did I let this happen? I overheard enough sad tales in the dorm about unwanted pregnancies. She thought of the condom machine she had seen in the restroom of a college bar. Someone had posted a large "Be Prepared" sign across the front of it.

Be prepared for an unexpected visit to a sheep wagon, from a usually unromantic husband? It hadn't even occurred to her.

Gracelyn felt shame. *Oh, Baby, I'm sorry to think such thoughts. I hope the tube that's sending food to you isn't piping in your mother's doubts.*

She thought of her own mother, who had not written once since she had filed for divorce from Daddy. *Were your children an unpleasant surprise? Had you had time to figure out your husband? Were you ready to give up your dreams of painting? Whoa! That's not mother . . . that's me.* Gracelyn plodded along the trail, confused and tired.

She glanced at Pete. "It started with you," she said aloud, and for one moment—hot, discouraged, breathing the dust kicked up by seven hundred sheep—she pictured herself back in the Subaru that first shocked moment after the impact, before she had gone to help Pete.

If I had just driven on . . . It made her feel sick to think of it. She reached out to pat the dog's head, and he licked her wrist.

She was so tired. Zandy had said they'd let the sheep rest near the next water tank. "Baby, I can see you're going to change a lot of things in my life." She said it aloud and then went on mumbling to the baby or to the thought of a baby. "You don't seem real, and right now, I've got a lot of problems you aren't going to help with." Gracelyn moved quickly to turn a lamb back into the flock and then went on with her monologue.

"You've already got an older sister of sorts. Josh said this ranch would take my artwork away from me. I've only just discovered how much it means to me. Please don't make me give it up."

Sweat ran down Gracelyn's face. She took her hat off and fanned herself. She looked out across the valley, but the heat lines made her dizzy, and she turned her attention to the sheep.

Now she was muttering to Mother Nature. "What sort of wicked creature are you anyway? Do you think I'm fit to be a mother right now? I'll be *worse* than those two-year-olds. My instincts are bad, and my heritage is worse. My own mother doesn't know how to be a mother, and besides, she's just been dropped off a cliff herself. How do you think she's going to help me?" Gracelyn was crying. "This little one you've planted in me isn't even going to get a fair start."

Good Lord. Zandy was riding her way. Gracelyn smeared her tears into the dust on her face and tried to hide her fatigue.

She didn't tell Zandy about the baby then, and the next day they were into weaning and shipping, followed quickly by the long-delayed second cutting of hay. It seemed as if there was always the noise of some piece of equipment to yell above.

At night, she was too tired to talk. Zandy was seldom home anyway. The CB squawked all the time. It interrupted meals and conversations; it disrupted shared work; it even ended lovemaking once in a while.

But Zandy had a want list a mile long, and he drove himself to make the veterinary calls. "My Cash Calls," he said to Gracelyn with a grin. "We need a clothes dryer and a flatbed truck and a harrow and a rake and more lambing pens and . . ." As he went on with his list, Gracelyn added silently, "and a doctor, and a hospital, and a crib, and some maternity clothes, and a fund for a college education."

That thought brought tears to her eyes and nausea to her stomach. She went to the bathroom and ran the water to hide the sounds she made.

Each day of October, Gracelyn vomited her coffee in the barn at the first smell of milk cow. Zandy happened into the corral one morning and came quickly into the barn.

"Are you sick?"

Gracelyn wiped her mouth and leaned against the stall. She tried a smile as she said, "Only in the mornings."

"You mean you're pregnant?"

She nodded, trying to read the tone of his words.

The familiar flush colored Zandy's neck and rose clear to his hair line. But was it anger or happiness or what?

"When are you due?"

"First week in May, I think."

"Lambing season."

"Good Lord, I hadn't thought of that. I'm sorry." But it was his fault as much as hers.

Zandy said, "Do you want me to take over the milking?"

No, Gracelyn thought, *I want you to tell me you're happy that we're going to have a baby.* But she said, "Maybe for the next month. Isn't morning sickness supposed to go away after the first three months?"

Zandy grinned at her. "I don't know. None of my patients ever had morning sickness."

Nausea boiled its way up again and Gracelyn ran outside.

Chapter Fifty-Two

THE next morning, Zandy sat at the breakfast table long after he usually went to work. He stared at her until Gracelyn got up and moved uneasily around the kitchen.

Finally he said, "Well, your coat looks good, and your wind is sound. Your head's not droopy, and your hindquarters seem firm. But maybe we ought to get a second opinion."

"Whose?" she said, a bit abruptly. She knew he was kidding her, but she didn't feel like being teased.

"I thought we'd go into Brandon today and find a gynecologist."

He cared enough to put a doctor at the top of his want list. Gracelyn smiled at him. "What a relief," she said. "I thought you might be planning to consult Old Daniel."

When they found a doctor and he had examined Gracelyn, he said, "You're in good shape. Your body is exactly right for carrying a baby easily and giving birth smoothly." Gracelyn felt absurdly pleased at the praise. The doctor set her up on a monthly schedule for the first four months.

As they left the doctor's office, Zandy said, "Let's get a milkshake and head for Larkspur. Jake Liggen's got a problem with one of his bulls."

"I'd like to meet him. I talked to his wife at the auction. She was real nice."

Bertha Liggen remembered her right away. "I didn't realize that you were Doctor MacNair's wife, though." Everyone seemed to know Zandy. The big-boned woman with the frowsy grey hair and weathered face smiled warmly at Gracelyn and once again Gracelyn decided that the woman was beautiful. Bertha said, "Most ranchers keep the coffee pot on, but I like a good cup of tea. Can I brew a pot for you?" Zandy left for the barn to find Jake.

Soon Bertha and Gracelyn were chatting over their tea. When they had finished talking about the sheep and the cold wind that had ended the Indian summer, Gracelyn said, "I bought an embroidered picture at the auction. I hung it on my living room wall with one of Maggie Norman's quilts."

"Isn't Maggie a genius?"

"Are you a quilter?"

"No, I prefer crochet." Bertha rose and led Gracelyn to a cedar chest at the foot of the master bed, and opening it, removed a rainbow of afghans.

"I make up my own designs," the big woman said. "I think those kit things would be boring."

Gracelyn sorted through the treasure of soft throws, crib blankets, and shawls, stopping at an afghan with a zig-zag design in Prussian blue and silvery-grey. She could feel the impact of its beauty in the pit of her stomach. She held it up and stretched it to its full length. "It's like lightning before a summer storm. How did you ever find time to do such intricate stitches?"

"Oh, I rest by crocheting. I usually keep a basket by my rocking chair, and when I'm taking a breather from barn chores, I concentrate on a few rows."

Gracelyn said, "Would you let me buy this afghan to add to my collection of handwork?"

"Heavens, no," Bertha said. "I wouldn't think of selling it, but I'd love to give it to you."

Gracelyn said, "Your work is lovely, but I value it too much just to take it."

The woman met Gracelyn's eyes and said, "Honey, I value it too much to sell it."

Gracelyn was ashamed. But she really wanted the

afghan. "Well, then, may I trade you some of my sketches?"

"Oh, I'd like that."

They spent the next half hour flipping the pages in the sketch books that Gracelyn carried in her purse, and before Zandy and Jacob Liggen had finished cleaning their boots on the back step, Bertha had opened the door.

"Look here, Jake. Isn't that the spitting image of old Bess?" She was holding a charcoal sketch of the Brown Swiss. The rancher joined them in looking at the sketches and he and Bertha chose the picture of the cow and another of her with her calf.

Gracelyn watched them with interest. This was the man who had flown to Washington to fight with the IRS because it didn't value his wife properly. He didn't seem to treat her in any special way. He handed the sketches to her, and looking around, said, "I asked Doc to eat with us. Is dinner about ready?"

Gracelyn helped Bertha in the kitchen. The four of them were joined by two hired hands at the big oak table covered with a flowered plastic tablecloth. The ranch hands and Jacob and Zandy talked about cattle diseases. Bertha ate quietly with an occasional smile at Gracelyn. She seemed at peace with herself. When the meal was finished, Bertha rose to clear the table while the men leaned back in their chairs and told stories. Gracelyn moved from the table to the sink, helping Bertha. Jacob laughed at the punchline of a ranch hand's joke, puffed on his pipe for a moment and began a tale of his own.

"This old boy, he figured to go hunting after roundup. He was foreman on the J-bar-J up in the Powder River country, and he'd been wantin' to go hunting all season, but he'd been hogtied by a bunch of green hands including the boss's two teenage nephews, who thought they knew all there was to know about ranching. When he finally got them steers rounded up and shipped, he told his boss, 'I'm going down to hunt in the Colorado high country for a couple of weeks.'" Gracelyn dried dishes, enjoying the word pictures Jacob made.

"The boss pushed his Stetson back, scratched his head, spit into the dirt, and said, 'Sure you kin go, John, but will you do me a favor?'

"Thinkin' his boss was going to ask for a big elk steak or somethin' like that, the old boy said, 'You name it.' "

" 'Well,' the boss said, 'them city kids of my sister's been wanting to do some trophy hunting. How about you taking them under your wing? You can use the big horse trailer and drive my pickup.'

"Wishin' he'd kept his mouth shut, the old boy loaded up three saddle horses and a pack horse, tossed in the grub box and bedrolls, took his rifles and his side arm and those two mouthy kids and started off."

Gracelyn glanced around the table. The ranch hands and Zandy were engrossed in the old man's story. Bertha was wiping out the sink, listening in a casual way that made Gracelyn think she'd probably heard the story before.

"The trip turned out even worse than he'd figured. Them two boys knew as much about hunting as they did about ranching and, between their loud talking and their careless shooting, they kept the game well out of sight. The old hand kept moving 'em higher into the hills hoping to calm 'em down some with the riding and the packing, but they grumbled about the work and kept shooting off their rifles and their mouths. They didn't like riding all day, they didn't like sleeping on the ground, and they bitched constantly about the food. The old boy had just about had his fill."

The rancher paused for a moment. Bertha took the pot from the stove and filled his coffee cup. He looked up and winked at her and then returned to his story.

"Late one afternoon, as they topped a high ridge to look for game, the sky started clouding up. 'We better look for shelter,' the old boy said.

"Before he could say another word, they galloped off, leaving him to grab the reins of the pack horse. When he finally caught up to them two, they'd found an old cabin. As soon as he rode up, they jerked their bedrolls off the pack horse and rushed inside. By the time he'd fed and watered the horses, the boys had rolled out their beds in the tightest corner of the old shack, leaving him a section of roof that was missing a few boards. He brought his bedroll in, spread it out upon his tarp, and tossed his slicker over it.

"And just as they was bedding down for the night, there come up a real gully washer. Those kids had a high time giving the old boy the hee-haw.

" 'Hey Old John, if you're such a smart camper, how come you're sleeping in the rain?' one of the kids said.

" 'Yeah,' said the other. 'Look at us. Our roof don't leak.'

"The old boy reached down inside his bedroll where he'd put his sidearm to keep it dry. Lifting the gun, he took careful aim and shot six fine holes in the ceiling over the boys' beds.

"As he rolled back into his bed and hunched the slicker up around his shoulders, he said, 'Now it does.' "

The laughter around the table was a warming sound. Gracelyn studied Jacob Liggen. He wasn't at all what she had expected of a man who was willing to beard the IRS in its den. He was shorter than Bertha, and stocky, with a belly that rounded the front of his wool cowboy shirt. The top of his head was shiny. His face was white to the hat line and tanned and leathery below. A network of squint wrinkles and laugh lines surrounded his eyes, but his eyes were shrewd and intelligent. He was obviously a successful rancher. The house showed it as much as the barns and other outbuildings. The living room beyond the kitchen door was carpeted and furnished with expensive overstuffed furniture. The kitchen was well-equipped with a freezer, a range with double ovens, and a microwave oven on the counter.

The men had stopped laughing and were getting up to retrieve their hats and go back to work. The cowboys shook hands with Zandy. Gracelyn turned as Jacob Liggen moved quietly to his wife.

"Good grub, kid," he said and pinched her bottom. She blushed like a young girl and, catching his hand, held it for a moment.

"You old rooster," she said.

Gracelyn looked away, feeling as if she'd witnessed an intimate bedroom scene. This unlikely pair of old country folk was obviously in love with each other. She felt a surge of envy as she picked up the afghan and joined Zandy in saying their goodbyes.

Chapter Fifty-Three

GRACELYN'S nausea eased by Thanksgiving, and she was able to enjoy Maggie's turkey, although she refused the sage hen Josh had shot. The weather turned stormy, and the outside work took more time as winter deepened. The week before Christmas, Maggie drove to the hay feeder to get Gracelyn.

"Your sister called. She sounded like she's wound tight and ready to blow. I told her you'd call her back."

Gracelyn climbed into Maggie's pickup. By the time they reached the other ranch, her hands were trembling.

Maggie said, "Now, don't you let her upset you. You've got to take care of yourself and that baby." Gracelyn nodded. Maggie added, "I'll be at the barn if you need me."

Gracelyn scooted a kitchen chair near the phone and sat down to dial Suzanne's number, grateful for Maggie's tact and the privacy. Her sister answered immediately.

"Suzanne?" Gracelyn said.

"Oh, Gracelyn," Suzanne said and burst into tears.

"What's the matter?"

"Everything's falling apart."

"I can't understand you. Can you stop crying?"

Suzanne choked back her sobs. "Gracelyn, it's terrible. Mother's leaving, and Daddy's going to marry that girl."

Gracelyn clutched the phone with both hands and took a deep breath to control her sudden nausea.

"Wait, Suzanne, tell me slowly. Is the divorce final already? No one has written to me for months."

"It was final yesterday."

"Well, what do you mean Mother's leaving? I thought they were selling the house anyway. Has she been staying there?"

"No. I mean, she's leaving the state." There was a sudden static on the line, and Gracelyn missed the next words.

"I can't hear you, Suzanne."

"She's going to Florida," Suzanne yelled.

"Why?"

"No one can talk her out of it. She's going to start an interior decorating company. Daddy doesn't think she has enough experience. Steve tried to give her advice, but she wouldn't listen to him. She's just cold and quiet and . . ." Suzanne was crying again.

I can't deal with this. "Suzanne, you'll make yourself sick," Gracelyn said firmly. She waited through more sobbing mixed with static. Finally she said, "Tell me about Daddy."

"He's getting married day after tomorrow."

Gracelyn leaned her head against the back of the chair.

"Are you there?" Suzanne asked.

"Yes, I'm here, but what do you think I can do about all this?"

"Could you come home?" Suzanne said.

"I don't think I can get away. You're surely not inviting me to his wedding?"

"Oh, no!" Suzanne sounded shocked. "They aren't having a real wedding. They're going to fly to Las Vegas."

"Does Mother need help moving?"

"Mother says she doesn't need anything from anyone." Suzanne stopped talking and for a moment the only sound on the line was the crackle of the static. Then she said, "Gracelyn, Steve and I are going to be all alone for Christmas."

Gracelyn remembered last Christmas at home and the drawing she had given her father. For Suzanne and Mother, it had been a happy Christmas. She could understand why

Suzanne was feeling so bereft, but having Gracelyn there wouldn't change anything.

"I can't leave here, Suzanne," she said as gently as she could. "We're feeding hay and cake every day. It takes both of us to keep up with the work."

"Well, you're not going to work on Christmas, are you?"

Gracelyn smiled. She had probably had ideas like that too before she left the city. "The sheep and cows have to eat on Christmas just like any other day."

Suzanne persisted. "You could hire someone."

"We're a little short on money right now. We just bought a machine to grind hay." It sounded too cold to leave it like that, and so Gracelyn said, "Suzanne, why don't you and Steve come to the ranch?"

There was another small silence before Suzanne said, "That wouldn't really be like Christmas at home, would it? I don't see why you can't come here."

"Suzanne, I am four-and-a-half-months pregnant, and I've just barely stopped throwing up my breakfast." She hadn't meant to tell her sister about the pregnancy just yet, and she wished she could take back the words as soon as they were out.

Suzanne burst into tears again. "Then that means you're really going to stay up there."

Whatever happened to "Gee, that's wonderful news"? Gracelyn thought, but she said, "You didn't think I was just visiting, did you?"

"Well, no, of course not, but the way you ran off so suddenly and you didn't really know Zandy that well and you came from such a nice background . . ." Suzanne's voice trailed away and Gracelyn wondered if she'd suddenly realized how insulting her comments were. Suzanne added a little lamely, "It's nice about the baby."

Gracelyn didn't respond at once. She was afraid she'd sound sarcastic. After Suzanne had seen the ranch, how could she so casually count out Gracelyn's home and the work she was doing, not to mention Zandy and his work? Suzanne certainly served roasted leg of lamb often enough. Where did she think it came from anyway? But Suzanne was already nearly a basket case. No point in adding to her woes. Gracelyn went back to the subject of Christmas.

"Why don't you think about it before you say no? You and Steve could drive up for a day or two."

"We'd be putting you out," Suzanne said, and Gracelyn translated, *You don't have a decent guest room.* "But we'll think about it. I'll write you. Okay?"

"Sure," Gracelyn said. "Do you have Mother's new address?" She copied down the general-delivery information her sister gave her. "Things will work out, Suzanne. Somehow."

"But nothing will ever be the same. Neither one of them cares about us at all."

Tears came to Gracelyn's eyes as she thought of her father and Arminda in some garish Las Vegas hotel, and her mother following a moving van to Florida.

"If you want to come to us, Suzanne, you're always welcome."

After they had hung up, Gracelyn sat numbly next to the phone. Maybe, despite what she had told Josh, she had always thought she'd go back, too. If she hadn't, why was it so hard to know there was nothing there?

She looked down, suddenly hugged her newly rounding belly and said out loud, "I love you, Baby. You hear me. I love you."

She found Maggie in the barn replacing a broken board in the side of a stall. Maggie looked up from her hammer. "Everything okay?"

"Aside from the fact that my entire family has lost its senses."

"Josh told me about your folks filing for divorce. I suppose it just came final. Is that what's upsetting your sister?"

"Among other things." Gracelyn could not talk about Arminda. What would she say? *My stepmother used to sleep with the boys in my dorm before she moved closer to home.* She changed the subject. "Did Josh ever tell you that he advised me to leave Zandy before I ruined my chances of being an artist?"

Maggie smiled. "Josh thinks it's all or nothing. Actually,

most men are like that. They get so dead set on the thing right in front of their noses, they forget everything else. Lord, the world would be in a mess if women couldn't manage two or three things at once."

Gracelyn laughed. "Josh also said that you're just like Zandy. All you care about is ranching."

"I'll bet he called my quilting a hobby."

"He did, but I didn't believe him. Tell me about it."

Maggie hammered in a final nail and stood up, rubbing at the small of her back with a leather-gloved hand. "I'm not concerned about quantity. I don't plan to make a quilt for every third bed in Montana."

She leaned on top of the stall and gazed out on the snowy pasture beyond the barn. "I am concerned with design and color and the quality of my stitches. I've collected patterns from the grannies who are now too blind to quilt. Some families brought patterns from the East and the South. When I make one of those patterns, I write down all the history that comes with it."

Maggie smiled at Gracelyn. "You've got me going. But I know that you understand. I feel that my quilts are a link with the women of the past and the women of the future. Did you ever know a woman who wasn't fascinated with a patchwork quilt?"

Gracelyn thought of Suzanne's greedy fingers tracing the sunbonnets on Maggie's quilt. "Do you think I can stay on the ranch and still keep drawing?"

Maggie laughed. "Gracelyn, you've been up here nearly a year, and I've never seen you leave your house without your sketch book."

"But I wasn't really working at it until just before I got pregnant. Since then, I've been so tired, I can hardly get my work done, let alone find energy to draw. Maybe Josh is right."

Now Gracelyn was the one who stared out across the snowy pasture. The casual words didn't come near expressing her feelings. Her artwork and her books were all that was left of her other life. She felt a steady thinning of the threads that tied her to college and to Dr. Carlson. She looked back at Maggie.

Maggie said, "You've taken on a tough job. It won't be easy to keep up with your art now that the baby's coming, but you can do it if you can stay focused. You're real good." She grinned. "Some of your sunsets are kind of watery, but that sketch you did of your slop bucket before you retired it made the bucket look so slimy I could smell the slop."

Gracelyn returned her smile, thinking of her sketches of romantic sunsets. Maggie's honesty was strong-tasting medicine, but it eased the pain of her family's lies.

"I'd better go home and focus then," she said. "I'm damned if I'll consent to being famous for my picture of a slop bucket."

"Are you going to Brandon this week?" Maggie asked as they climbed into her truck.

"Yes. It's time for another check-up and my latest treasure hunt." Zandy had taken her with him on calls to several ranches after her last check-up and she had asked each time about handwork.

As Maggie returned her to her front gate, Gracelyn said, "I have been in some of the messiest rooms I've ever seen, where the sewing machine was buried, and you might find a pincushion in the chair. And I've been in rooms so tidy they rival yours. No matter which, the handwork is usually wonderful. I never cease to be amazed at what these women are doing in their spare time."

"You can do it too," Maggie said.

As she slipped from the truck seat, Gracelyn said, "Thanks for everything. You always manage to cheer me up."

"You're quiet these days," Zandy said as they drove to Brandon later that week. Gracelyn smiled at him and then stared out over the snowy prairie. Nothing moved. Neither hawk nor eagle marked the ashy sky. There weren't even any shadows.

"I've been thinking about Christmas," she said. "Suzanne

loved that quilt Maggie gave me. I wish I could afford to buy her one for Christmas."

"You'll have a devil of a time getting Maggie to take any money."

"I know that. And yet quilts not near as nice as hers are priced at two hundred dollars in the city." She looked deep into the barren landscape, seeking a focal point, a perspective. This land was tough to draw in wintertime.

Zandy said, "Maybe you could deal through Josh. He can sometimes get Maggie to do things when no one else can."

"He calls her quilts 'a nice hobby,'" Gracelyn said, hearing the edge in her voice.

Zandy raised his right hand. "I swear, on my honor as a sheep rancher, I never once called your sketching a hobby."

Gracelyn laughed. "I guess I do feel a little touchy about it." *Wow*, she thought, *we're almost dealing with an emotion.*

"What about your folks?"

"My mother could use some money. She's trying to start a business."

"I'll look at the books. We might be able to send her a check."

Gracelyn felt like crying. When she told Zandy things, she always made them sound so normal, so nice. Why couldn't she tell him about that poor, frightened woman running blindly toward the farthest spot she could think of to get away from the man who had rejected her?

Because I'm ashamed of it.

Gracelyn was startled. That thought was clear enough. *I'm ashamed to tell him the truth about my family soap opera.* She felt a moment of discomfort. *Or maybe I'm ashamed of the feeling that my father rejected me.*

She reviewed all the things she had never mentioned to Zandy. Did he hide just as much behind his jokes? Did he have doubts about the baby? Or was he beginning to think about the baby with love sometimes, too, as she was?

"Shall we accept Maggie's invitation for Christmas?" Zandy asked.

"If she'll let me help fix dinner."

Josh persuaded Maggie to accept payment for Suzanne's quilt, and Gracelyn decided to fill the whole Christmas box to Suzanne and Steve with specialties of the country. Zandy brought home dry ice, and they packed a large chunk of her homemade butter. She sent cottage cheese that she had made and wild plum jelly from one of the ranches and a pair of lovely pillowcases with delicately tatted edges that she bought from another ranch wife.

Gracelyn wrote cards giving the history of each gift, aware even as she packed the box that her desire to prove that her ranch country had something valuable wasn't totally in the Christmas spirit. She could still hear the insulting tone in Suzanne's voice as she wailed about Gracelyn's staying in Montana.

Christmas Day was fun. They did only the necessary chores and then joined Maggie and Josh in front of the fireplace in Maggie's living room to sip hot buttered rum and open presents. Zandy and Gracelyn gave Maggie a carved sheep for her mantel; they gave Josh new leather gloves. Maggie gave Gracelyn a quilt with matching pillow shams for their bedroom.

"Oh, Maggie," was all Gracelyn could say. She cried as she hugged her neighbor. Josh gave them each a huge red stocking filled with nuts and candy.

During dinner, Gracelyn said, "We're a nice family. There's Mother Maggie, and the MacNair twins, and big brother Josh."

"Thanks a lot," Josh said, but he smiled at her. "Wish big brother luck at the Stock Show in Denver next month."

Maggie glanced at him. "You didn't tell me you were going to ride."

There was an uncomfortable silence until Gracelyn said, "Good luck, Josh. Or are you supposed to use theater talk and say 'break a leg'?"

"'Good luck' will do fine," Josh said.

Later he played the accordion while Zandy played his harmonica and Maggie strummed her guitar. They sang Christmas carols before heading out to do their evening work.

"Guess who else is pregnant," Zandy said that night. He was sitting on the edge of their bed pulling off a sock.

"Someone I know?" It couldn't be Maggie or Bertha Liggen, so who was it?

"Crybaby."

"You're kidding. When is she due?"

"She's getting pretty close."

"Fine vet I'd make. I thought she was just getting fat on all that cream and butter."

Chapter Fifty-Four

CRYBABY gave birth to her kittens the first week in January, as Zandy had predicted, but Zandy wasn't there to help with the birth. While she was in early labor, Crybaby would not stay in the box Gracelyn had prepared in the stove corner. The cat prowled the house until the babies began to appear and then lay down on the bedroom rug.

"Damn it," Gracelyn said, kneeling beside the cat. "Where is the veterinarian when you need him?" The kittens were large. Crybaby was small. Gracelyn was afraid to try to help the cat for fear she would harm her. Clutching her own belly, she watched as each of the five kittens was born, causing agony to the mother. During the birth of one kitten with a huge head, Crybaby clawed her way, screaming, up the bedroom door. Gracelyn put her hands over her ears and cried.

The kitten was finally expelled, and Crybaby fell to the floor exhausted. But as soon as she regained a little strength, she began to clean the kitten with her tongue.

When the final kitten was born and cleaned, Gracelyn carefully lifted all five kittens into the box. She picked Crybaby up and held her close, caressing her. When the cat looked anxiously toward the mewling kittens, Gracelyn put her into the box with them.

Zandy came home just in time to help with evening chores. Gracelyn milked the cow in her stall silently while

Zandy chatted about his vet call and the drive from Brandon. His day seemed totally disconnected from hers.

When he checked the cat that evening, he said, "She's fine. It was a normal birth." Gracelyn shuddered and made no reply.

All night long, Crybaby made trips from the kittens' box to Gracelyn's side of the bed. Gracelyn hung her hand down, and the cat leaned into the curve of her palm and rested there until the kittens cried, and then she ran to the box again.

For the next few days, Crybaby yowled whenever Gracelyn left the living room. Gracelyn took her churning and every other portable chore in near the stove and talked to the cat while she worked. One afternoon, while Crybaby was nursing her kittens, Gracelyn felt her own baby move.

That evening at dinner, she said, "What if you're not here when it's time for the baby?"

"Maggie asked me that yesterday."

Bless her, Gracelyn thought. "What did you tell her?"

"I didn't have a real plan then, but I've been thinking about it." Gracelyn waited. He said, "I'll hire Old Daniel when it gets near lambing season and your time."

"It will be nice to have someone around here about then."

Zandy looked at her. "I don't mean for *you* to be here."

"Well, where am I going to be?"

"Maggie has a friend in Brandon. About a week before you're due, we'll move you to her place. Then you'll be near the hospital."

"Won't you be with me?"

"I'll try to be. But at least I'll know you aren't stuck out here." Zandy grinned. "I'd hate to have to fix you a box behind the stove."

"The baby moved," Gracelyn said. She wanted to talk about what was happening inside her, but Zandy's response was disappointing. He was looking ahead to a baby outside of her, unaware of how real the child was right now.

He said, "Should we be thinking of names?"

"Do you have any favorites?"

Zandy considered. "My mother's name is Emma. If it's a girl, we could combine Mother's name and yours and call the baby Emmalyn."

"That's pretty. Will a boy be Alexander?"

"Nope. No juniors."

"What would you think of calling a boy Daniel?"

Zandy laughed. "If we name a kid after him, Old Daniel will be ours forever."

"Speaking of Old Daniel, could you talk him out of a pair of his coveralls?"

"What for?"

"For me to wear. Nothing fits me anymore."

Zandy turned bright red. "Good God. I'm sorry. I treat old Soot better than that. At least he has a blanket." He took out his wallet and thrust some bills at her. "Here, keep these, and you can go shopping next time we're in town."

Tired as she was, Gracelyn still took her forty-one minutes each day. She had decided to concentrate on sketching the kittens. Four of the kittens were black and white; the other was black and white with a cadmium orange spot on his nose.

"Sometimes I wonder about the father of those kittens," Gracelyn said. "His colors certainly didn't dominate."

"He was barn-cat yellow," Zandy said.

"How do you know?"

"Fatherhood seems to have been his last act in this life. I found him dead in the lambing shed."

Gracelyn thought of the agonies of birth that Crybaby had gone through. "I'm not too sorry for him," she said.

Zandy misunderstood her. "Plenty of human tomcats wouldn't mind ending it that way."

Gracelyn put aside a sudden picture of her middle-aged father and his new young wife and silently began a sketch of the kittens in the box with their mother, looking at shape and shadow, highlight and hollow.

She drew only the cat and the kittens now, but other animals caught her attention in a new way. One morning while she was milking, she began to think about the cow as one giant art lesson: the pink rubbery nose, shiny with the slime from the constant upward swipe of the rough tongue; the thick neck and bulging belly, the high hip bones separated from the knobby spine by smooth hairy hollows as deep as a cupped hand; the slicked-down look of the belly where it dipped in toward the hind leg; the hairy bloated udder; the puckered maw under the tail; the tangled manure-fouled hair at the end of the tail. Heavens . . . the textures and lines and shadows and play of light.

As she became more awkward in pregnancy, milking became a ridiculous chore. "By the time I'm really showing," she said to Zandy, "my belly will bump against the cow's belly, and my arms won't reach the teats."

Feeding the sheep was no longer a pleasant part of the day's work either. It wasn't the change in her, but the change in their feeding methods, that made it so unpleasant.

The new hay grinder was a monstrous, noisy, dusty machine. It ate the bales of hay that Zandy fed it; it chewed up the oats he dumped in the hopper. An augur mixed them all together, another augur sent the ground hay to the rounded, pipelike dispensing arm, inside of which was still another augur that moved the ground-up hay to the spout. All that motion kept the air full of dust. Zandy wore a mask over his nose and mouth when he ground the hay. Gracelyn wore a mask when she walked along the feeder troughs, directing the spout. But nothing could keep the fine-ground itchy hay from her hair, her skin, and her clothes. The shower could not wash it all away; the prickly itch of fine hay became a part of her, like the smell of manure that lingered on her boots.

Feeding hay with the grinder was not the companionable work they had shared when they fed with bales, taking turns driving the pickup, joking and talking. With the hay grinder running, they couldn't even hear each other. Everything was noisy: the engine, the hammer mill, the gears, the augurs. They communicated with hand signals. Zandy was proud of the machine; Gracelyn was lonely in the middle of the noise.

But the sheep thrived. They ate more of the hay, wasted less, and grew fat. "I'm thinking of putting you on a ground-hay diet," Zandy said.

"Oh, no you don't," Gracelyn said. "I'm not ready for twins or triplets."

The eighty-mile round trips to Brandon for her check-ups were exhausting in the heavy snows of late January and February. Gracelyn began to lose weight. She yearned to sleep through her forty-one minutes, but she was determined not to give them up. If she lost the thread of what she was reading, she went back and re-read it. Her back ached as she bent over her sketches. She wept easily and Zandy's jokes hurt her feelings more often than they amused her.

The baby seemed the only one close to her. As the baby moved inside her and her belly grew, Gracelyn had an exalted private sense of being part of Creation. And when the baby kicked as she sketched, the sense was doubled. Her mind and fingers and belly were all pregnant.

One evening, Zandy said, "I've finally found a hand to help us out for awhile, fella named Bill Riley. He's coming in the morning. He can do some of the feeding, clean the chicken house if you want him to, and later take over the milking."

Then, instead of feeling exalted, Gracelyn felt guilty for causing extra expense. The glut of conflicting feelings kept her silent. How could she explain anything to Zandy? He was still talking about Bill Riley.

"I hope he works out. Since the oil companies came in and hired so many men, the ranchers are hurting for help. At least this guy seems to have some savvy about sheep."

Zandy was called away before the new hand arrived. He leaned from the pickup window to say, "Tell Riley to scatter the cake and then put him to work wherever you want him. He could haul bales, but wait until I get back to grind hay."

A strange pickup pulled up in front of the house just as Gracelyn started the separating. A young man in denim work clothes and a battered black hat jumped down. She met him at the door. "Hi, I'm Gracelyn MacNair. Are you Bill Riley?"

The young man was short, rough-skinned, red-faced and surly. "Yeah, I'm Riley. Is the doc here?"

"He'll be back." Gracelyn smiled. "We might as well get to the work. If you'll go ahead and break the ice in the stock tanks, I'll meet you at the barn in a few minutes to help load cake." She stepped back inside for warmer clothes and gloves.

The morning didn't go well. The man was supposed to scatter the cake, but when she repeated the instructions, he just looked at her and continued to dump it in piles that caused the sheep to bunch up. She didn't know what she was doing wrong, but she and the man simply did not work as a team. Finally, she said, "I've got to get back to the house. When you finish with the cake, please start hauling hay from the meadow. Just stack it by the grinding machine, and my husband will grind it when he comes home."

It would be a big help to have the hay at hand. Zandy wouldn't let her lift bales anymore and it slowed up the grinding when he had to go and load the pickup. But by noon, when Bill Riley came to the house and asked about lunch, she could see nothing stacked by the grinder. He hunched over his plate and shoveled his food in. She hated to ask what he'd been doing. As he rose to leave, she said, "When you're done with the hay, will you clean out the chicken house? There are tools in the barn." He jerked his head and grabbed his hat from the hook on his way out.

When Gracelyn went to feed the chickens, their house had not been touched by fork or shovel. Bill Riley's pickup was near the barn, but she saw no sign of the new hand.

Gracelyn met Zandy as she walked slowly to the house for the milk buckets. She hated to complain to him, but she had to give him some explanation about the hay. She raised a hand to stop his truck.

He rolled down the window and smiled at her. "Hi, how's it going?"

She returned his smile, but said, "I don't think I'm much

of a boss. That man you hired yesterday didn't do any of the things I told him to do."

"Why not?"

"I don't know. He scarcely spoke to me."

"I'll talk to him as soon as I unload this grain for the milk cows."

Gracelyn took a moment to get a drink of water and then carried the buckets back to the barn. She was about to enter when she heard Zandy's voice. She stopped. She didn't want to get involved with Bill Riley again. If she stayed out of the way, maybe Zandy could get him started catching up with the work. But she lingered instead of walking out into the near pasture for the cows. She wanted to see how Zandy handled the situation.

"It doesn't seem like you got a lot of work done today," Zandy was saying. "My wife told you what was on line, didn't she?"

"I don't take orders from no woman." The voice was rude. Gracelyn could see the sullen face in her mind. Her anger rose. He had wasted his day and hers too.

Zandy said, "My wife is my partner. If you *won't* work for her, you *don't* work for me. You'd better pack up your gear." Gracelyn took a deep breath, her anger gone in an instant, replaced with a tremulous joy.

"You're not serious!" Riley said. "As scarce as help is you'd fire a good hand because some woman came whining to you?"

Zandy's reply was swift and in a tone so angry that Gracelyn winced. "My wife is a better hand than you'll ever be and a helluva good sport besides. She does three times her share of the work and in all the time I've known her, she's never whined about anything." Now Zandy's voice was hard and cold. "Get in your goddamned truck and get the hell off our ranch."

Gracelyn turned quickly away, afraid to be caught eavesdropping, but as she hurried out toward the milk cows, she felt as if she were floating. The wonderful phrases Zandy had used sang through her mind: *My wife is my partner . . .*

a better hand . . . a good sport. Zandy had actually said "our ranch."

When Zandy joined her later as she was pitching soiled straw from the chicken house, she said, "That Bill Riley sure left in a hurry," and waited with a smile for Zandy to tell her about the conversation.

"Yeah," Zandy said. "He had a mistaken idea about who's bossing this spread. I tied a can to his tail." Zandy began to scrape the chicken-house floor with a shovel.

Gracelyn's smile faded and her feeling of anticipation vanished. He wasn't going to tell her the rest of it. If she had not eavesdropped, she would never have known what Zandy said. She jabbed her fork into a matted clump of straw, silent as her silent husband, feeling cheated.

Chapter Fifty-Five

AS the kittens grew, Crybaby began to teach them. Gracelyn watched with apprehension as she saw how completely the kittens dominated their mother's day. She clung more fiercely to her own block of time.

One day she heard Zandy and Josh come into the kitchen. Zandy said, "Gracelyn has put her brand on forty-one minutes each morning. I'd better make the coffee." And somehow, it was accepted on Plum Creek that Gracelyn was not to be disturbed.

Another morning she heard Maggie ask Zandy, "Has Gracelyn done her forty-one?" She would have enjoyed seeing Maggie, but Zandy said "No, she's still working," and Maggie left without even sticking her head in the door. The words she overheard didn't seem to come from the same man who teased her about her art.

"Pretty soon, we can paper the bedroom," he said one morning as he studied an array of sketches. "If you keep at this, we can even paper the barn."

Her baby grew and her belly grew and the kittens grew. In the old grass outside the front door, Crybaby taught them stalking. Gracelyn could hardly sketch for laughing when the fat kittens went down on their bellies and waddled. "You're supposed to slither," she said.

Zandy was keeping the milk cows close in the creek pasture, so that Gracelyn didn't have so far to go to bring them in for milking. She enjoyed the walk along the meadow. One balmy day in late March, Zandy yelled from the corral, "Look behind you."

Gracelyn turned. She was leading a parade. Crybaby and the kittens were following her single file. She had never seen a cat follow along like a dog, but her cats stayed with her as she turned the cows and took them to the barn. There, the cats formed a patient circle. Zandy came in to watch them.

"They're here for dinner," he said. "I'll go find some cans to feed them in."

Every day as the early spring stayed nice, and the out-of-doors was sweet with promise, the cats followed Gracelyn and the cows to the barn for warm milk.

"Maybe they'd stay up here if we made a bed for them," Zandy said. "Six is at least five too many house cats."

Gracelyn thought of her sketching. Zandy knew she was trying to capture the phases of the kittens' growth. It would be harder and take more time if she had to make trips to the barn or hunt for the cats in the grass. But Crybaby made her own decision.

One night, the cat meowed to go out. The kittens followed. All six of them disappeared into the darkness and did not return. The next morning when she went to milk the cows, Gracelyn found the cat and the kittens in the barn. Near them were two little white fluffs of fur, round like cotton balls.

"What are they?" Gracelyn asked, showing them to Zandy.

"They look like the tails from cottontail rabbits," he said.

"But there was nothing else there. They can't have pulled the tails off the rabbits, can they?"

"Gracelyn, I think they ate the rabbits."

"Ate them!" Gracelyn leaned back from the Brown Swiss to stare at Zandy. "Bones and all?"

"From nose to tail," Zandy said. He propped his arms on the stall, looking at the cats.

"I don't believe it," Gracelyn said.

"Well, we can't know for sure, but they were out all

night hunting, and they aren't hungry, even for milk, this morning."

Gracelyn thought she had known Crybaby. Now, thinking of the cruelty, thinking of the pain for the baby rabbits, she felt that her pet was a stranger. She started to cry.

Zandy said, "Gracelyn, are you always going to cry over perfectly natural things?"

"But it's so cruel."

"Nature is cruel. People who babble about going back to nature don't know what they're talking about. Nature will take us back when she wants us—in some flood, earthquake, or raging blizzard."

Gracelyn thought of their first lambing season. She stood up and carried her bucket and milking stool to the holstein's stall. "Well, I don't want my cat to eat rabbits alive," she said. She balanced herself on the one-legged stool. As she leaned toward the cow, the baby objected to being squashed and kicked Gracelyn. She patted her stomach.

"A lot of us make the mistake of thinking we own our animals," Zandy said. "That cat belongs to herself."

Gracelyn wasn't thinking about the cats anymore. She was thinking about the baby. It was odd that Zandy wasn't even aware of his child at this moment when the child was so vigorous inside her.

Zandy said, "Well, enough of this weighty discussion, I've got to go grind hay."

Gracelyn went on with her milking, thinking of Annie's latest letter. After Maggie had called her sunsets weak, Gracelyn had sent Annie some sketches to evaluate.

Dear Gracelyn,

You're really making progress. When you draw the things you know and work with . . . the milk buckets, the separator, the churn, you show a style of your own. The picture of the windmill from your window is superb. I've stolen it from you to frame and hang on my wall.

I agree with your neighbor, though, about your pictures of the land and the sky. Only I wouldn't call them weak. You're not a weak artist. I would call them indecisive.

Gracelyn, I can tell that you have not yet decided if the land is yours, despite your obvious attraction . . . maybe obsession. You romanticize it in one sketch, making it pretty; the next you ignore its beauty and present only that which is harsh.

Why not let the land alone for the present. Paint those things that are yours to paint. Some day, you will know if the land is yours, and then you will know how to paint it.

Craig and I are slowly working things out. He actually put a casserole in the oven the other day. I read your letters aloud. Craig enjoys them too. Hope your pregnancy goes well.

Love, Annie

Gracelyn poured milk for the cats and carried her buckets to the house, aware of how routine ranch life was when it wasn't dramatic. Annie's letters fed her mind.

Dear Annie,

I don't know if people *can* make the land their own. We can't even agree about its use. I ache for the ranchers who lose lambs to coyotes, but I wouldn't put out bait for fear of killing an eagle.

One day, as I was hunkered down on the ground near the barn, Zandy came by and asked what I was doing. "Looking at an ant hill," I said. He was shocked that I'd never seen an ant hill.

Annie, where would I have seen an ant hill? Silver Crest would never permit one. The land around the college is paved or grassed over. The land at the country club is equally sterile. Can you imagine putting asphalt over several acres of land, installing grass that is never allowed to bloom or to go to seed, filling a concrete pool with chemically treated water and calling it civilization? And Suzanne calls our pastures barren!

But I'm not wise enough to think I know what to do with the land. So perhaps I will take your advice and leave the land alone for the moment.

As I re-read these lines, it occurs to me that perhaps I never did belong in the city. I hope I have the courage to let my child find its true place without making it miserable for years as I try to mold it to my plans.

I am so proud to think of *my* windmill hanging on your wall!

"We've got a lot to do today," Zandy said as they drove toward Larkspur the next day. "See Jake Liggen's sick cow. Shop for groceries. Take you to the vet." He looked at her and grinned.

Jake and Bertha were loosening the fence at one end of the garden. "He'll plow it for me," Bertha said. Zandy helped them to roll the wire back so a tractor could pass through, saying, "We probably ought to be thinking about a garden." Then they all stood for a moment, chatting.

Jake Liggen didn't seem to be in any hurry to get to his sick cow. He leaned on the pickup box in the spring sunshine and told them a story. To herself, Gracelyn called Jake's stories "This Old Boy Tales." Jake always started his stories in the same way.

"This old boy, he worked at one of them open-pit coal mines in Wyoming. He was the day mechanic on the coal-hauling rigs and his buddy was the night mechanic. Happens that they had a fishin' hole they liked to go to, but the operation was working seven days a week, and they never could seem to get the same day off.

"So this old boy, he'd go fishin' alone and tell his buddy all about it the next day. And then his buddy would go fishin' and tell *him* about it. As time went by, the telling was as much fun as the fishin'.

"So one day when they met at shift change, this old boy says, 'I had real good fishin' today. I caught me a big old bastard. Yessir, I caught a trout two feet long.'

"His buddy said, 'Two feet, huh. Well, wait 'til you hear about *my* catch the day before yestiddy. I was fishin' the hole pretty serious and suddenly I hooked onto something big. I reeled 'er in slow. When she broke the water, I could see that I'd latched onto one of them old kerosene barn lanterns. And by damn if that lantern wasn't still lit.'

"'Whoa there,' this old boy said, pushing back his hat and scratching his head. 'Tell you what I'll do. I'll take a foot off my trout, if you'll blow out that lantern.'"

The others laughed, but as the men headed for the barn, Gracelyn settled gloomily into a chair in Bertha's kitchen. Bertha poured tea and studied Gracelyn quietly a moment before asking, "Jake's jokes lost their charm?"

Gracelyn held the warm teacup to her cheek. "Jake's— Zandy's, *everybody's* jokes." She glanced up, hoping she hadn't offended her friend. To her surprise, she saw a spark of light in Bertha's eyes as if she had opened a window into some other part of the old woman.

"My dear child," Bertha said, showing unusual emotion, "you need to understand the humor. If you're going to survive . . . if you're going to stay." Gracelyn stirred her tea, waiting while Bertha seemed to gather her words, wishing people wouldn't question her staying on the ranch.

"When I met Jake," Bertha began, "I was visiting my sister in Kansas City. She'd gone out from our home in Philadelphia with her husband. He worked as a buyer at the stockyards, and he brought Jake home one night."

Bertha had been a city girl, too. Gracelyn could hardly believe it, looking at the weather-roughened face across the table.

"I thought he was the most attractive man I'd ever met. He kept us laughing the whole evening . . . and for a week after that, while I delayed my return to Philadelphia and he hung around my brother's place instead of taking the train West."

Bertha looked into her tea cup. "Even his proposal was

funny." She met Gracelyn's eyes. "I accepted it, thinking only of what fun it would be to live with so humorous a man. I never considered how hard it would be to live with a man who never spoke of his feelings and never mentioned love."

"But it's obvious that he loves you."

Bertha nodded without a smile. "I had to learn about his humor before I could see that for myself."

Gracelyn prayed that Jake and Zandy would stay in the barn so that this conversation would not be interrupted.

Bertha said, "Little by little, watching Jake and the other ranchers, I began to figure out the complicated reasons behind their humor. First of all, it was an admission that they were smaller than this land—that they would never have complete power over it. But it was also a way of saying that, by God, nature wouldn't beat them. They would endure. So when nature slapped them down with crop loss and the death of their animals, they joked and plowed up their hailed wheat—told a story and hauled their lambs to the bone pile."

Oh, this rang true. Zandy had said, "How can you not joke?" Gracelyn held her breath, hoping Bertha would not stop. But Bertha seemed to need to talk as much as Gracelyn needed to listen.

"Jake also used humor then, and even more often now, to rest for a moment, to ease the stress on his mind and his body. He knows that from dawn until well after dark, he'll be driving himself. The work will never be done. He won't admit that his back is stiff or his hip aches from the time he was thrown from his horse. He won't say that he needs to rest against something. No, he leans against the pickup casually, grins, and tells a story."

Gracelyn thought of Zandy's little jokes about the Hershey Kisses during lambing season when he leaned against the fence and peeled away the foil around the candy, looking ready to collapse.

"Of course, there's a little more to it with Jake," Bertha said. "I swear that man just likes to play with words and ideas. He tells stories in bed." She laughed.

Gracelyn hadn't yet heard all that she needed to hear. "But why don't they tell us how they feel? We're in it with them."

Bertha reached out and patted her hand. "Honey, put yourself in their place. They know they work their women too hard as they go after their dreams, and they know they couldn't reach those dreams without us. Who is there to help on a ranch but the women? How can they put that into words?

"They can only hope that we'll come to share their dreams—that someday they'll be able to show us that we weren't wasting the years we struggled along with them." Gracelyn thought of Zandy's words to Bill Riley: *She's my partner.*

Bertha gestured toward her living room. "Look at all the stuff Jake buys me now. I have to be careful not to admire something I don't really want. If I as much as say, 'Isn't that pretty,' Jake buys it." She grinned. "Mind you, he doesn't do it without a joke, but he buys it."

"What if you have dreams of your own?"

Bertha said, "Your art." A flat statement, not a question.

Gracelyn nodded, warmed by her understanding.

Bertha said, "You fight for them. Sometimes your own dreams are all that sustain you. You'll come to love the ranch, if you love Zandy, but it won't replace your art."

She grinned, and a wicked twinkle danced in her eyes. "A good fight never hurts a marriage if you know what you're fighting about and what you're fighting for."

"Can you fight for love?"

Bertha's eyes lost their twinkle. "No, if it's not there, you can't fight for it. But you can look for it; you can learn to recognize it. Just don't look for it in words."

Gracelyn was quiet on the way to town from the Liggen ranch, her mind busy with Bertha's parting words. Bertha had given her a warm goodbye hug and whispered, "Fight for your dreams and learn to laugh."

Zandy said, "We might as well shop in Larkspur. We're closer to it than Brandon." And there in a little shop next to the grocery store in Larkspur, Gracelyn found a poster that set her to laughing so hard she couldn't stop. It was a Leanin' Tree poster of an unshaven cowboy in a greasy Stetson, a grim look on his face. Underneath the painting, it said, "There were a helluva lot of things they didn't tell me when I hired on with this outfit."

Gracelyn pointed to the poster and sputtered through her laughter, "Buy me that." Zandy looked at the poster. He was slow to grin, but since Gracelyn was still pointing, he took the poster to the cash register.

"I don't see what you find so damn funny about that poster," he complained as Gracelyn continued to giggle in spurts on the way to the truck. She couldn't tell him; she just knew that the disreputable-looking cowboy mouthing the disgruntled words on the poster was going to bring her a great deal of comfort in the years to come. "There were a helluva lot of things they didn't tell me when I hired on with this outfit," she said to herself and climbed into the truck, still laughing.

"Where did the year go?" Zandy said as they headed back toward the ranch with a truckload of supplies. "I didn't work on half the equipment I laid out to fix during slack time this winter, and we're already into the busiest season again."

"Have you hired the same shearing crew?"

Zandy grinned. "Well, I tried to, but they weren't sure they wanted to come if I still had the same old cook."

Gracelyn punched his arm. He laughed and said, "Yeah, we've got that wild bunch of shearers again." He took his eyes from the road. "Are you going to be able to tie fleeces?"

Gracelyn held her hands up, palms forward. "My hands aren't pregnant." She looked down. "But I don't think you'd better plan on my pulling any lambs. I can't hunker down very well at the moment."

Zandy sobered. "God, I hope we have better weather for lambing this year."

"I do too," Gracelyn said, but she was thinking of what the trip to the hospital would be like if she went into labor during a snowstorm.

Chapter Fifty-Six

LAMBING season started later in the spring than it had the first year, and Gracelyn didn't get a chance to do more than walk through the drop bunch a time or two. Zandy insisted that she move into Brandon on the third of May. And on the seventh, Emmalyn MacNair was born, without her daddy in attendance. He arrived when she was four hours old.

"I should have been here," Zandy said when he kissed Gracelyn. She had a fleeting memory of the day that they had lost the ewe. He had said those same words then.

She smiled. "There wasn't anything you could have done. Mother Nature and I were right in tune this time. Your little red-headed daughter just popped out and hollered, 'Here I am.'"

Zandy called Suzanne, who called her parents. The newspaper in Brandon told everybody else. Gracelyn was touched to the point of tears at the number of gifts, cards, and bouquets that were sent to the hospital by Zandy's clients.

Zandy visited every day of the three days she spent in the hospital with the baby. Gracelyn's mother called from Florida. "I wish I could have been there with you," she said, "but I couldn't afford it. Are you all right? How's the baby?"

After Gracelyn assured her that everything was fine, her mother said, "Thank you and Zandy again for the money you sent at Christmas."

Gracelyn said, "I think you'll be a terrific decorator, Mother."

The words opened the door to real communication. Her mother sounded shy, but pleased. "I'm glad you think so, Gracelyn dear." Gracelyn felt a wave of warmth, hearing her name that way. It eased her homesickness to know that some things didn't change.

"How is your business going, Mother?"

"Well, of course, businesses do take some time to get started, but I'm fairly sure that I've got my first contract."

My God, Gracelyn thought. *She's been down there five months and is just now getting her first contract. She must have been through hell.*

"Are you really all right, Mother?"

It was the wrong question. The door closed. "Why yes, I'm just fine. I manage on my own quite well." And in a moment, she had hung up. She had only mentioned the baby once.

Gracelyn's father and Arminda had sent an arrangement of silk flowers in a blue-and-pink ceramic vase shaped like a baby's shoe. The vase had been made in Taiwan. I'll bet Arminda ordered that, Gracelyn thought, resisting the temptation to knock it off the hospital table.

When Maggie came to visit, she said, "I swear I saw Old Daniel looking through the nursery window."

Gracelyn smiled. *My father and mother may not be here, but I have family. We're kinda like my odd colored sheep,* she thought, *but we're a nice little flock.* She said to Maggie, "Where's Josh?"

"Gone rambling."

Zandy took them home from the hospital on the eleventh of May. "I didn't want to mess up the house, so I fixed the baby a spot in the lambing shed," he said with a grin as he took Emmalyn from Gracelyn's arms and helped Gracelyn from the pickup.

Gracelyn knew that he had bought a crib, but she was not prepared for the nursery corner that had been created in the living room. A folding screen had been set up as a divider in the corner nearest the bedroom door and opposite the stove. Within the private space, there was a crib complete with sheets and a bright quilt. Gracelyn recognized Maggie's touch there. Next to the crib stood a wooden dresser with a wide flat top, perfect for a changing table. Hanging above the crib was a mobile with tiny wooden farm creatures suspended from the strings.

"Well?" Zandy said as Gracelyn stood speechless, staring at the little room.

"It's wonderful," Gracelyn said and began to cry.

Zandy just grinned while she sniffled. When she finally wiped her eyes and took the baby from him, he said,

"Of course, I didn't do it all. I bought the crib and the sheets. Maggie provided the quilt and the screen. Josh built the dresser."

"What about the mobile?"

"Old Daniel came by one day with that in a paper sack. He made it, carved the animals, everything."

"He made it! Oh, it's perfect." Gracelyn laid Emmalyn in the crib. The baby was so tiny, Gracelyn was suddenly scared.

"How am I ever going to take care of her by myself," she said. "She seems so fragile."

Zandy said, "I predict that you'll soon be hauling her up to the barn and to the lambing sheds." He patted her on the shoulder. "If we get you one of those canvas slings modern mothers are using, you can even take her out to get the cows."

"Well, I'm sure she misses the cows," Gracelyn said. "She's been listening to their heart beats and belly gurgles for nine months."

Before the week was out, Gracelyn said to Zandy, "Whatever made me think I was going to be alone with this baby?"

Maggie had been in every day to see her. Josh dropped by when he came back from his rodeo. Old Daniel had made some excuse to come to the ranch.

"I can't remember his being in this house more than twice before now," Zandy said, "and he's already seen Emmalyn three times this week."

"There are so many things I wonder about Old Daniel,"

Gracelyn said. "Has he ever mentioned a home or a family or children?"

"Nobody knows anything about him except that he's good with sheep, and if he takes on any other chore, he'll do a good job of it, but he won't hire on permanent anywhere."

"Where does he live?"

"In one sheep wagon or another from here to Larkspur and beyond."

"Hasn't anybody ever asked him where he goes?"

Zandy laughed. "What? And break the code of the West?"

Gracelyn said, "It suddenly occurs to me that you've been spending a fair amount of your time in the house, too. Don't any of you guys think I can take care of this baby?"

"We're just making sure that you don't burn her out," Zandy said, but he was hanging over the crib poking his finger between the baby's finger and thumb. Emmalyn closed her little fist around his finger. "Did you know your mama used to be a lamb-licker?" he said to the baby. Then he said, "You're a pretty little thing."

Gracelyn felt a sudden surge of jealousy. *I want to be a pretty little thing*, she thought. She turned away, sick with her strong feelings. *Emmy's my child! How can I be jealous of my own baby? She needs for her daddy to love her.*

Zandy turned from the crib. "I heard from the wool people. Our check should be pretty good. The wool was real clean."

"Probably because we weren't dumping bales on the sheep's backs." Gracelyn was glad that the hay grinder made something better.

Gracelyn was tired, and nursing in the night left her sleepy all the time. Zandy was patient, and he tried to be helpful, but she could see that he was over-burdened with her chores on top of his own, and the summer work was just beginning.

After ten days, she said, "If you can build me some sort of portable baby box with a frame and some mosquito netting around the top, I could take Emmy with me and start doing my own barn work again."

"We won't want to take her out there when we run the grinder," he said, "but I think she'd be okay while you're milking and doing chicken chores." He ran a hand through his mop of hair and grinned at her. "I sure hate earning that butter and egg money." Gracelyn thought of Bertha's advice and looked past the words to the appreciation behind them. Zandy was trying to say thank you.

"I can fill water tanks and feed bums, too," Gracelyn said.

Zandy brought a little canvas front pack from town. He started to build a box, but Josh found him at it and said, "Let me do the finish work. As a carpenter, you're a great veterinarian." Zandy relinquished the job, and Josh took the box home, returning it the next day, smooth-sanded, with a domed, hinged lid covered with fine netting.

Gracelyn was grateful for the safe little bed for Emmy, but she thought ruefully of Maggie. At this time of year, Maggie was overworked and tired. *Josh should be helping her instead of designing and building things for me. Josh always seems to have time to do what he wants to do.*

Gracelyn rested her hand on the smooth box, wishing that she could take off and draw all day. Her forty-one had been a jumbled collection of fives and tens since she had come home from the hospital with the baby. There were no solid chunks of uninterrupted time.

When she didn't draw, she felt empty and irritable. Somehow, just opening her sketch book centered her mind and feelings and helped her to absorb the things that happened to her. *Maybe when I criticize Josh for doing whatever he wants, I'm just envious of his freedom.* She pictured herself roaming around the country with her paint box and easel, then Emmy cried in her crib, and Gracelyn let the picture go.

Chapter Fifty-Seven

"WE should start night herding sooner this year," Gracelyn said to Zandy just before they moved the herd to summer pasture. "The lambs are so vulnerable." She had been doing her own work for nearly three weeks.

Zandy looked startled. "I didn't figure you'd want to spend the nights up there now that Emmy's here."

"I can take Emmy with me. Pete's a good watch dog, and we were always perfectly safe." She grinned. "Except from you."

Zandy laughed. "I won't go shopping for Brie this year. But, I'm going to miss you two girls here in the house."

"I have a confession to make," Gracelyn said.

"What's that?"

"I'm offering to night herd so you won't insist on planting a garden. I heard what you said at Liggens' and saw the look on your face when Maggie was promising us green peas and new potatoes from her garden."

Zandy said, "I'd plow the garden and get it ready if you wanted to try it."

Fight for your dream. Gracelyn shook her head. "Nope, I'm an artist, not a gardener. I don't care how many blue ribbons Maggie gets on her squash and beans at the fair."

"But I like young radishes and fresh spinach."

"I'm sure you could trade some vet work to Maggie for all the radishes you can eat."

Zandy said, a little mournfully, "And I miss the smell of dill."

"Oh, oh," Gracelyn said. "Dill means dill pickles, I think." She reached for her sketch book and held it close to her heart. "We're besieged. He wants us to start pickling and preserving."

Even though she spoke lightly, she felt threatened. She flipped through the sketches of the kittens. "I'd like to hang a cat picture on Emmy's wall, but the way things are going, she'll be reading books before I finish a picture."

"I hate to change the subject," Zandy said, "but do you think Emmy would be okay if we took her haying with us?"

Gracelyn felt herself flush. She had been trying to tell him how discouraged she was feeling, but he obviously thought she was just chattering. At least he'd dropped the subject of a garden. She glanced at the poster of the cowboy, which she had hung above the kitchen table, and was able to smile as she answered his question.

"She'll enjoy haying, if we can find a cool place for her box." Gracelyn checked the baby, who was happily reaching for Old Daniel's mobile.

To Gracelyn's surprise and secret delight, Emmy loved her mama better than anyone else on either ranch. The first time Maggie held her, Gracelyn had thought, *Maggie makes a better mother than I do. She knows how to hold her and the right words to say.*

But Emmy let it be known that her favorite place was near Gracelyn. She didn't care if she was in the Subaru heading for the pediatrician in Brandon or on the ranch in the little canvas tote sack, in the box, or slung across Gracelyn's hip, just as long as she was with her mother. By the time Emmy was three months old, she and Gracelyn had a comfortable, busy schedule worked out.

They woke in the sheep wagon before the sun rays that reddened the bluffs had reached the pasture. Pete helped them check the flock. They usually completed their walk through the sheep just as Zandy drove through the gate.

Back at the ranch house, Gracelyn took a shower. Emmy nursed before morning chores and then went along to the barn. The tote sack that held her close to her mother's heart kept her head at just the right height for kissing. They walked through the dewy grass listening to the meadowlarks in the creek pasture. Pete peg-legged his way across the bridge and was ready to terrify the cats as soon as Gracelyn opened the barn door.

In the barn she usually found the little powder puffs that meant that the cats had gone rabbit hunting in the night.

"I understand you better since I've got a hungry child to feed," she said to Crybaby, "but you could have trusted us. We were planning to take care of you all."

Crybaby wound herself around Gracelyn's ankles. Gracelyn knelt and helped the baby touch the cat.

When the milking chores were done and the chickens fed, they returned to the house to separate the milk. Zandy, who had been fueling and servicing the tractor, joined them for breakfast. He held the baby then. He was sweet with the baby and, watching them play, Gracelyn missed her own father. She wished she could go back for a visit and play golf with him and go to lunch and feel his arm across her shoulders. But thinking of her mother . . . and of her stepmother . . . she turned away and took her bucket of bottles out to the pickup. She drove to the pasture near the lambing shed to feed the bum lambs. After that it was Emmy's bathtime.

The nurse in the pediatrician's office had said, "She's such a pretty little girl, with her mama's big brown eyes and her daddy's dark red hair."

Gracelyn agreed entirely. Her little girl was the prettiest child she'd ever seen. Her skin was creamy and smooth. *And I know what creamy is now,* Gracelyn thought, washing the chubby arms and legs. The wide kitchen counter was a pleasant spot to put a baby's bath tub. The sun came in through the windows and made rainbows in the water drops on Emmy's tummy.

She let Emmy play naked on the bed while she made it, stealing a moment for one quick gesture drawing of the baby's chubby hand reaching toward her pink toes. She nursed the baby again and dressed her before tossing a load of laundry into the machine. Gracelyn would have loved using throwaway diapers, but there just wasn't any place to throw them away. She didn't want to send them over the bank and pollute the creek. They couldn't burn them, didn't have time to bury them. So, she used cloth diapers, and washed every day, grateful for the new dryer Zandy had bought with the wool check. Then she settled the baby into her traveling box on the pickup seat for a nap while they hauled salt to the sheep, checked water tanks and carried parts and supplies to whichever field Zandy was plowing, harrowing, planting, cutting, raking, baling—his activity varying month by month through the summer.

By the time Gracelyn had driven back to the ranch house, Emmy was awake and hungry and it was time to start lunch. Gracelyn washed the separator, milk buckets, bum bottles, and dishes. When she was interrupted by the CB, she took Emmy and went to the fields to tell Zandy.

After lunch, she had to think of supper, devising food that would cook slowly in the oven because by the time she nursed Emmy again, the bums would be bleating for their next feeding. And then it was off on old Soot, with Emmy in the tote sack, to find the milk cows and bring them in for evening milking.

After dinner and dishes, Gracelyn put her eggs into cartons and poured her sweet cream into cream cans for Zandy to take to town, set her churning cream to sour, heated milk for cottage cheese, and hung the cheese to drain before going back to the barn with Emmy to gather more eggs and shut up the chickens.

Emmy was always ravenous. "She doesn't bump me to make me let down more milk like the lambs do their mothers," Gracelyn said to Zandy, "but she would if she could."

"Maybe you'd better ask the doctor about solid foods," Zandy said, grinning, as he added, "That, or get Crybaby to take her hunting."

"I'll talk to the doctor. Sometimes I feel like there's nothing left of *me* but a powder puff."

It was a relief to get to the sheep wagon. Emmy was especially peaceful there. As the sky darkened, the sheep moved in toward the wagon, sometimes crowding against the wheels, rocking the wagon gently as they turned and settled. The sounds of the animals were comforting. Mothers cried softly, and the lambs answered in tiny voices. Gracelyn sat on the steps, holding Emmy and watching as the lambs stretched out across their mothers' front legs. She put her own chin across Emmy's head, imitating the ewes.

Had she and her mother ever shared moments of such peace? What had happened to them? It frightened her to think about her mother, for she knew that Emmy couldn't live in a box forever. She would walk and talk and want things. *What if I don't understand her any better than Mother understands me? How lonesome it will be.* Gracelyn's eyes filled with tears, blurring the rising moon.

Chapter Fifty-Eight

GRACELYN hadn't heard from her mother since the day of Emmy's birth. She had sent pictures of Emmy and she had written, but she never said what she really wanted to say: *Dear Mother, I know you are wounded and trying to find a way to heal, but don't you care that you're a grandmother? Or is it too scary to become a grandmother when you've been replaced in your own marriage by a young girl? Daddy doesn't seem to mind being a grandfather. When we sent pictures of Emmy to him, he sent back a bond in her name. Do you think that's guilt money, Mother?*

And what would she say to her father? *Dear Daddy, I hate it when Arminda picks baby clothes and signs your name. Her handwriting is just like her—so cute.*

Dear Suzanne, I don't have "a baby," I have Emmy. And I love having Emmy, no matter how I thought I felt about having a baby. I'm sorry that your visit to Florida wasn't as pleasant as you had hoped. You might be more welcome if you'd stop carrying your panic to Mother.

Dear Dr. Carlson, You were wrong about me and sheep ranching. I'm not the failure you predicted. And you were wrong about talent. It isn't like a wolf, it's like a coyote. If you're not paying attention, it sneaks in and goes for the jugular, and you bleed down your front as you die.

Dear Zandy, I love you, but I won't give up being me and plant some dumb old garden when I'm hurting for time to draw.

It was getting late. There was no time to write letters even if she dared express those thoughts. Emmy was asleep in her arms, and if Gracelyn didn't sleep while Emmy slept, she would be exhausted all day tomorrow. She rose to put Emmy in her box and then slid into the bedroll herself.

Emmy had brought something new to Plum Creek. Despite the abundance of lambs and chicks and calves and colts, it seemed to Gracelyn that the adults couldn't get enough of babies unless they saw Emmy every day. She didn't know how they found the time, but she began to keep the coffee pot going all day and planned for extras at lunch.

Old Daniel had never eaten a meal with them before Emmy was born, but now he often accepted Zandy's invitation at noontime.

Zandy and Old Daniel had scarcely driven through the pasture gate, heading back to the hay field, when Maggie's pickup crossed Plum Creek and swung up in front of the house. Gracelyn gave Emmy to Maggie while she did dishes.

"I'd be glad to babysit when you need it," Maggie said. "I'll show Emmy all my carved animals. She certainly likes the ones in Old Daniel's mobile."

"Did you and Howard ever think of having children?" Gracelyn wasn't sure her question was tactful, but she was interested.

Maggie reddened. "I wanted children dreadfully, but Howard had the mumps when he was a teenager, and they went down on him. He couldn't have kids."

"I'm sorry," Gracelyn said. "I should have kept my mouth shut."

Maggie laughed. "I'm glad you didn't because now I can be tactless and ask about something."

"What's that?" Gracelyn asked, feeling wary.

"I was just wondering the other day how you and Zandy manage to—uh—get together when he's gone all day and you sleep at the sheep wagon at night."

Gracelyn smiled. "A bedroll under the stars is a pretty romantic spot, Maggie." Gracelyn had taken her diaphragm to the sheep wagon with her this summer. She didn't want another baby so soon, but she enjoyed the nights when Zandy joined her at the summer pasture. She never knew when he would show up at the sheep wagon, and they never talked about it later, but making love in the lustrous night air with the stars silvering the sky made Gracelyn feel beautiful. She was grateful to Zandy for that.

Emmy fussed and Gracelyn took her to nurse. "How's your sketching coming along?" Maggie asked.

Gracelyn wrinkled her nose. "It isn't. I'm too tired. When I try, there's such a logjam inside me, I can't get it right." She sighed.

Maggie stood and patted her shoulder. "You'll get to it, Gracelyn." She rinsed her coffee cup and set it in the cupboard. "I've played hookey long enough."

Josh dropped by the next morning. "Maggie says to tell you that she wants you to come to the county fair August 30. She's showing her beans and pickles and one of her quilts."

"I'll ask Zandy. Maybe we can have a family outing."

"I'm riding. Come cheer me on."

Gracelyn smiled, but she thought, *Riding at the county fair. Is this another downward spiral?* Josh hadn't done too well at the stock show. He'd come home in February morose and silent. "You're not riding bulls, are you?"

"Nope. Saddle broncs. And I'll do some calf roping."

Josh was holding Emmy now. Her hand looked white against the black hairs on his arm. When he gazed down at the baby, his face softened. Gracelyn spoke to break the awkward silence.

"Tell Maggie we'll come to the fair."

Josh handed her the baby. "I better get going. Maggie threatened me with death or no dinner if I didn't help her out today." They went outside to Josh's truck. He looked down at Emmy again and touched her hair lightly. "She makes me feel peaceful," he said and then climbed into his truck.

Gracelyn rocked Emmy gently and stood for a moment

in the yard thinking about the love that surrounded her baby.

When they found the quilt display at the fair, a wide, gold-stamped purple medallion, trailing purple ribbons, was pinned to Maggie's quilt. Maggie blushed and smiled as people stopped to congratulate her on winning the grand champion ribbon.

"My beans only got a red, second-place ribbon," she confided to Gracelyn.

They looked at some of the other crafts and then walked through the sheep barns to see the prize ewes and rams and watch the shearing competition and spinning demonstrations. At the wool exhibit, Gracelyn fingered the beautiful yarns. She gave her name to a woman who was interested in buying colored wool and then they went to the rodeo.

In the grandstand, they stood to honor the colors as the riders displayed them at a gallop around the ring. The cowboys followed the color bearers, standing in their stirrups with their hats held high.

Before the rodeo began, Zandy was called to one of the barns where they needed a vet. Maggie and Gracelyn chatted until Josh rode in on his roping horse and then cheered him on as the calf was released from the chute. Josh caught the calf with the first loop and was off his horse to secure the calf's legs with the tie string. His time was good. He had a chance at winning some money for the event.

"I had no idea he was that skillful with a rope," Gracelyn said.

"He's good at everything on the ranch, when he wants to be," Maggie said.

Zandy rejoined them in time for the saddle bronc riding. Josh was having a good day. He was in the money in that event, too. After the rodeo, they walked Maggie to her pickup and congratulated Josh when he joined them. He had bought a little stuffed monkey for Emmy.

"You didn't need to do that," Gracelyn said.

"Yes, I did," said Josh. "I like to buy presents when I'm riding high. And Emmy's my best girl." He looked at Gracelyn with an oddly sober look that made her uncomfortable.

She dropped her eyes to the toy.

Chapter Fifty-Nine

"WE must be getting old," Zandy said to Gracelyn one morning at breakfast, several weeks after the fair.

"Why do you say that?"

"Time never went this fast when I was a kid. Summer and fall are already gone and we're heading into our third season. I turned the rams in with the ewes today. In about five months, we'll be lambing."

"Hey," Gracelyn said. "You just skipped your birthday and Thanksgiving, Emmy's first Christmas, and our second anniversary."

"And about four months of grinding hay," Zandy said as he rose. "I'd better get to work fixing the tractor."

"Seems like that old tractor is always breaking down," Gracelyn said. "I hope we don't have to buy a new one before we get Emmy's Addition on the house." Emmy's Addition was the small room they were planning that would give the baby a real bedroom and square up the house.

"Well," Zandy said, "you know what Josh says about everything I do. It's the same with fixing the tractor. As a mechanic, I'm a pretty good veterinarian." He picked Emmy up and held her close for a moment. "What do you think, little girl, will you grow up to be a mechanic? We need one of those."

Emmy made a little sound and waved her fists in the air.

"She's telling you 'no,'" Gracelyn said. "Emmy and I are

sheepherders, but we're temporarily out of a night job, so we're thinking of going rambling like Old Daniel."

"In that Subaru? It was okay to take for Emmy's checkups last summer, but with bad weather coming on, we'd better start going in together in the pickup again."

"Oh, good. I can start Christmas shopping at all the ranches."

Time did pass quickly. Before Gracelyn had a moment to sketch the golden leaves on the cottonwoods, they had fallen, and just as she resigned herself to painting an autumn picture with heaps of darkening leaves, the first snows covered them over.

Emmy was growing. She no longer fit the little canvas front pack, so Zandy bought Gracelyn a back pack. Maggie made the baby a warm snowsuit for Christmas. Josh gave her a tiny pair of fur-lined cowboy boots. "Ridiculous!" Maggie said.

Christmas morning, before they had gone to Maggie's, Gracelyn had given Zandy a framed sketch of Emmy asleep in her crib. Zandy gave Gracelyn several packages.

"So many!" she said.

"Well, we seem to forget your birthday pretty regularly," Zandy said, "and you've been doing double-duty all summer. And the lambs sold well." Gracelyn thought of Bertha Liggen. *Jake buys me things . . . Don't look for love in words . . .* She stretched upward to kiss Zandy's cheek before she opened the gifts.

There was a warm honey-colored robe a little darker than her hair. And slippers to match. Three canvas panels, several tubes of paint, and a matting tool with Exacto knife blades.

"Oh, look, Emmy," Gracelyn said, holding up one gift and then another. "Your daddy is a real Santa Claus."

Zandy hung her sketch of Emmy on the bedroom wall. Then, stepping to the refrigerator, he said, "I have one more present." He handed Gracelyn a package wrapped in white butcher paper.

Gracelyn blushed as she took out a good-sized chunk of Brie cheese. She looked up. Zandy was blushing, too. But all he said was, "Come on, we're going to be late for Maggie's dinner."

Zandy's vet calls during Christmas week had taken him miles in the other direction from Brandon, so they didn't get their Christmas mail and packages until after New Year's Day.

"Everyone sent things for Emmy," Gracelyn said to Maggie, who had braved the drifts for a cup of coffee. "She has three ruffled pink dresses and two pairs of white booties with lace edging." *Arminda looks fantastic in pink*, Gracelyn thought, *but after the pictures I sent, how could she choose pink for my little redhead?*

"Suzanne sent the green terrycloth sleepers she's wearing." She offered Emmy to her neighbor. "I'm churning. Would you like to hold her?"

Maggie took Emmy on her lap. "Your sister's gift is sensible. Must have done her some good to see the ranch."

"Suzanne blows hot and cold about the ranch. In one letter, she speaks of some nice thing she remembers about the sheep; in the next, she wonders why Zandy doesn't get a small animal practice in town."

Gracelyn set her churn on the table and began to turn the handle that worked the beaters inside the big glass jar.

"Do you ever wish that he would?"

"No, I never miss the city, except for art galleries and libraries and time to draw."

"You should have more kids," Maggie said with a smile. "They'd grow up to be ranch help, and you'd eventually have more time."

"I saw a whole lot of mamas at the fair helping kids with 4H projects," Gracelyn said. "Seems *more* kids would take *more* time for a *lot* of years."

"I'll bet Zandy wants a son."

"I suppose he does," Gracelyn said, "but Emmy's only eight months old." The cream in the churn began to change as little bits of butter separated from the liquid.

She thought of the conversation Zandy had started in the barn one day.

"If we had a son about ten years old," he said, "he could shovel out that milk-cow corral."

"It takes eleven years to get a ten-year-old son," Gracelyn said.

"That pile of cow manure is sure gonna get high by then," he had said with a grin, "we'd better hurry."

Maggie spoke, bringing Gracelyn's thoughts back to the kitchen. "Has Emmy had any more croup?"

"Once, just after Christmas, but the croup tent we made and the steamer the doctor ordered cleared it up quickly." She reached for the butter paddle and, removing the lid and beaters from the churn, she began to push small pieces of butter together into larger and larger clumps.

"She sounds so sick when she gets croupy," Maggie said.

"I know. It's scary when she doesn't breathe right."

Emmy began to fuss. "Here," Maggie said. "Why don't you nurse her, and I'll wash the butter."

"How do you find time to come up here and help with my chores?"

Maggie flushed. "I had a row with Josh and I needed to cool off."

"What are you fighting about now?"

"Same old thing. Since he did so well at the fair, he thinks he should give the National Western another shot."

Gracelyn held her fingers on her breast, aiming the nipple at Emmy's mouth until the baby took hold and began to suck. She didn't know what to say about Josh.

Maggie ran cold water over the butter. "What do you hear from your mother? Is her business doing any better?"

"It's a bit hard to tell. I have to read between the lines, but at least she writes to us now."

Maggie pressed all the water out of the butter and formed it into a flattened sphere. "It's tougher to start over after a divorce than it is when you're widowed," she said. "At least, when a man dies, he leaves *his* money and *your* self-esteem intact."

As she buttoned her shirt and put Emmy to her shoulder to burp her, Gracelyn thought, *And when he dies, it's over.*

He isn't flaunting his new wife while you fumble with the worn-out pieces of your life.

"Do you need this butter, or shall I freeze it?"

"Freeze it, please."

Maggie opened the refrigerator door. "Isn't electricity wonderful! I started with a well house where my butter hung in jars in the water, and then I got an ice box which leaked all over the porch." She stuck the package in the freezer section and shut the refrigerator.

"Are you going to tie fleeces this year?"

Gracelyn had gone to put Emmy in her crib. She came back and said, "Yes, I am. We're making a playpen in the back of the Subaru and we'll just drive the car into the lambing shed."

Emmy walked before her first birthday. At her party on May seventh, she took a few steps from Zandy to Maggie, then to Josh, then Daniel, and then with a big smile and several staggering steps, she headed for her mother, who caught her in her arms and held her close.

Another season went whirling by. Lamb, dock, castrate, vaccinate. That summer Emmy walked part of the early morning rounds from the sheep wagon, holding on to Gracelyn's hand and patting the sheep as she passed them and answering their greetings with a piping little "baa."

When they shipped in the fall, Zandy said, "It's a good thing we're getting Emmy back into the house. I think she talks more sheep than she does English."

Into the house did not mean into the addition. There was no time to work on the house. They had put up the studs just before they started haying, and that's the way they stood.

"Looks like you're building a cage for the little critter," Old Daniel said.

On the eve of Emmy's second Christmas, Gracelyn cleaned out her art dresser so that she could have more space for the baby's things. She spread her sketches on the bed. So few.

Zandy had been called away. "I hate to leave you on Christmas Eve. What do you want in your stocking?"

"Time, Zandy. Time to paint."

He grinned. "I gave you that once, on your first birthday on the ranch. Did you use it all up?"

Gracelyn smiled, but she felt a little rise of anger. Why was time his to give? Where was her time?

After he left, she sat on the bed and studied her work. She picked up the unfinished cat picture, suddenly excited. She would finish it right now. The gifts weren't wrapped, the kitchen was a mess, but it didn't matter.

Chapter Sixty

THE hours flew. She was just stepping away from her easel when she heard Zandy's truck. It was three o'clock Christmas morning, the house was a disaster, and she'd be dead tired all day. But she didn't care. She looked again and again at the picture: The black and white kittens played in the creamy sunshine at the door of the barn. Crybaby was skinny and tired, but her eyes focused on her babies with an intense yellow shine as she crouched near the battered milk pans. Behind her, you could see the individual hairs on the fuzzy little powder puff rabbit tails.

When it dries, there will be two of my pictures on our walls. She looked at the sketch of Emmy where Zandy had hung it. Then she stepped into the living room to look at Mrs. Tyler's solitary embroidered wall hanging. Two pictures.

After the holidays, it seemed that the snow never stopped. Emmy had croup several nights in a row. Gracelyn stayed inside. Zandy worked alone, coming in exhausted after hours of grinding and feeding, to rest and babysit while Gracelyn caught up with her outside chores, fighting the pickup over the icy bridge, wading through the drifts to the barn, trying to fix more shelter for her chickens as the wind blew in circles.

The wind slopped the milk from the buckets as she carried them to the truck; the wind piled up drifts in front of the house. Zandy broke drifts on the bridge and road as he went to his calls. The wind blew them back. The wind blew down the studs for Emmy's Addition.

In the house, they burned coal and coal and more coal to stay warm. Gracelyn took Maggie's quilt and then Mrs. Tyler's wall hanging from the wall to protect them from coal dust and smoke.

But Emmy was a joy. She "helped" with everything. Her fingers were in the cream, in the butter, in the cheese. She wallowed across poor, patient Pete when he flopped down to rest. She pulled her daddy's hair when he held her to his face. And she followed her mother from room to room, totally happy, involved in Gracelyn's chores.

Zandy hired a complete crew for shearing in April that year, and Gracelyn neither tied fleeces nor cooked for the men.

"Sounds ornery of me to say so," she told Zandy, "but I feel kinda left out of things since I don't smell like fleeces and you do." They were sharing the noontime meal for a change.

Zandy leaned over and sniffed her. "Why, I think you smell as sheepish as always." They laughed, and he kissed her cheek. Emmy watched them from her high chair where she was stirring her dinner with her fingers.

Since the lambs were due during the week of Emmy's birthday, they celebrated for Gracelyn and Emmy together on the twenty-eighth of April. Gracelyn was twenty-three; Emmy would be two. And when lambing season, with its hard-won gains and inevitable losses, was completed once more, Gracelyn and Emmy moved their bedroll to the sheep wagon in the summer pasture. The summer flew happily away, despite the hard work and despite Emmy's new determination to be independent.

The little red-headed two-year-old wanted to be in the midst of everything. Gracelyn would turn away to pick up a bucket, and Emmy would be gone, walking right into the crowd of bum lambs, patting their sides and babbling a language strange to Gracelyn and Zandy.

"Look at that little monkey," Zandy said, resting a moment on the tailgate of the truck before unloading another sack of cake. A lamb turned too quickly and knocked the little girl down. Zandy swung over and picked her up. She wasn't crying when he reached her, but the moment he lifted her away from the sheep, she began to kick and cry. "The yams. I wants the yams."

Gracelyn, who had dealt with dozens of similar scenes, watched and laughed as Zandy's face turned red as he tried several ways to divert Emmy's attention, failing with every one.

Finally, he set the little girl on the back of a docile old ewe they had kept down from the summer pasture for treatment of a caked bag. Emmy dug her hands into the wool, her tears forgotten as Zandy led the ewe slowly around the pen.

When he brought the baby to Gracelyn, he said, "This one sure shows her breeding. She got two doses of stubborn."

Gracelyn set the little girl on her hip and held her close with one arm. "We'll probably have to talk about some other night herding plan next summer. I woke up about three o'clock Wednesday morning, and she was just climbing down from the wagon to check out the herd by herself."

"That's how you get your sheepherders," Zandy said with a grin. "Catch 'em young and raise 'em right." He went back to unloading sacks of cake, stacking them inside the shed. Then he came back to where Gracelyn and Emmy held the bottle board for the bum lambs. "I'll figure out some way for you to ride herd on Emmy a little better at night. She can't go running around in the dark."

One unusually hot evening in late August, Gracelyn and Emmy took a giggling bath in the sheep tank at the summer pasture. Emmy's damp hair curled around her ears and settled in little red coils on her forehead.

Gracelyn rubbed the little girl's skin rosy with a big towel. "Let's put on your green jammies, honey lamb." She laid the little girl on the bed in the wagon and took hold of her feet. "Kick, kick," she said pumping the sturdy legs up and down. Emmy laughed and pushed against Gracelyn's hands with her tough little feet, echoing, "Kick, kick." When Gracelyn held the pajama legs up, Emmy pushed her feet into them.

"Now for your story." Emmy and Gracelyn sat on the bunk to read the book filled with pictures of animals. Gracelyn felt a whisper of worry as she got up to light the lantern. It was too early for it to be this dark.

Emmy ran her fingers over the pages, saying animal names aloud and making animal noises.

"That's right," Gracelyn said, but she looked toward the storm that was gathering around the highest part of the rock formations above the pasture. There were always summer storms, but this one was higher and darker than usual.

The last rays of the sun filtered through thick clouds, sulfuring the air. The sheep huddled, but didn't settle. As Gracelyn watched, a whiplash of lightning cut the clouds. Thunder rumbled around the rock rim. She turned to Emmy.

"Good, honey. You named all the animals and made their noises. Now into bed."

A new shelf had been added to the wall of the wagon, with a small crib-type bed attached to it. Zandy had said, "I hate to put her in a cage, but it's not safe for her to wander. Isn't she afraid of anything?"

Gracelyn replied, "She doesn't seem to be. Wouldn't it be marvelous to face the world like that . . . knowing that you're wonderful and powerful?"

Zandy laughed. "She's got all five of the adults on Plum Creek assuring her that's she's absolutely perfect. Where would she get any different idea?"

Gracelyn glanced at the queer light outside the sheep wagon and then tucked the blankets around Emmy. She stood patting the little girl's back until her breathing became light and regular.

She rested her hand on the child and looked toward the mountain. The thunderheads were massed in high castles. A raw, hot wind stirred the cedars on the slopes. She thought of El Greco's "View of Toledo in a Storm." It had the same breath-held feeling.

The lantern light was bright. It put the strange dusk at too much of a contrast. Gracelyn turned the lantern out and, bending to slide past Emmy's bed, sat down on the step.

Chapter Sixty-One

PETE was moving around the flock. He came back and nosed Gracelyn's leg. She put her hand on his head. "It's a scary old sky, isn't it boy?" Pete licked her hand and flopped down by the wagon tongue. It was muggy. All of August had been hot, but tonight there didn't seem to be enough air to breathe.

Gracelyn stepped from the wagon and walked slowly down slope to the tank. Pete followed. She cooled her face and hands with water, then started back wondering if *anyone* could paint the fullness of the dusk: the air was a shawl of somber grey, lined with that evil yellow light. The eerie drapery changed the look of everything. It seemed as if there were shapes moving around the edge of the flock.

Gracelyn went slowly through the herd, talking softly, touching the sheep with her fingertips. She headed back toward the wagon just as a streak of lightning zigzagged across the sky, followed at once by a crack of thunder that left her ears ringing. Emmy woke and began to cry. Gracelyn put her hand on the little girl's head and she settled back into sleep. Lightning flashed again farther away and thunder grumbled along the ridge.

Would the wagon attract lightning? There was iron in the tongue, but the wagon sat on rubber tires. Maybe that helped. She was glad they weren't on the highest ridge.

Fascinated by the storm, Gracelyn tried to store visual memories as she studied the light. But her thoughts were divided as she worried about Emmy's being on the mountain too. What could I do to protect her from lightning?

She moved to the step and watched as darkness slowly erased the greyish-yellow light. She was glad to see the light disappear, taking with it the gray shapes that floated in the haze.

The storm was centered on the peaks above her. The air was pregnant with rain, but no rain fell. The wind had risen. It tore through the trees on the hill, roaring like an incoming tide. It slammed against the wagon, rocking it on its wheels. What if the wagon blew over? Gracelyn rose to check on Emmy.

She went back to the step and looked up at the peaks. The clouds were huge, a colossus of black against the indigo sky. Lightning streaked through them and around them, lighting the sky for a moment, followed by thunder and darkness. The sheep were nearby. She could see the huddle of white when the lightning flared.

Pete whined. "Come on up, fellow." Gracelyn reached a hand to the dog's collar and helped him into the wagon. He turned around and lay down along her leg. She put her hand on his head and fingered his ears. He was a comforting old beast.

Gracelyn began to enjoy the storm as she caught brief glimpses of the tossing trees and waited for the thunder after each stab of lightning.

Her senses were fine tuned. She could hear the wind in the grass and the change of its tone in the brush and trees. The small sounds of the restless sheep came clearly to her. Then the thunder exploded, and the other sounds were lost until the grumble faded away.

The air was tight with expectancy. As the alternation of lightning and thunder continued, Gracelyn reached to loosen her shirt and bra. She inhaled deep reservoirs of air, caught up in a wild combination of elation and despair. Even as she hummed in vibration with the life and beauty of the storm, she quivered with the sense of loss. She would not paint this sky.

It was increasingly hard to fight for her art work. There

wasn't time or room in the house. When they had finally gotten the addition roughed in, Gracelyn had moved her art dresser into Emmy's room, turning over three of the drawers to Emmy's clothes. She felt crowded and cross—and guilty for feeling that way.

Two pictures. In three years, I've finished two pictures. Her anger and frustration rose and blew across her mind as the wind was blowing the trees. Would they ever get to the point where she could demand time of her own?

The sky in front of her split wide open with light. The thunder slapped the hill. It began to rain. The wind whipped the water toward the door of the sheep wagon.

Gracelyn scrambled up. Pete followed as she retreated. She sat down on the bed in the dark, listening to the hammering of the rain on the roof and the splashing of the water as the torrents joined on the ground and raced downhill.

Gracelyn pulled Pete close to her knees and hugged him as she huddled in the dark. Her bed was getting wet.

She got up and, reaching out into the downpour, unhooked the latch that held the door open. She swung the door shut and re-latched it. She re-lit the lantern. She'd forgotten how small this place was with the door closed. The rain continued to pound on the wagon top.

Emmy stirred and cried out. Gracelyn took her from the crib. She pulled the blanket around them both and rocked Emmy gently on her lap.

When Zandy banged on the door and called her name, she lurched upward in shock. She had not heard the truck.

"Let me in, Gracelyn. I'm drowning."

Gracelyn put Emmy down and opened the door. "What are you doing here?" she said. She grinned at her husband, who stepped in, drenched to the skin, "Don't you know it's raining?"

Zandy shut the door and took the towel she handed him. "I was on my way home from a call. I could see the lightning from the top of Maggie's hill. I think you three should get in the truck with me and come on home."

"What about the sheep?"

"There isn't room in the truck."

When you can't do anything else, make a joke. Gracelyn smiled and began gathering Emmy's things.

Back in the ranch house, they dried off and Gracelyn made hot cocoa. She said, "I hope the sheep will be okay."

Zandy shrugged. "We can't control everything. That lightning was too damned close to the wagon."

"Thanks for rescuing us. I worry about Emmy."

"Was she upset?"

Gracelyn laughed. "No."

Zandy said, "She thinks her mama can do anything, so she never worries."

Gracelyn kissed the top of the baby's head and set a small cup of warm milk lightly flavored with chocolate on the high chair tray.

"That was a wild storm. Mother Nature isn't the sweet homebody you see on TV."

"Stop picking on Mother Nature," Zandy said. "She's a lot sweeter than Father Time."

Emmy was looking from one to the other of them as they bantered. Zandy laughed. "That kid's getting *some* education. So far she hasn't had ten days of normal upbringing."

"I still haven't told my mother that her granddaughter sleeps in a sheep wagon in the summer."

Zandy said, "We'll have to air her off good for her first day of school. Some folks have the opinion that sheep don't smell nice." He reached out to wipe cocoa from Emmy's chin.

"Cattle rancher said to me the other day, 'Well, Doc, you're a damn fine vet, and I only got one thing agin' ya.'"

"I said, 'You think my fee's too high?'"

"'Naw, that ain't it,' he said. 'You're worth your pay. Only thing is, I hate to tell anybody that I'm letting a sheep rancher work on my cattle.'"

Gracelyn laughed and rose to take Emmy from the high chair. "They probably don't know how they managed without you."

"I'm hoping I can cut back a little on vet work if the lambs sell well."

"What do you think about my mother's invitation? If the lambs sell real well, could we go to Florida so she can meet her granddaughter?"

"Seems like it would be easier for *her* to come here."

"She says she can't get away, and besides, if Suzanne can't bear to come back to the wilds of Montana, you'd never get Mother up here." Gracelyn rubbed her chin lightly over Emmy's soft hair. "You can be sure Suzanne has filled Mother in on life in the real West."

"You want to invite them all here for Christmas?" Zandy was grinning.

"Sure, and while we're at it, we'll invite Annadean and Maggie's other relatives."

Zandy laughed as he rose from the table and reached for Emmy. "Come on, kid. If you don't get to bed, it'll be morning chore time."

Gracelyn watched as he stepped into the addition and put Emmy in her bed. Not one set of grandparents had seen the baby. As far as Emmy was concerned, her extended family was Josh and Maggie, Old Daniel, and the sheep. Zandy's mother and stepfather sent gifts occasionally, but their place in Oregon kept them busy.

Zandy came back. "Maybe you and the baby could go to see your mother, Gracelyn, if the lambs sell high. I don't think I should leave at the same time."

Gracelyn relinquished the whole idea. A trip to Florida didn't seem real to her anyway. Suzanne had complained about how small her mother's apartment was. No point in putting her mother to a lot of expense and trouble.

"Your father's new wife doesn't seem eager to meet her grandchild," Zandy said. "Maggie's keeping track of how many times she has called to postpone the visit they promised."

"Maybe he tells her to call." Gracelyn was sure that her father could do exactly what he wanted. But as Zandy went into the bathroom, Gracelyn wasn't thinking about her father and Arminda. She was thinking about the storm.

She sat down at the table and made several quick sketches. If the lambs sell well, I won't go to Florida, I'll ask Old Daniel to work for me and I'll try to paint a picture of the storm.

Gracelyn and Emmy were at the chicken house when Zandy drove down from the high pasture the next morning. The storm had died away some time after midnight. The new morning brought a gentle, fresh-smelling breeze that rippled the tawny grasses on the slope behind the barn. Zandy had gone to the summer pasture just before dawn.

Gracelyn gave Emmy a small can full of chicken feed. Emmy dipped out a handful and scattered it around the pen, calling "Here, shickie, shickie." Gracelyn stepped to the fence to meet Zandy as he got out of the truck.

He said, "I need you. Take Emmy down to Maggie's." His face was white. "Tell Maggie we'll get her tonight."

Chapter Sixty-Two

GRACELYN turned for her daughter, sick with dread.
She took Zandy's truck and roared across the bridge to
the house. Packing Emmy's things with trembling hands,
she ran the possibilities through her mind: lightning strike,
drowning, coyotes, cougar. Had that mountain lion come
back?

"I don't know," she told Maggie. "He was too shook up
to say anything else. But something awful has happened up
in the summer pasture."

She raced the three miles back to the ranch and picked
Zandy up at the garage where he had amassed his veterinary
supplies.

"What is it?"

"Coyote kill," he said.

"How bad?"

"I don't know the extent of it. But it's god-awful." He
looked at her. "Be prepared. I wouldn't let you go up there
if I didn't need you."

There was no way to get prepared for such a scene. As
they came up the muddy hill past the tank, Gracelyn began
to see the bodies of the lambs. Dozens of them. She gasped
and bit her lip to keep back the tears.

"Are they all dead?"

"The lucky ones."

Zandy stopped the truck and handed Gracelyn some of
the supplies. They walked to the first lamb. It was dead. Its

belly had been ripped open; the heart and liver were gone. Rib bones stuck out of the mangled chest. The hind leg bones were picked clean. Gracelyn swallowed to keep from throwing up. Zandy had all he could handle without her falling apart.

"Are you sure it was coyotes?"

"No mistaking the sign. This time of year, the pups are ravenous, and the mother moves into a flock to teach them to hunt for themselves."

Gracelyn remembered how Crybaby and her kittens had hunted rabbits. They were approaching another lamb. It was still alive, but it was ripped in the flank.

"If we can even save this one, it will be crippled," Zandy said as he prepared to work on the torn flesh.

"I should have let you take Emmy home, and I should have stayed at the wagon," Gracelyn said, as she held the leg of the suffering lamb. Its blood had dried around the edge of the tear.

Zandy glanced up. "It's not your fault. I made the decision. And I still wouldn't risk you and Emmy around those lightning storms."

He finished his work on the lamb. "Can you lift him into the truck? I'll get started on the next one." He moved to a lamb who stood head down, one ear and half his face torn away, blood dripping onto the grass.

Gracelyn knelt to gather up the crippled baby they had treated. He was heavy, but he didn't struggle. She put him on a bed of hay and went back to Zandy.

They worked steadily. When Zandy didn't need her to help with the living, Gracelyn dragged the dead lambs away from the flock. Each corpse was torn open, the insides ripped away. Many of the bones were stripped of their flesh. Gracelyn swallowed and gagged.

She made a bloody bone pile behind a clump of trees, sobbing as she pulled the carcasses out of Zandy's sight. Not three months ago, they had worked around the clock to bring these babies into the world. It was so cruel, so useless.

Damn the coyotes. How could a mother destroy another mother's child? Damn the Sierra Club. Damn the whole ranching

business with its high hopes and its bloody awful disasters.
Gracelyn leaned against a tree, crying and shaking. What
was she doing here? It was more than any human could
hope to endure. She thought of Zandy and tried to choke
her sobs. He needed her help.

Finally, she stopped crying, wiped her nose on her sleeve
and went back to help lift two more crippled lambs into the
truck. Zandy glanced at her. His face was red except for a
white line around his tight lips.

Gracelyn turned away, ashamed of her weeping. Zandy
kept trying to ease the pain of the damaged creatures around
him. She wasn't doing anything. She looked across the
pasture for more dead lambs and went back to her grim job.

The sun rose hot and high, steaming the flesh they
worked with, adding their sweat to the blood. They used
the tarp to make shade for the crippled lambs in the truck.
They dunked their heads in the sheep tank to cool themselves and kept working.

Around noon, Josh drove up to their truck. He got out,
looked around, and shook his head. "Maggie sent lunch,"
he said. He looked a little green around the gills, Gracelyn
noticed, as he turned away from the scene of slaughter. "I
fed your bums," he added before he drove away.

She had not thought she could eat. *But I'm like all the
rest of the animals. I have to have food, no matter what else is
going on.* She was too tired now for hating anyone. She only
wished they could be done, and she could go home and
hold Emmy and not think about anything at all.

Late in the day, Old Daniel came to the pasture. "How
many dead?" he asked.

"Seventy-three," Zandy said, "and fourteen crippled."

Gracelyn could not help herself. She multiplied the number by the dollar loss. At least $5,000, probably more.
$5,000 lost in one night. *I should have come back to the
wagon. I will come back to the wagon. We cannot afford to lose
one more lamb. That damned old coyote is not going to feed any
more of my babies to her babies.*

But Old Daniel was the one who stayed the night. Zandy
and Gracelyn went home to fix a pen for the crippled lambs,

to milk cows, feed bums, and shut the chickens in before some fox and her kits decided to have a nighttime lesson.

They showered and put their bloody clothes to soak. Zandy sat down at the table and put his head in his hands. He looked so exhausted that Gracelyn felt a rise of panic. Would he be all right?

He finally looked up at her. "I'm really going to have to hit the veterinary trail now."

"You're already working too hard . . ." Gracelyn hesitated, and then said, "Maybe we should follow Suzanne's suggestion, move into town, open a vet clinic . . ." Her voice trailed away as she saw the line of Zandy's jaw harden.

"I'm *not* going to give up my dreams just because we've hit a stroke of bad luck. I went to vet school because my grandfather wanted me to, but sheep ranching has always been my dream. We can do it."

Gracelyn was stung to anger. "What about *my* dreams? You never asked me if sheep ranching was my dream!"

Zandy wiped a hand through his hair and met her eyes. "When I met you, I didn't know you had any dreams. You were running away from school and everything else as fast as you could." He looked as if he might cry. "Good God, Gracelyn, if I had known how much you really care about your art, do you think I would have dragged you up here?"

She turned away too confused to respond. On the surface, she felt a surge of joy that he did understand about her work, but at some deep level, a part of her cried out, *Yes, if you loved me, you would want me to go with you—wherever you went—no matter what.* But just knowing that he was aware of her dreams eased some of her despair.

She turned back to him. "Can we make it until the wool check?"

She saw the relief in his face. "If I get enough calls, if you can feed when I have to leave the ranch, if we can get through shipping with minimal loss, if the bank will advance me a little more money . . ." He stopped talking and attempted to smile.

Gracelyn tried a joke. "Well, then, if our future is all that secure, we might as well have supper."

Zandy stood up to hug her, and they forgot supper and they didn't hurry to Maggie's to bring Emmy home, because somewhere in the middle of the hug, Zandy and Gracelyn became aware of the empty house and the silent CB and their need for each other. Gracelyn closed her mind to storms and tragedy and thought of nothing but the man who caressed her body. He never said the words, but every stroke of his hands said, "I love you," and that night she almost believed it.

Chapter Sixty-Three

ZANDY had said that ranching was a gamble. They were on a losing streak. Before the thunderstorms in the mountains were over, a ewe, one of Gracelyn's Odd Bunch, was struck by lightning and killed. Two of the crippled lambs had died. A bum lamb got crowded into the feeder and suffocated.

When Maggie dropped by in mid-September to talk about shipping, Zandy said, "I'm short on cash, Maggie. I may have to find a cheaper trucker."

"I hate to see you use a fly-by-night trucker, Alex. Those cheaper guys don't carry enough insurance."

Gracelyn was busy at the sink, but she turned to look at her husband. He seemed thinner than ever. He was up every day before the sun. She tried to take over as many of his chores as possible, but she couldn't fix machinery, and she had never completely mastered the tractor. She took Emmy in the truck and loaded bales, but she couldn't work as quickly or do as much with the little girl to care for. Though Zandy's wheat had done all right, *it* had to be harvested too, and Zandy worked with every crew to save money.

"Maybe I'll just sell to a buyer," Zandy said. "Save the stockyard commission and let him worry about the trucking."

"That's okay if you get an honest buyer," Maggie said. "You can come out close."

Gracelyn listened to their conversation feeling as if she were a split personality. She cared every bit as much as they did about shipping the lambs safely, and she knew the details were important, but she had not even opened her sketchpad since the day the coyotes had killed the lambs, and she felt barren and irritable. She thought of Dr. Carlson more and more often. She would picture a lecture in class and try to recall everything he had said. She disassembled the separator, washed it, and reassembled it, not even thinking about it.

She now did most of her housework without conscious effort. She whipped the bedclothes into order in the morning, ran a cloth across the dresser, and picked up the clothes box, stopping only occasionally to admire the quilt and pillow shams Maggie had given her. It was the only thing in their bedroom that she found satisfying. The straight lines and bare flat tops left her feeling hungry. And she resented them more now because she had lost her forty-one minutes to the pressure of the outside work. But Zandy liked the room. He was careful to put his dirty clothes into the box.

Emmy fussed and Gracelyn left the sink to lift her from her crib. Emmy was dry. She seemed to be completely potty-trained now. Gracelyn put her into Maggie's open arms.

Emmy was happy to play with the buttons on Maggie's shirt, so Gracelyn stepped outside. The cottonwoods along the creek had leaves like golden glass as they shimmered in the sun. Gracelyn walked behind the house and halfway up the hill to get a view of the valley. The aging paint on the house was just right for this time of year. Like sensible brown shoes, it kept Gracelyn in touch with reality when she leaned into the glory of the leaves and the endless blue sky. Annie continued to advise her to draw the small, ordinary things she knew, but Gracelyn studied the vast, hot, sweet, bright, ripe, rich autumn valley and sketched the scene into her mind before returning to the house where the discussion of buyers and truckers and lamb markets had gone on without her. Neither Maggie nor Zandy had any idea of the war that raged constantly inside Gracelyn. She gritted her teeth and decided, absolutely, to set aside Emmy's naptime for sketching.

Zandy welcomed the buyers when they came around, and Gracelyn cooked meals for various men who sat at her table after dinner, ignoring her as they talked contracts with Zandy. "I'll give you seventy-five cents a pound for your wether lambs if they don't weigh over eighty pounds, seventy-two if they weigh between eighty and ninety-five, over ninety-five, seventy cents." The numbers were dizzying. She let them slide across her mind and went back to memories of Dr. Carlson's class.

And finally the lambs were shipped. Frustrated because the buyers didn't offer enough, Zandy gambled one more time—on a "fly-by-night" trucker—and lost one more time. Ten lambs went down in the truck and couldn't get up. As Maggie had warned them, the trucker didn't have insurance for that kind of loss.

"This season's losses come to over $6,000," Zandy said. "I've got to make up $6,000."

"No," Gracelyn said. "You can't. You'll kill yourself." It was only later that she began to worry about her own survival.

They were running the herd through the chute to vaccinate for worms when Zandy leaned against the rail, vaccine gun in hand, and said, "If you could learn to grind hay, you could feed without me."

Gracelyn shoved another ewe into the chute and pushed the sheep along toward Zandy. She hated the thought of dealing with the hay-eating monster, but she asked, "Could I do it?"

"The machine does most of the work. You'd be lifting a bale at a time and adding a few buckets of grain."

"I could never take Emmy into all that dust."

Zandy said, "I was hoping you could grind hay during nap time."

Gracelyn bit her lip and remained silent because she suddenly felt so angry about Zandy's encroachment upon her few quiet moments that she could not be sure of what she would say. Zandy released the ewe he had just vaccinated, and Gracelyn climbed up on the runway fence. She prodded the sheep forward with a sheep hook before asking, "Zandy, does everybody pay you?"

Zandy's face reddened. "All except the real hardship cases. Why do you ask that?"

"Well, Josh asked me, and then Maggie asked me." Gracelyn watched as Zandy jammed the vaccine gun against the rump of one of the ewe lambs they'd kept to replace the ewe that had been struck by lightning. "I think *everybody* should pay. Right now we're the real hardship case." She opened the chute gate and pushed more sheep into the runway, then jumped down from the fence and faced her husband.

"I'll learn to run that hay grinder, but only if you make everybody pay us what they owe."

"I'm not sure I can do that," Zandy said.

"Well, *I* can," Gracelyn said. "Other people send bills. I can send bills."

"You're still upset because I hired that trucker."

"No, I'm not upset. It's just that my father would say that the cheapest investment is not always the best investment. And if people didn't pay their insurance premiums, you can be sure his company canceled their insurance. Why should you work for free?"

"That's the first time you ever quoted your father to me."

Gracelyn was startled. For the first time since she'd been on the ranch, she had thought of her father without thinking of Arminda.

She said, "He's a good businessman. If I had paid more attention, I might have learned a lot from him." *When did I realize that?*

"Would you really like to take over the billing?"

"I'm willing to try." *If it means that we can collect some overdue debts.*

Zandy fixed her a desk with a good light and a nice broad top. It would have been perfect for drawing, placed as it was, next to the window in their bedroom. Sitting there, she could see the road slope downward toward the creek and the north pasture rise toward the cedars.

At first the bills were like a foreign language, but gradually, as Zandy explained the medical terms and his price list, she began to get a broader picture of what her husband had been doing all those days and nights away from the ranch. She was soon familiar with the names and addresses and veterinary problems of ranchers for miles around. She began a list of money owed for months by certain ranchers, angered to discover that some of them were well-established, even if they didn't have a lot of cash. How long did they think Zandy was supposed to carry them? She added a "Please" to her second billing, and "Past Due" to her third billing. Zandy didn't like it. It made him uncomfortable. "They all have money troubles," he said.

And with stony determination, thinking of her lost forty-one minutes and the stolen nap time, Gracelyn said, "That's not my problem. They owe you the money. You drive a hundred miles round trip without charging them mileage. They're getting off easy when they do pay."

Slowly, some of the long overdue checks arrived in the mail. Gracelyn recorded each one in the book with a grim sense of triumph. She was improving their odds.

But it took time, and even more time when Zandy suggested that she take over all the bookkeeping, which included keeping tax records and inventorying supplies.

Counting things! Dear God. She who hated a tidy room was making tidy lists, balancing the checkbook, keeping meticulous records for Uncle Sam, the bank, and Mr. Radson.

Handling the books made her understand just how close to the edge they ran. Money went out constantly for such things as diesel fuel, feed, payments and repair parts for equipment, sheep spray and vaccine, seed, wages to Old Daniel and various temporary crews, and on and on. "Support the barn and the barn will eventually support the house." Maggie had quoted that saying to her at least two years ago. Gracelyn was willing to give up things in the house, but she dreamed of a hired hand to do some of her chores.

Twice a year, they got a large check. The wool check in

the spring and the lamb check in the fall. They had to make it last or collect more of the vet bills.

"It's too bad you didn't get a dowry from my folks when you married me," Gracelyn said once when Zandy and she were shaking their heads over the bank statement.

"What makes you think I didn't," he said, putting his hand on her shoulder as she sat in front of him at the desk. "They gave me a lamb-licker, a ranch hand, a ranch cook, and a bookkeeper all in one."

Gracelyn looked up in surprise. His tone was full of emotion. He met her eyes and said, "Do you realize how little you ask for? You haven't had a hundred dollars' worth of new clothes this year and that old Subaru of yours needs a tune-up. I'm damned glad your dad hasn't made that visit." Zandy's face was very red. "He'd probably horsewhip me for what I've done to his daughter."

Gracelyn was pleased. She had noticed how few of the expenses recorded in the ranch books were hers, but she hadn't known that Zandy paid any attention to the fact.

Zandy said, "Gracelyn, I promise you that as soon as we can afford help, you'll have more time to draw." He swallowed, before adding, "And if you need to leave the ranch and go back to school, I'll try to pay your way and get along here without you."

She reached up, grasped the hand that rested on her shoulder, and put her cheek against it. She was overwhelmed by his words and too deeply touched to reply. She could not cover her emotion with jokes as he did, so she simply sat silently holding his hand, knowing what a promise like that might cost him, and loving him for making it anyway.

Gracelyn could tell by looking in the mirror that she was grinding hay and feeding every day in the cold wind of mid-November. The hay caused a constant itchy rash around the inside of her collar, leaving a red line that made her look as if someone had tried to slit her throat. Her skin was wind-burned and dry no matter how much she creamed it. Her hair looked like hay—baled poorly and stacked crooked. *I'm glad Mother can't see me,* she thought.

They had written to postpone Gracelyn's trip to Florida with Emmy and invited her mother to come for Christmas, but her mother's reply was full of news about a decorating job she had bid on. She didn't mention their invitation in that letter. So it was with a sense of panic that Gracelyn ran to the garage on Thursday of the third week of November with the letter Zandy had just brought from Brandon.

"What am I going to do?" she said, waving the paper at him. "Mother is coming here for Thanksgiving!"

Chapter Sixty-Four

SHE scrubbed and cleaned. She hung the quilt and the embroidered picture back on the wall and spread Bertha Liggen's blue-and-silver afghan over Zandy's old chair.

She consulted Maggie a dozen times a week about bread and pies and new recipes for meals. She wrote an extravagant grocery list.

"You and Josh have to come for Thanksgiving dinner," she told Maggie.

"We'd be intruding."

"No you wouldn't. You're our Plum Creek family. I want my mother to meet you."

"Are you sure?"

"Absolutely sure. You and Josh have always invited us for Thanksgiving. Now it's my turn." She smiled at Maggie. "Besides, if you're not here for moral support, I won't be able to get the meal on the table."

Zandy promised that he'd stay home all day unless there was a life-or-death emergency on some ranch. To Gracelyn's surprise, her mother had told them not to meet her. She was renting a car at the airport in Brandon, Suzanne had told her how to get to the ranch, and she would be there the day before Thanksgiving.

There was snow on the ground and a bite to the air on the morning that Gracelyn's mother was to arrive, but the sky kept its remote, icy blue, and no new snow fell. Just after Gracelyn finished the separating, a grey Buick pulled into the yard.

Emmy was dressed in her prettiest playsuit. Gracelyn had planned to dress fancier, but it wasn't sensible to wear anything but jeans to the barn. She picked Emmy up and stepped outside the house as her mother, in a stylish coat and hat, got out of the car.

They stood uncertainly, looking at each other, until Gracelyn stepped forward and pecked her mother's cheek. She gave her a one-armed hug. "Emmy, this is your grandma."

Her mother came into the kitchen and sat down at the table. Gracelyn put Emmy in her high chair and said, "Would you like a cup of coffee?"

"Oh, Gracelyn dear, I'd love one. Suzanne told me you were forty miles from Brandon, but I didn't realize that there would be no place to stop."

Gracelyn filled two cups. She gave Emmy a cracker and then sat down across the table. In four years, her mother had aged. Fine lines etched the corners of her eyes, her face was thinner, and her hair had a sheen of grey. Gracelyn thought of all that her mother had gone through alone. For a moment, her anger at her father burned hot. She could feel it in her face. She took a deep breath.

"I'm so glad you could come," she said. And it was true. She hoped that her mother would try to understand the problems of keeping a decent house with all her other ranch work, but it didn't seem to matter so much now. She was just glad to have her mother there to share her daughter.

Emmy was fascinated with her grandmother. She leaned from her chair to touch the beads at the neck of the trim suit. "Pretty."

Gracelyn's mother smiled and patted the baby's hand.

"Would you like to hold her?"

Her mother seemed shy. "May I?"

"Of course."

Gracelyn put Emmy into her mother's lap. Emmy put her hands to the beads again. Gracelyn's mother unclasped the necklace and placed it around the baby's neck. She glanced at Gracelyn. "Is it all right?"

Gracelyn had never seen her mother so unsure of herself. "It's okay, Mother."

"I have some real baby things in the car."

Gracelyn was glad for something to do. She brought her mother's luggage in and set it in their bedroom. She and Zandy had decided to use the living room, so that when they got up early to do chores they wouldn't disturb her mother.

Her mother looked around the bedroom. "It's nice and tidy, dear. And that's a lovely quilt."

"My friend made it. You'll meet her tomorrow. She and her brother are coming for Thanksgiving." Gracelyn felt as if she were pulling the conversation through a snow drift. Her mother ventured nothing about herself. She unpacked a little valise full of baby clothes and bright-colored toys. Gracelyn was touched because she knew that her mother's money was limited. Emmy bounced up and down on the bed, her brown eyes sparkling. For a moment, her grandmother smiled, and then the smile faded, leaving a sad, tired look.

"Would you like to rest awhile, Mother?"

"No. I'm fine." They stood near the bed watching Emmy. Gracelyn tried again. "Suzanne writes that you're buying a small house."

Her mother's face brightened. "Yes. That was such luck. I decorated a home for the owner, and she made me a good deal. It looks out on the gulf. I could never have afforded it . . ." She stopped for a moment and then said, "I still want you to come and visit. It doesn't have a guest room, but I'll get you a motel room, and you can eat with me."

Gracelyn was swimming in words, confused. Her mother's invitation was so tentative. Come close, but not too close. She spoke to the subject of the house.

"Tell me about it. You never write details."

"I don't really have time to write letters. I have to keep constantly at my business. Some day I'll be able to afford a bookkeeper and perhaps someone to do some advertising, but right now, I do the books, the bidding, the buying, all the customer contacts, and the actual work."

"Well, we're not so different in that. I've recently taken over our books and some more of the ranch work."

Her mother looked at her. "You've changed."

For a moment, Gracelyn felt criticized. "I know. Aren't I a mess?"

"I wasn't talking about your looks. You seem more sure of yourself."

"I've had to learn to do a lot of things. And I'm often alone." She hoped that didn't sound like criticism of Zandy.

Her mother nodded. "Being alone teaches you things."

That was the nearest they came to discussing the divorce. Her mother didn't mention her father. Gracelyn was hesitant to ask questions. She felt a rush of sympathy. Despite her mother's reticence, Gracelyn knew that there had been bitter times, worry about money, self-doubt.

Her mother said, "Are you doing any art work?"

Gracelyn could feel herself flush. Her pain was intensified because she had to admit her continuing failure to her mother. "No."

But instead of saying *I told you so,* which she had every right to say, her mother said, "I know how hard that is for you, Gracelyn dear." And the words seemed like a caress.

Gracelyn's eyes filled. Her mother and her daughter blurred and swam. If Zandy had not stepped into the house at that moment, she would have burst into tears. She turned and smiled at her husband, who came forward with his hand outstretched, smelling of fresh air and hay.

During dinner, Gracelyn's mother was as attentive to Zandy as Suzanne had been, but with the difference that she seemed truly interested in the ranch and its work.

Gracelyn watched and listened. Her mother asked good business questions. That was surprising, because her father had always made the business decisions in the family.

Gracelyn said, "How did you learn so much about business so quickly?"

Her mother's mouth tightened slightly. "Your father wasn't always in the Million-Dollar-Medallion class of insurance salesmen, Gracelyn. Like you and Zandy, we had to start small."

And he dumped you for a younger woman after you helped him make it big. Her mother must have had the same thought. Gracelyn saw the pain that crossed her mother's eyes, and she changed the subject.

"Would you like to learn to milk a cow?"

Her mother laughed, and the pain left her eyes. "No, but I want to see everything while I'm here."

"It's the real thing. Not Disney World," Gracelyn said. "I hope you brought some old shoes."

"Why don't you stay the winter?" Gracelyn said that afternoon after the chores were finished, and they were riding toward the house in the Subaru with Emmy on her grandmother's lap, a bucket of milk at their feet. "With a grandma around to babysit, I could get my work done in half the time."

"Grandma," her mother said, as if the word tasted funny in her mouth. Then Emmy said "Gramma," and reached up to touch her grandmother's face. Gracelyn yearned for a sketch pad and pencil to capture the scene. Her mother met her eyes. For one moment they were in tune as they had never been, and it hurt to understand so much. *She's lonely, and this is not the picture of herself as a grandmother that she held through the years she lived in her beautiful house with her dynamic salesman.* For an instant, Gracelyn felt as if she had two children.

Despite Gracelyn's worries and her mother's early nervousness, Thanksgiving dinner was a huge success. Zandy had managed to convince Old Daniel to join them, along with Josh and Maggie. Maggie had helped Gracelyn with some of the relishes, and, at Gracelyn's urging, she made the gravy after the big golden turkey was on the platter. Gracelyn's mother talked about Florida and asked about Montana. She praised Maggie's quilts and the frame that Josh had made for the one on the wall. She charmed the Plum Creek family, and Gracelyn felt proud.

Josh talked about his rodeo work. He had had a better year. *A spiral upward?* Gracelyn wondered. Josh said, "Maggie has agreed to go to the Stock Show with me in January. She hasn't been away from this place overnight in years."

Maggie smiled at her brother. "He bribed me. Swears that all he wants for Christmas is my promise to go to the Stock Show with him."

Old Daniel was listening and nodding and filling his mouth with one forkful after another of turkey dressing and gravy. Gracelyn looked at her husband. He winked at her and sent his wide smile around the table like a lighthouse beam.

And the next morning, her mother went away again. Gracelyn had said, "You've come so far. Can't you stay longer?"

Her mother shook her head. "I shouldn't have left my business for as long as I have, but I wanted to see my daughter and my granddaughter." She was dressed in another lovely suit, as elegant as Gracelyn had ever remembered her.

"You look like a successful business woman," Gracelyn said.

Her mother flushed and her eyes brightened. "Thank you," she said, and while her mother was still open to emotion, Gracelyn stepped forward and hugged her, cherishing the return hug.

Her mother stooped to kiss Emmy, who was standing by Zandy. Then she held out her hand to him. "Thank you for sharing your family holiday with me," she said.

Zandy swung a big arm around her. "Why, you're part of our family," he said, sounding surprised. As her mother turned toward the car, her eyes were shiny with tears and her face had a tight look of suffering that stayed with Gracelyn long after the grey Buick had gone out of sight.

The rest of the year was an anti-climax. It seemed that every rancher in a fifty-mile radius had a veterinary emergency between Thanksgiving and Christmas. Gracelyn had never been so tired. Emmy suffered with frequent bouts of croup. Maggie had the flu during Christmas week. Zandy and Gracelyn helped with their neighbor's feeding after they did their own. Josh was working steadily, but Old

Daniel had gone roaming after Maggie had extracted a promise from him to come back and spend two weeks on her ranch in January while she went with Josh to the Stock Show in Denver.

Christmas Day everyone stayed home. Emmy brightened the morning for Zandy and Gracelyn, as she explored her Christmas stocking with happy excitement, her red curls prettier than the coils of ribbon on the packages.

Zandy was gone most of the week before New Year's and Gracelyn was beginning to wonder if she would have to spend New Year's Eve alone, but he showed up about ten-thirty with a bottle of champagne, a pound of Brie, a bottle of Greek olives, and a big smile.

"All we need is Guy Lombardo," Gracelyn said as she spread the feast out on their bed and fluffed up their pillows.

"Let Guy Lombardo find his own girl," Zandy said and toasted the New Year with a coffee mug full of champagne.

And then it was the tenth of January and time to wave goodbye to Maggie and Josh as they headed down the Plum Creek Road with Josh's saddle in the back of the pickup.

Chapter Sixty-Five

ZANDY groaned as the CB radio crackled into life on a freezing morning ten days later. He turned over in bed and snuggled closer to Gracelyn. "Cold-blooded damn machine doesn't care that it's below zero outside." The call was repeated.

Gracelyn was sleeping in the middle. The electric space heater in Emmy's room was overpowered by the relentless January cold, and they had brought the little girl to bed with them. When Zandy sat up and pushed the covers back, a rush of icy air took his place. He stood up and pulled the blankets over Gracelyn's shoulder.

"How cold is it?" Gracelyn asked as Zandy turned on the light in the room. He leaned close to the window and squinted at the thermometer mounted outside.

"Somewhere between twenty and thirty below—real Stock Show weather." He turned. "You two stay under the covers until I find out what that box is squawking about. Then I'll build a fire."

"No, if you have to leave, I'd better get up and get the milking done. I don't want to take Emmy out until the sun is up."

"I'll go call the guy, but I'll try to postpone a real trip until I finish feeding," Zandy said. As he shook down the ashes in the stove, Gracelyn shivered her way toward the bathroom.

Zandy returned from Maggie's place just as Gracelyn

dished up scrambled eggs. "How is Old Daniel doing?" she asked. "He's been pretty faithful up there for the last ten days. Is he getting ready to ramble?"

"Didn't talk to him, but I wouldn't be surprised if he took off. Maggie's due back. Is Emmy still sleeping?"

"Surrounded by blankets. I left the bedroom door open so some of the stove heat would get in there." Gracelyn had made hot oatmeal as well as eggs. Feeding sheep in such extreme cold took extra energy. She was grateful now for the big mechanical snout that filled the hay troughs. The machine never tired. It was enough for Zandy and her just scattering cake. "Do you have to leave?" she asked.

"Yeah, but it's no life-or-death thing. I'll feed first."

Gracelyn separated while Emmy slept. The little girl woke up cranky. She refused to eat breakfast. Gracelyn tried to interest her in a game.

"See the choo-choo train, Emmy. It's coming toward the tunnel. Open the door so the train can come in." Gracelyn brought the spoonful of oatmeal close to Emmy's mouth, but Emmy turned her head aside. "Here, try eggs. You like scrambled eggs." Emmy pushed the spoon with her hand, spilling eggs on the high chair tray.

Gracelyn took the little girl from the high chair. "What's the matter, Emmy? Don't you feel good?" Emmy hid her face in Gracelyn's neck. "Do you want to help Mama do dishes?" Emmy shook her head. Gracelyn took her to the bed in the living room and laid her there with blankets around her, but when Gracelyn went back to the kitchen, Emmy followed, clinging to Gracelyn's legs as she moved about trying to finish up the dishes and clear away the clutter on the counters.

Finally Gracelyn left the separator sitting in the dishwater and picking up her sketchpad, sat down at the kitchen table and took Emmy on her lap. "I'll draw you a story." Emmy put her thumb in her mouth and leaned back against Gracelyn's breast.

"See," Gracelyn said, swiftly sketching a horse, "this is a horse." Emmy lay still. "And this is Uncle Josh on the horse." Emmy sat up. "And this is Aunt Maggie watching Uncle Josh ride the horse." Gracelyn sketched a few lines for a seat and put a fair likeness of Maggie on the seat. This was fun. Why hadn't she thought to entertain Emmy with sketches before?

Emmy leaned forward, thumb in mouth, to watch as Gracelyn drew a dividing line and sketched another horse, this one bucking. "See the horse buck. Uncle Josh is trying to stay on the horse until the buzzer rings."

Emmy took her thumb from her mouth and said, "Horse bucks."

"Here's a man with the buzzer. Hurry up and ring the buzzer, man."

Emmy said, "Hurry up, man." Gracelyn hesitated. She wondered which way Josh's Stock Show spiral was going today. She decided to help him out. "Bzzzz!" she said, sketching sound lines in the next frame of her comic strip. "The buzzer rings just in time."

She sketched a man with arms and legs akimbo. "There goes Uncle Josh flying through the air. But he beat the buzzer. Hurrah for Uncle Josh."

Emmy didn't laugh. She just put her thumb back in her mouth and leaned against Gracelyn. Gracelyn closed the sketch book and put her hand on the little girl's head. She seemed warm.

The CB crackled. Gracelyn took the call, hoping that Zandy was somewhere near his truck so she could relay the call to him there. He didn't answer. He was probably on the tractor pulling the grinding machine. She checked the outdoor thermometer. It had warmed up to nearly zero.

She dressed Emmy and zipped her inside her furry snow-suit, a Christmas surprise from Gracelyn's father and Arminda. The surprise was that it wasn't pink. It was made of fake rabbit fur and was all white, with a quilted lining. Gracelyn wondered if her father was ever going to drive to Montana to meet his granddaughter as he and Arminda had so often promised. She flipped the rabbit ears on the hood as she pulled it over Emmy's red curls, and Emmy giggled.

"I'm glad to see you smile, baby." She hugged her daughter and tickled the corner of her mouth. Emmy showed her teeth in another grin.

"Here, honey," Gracelyn said, handing Emmy a biscuit. "Chew on this, and I'll fix you some hot cocoa when we get back from the feeding pens."

She put on her coat and boots and wrapped a blanket around Emmy. Pete bounded through the door as she opened it. There wasn't much snow on the ground, just a gritty coating of hard frost.

Pete jumped into the back seat of the Subaru, and Gracelyn settled Emmy in the front. She floored the accelerator and tried the starter, repeating the process several times before the sluggish engine turned over. Her fingers were cold in their gloves, but Emmy seemed cozy in her rabbit skin. She chewed on the biscuit.

"No, honey," Gracelyn said as the little girl started to offer Pete a bite. "His mouth is too big. Sit down, Pete." The dog sat, but he rested his muzzle on the back of the front seat and, drooling, eyed the biscuit. Gracelyn laughed and revved the engine.

By the time she started over the bridge, Zandy's pickup was coming down the slope from the barn. Gracelyn backed the Subaru off the bridge and turned toward the house. Zandy stopped by the car, and she hollered "Clayborne." He made a face and drove on down the road.

Zandy radioed back from Maggie's place. For a change the transmission was clear. "Clayborne's got a real emergency with his prize bull," he said. Gracelyn sighed. Clayborne's ranch was at least ninety miles from Maggie's place. She pressed the transmitter button.

"Do you think you can be back by chore time? Emmy's acting like she may be getting croupy again, and I think she's a little feverish."

"I'll do my best, but I'll probably be late. Don't take her out. If I'm not back, the chores can wait."

Gracelyn laughed and punched the button again. "In this weather, the cows will make ice cream." She let go of the button and heard Zandy laugh. "Keep warm," he said.

Gracelyn ran hot water and started the dishes again, thinking of the weather. The dry cold was unusual. She was used to slogging through snow drifts in the winter, but the sun usually burnt off the morning fog, and she could put Emmy to play in a clear spot on the south side of the barn or the lambing sheds while she loaded cake into the Subaru. From time to time, she would go and sit in the warm spot and help Emmy dig in the dirt. Or they would look up into the sky.

"Sky," Emmy had said as she bent her head back, her arm extended, pointing.

"Blue sky."

"Boo sky."

"Blue . . ."

"Baloo," Emmy said, sticking out her tongue as she struggled with the word. She giggled and dug a spoonful of wet dirt. "Eat, Mama." Gracelyn pretended to eat the dirt, then made a face. "Too hot." She had been reading Goldilocks to Emmy. Emmy giggled again, "Too hot."

But this weather was different. Too dry, terribly cold. Zandy worried about drought. The winter wheat would need more moisture in the soil. Grasshoppers loved dry years. That worried Zandy, too. He might lose his wheat altogether. He ranged farther and farther in his vet calls. This Clayborne call. Surely there was some closer vet. A hundred and eighty miles round trip.

Gracelyn sighed and finished up the dishes. Emmy was dozing on the bed by the big stove. Gracelyn thought of starting on the bills and record books, but decided first to put in a load of wash. Pete went to the door to be let out. Gracelyn stepped to the door and opened it. The sky was a flat grey ceiling. The cold air rose toward it like thick prison walls, invisible, but as confining as stone. She glanced up the hill toward the feeding pastures. She hoped that the sheep weren't crowding the troughs. She and Zandy didn't need to find another yearling smothered in the hay or suffocated by his own kin. Sheep were so dumb. Gracelyn shut the door.

She set to work on the books while the machine finished

its cycles. Emmy was content to lie on the big bed in their room and watch her mother at the desk.

By two o'clock, Gracelyn had brought the billing up to date and washed three loads of clothes. "Let's eat some soup, Emmy. Then Mommy will fold clothes."

Emmy crawled quietly into Gracelyn's lap. Gracelyn decided to take her temperature before she fed her the hot soup. It was only ninety-nine. Must be a tooth. She ran her finger along Emmy's gums. Emmy sucked on her mother's finger, and then accepted several spoonfuls of soup before sliding down and returning to the bed in the living room.

"Let's bring your crib in here, chickie, and you can take your nap by the stove."

Emmy watched Gracelyn slide the crib through the door into the living room, Old Daniel's wooden mobile clattering as it swayed. Gracelyn picked her up and rocked her gently in her arms, her cheek on Emmy's hair. "Poor baby," she murmured, "you can't tell your mama what's making you so droopy, and your dumb mama can't figure it out for herself." Emmy patted her mother's cheek with three soft fingers.

Gracelyn held her a few moments and then put her into the crib with Josh's monkey. Emmy took the monkey's paw into her hand and lay down.

Gracelyn slipped outside to replenish the wood box. A swift breeze was blowing. She looked at the sky. The wind hadn't blown for several days. Maybe the weather was changing. She rubbed her hands for a moment, then took an armload of wood and went inside.

Zandy had not returned by chore time. The chicken water and the water in the milk cows' tank would be frozen. She hated to think of leaving the cows with swollen udders. Maybe she could do the chores a bit at a time, returning to check on Emmy in between.

Emmy had fallen asleep clutching the monkey. Gracelyn left Pete with the little girl and drove to the barn with the milk buckets. She fed and watered the chickens and broke the ice in the stock tank at the milk barn before driving back to the house to make sure that Emmy still slept.

She milked as quickly as she could. The barn was cold and the milk steamed in the buckets. Crybaby and the kittens—who were all fully grown cats now and some of them obviously pregnant—sat in a half-circle and meowed, waiting for her to fill their supper pans.

Emmy was still asleep when Gracelyn finished separating. She decided to chance a quick swing through the sheep. She couldn't feed, but she might check the water tanks.

A few hard kernels of snow peppered the windshield as she pulled into the sheep pasture. The sheep were bunching in the dusk, but one ewe had gotten her leg tangled in the wire by the water tank. She reared and struggled as Gracelyn came near and wouldn't let her get at the leg.

Gracelyn went back to the barn for a sheep hook. She grabbed the ewe by a hind leg and, setting the sheep hook on the ground, held it steady with her foot while she freed the sheep's front leg.

The ice in the tank was too tough for the sheep hook. She had to break the ice with an iron bar. By the time she finished, the unseen sun had set; the January night was darker than usual. The clouds that had masked the sun all day were thickening. Gracelyn closed the chickens' door and went back to the house.

Emmy was crying with the hoarse crusted sound that meant croup. Gracelyn flung off her coat and swept the baby from the crib. "There, there, honey. Mommy's here. We'll get your steamer going right away." It hurt her to listen to the rasping sobs.

By the time she had the croup tent over the crib and the steam misting the air, Emmy was burning hot. Gracelyn took her temperature with the rectal thermometer as gently as she could. "Oh, my God!" she said as she traced the silver line. It rested just below one-hundred-and-four degrees.

Chapter Sixty-Six

GRACELYN'S heart began to pound. She took several deep breaths as she slipped the thermometer into its case. Her hands trembled, and she clenched her fists to still them. What should she do first? Emmy had never had a temperature this high.

She moistened a cloth and bathed the baby's forehead and then her arms and legs, uncovering one at a time. Emmy's breathing was rough; she tried to say "Mama," but her voice was no more than a whisper. Gracelyn wanted to pick her up and hold her, but she didn't dare take her away from the steamy tent. Inside the sheet that made the tent, the air was moist and warm. The room seemed chilly by comparison. Gracelyn added wood to the fire.

She poured baby Tylenol into a teaspoon and coaxed Emmy to sip it. Emmy's eyes were dull. She whimpered and turned her head from the spoon. Gracelyn re-filled the spoon and lifted Emmy. "Please, honey, you need the medicine." Emmy opened her mouth a little, and Gracelyn slowly poured the Tylenol onto her tongue. Emmy tried to swallow, but most of the liquid ran from the corners of her mouth. Gracelyn let her lie down again.

She bathed the baby once more, feeling sick as the washcloth turned hot from touching Emmy's skin. She pulled the sheet close around the crib and went to the CB.

She pushed the transmitter button and began calling for Zandy. "Calling Doc or anyone in the vicinity of Doc.

Emergency." She should look up the code number, but she didn't have time. "Emergency. Doc is needed at home. Repeat. Anyone knowing the whereabouts of Doc, please relay the message." When she let go of the transmitter button, the incoming sounds were so static-filled she had no idea if there was a human voice in the noise.

She took Emmy's temperature again. The silver line was now above the hundred-and-four marker. Biting her lip to keep from crying, she began to bathe the little girl once more. Then she mixed a spoonful of Tylenol in orange juice and tried to get Emmy to drink from the glass. The baby turned her head from side to side until Gracelyn held her head still and sip by sip put the liquid down her throat. Pete got up and paced around the room. The wind was rising. It rattled the windows in Emmy's Addition and squealed around the stove vents.

Gracelyn sent another call out on the CB. Surely people would relay her message. She looked at the clock. Six-thirty. Dinnertime. *Darn.* Trucks would be idling outside of cafés; pickups would be parked at ranch houses. But she sent the emergency call again and again until she heard Emmy coughing and went back to her.

Emmy's eyes were glazed with fever; her hoarse coughing raked her throat. It sounded so painful. Gracelyn refilled the steamer, trying to think what else she could do. Bring the temperature down, get some liquid into her so she wouldn't dehydrate, run the steamer to clear the breathing passages. But how could she bring the temperature down?

She bathed Emmy over and over, changing the water as it warmed from the cloth. She held the little girl up and urged her to drink the juice, then water, but Emmy rolled her head away and gasped for breath, crying with the croaking sound that wrenched Gracelyn's heart.

She picked the baby up and held the hot body close, rocking her back and forth. "Mommy's here. Oh, baby, I know you're sick."

She mustn't keep her out of the steam. Putting Emmy back into the crib, she took her temperature again. By now the Tylenol should have done something.

But the terrifying silver line had moved up again. *Oh, God, I can't let her temperature get to a hundred and five. Zandy, where are you?* She looked at the clock. It was nearly seven.

Once more Gracelyn put Tylenol in Emmy's mouth and tipped her head to make her swallow. Emmy made a fretful sound and rolled her head away from Gracelyn's hand. Her skin was parched even though Gracelyn had bathed it only a moment before. Her breath scraped in and out.

Gracelyn bathed her daughter again. Just as she pulled the covers back over Emmy, the little girl's body stiffened, her eyes rolled back in her head, and her arms began to jerk. Gracelyn cried out and stood stunned for a second.

What should I do? Her tongue. I can't let her tongue choke her. Gracelyn slipped her arm around Emmy and pulled her body upward. Forcing her finger into Emmy's mouth, she felt for her tongue. *It was properly placed, thank God.* Gracelyn quickly rolled the wash cloth into a pencil shape and inserted it between the tiny teeth.

The jerking of the arms went on and on. *God, how can I make it stop?* When Emmy's body finally relaxed, it seemed to Gracelyn as if she had been standing there forever. She removed the cloth and put Emmy back into the croup tent. Then she glanced at the clock. She couldn't believe it. It was only a minute or two after seven. The seizure had lasted less than thirty seconds.

Crying now, Gracelyn ran again to the CB and screamed her message again and again. No answer came through the crackling receiver.

I have to get to Maggie's and the phone. Emmy's got to have a doctor. She turned and looked at the crib. *But I can't leave her.*

She dressed Emmy in her footed pajamas and then in the fur snowsuit and wrapped her in a blanket. She put the orange juice and a glass and the Tylenol in a sack, then put on her outdoor clothes, pulling an orange knit cap down around her ears before she picked up the sack, the bundled baby, and her purse.

"Stay, Pete." She pulled the door shut behind her and blinked in dismay as she stepped into the wind. The air was warmer, but a fine mist settled on her face. She turned Emmy inward toward her body and hurried to the car.

The Subaru was only beginning to warm as she drove up the road from Maggie's gate. The light on the pole at the barn was burning, but there were no lights in the house. Old Daniel's pickup was gone.

Gracelyn shielded Emmy from the mist again as she felt her way up to Maggie's door and let herself in. Thank God for ranch people who never locked their doors. She found the light switch and the phone, but when she dialed Clayborne's number, the line was busy. She asked the operator to interrupt, but the operator said, "I'm sorry, Ma'am. It's not busy. There's trouble on the line. You know it's storming in that area."

Of course she hadn't known. She was out of touch with everyone in the world. "Please, operator, this is an emergency. I'm trying to get my baby to a doctor. As soon as those lines clear up, will you call this number and tell them to send Dr. MacNair to meet his wife."

"Dr. MacNair?"

"Dr. MacNair is a veterinarian. He's my husband. Tell him, tell him . . ." For a moment she didn't know what to tell him. "Tell him I'm taking the baby to Brandon to the hospital where she was born."

Emmy's body began to tighten and her arms began to jerk again. Gracelyn dropped the phone and put her finger between Emmy's teeth, wincing as her jaw tightened and the sharp teeth bit into her flesh. She had to go. There wasn't time. The moment Emmy started to relax, she picked her up and left Maggie's house.

The soft rain had turned to sleet, and before she was two miles down the Plum Creek road, it was snowing—thick wet globs that clung to the windshield and to the windshield wiper. Gracelyn kept one hand on Emmy and drove with the other, peering through the coated glass and through the tears that ran down her face unchecked.

She stopped once to give Emmy more orange juice and Tylenol. Most of it ran down the sides of the baby's mouth, but Gracelyn tipped the glass again and rubbed Emmy's throat the way she rubbed a lamb's throat when she was teaching it to bottle feed. Emmy swallowed. Gracelyn shifted into gear and moved on down the road.

The farther she went, the more snow was on the ground. The blizzard thickened. The headlights mixed with the whirling snow, blinding her and not penetrating the sooty darkness beyond. The hand that rested on Emmy grew hot from the contact. The baby moved restlessly on the seat. Her breathing sounded like dry leaves breaking.

A vast windblown bench of snow suddenly loomed out of the darkness, blocking the road. Gracelyn accelerated and aimed at the lowest spot. The Subaru was struggling through the drift when Emmy's body tightened. Gracelyn stopped the car and took the baby in her arms, checking her tongue first and then forcing an edge of the blanket between the clenched teeth. Emmy's fists knotted tight and her arms began the rhythmic jerking. Gracelyn felt as if the blizzard had entered her mind. She whirled upward into the snowstorm, her senses spinning.

When the convulsion eased, Emmy lay limp in her arms and Gracelyn was wrung out. Confused for a moment, she shook her head. Then she bent to listen to Emmy. Her breath was faint. *She can't take this much longer. I've got to get her to Brandon.*

Gracelyn put the baby onto the seat and tried to push the Subaru forward. She had to back out of the drift to gain traction and then speed. The Subaru hit the drift like a battering ram and broke through, almost running into the headlights of the vehicle on the other side.

"Thank God. Zandy."

No, it wasn't Zandy. It was Maggie's truck that had braked hard at her abrupt appearance out of the drift. Shutting off the car, Gracelyn pulled Emmy into her arms and rolled the blanket over her head. Staggering through the snow, she went to the passenger's side of her neighbor's truck.

"Josh, Maggie. We've got to get Emmy to the hospital."
But Maggie was alone. Gracelyn put Emmy on the seat and
pulled herself up into Maggie's pickup.

Maggie touched the baby's forehead and without a word
backed the truck around and headed toward The Silos and
the highway.

The storm was even worse toward Brandon, but whenever
there was a let-up, Maggie pushed the truck faster. Gracelyn
loosened the blanket around Emmy. The poor baby was so
hot.

"How long has she been sick?"

"Her temperature went up just after chore time this evening. I bathed her; I gave her Tylenol; I tried the steamer.
Nothing helped. Maggie, her temperature was nearly one
hundred and five and it was still going up." Gracelyn's
voice broke on a sob and she turned her head toward the
window.

"My God," Maggie said and increased their speed.

Gracelyn turned back to Maggie. "Where's Josh?"

"In St. Luke's Hospital in Denver. His leg is busted in
two places and where he doesn't hurt, he ought to."

Gracelyn thought of her sketch of Josh flying through the
air. So his spiral was downward again. "What was it? A
horse or a bull?"

Maggie snorted. "Neither. The damn fool went out
drinking with a bunch of cowboys and got into an automo-
bile accident. He's lucky to be alive."

Thinking of the little monkey Josh had bought for Emmy
from his winnings at the county fair, she asked, "Did he
win anything?"

"Enough to pay for a couple of days in the hospital."

"Poor Josh."

"Poor Josh, hell. Poor Maggie. I'm coming into shearing
and lambing without help." She glanced at Gracelyn. "I
don't suppose there's a chance that Old Daniel is still out
on the place?"

"I didn't see his truck, but the yard light was on at the
barn."

Maggie was silent then as she peered into the blizzard

and pushed the truck forward. Emmy lay heavily on Gracelyn's lap, her breath rattling in her throat.

"She's been having convulsions." Gracelyn smoothed the little girl's forehead with her hand.

"Her temperature's too high. I guess that can cause convulsions."

"The doctor never told me croup could cause a temperature this high. I didn't know what to do."

Maggie rested her hand on Gracelyn's arm. "You've done everything you can. We'll get her to the hospital. Do you know where Zandy is?"

"He got a call from Clayborne. I tried to get him on the CB and then I phoned from your place. But the lines were down."

"Yeah, they've had a monster storm. The drought is broken for damn sure." Maggie fell silent, and Gracelyn leaned toward the windshield, willing the truck to more speed.

Emmy's body went into its agony of jerking again just as they pulled into Brandon. Maggie raced toward the hospital while Gracelyn tried to ease the contortions of the little body. When Emmy relaxed into her lap, she was heavier than ever. Her head lolled over Gracelyn's leg.

Maggie pulled into the emergency entrance and jumped from the truck. Gracelyn, suddenly full of a terrible dread, lowered her head to listen to Emmy's breathing. The rasping sound had stopped.

"No, Emmy, no. We're here. The doctor's coming." She picked up the weight of her child and held her ear close to the mouth.

The door of the truck opened and a male voice said, "Let me take the little girl." Gracelyn released Emmy and followed the green-coated figure.

Gracelyn was shunted into the admitting office with Maggie, who answered the clerk's questions because Gracelyn had buried her face in her hands and was sobbing in great shuddering gasps. Her thoughts ran in wild circles. *Too late.* Their questions were futile. *No point in answering questions.*

Emmy had stopped breathing. That was the only answer that mattered.

A man in a green medical coat came into the office. "Is this the baby's mother?"

Gracelyn looked up and swallowed back her sobs. She wiped away the moisture on her face and said, "I am Emmy's mother." She did not have to ask him anything. His face was white with his own pain, but he told her anyhow.

"I'm sorry, but the baby was dead when we took her from the truck."

Gracelyn said, "I know," and a calm grey cloud settled down around her, blotting out all the sounds. She watched through the mist as Maggie touched a pen to the white paper on the brown desk. The man in green stood in front of her, his mouth moving, but the cloud insulated her, and in a moment he stepped away. When he returned he held a capsule and a paper cup full of water. She opened her mouth when his fingers touched her lips. She swallowed when the water filled her mouth.

She heard nothing until Zandy spoke to her. She was sitting in the chair by the desk, staring at the brown and beige tiles on the floor when Zandy spoke her name. She looked up. His face was pale. His eyes were red. She stood and her legs wobbled. Zandy reached a hand toward her, but she backed away.

"Gracelyn," he said and stepped forward. She took another step backward. He stopped, and she met his eyes.

"You should have been there," she said.

Chapter Sixty-Seven

SITTING in the mortuary office with Maggie, Zandy and Gracelyn consulted each other with distant courtesy, as if they were strangers. Gracelyn felt nothing at all as Maggie and the funeral director arranged for a church and a minister and a hymn. Zandy nodded his head when Maggie suggested a particular casket.

It was only when it was time to choose a cemetery that they disagreed. Gracelyn wanted Emmy's grave at least as close as The Silos.

"No," Zandy said. "We'll bury her in Brandon."

"It's too far," Gracelyn said.

"I won't have her buried by the railroad tracks in that dump of a cemetery. It's all weeds and trash." Zandy's voice broke.

Gracelyn half rose from her chair and then she sat down again. "Brandon is too far away," she said in a flat, stubborn voice.

Maggie intervened. "There's another cemetery—an old homestead cemetery about seven miles from your place on the Plum Creek road."

Zandy and Gracelyn turned toward her.

"Of course it's buried in snow right now, but in the springtime, the wildflowers grow on the slope, and the rabbits play in the grass near the headstones." Maggie's voice faltered on the word, but she went on. "There are only a few graves, but it's on a southern slope where the sun warms it in the winter, and it's high enough that the cedars provide a shady spot or two in the summer."

"I know that cemetery," the funeral director said. "We buried old Sadie McCormick there two winters ago."

Gracelyn looked at him. "Why?"

"Her husband's been buried there for nearly thirty years. She wanted to lie beside him."

Gracelyn glanced at her husband. He had not touched her since she had backed away from him in the hospital. And she didn't want him to touch her. He had been off following his dreams when she needed him. Why should he expect her to want him now? She didn't need anybody or want anything except to bury Emmy close to home.

She looked at the funeral director. "Can you get someone to dig a grave in the Plum Creek cemetery this time of year?"

The director looked at Zandy. "Is the Plum Creek cemetery acceptable to you?"

Zandy nodded. "I'll take Maggie's word for it."

Emmy was ready for viewing before they left Brandon. Zandy shook his head. "I want to remember her alive." Gracelyn went in with Maggie.

The little face was quiet as when she was sleeping, but her curls weren't right. Gracelyn took a comb from her purse and twisted each red curl around her finger, then placed it carefully on Emmy's head. Something still wasn't right. She began again and wound the curls tighter before she let them go. Shaking her head, she started with the first curl once more.

Maggie took hold of her arm. "Gracelyn, that's enough."

"She doesn't look right, Maggie. Something's wrong."

Maggie pulled her out of the room. Gracelyn started to twist away to go back to Emmy. Maggie said, "Gracelyn, stop that. You are coming with me."

She could not break Maggie's grip on her wrist. She followed her neighbor into the snowy day. Zandy was standing by the truck.

"Shall I take you back to the motel?" he asked. "I think I'd better get out to the ranch."

"I've got to check my place, too," Maggie said. "There's nothing else we can do here."

Zandy looked at Gracelyn. "Do you want to stay here? I can bring the clothes you need."

Gracelyn glanced from Maggie to Zandy and back to Maggie. "I have chores to do, too. My cows will be bursting. You don't have to treat me like a mental case. I left Pete in the house, and he'll be miserable."

She saw Zandy glance at Maggie, who shrugged. "Maybe it's best for you to go home, Gracelyn."

They didn't speak for twenty miles, and Zandy didn't turn the radio on. They just rode through the white landscape, the snow tires droning. Hanging above her at the edge of her awareness, Gracelyn could feel the grey cloud that had smothered her in the hospital.

Zandy said, "Gracelyn, you should cry. It always helps you to cry."

She looked at him. How did he dare to say what would help her? Where had he been when she was calling for help?

"I cried when they took Emmy from me at the Emergency Entrance. Before you came. I'm through with crying. I'll never cry over anything again."

Zandy's face grew red, but he didn't say anything else. They were nearing The Silos when Gracelyn asked, "What about Clayborne's bull?"

"He's alive."

Some time while Gracelyn was milking the cows, Zandy put Emmy's crib back into the addition. Gracelyn noticed that the little monkey had been set to lean against the pillow. Her mind went around and around with the separator handle; the droning sound of the machine blotted out all her feelings.

Gracelyn took the pickup to the barn and loaded cake for the sheep. Her Subaru was still sitting in the snowdrift on the Plum Creek road. Zandy ground hay and filled the feeders.

The sheep were just fine. Not one had gotten onto its

back and died before it could get up. There were no suffocated yearlings in the hay troughs. The coyotes had not come down close to the barn. No mountain lions had left their track. Gracelyn stood looking at the contented, quiet sheep, bedding down after their stomachs were full, and for a moment she thought she saw a little red-haired figure moving among them. She shook her head and her eyes cleared. She turned away from the sheep and drove down the hill to close the chicken coop.

When Gracelyn put supper on the table, they both ate. Gracelyn remembered the lunch Josh had brought to them at the summer pasture the day of the coyote kill. *We are always animals*, she thought.

She cleared the dishes away and washed them without feeling the water on her hands. She set milk to sour for cheese and cream to sour for butter and then stood looking at it, forgetting that she had done it. She swept up the ashes around the living room stove. She fed Pete and filled his water dish.

When the house was in order—all the surfaces cold and bare and alien to her—she went into Emmy's room and sat down on the little chair that Old Daniel had made for Emmy at Christmas. She wrapped her arms around her knees and looked at the monkey in the crib.

Zandy came in from the shop and spoke her name, but she didn't answer. The CB crackled. She heard someone say, "Doc," but Zandy did not leave the house.

She did not know how long she had been sitting there when Zandy came into the room. "Gracelyn, it's too cold at night for you to stay in here." She looked up at him. She didn't move. He went out and, in a little while, the lights went off in the house.

The darkness was encompassing. Gracelyn could no longer see the crib or any of Emmy's things. As the fire in the living room stove died down, she began to shiver. Finally, she rose and stumbled into the living room. Zandy had left blankets on the bed there. Didn't he want her to sleep in the bedroom?

She sank numbly onto the living room bed and pulled

the blankets around her. Pete stirred and came to the edge of the bed. She put her hand on his head.

It stormed in Denver on the day of Emmy's funeral. Gracelyn and Zandy were at the motel in Brandon. Gracelyn's mother called from Stapleton Airport.

"Suzanne and I are snowed in. All flights have been canceled for twenty-four hours." She was weeping.

"It's all right, Mother. Suzanne shouldn't be traveling in her condition anyway." Suzanne was finally carrying the baby she had talked about for so long. "Don't worry, Mother. The Plum Creek family will be with me."

That wasn't exactly true. Josh was still in the hospital in Denver, and no one seemed to know where Old Daniel had gone after he'd left Maggie's place. He probably wouldn't show up again until lambing season.

"Let me speak to Zandy."

Gracelyn handed the receiver to her husband. He spoke in a comforting tone to her mother. The tone cooled when he spoke to Gracelyn. "She wants to talk to you again."

But her mother only sobbed, "Gracelyn dear, oh Gracelyn dear."

Suddenly irritated with her mother's weeping, Gracelyn said, "I'll be all *right*, Mother. It's not your fault that you are snowed in. God knows, no one can control the weather."

There were many people in the church, a sea of faces. She glanced at Zandy. He was staring at the opposite wall. She looked at the coffin. Emmy. Maggie's hand covered hers, and she sank into the warmth of it, feeling nothing else.

The cemetery was cold and snowy. Gracelyn looked away from the brown maw of the newly dug grave. She could see the crestline of the bluffs that stretched along the valley. A hawk was circling above the bluffs. New snow had broken the impacted sky and, behind the bird, the blue was flat and empty. The sky and the barren, uncaring rock would be there when spring came; and more lambs would die; and Zandy would never quit. *I will be like those rocks*, Gracelyn thought. *I can be like the rocks.*

People came to offer words of sympathy to her. Jacob

Liggen took both of her hands in his gnarled hands and looked quietly into her eyes. She wished she were only waiting for him to begin, "This Old Boy." Bertha Liggen hugged her silently.

The minister invited the cold mourners to Maggie's house for food and hot drinks. Gracelyn bent her head and hurried unseeing to the limousine.

Gracelyn was holding a cup of coffee in her hands when her father spoke her name. The coffee splashed over the rim, puddling in the saucer. She turned.

"Daddy. I didn't know you came."

Her father looked old. His skin was mottled from the cold. There were lines around his eyes. "We were late. God-awful drive in that storm."

She didn't know what to say. Her father took her arm and moved her away from the kitchen into a small open space by Maggie's fireplace. "Gracie, I wanted to tell you . . ." His voice broke and he began again. "Sometimes things happen to us. Sometimes we hurt people we love. We blame ourselves. Gracie, don't blame yourself. You can't live the rest of your life blaming yourself. We do the best we can . . ." He broke off and Gracelyn stood for a moment remembering the first time she had taken Emmy's temperature the day she got sick. It was only ninety-nine then.

"Gracie?" Her father's eyes were bloodshot, but they were full of feeling. "I wish I had come to see her. I thought I had plenty of time. I am so sorry."

Suddenly Gracelyn realized how tired she was, how much she wanted to go home. She took a step forward and raised her arms, ready to embrace her father.

But at the same moment, Arminda appeared at her father's side. She slid an arm through his and said, "Hello, Gracelyn. I'm awfully sorry about your little girl."

Gracelyn could only stare. Arminda's small frame bulged under the stylish maternity dress she wore. Gracelyn's arms fell to her side. She said to Arminda, "It was kind of you to make such a long, cold trip." As she turned away, the coffee cup rattled on the saucer in her hand.

Chapter Sixty-Eight

THE last week in January and the first two weeks of February were one long blizzard through which Gracelyn moved blankly, impelled by the needs of the animals on their ranch and on Maggie's ranch. Every day, though she seemed to wake to the sound of Emmy stirring in her crib, it was the bleating of hungry sheep that filled her ears, hour after hour, as she and Zandy or she and Maggie tried to keep the herds near shelter, to find a dry spot for feeding, to break a trail for the pregnant ewes.

Her clothes were always wet and filthy. She came into the house from milking with the buckets held well away from her, and she stripped before she even strained the milk. And when she had set the dirty strainer aside, she sank to a chair, lost in a miasma of sheep and fatigue and the grey numbness that had settled over her in the emergency room at Brandon.

"Gracelyn?"

She started up. "What?" She shook her head and looked up at Zandy.

"I've got to go out on a call. I shut the chicken house. The outside work is done. We need wood for the stove, though."

She hadn't even heard the CB. She stood up and looked down at herself. She was wearing long underwear and heavy wool socks. She stumbled into the bathroom. In the mirror over the sink she saw a face she scarcely recognized. Her hair was the color of a lion's mane and showed the same disorder. Her eyes seemed to be browner than ever, lost in deep sockets that reminded her of the old skulls in the bone pile. She washed her face in cold water, feeling the boniness under her hands.

Zandy came in and set a box of veterinary supplies on the table. "Is Maggie's work all done, too?" Gracelyn asked, "Or should I go down and help her finish up?"

"Her work's done for now, but she's going to Denver tomorrow to get Josh. I told her we'd do both places for a couple of days." His tone was impersonal, as if she were just someone who worked for him.

"Can Josh walk?" Her tone matched his.

"Only on crutches. He broke both the tibia and the fibula in his left leg. They had to fasten them together with a metal plate. He'll be in a cast for months."

Zandy didn't seem to be in any hurry. He sorted the supplies slowly. She wondered what he was thinking about. Did he see Emmy as she did, every day, everywhere?

In the milk cow barn with her head against the Brown Swiss, she could see Emmy's red curls from the corner of her eye as the little girl bent to play with Crybaby. Before she reached the chicken yard, she heard a little voice calling, "Here, shickie, shickie." And in the crib in Emmy's Addition, the little hand reached toward the carved animals on Old Daniel's mobile, clicking them softly against one another.

"Where do you suppose Old Daniel is?" she said.

"I've been asking around. A fella who's helping out at Miller's place said Daniel had talked some about wintering in New Mexico this year."

I hate for him to have to find out about Emmy. She only thought the words. She and Zandy had not mentioned Emmy's name since they had planned the funeral.

After Zandy was gone, Gracelyn put her outdoor clothes on again, and she and Pete went back and forth to the garage. The coal had been long since burned up. Gracelyn hauled armloads of wood; Pete trotted along with her on his three legs. Even when the stack behind the stove was fully replenished, she hated to stop. The wood was her last excuse for being away from the house.

The chores were like a stair railing. She pulled herself upward through the days, one step at a time, grasping at the chores through habit, forgetting them as soon as they were done, planning nothing until the next chore demanded that she focus for a few moments.

She leaned against the hood of the broken Subaru, which Zandy had towed home. The evening was calm. Maybe the three-week storm was over. The clearing sky brought icy air, and her toes and her cheeks tingled with frost. She rubbed her cheeks with her hands. If she went in, she would sit in Emmy's room.

She knew she shouldn't go and sit in Emmy's room the way she did each night, but the rest of the house was so empty. Even when Zandy was home, it was empty. He sat in the big chair in the living room reading his sheep manuals and the woolgrowers reports. He seldom spoke. At nine, he would tip the recliner forward and pull on his boots.

"I'm going to check the sheep," he said, every time.

And when he came back, he drank a glass of milk, used the bathroom and went to his bedroom. It had really always been his bedroom, bare and square the way he liked it. She only went in there now to make the bed or to do the books. Her pile of blankets was folded in the daytime at the end of the living room bed. When she got cold in Emmy's room, she settled in the living room and waited for sleep to come, for the night to pass.

She couldn't remember what she did when Zandy was away in the evenings. It seemed that the laundry was always folded and in its proper place, and there was cream to send to town, and cheese—so much cheese since it was winter and there were no bums to feed. She didn't recall making all that cheese.

Sometimes, when she saw three or four bowls of cheese in the refrigerator, she fed the new skim milk to the chickens.

Pete nosed her side. How long had she been standing there? "Let's go for a walk, Pete. The moon is out."

Pete was silly with joy as they started up the hill: He

went looping through the snow in wide swings around Gracelyn. She followed a trail the tractor had made, peering into the night, seeking the beauty she remembered, but she saw no depths of shadow, no variation in shade. It was simply dark.

An aching sense of loss pierced the numbness. She had wanted to show Emmy how beautiful the night could be and teach her how to see shades of color in the darkness. But there was nothing in the darkness, no color but black. She turned back down the hill. Entering the house, she went to sit in Emmy's little chair.

Maggie said, "Josh is exhausted from riding in the pickup all the way from Denver with his heavy cast propped up, with his foot resting on the dash." Gracelyn and Zandy stood with her outside of Josh's bedroom door. Maggie tapped lightly, but there was no answer. "I guess he's asleep." She turned to them. "He tried a joke or two as we drove, but he couldn't keep that up, so he just listened to the radio and scowled out the window." She grinned at Gracelyn. "It was a real pleasant journey."

They left Josh there asleep and helped Maggie feed her sheep. When they came in for supper, Josh called out, "Come see me."

Gracelyn went into the bedroom. Josh's leg was elevated on pillows, but he swung it around and sat up on the edge of the bed, the leg aslant. He held out his hands to Gracelyn.

She took them and met his eyes. There was no need for words. He suffered with her. When she could no longer endure the pain in his face, she turned to leave the room. Zandy was standing in the doorway watching them, and for a moment his eyes were bleak. But then he stepped forward and said, "I'm sorry you're all banged up, Josh."

Josh's face twisted in a wry grin. "I rode the wrong horse, buddy."

Maggie said, "Come have a cup of coffee, Gracelyn, and let Josh and Zandy talk. Josh and I are sick of talking to each other."

Gracelyn allowed herself to be pulled along to Maggie's

kitchen and seated in a chair. It seemed that ever since the ride to the hospital in Brandon, it had been Maggie who moved them through the days. She had practically arranged the funeral, calling all the people and planning the food afterwards. Now she was bustling around the kitchen putting cookies on a plate, setting coffee mugs on the table. How could she just go on like that? Didn't she care that Emmy had died?

Maggie filled the cups and sat down at the table. She took a sip and then said, "Honey, I'm kind of worried about you. Zandy tells me you're still sitting in Emmy's room every night."

Gracelyn looked away. "Zandy shouldn't talk about me to the neighbors."

"Gracelyn, I'm not some stranger. I'm your friend. And I care what happens to you. He says you just sit. You don't cry. You don't even draw."

"I can't draw."

"Have you tried?"

"You don't understand, Maggie. There's no point in my picking up a pencil. That's just doodling. Maggie, I can't see. I can't *see*, Maggie."

Maggie didn't reply. Gracelyn thought, *She doesn't understand. She really thinks that picking up the pencil is the important part. She doesn't know what I mean when I say I can't see.* Gracelyn sat in misery. *Dr. Carlson would know what I mean.* But she was silent because there was no way to make Maggie understand her other loss. They drank their coffee. Finally Maggie said,

"Don't you think it might help if you put Emmy's things away? It only keeps you from accepting her death to sit in there and pretend that she's still alive."

"I don't."

"It would be better to send the baby things to Suzanne . . . or even Arminda."

Gracelyn's breath hissed as she drew it in sharply. "I won't." She glared at Maggie. "How dare you suggest giving Emmy's things to that tramp?"

Maggie blinked. "Gracelyn, I didn't mean to upset you. I just think it's time for you to get on with your life."

"Don't you want to remember Emmy, Maggie?"

"Oh, honey, none of us on Plum Creek will ever forget her." Maggie's eyes filled with tears. Gracelyn felt the numbing grey cloud settle back over her as she watched the drops spill and run down Maggie's cheeks.

February was gone and March nearly so. Gracelyn stood by the barn looking at the hill behind it.

"What do you see?" Zandy asked.

Nothing, she thought, *The hills have no weight, the gulleys have no depth*. But she said, "Green grass at the edge of that melting drift."

"Spring comes regardless," Zandy said in an odd voice and turned and walked with her to the pickup. Gracelyn matched his silence, feeling strange. Emmy seemed to be right beside her, and Zandy seemed to have gone away. She was relieved to find Maggie's truck by their gate.

"Hi," Gracelyn called as she slipped down from Zandy's pickup. "Have you brought me that cranky old bullrider to babysit again?" She smiled at Josh, who came almost every day now to visit and to help her in the house.

Maggie grinned, "I'm going to owe you a lot of hours of cleaning sheep pens for taking him off my hands."

"Thanks a lot," Josh said, lowering himself awkwardly from the truck onto his crutches.

"He's a pretty good butter churner," Gracelyn said, "and he's re-varnished every chair in the house."

"Keep him busy," Maggie said and headed back toward her ranch.

Zandy was leaving for town. "I should be back by lunchtime," he said to Gracelyn.

"Fine," she said, holding the gate for Josh to hobble through.

When Josh was seated in Zandy's recliner where he could elevate the leg and the heavy cast, Gracelyn took him a cup of coffee.

"Sit down a minute," he said. "You and Maggie are always doing something. You make me nervous."

"Well, Maggie and I are never caught up."

"Sit down anyway," Josh said. "I want to talk to you."

Gracelyn sat on the edge of the living room bed. Was he going to talk about Emmy's room, too?

But Josh had something else on his mind. He said, "Don't you think it's about time you let up on Zandy?"

"What do you mean?"

"Don't give me that blank stare, Gracelyn. You must know that your voice alternates between venom and icicles when you talk to your husband." He shifted in the chair to look directly at her. "Why don't you give him a break? He's not to blame for Emmy's death."

At that moment, Gracelyn hated Josh more than she had ever hated anyone, even her father. She could hear the edge to her voice as she said, "Are you saying that Emmy's death was my fault?"

Chapter Sixty-Nine

THE recliner slammed forward as Josh sat up. "Good God, no! You did everything you could. Maggie told me all about it. What I'm trying to say, Gracelyn, is that no one is to blame."

"Zandy was gone."

"Be fair. How could Zandy know that Emmy was going to get sick that night?"

"He doesn't care anyway."

Josh's face turned bright red, and he was almost yelling at her, "Are you blind and deaf, Gracelyn?"

"What do you mean?"

"Your husband is a walking scarecrow, and he hasn't made a joke since the night your baby died. And you just sit in that goddamned room as if it were some sort of shrine."

Gracelyn clutched her hands tightly together in her lap. "You know," she said in a cold voice, "it's really none of your business."

Josh reached down beside the chair and grabbed hold of his crutches. Struggling to his feet, he picked up his hat and his coat. Leaning on one crutch at a time, he put the coat on. Then he made his way slowly to the door. Gracelyn heard him open it. She got up and went to the kitchen.

"Where are you going?"

"Home," Josh said.

"You can't walk three miles; you have a broken leg."

Josh met her eyes. "That's really none of your business," he said and went out the door. Gracelyn followed him.

"That's crazy, Josh. You'll hurt that leg all over again. How can you heal if you do something so senseless?"

Josh just gave her a long look and kept on hobbling toward the gate.

"Josh, you stupid, crazy cowboy, you can't do this."

But he kept right on inching along without another word to her. Gracelyn watched him as he started downhill toward the bridge. Then she wheeled and ran inside.

Grabbing the CB transmitter, she called for Maggie, breathing a sigh of relief when Maggie answered after the second call. "Maggie, come and get Josh. He got mad at me and he's walking home."

Josh didn't come back. She missed him, but she was relieved not to have to talk to him, because he was right about Zandy. Zandy had stopped joking, and she had never noticed.

Zandy went about his work with a fierce intensity that was like a thick wall around him, and when he stopped to rest, he only looked toward the bluffs for a moment or two, and then went back to work. He never joked about anything. He seldom smiled. He spoke only when it was absolutely necessary. He never mentioned Emmy.

And now, during those times when Gracelyn wasn't lost, deaf and sightless, in her own fog, she watched her husband and saw him get skinnier and grimmer. One day, as he bent over a ewe, the sun sparkled on new silver hairs in his red thatch. Gracelyn's throat ached. She turned away and clutched the railing on the fence. She should never have blamed him. Emmy's death was her fault.

When the shearing crew came along the third week in April, they were short-handed, so Gracelyn tied fleeces, listening to the normal, foolish conversation among the men as if it were a foreign language. Zandy never once joined in the kidding.

I owe Josh an apology, Gracelyn thought one night after the shearers left. She was sitting in Emmy's room. She looked at the little monkey. Then she went to the kitchen for a paper sack. She put the little monkey in the sack and wrote Josh's name on it. When Maggie came by again, Gracelyn gave her the package for Josh.

At the end of April, there were birthday cards in the mail, marking her twenty-fourth birthday. Her mother and Suzanne and Arminda and Annie kept writing, even when she didn't respond. She didn't care about her birthday.

Lambing started the first week of May, and Zandy and Gracelyn worked side by side, their conversation so economical they could go for hours with only a word or gesture.

As Emmy's birthday approached, Gracelyn felt as if she were suffocating in the grey cloud. She couldn't sleep; she didn't eat.

Every step to feed Soot or the chickens took an effort of will that left her shaky. When she reached to pull the cow's teats, her arms seemed elongated and heavy. Sometimes, she just leaned against the side of the cow.

Maggie came to talk to her. *Bless Maggie. She doesn't mind saying Emmy's name.* "Remember how she walked at her first birthday party?" Maggie said, and for a moment, as they talked about the little girl, the cloud lifted away from Gracelyn.

"Nobody ever mentions Emmy in a letter," Gracelyn said. "Suzanne and Arminda write about their little boys. Mother never speaks of babies at all. Nobody talks about Emmy."

"It's hard," Maggie said. "They don't want to hurt you."

"It hurts more to think that no one remembers her; that for everyone else, she's just gone."

"I think about her every day," Maggie said. Gracelyn felt an overwhelming rush of affection for her neighbor.

"And Josh thinks about her. He cried when I gave him the monkey."

Gracelyn stared into her coffee cup, feeling odd. She was so grateful to Josh for crying.

Maggie said, "I wish Zandy would give in and cry. This thing is eating him up inside."

Gracelyn said, "He won't even talk."

"I think the vet calls are good for him now," Maggie said. "At least he can get away for awhile and see that the world goes on." *The world goes on.* Gracelyn did not want to think that the world could just go on.

Gracelyn's back and legs ached as she labored in the lambing pens. It seemed that every difficult ewe in the drop bunch had decided to deliver on Emmy's birthday.

Gracelyn helped Zandy perform a cesarean on a ewe who couldn't deliver. She pulled lambs. She wrestled with stubborn ewes to make them let their babies nurse. It rained and they spent hours rubbing lambs with sacking and setting up heat lamps. The crowd in the bum pen increased by the minute.

By the time the day was over, Gracelyn and Zandy were too tired to eat supper. Zandy sat down in the recliner and fell asleep. Gracelyn collapsed on the living room bed. *What is the point of all this?* She drifted toward sleep thinking of being with Emmy.

Gracelyn rode an erratic elevator. Sometimes she remembered a cute thing Emmy had done and her spirits rose with the memory. But when she glanced at Zandy, his somber face reminded her that Emmy was gone. Then one day, standing near a group of new lambs, Zandy suddenly clapped his hands, startling the babies into action. He smiled as the lambs scooted down the hill, their stubby little tails bobbing. Watching the lambs, seeing Zandy smile, Gracelyn felt the elevator plunge, taking her into a dark, lonely place.

Sometimes when they worked side by side and their hands touched, Gracelyn wanted to lean against Zandy. She needed his arm around her. But his body was stiff beside her. She could not chance it; could not bear it if she moved toward him and he backed away.

He asked at dinner one night, "What do you think we should do about summer herding?"

"I'll go up there," Gracelyn said. For a moment every memory they had about the summer pasture shimmered in the air between them. Zandy's fingers curled slightly as if he grasped at something. But the moment slid away and Gracelyn said, "I'll take Pete."

Chapter Seventy

Oᴸᴰ Daniel did not return until after the flock was in summer pasture. "Went clear down to Mexico," he told Zandy and Gracelyn as they stood beside his pickup on the first day he drove into the yard. "I didn't know about the little girl."

Zandy hired him to help with the farming. Gracelyn worked in the fields too, until chore time, then did the chores, fed the bums, saddled Soot, and rode to the sheep wagon with Pete trotting along behind.

She bathed in the tank, ate supper, and walked around the herd. When she felt Emmy's hand in hers, she stood still and let the pain flood her. The pain eased faster than the depression that came when she refused the pain.

One June night, the clouds rolled over the bluffs. A violent thunderstorm deluged the summer pasture, and memories of her last night in the wagon with Emmy pounded her like hailstones. Unable to endure her thoughts, she ran out into the storm screaming, clenching her fists, and howling with the wind. She screamed until she was exhausted.

Old Daniel showed up at the summer pasture on an evening in mid-June. He greeted Gracelyn, but refused refreshment. Settling himself on the step of the sheep wagon, he took out his pocket knife and a piece of wood. He whittled quietly. Gracelyn sat on the bed and watched him. After a while, he began to speak softly, as if he were talking to himself.

"Long time ago, when I was about the age of the Doc, I had a little bunch of sheep on a small spread in South Dakota."

Gracelyn caught her breath. No one had ever heard Old Daniel say where he came from. She didn't speak. Old Daniel went on whittling and speaking in that low rumble, as if he were riding a slow freight back into his memory.

"I married a girl from Sonora. Her folks had been working sheep for a rancher outta Belle Fourche."

A pile of shavings grew under the wagon tongue as Old Daniel whittled. "We had a little boy." Gracelyn's stomach tightened.

"I was lookin' to upgrade my herd, and I bought me a big new ram; a strong feisty buck with a head of curved horns."

Old Daniel stopped whittling for a moment and looked out over the sheep. Then the knife began its whispering strokes and he took up his story again.

"Young Daniel was like Emmy. He wanted to be with his folks, and he trailed us out to the barns and lambing sheds like a pup. She . . ." the old man's voice faltered . . . "Juana picked him out of the lambing pens and cleaned him up when he dabbled in the chicken's milk. He was always laughing, always ready to try something new."

Old Daniel turned the piece of wood between his fingers, looked at it for a moment and began to whittle again. Gracelyn gripped her hands in her lap.

"One day, the little fellow wandered away from us and climbed into the ram's pen." Old Daniel stopped his knife and was silent for a long time.

"Afterwards, she just faded away. Flu got her down that winter, and she didn't try to get well. Her folks took her body down to Sonora to bury it. The boy stayed behind in an old cemetery out there near my place."

He cut away at the wood again, silent on the doorstep. He didn't say anything else until he got up to leave. "You don't ever forget," he said, "but you go on." He turned and offered Gracelyn the lamb he had carved. She took the lamb, holding his hand with it for a moment. "Thank you, Daniel, thank you for telling me."

The summer became a time of bitter contest. Zandy seemed determined to wrest everything he could from the land, and Gracelyn joined him.

She drove the truck; she improved her handling of the tractor, letting her thoughts of Emmy be engulfed by the engine's roar. She loaded bales; the few inches of her skinny, brown arms that stuck out between the cuffs of the old plaid shirt and the edge of the heavy canvas gloves were scarred and scratched by the hay.

Her work clothes were wearing out. She never went to town. Zandy did the shopping, and she didn't mention clothes. It didn't matter.

The sun beat down upon them all day long. The temperature was ninety, ninety-five, ninety-nine, one hundred and two. Her body became sticky with sweat and then crusty where the hay dust dried on it. Under the hat she wore, her matted hair grew damp, stinking of the sodden leather hatband.

But the days were easier than the nights. Gracelyn could not sleep on the mountain. When the sun had gone beyond the bluffs and the flat grey dusk descended, questions swarmed like gnats.

Why? she asked. At first it was only, Why did Emmy die? But as the summer nights went by, the question broadened to include all the pain and suffering she had seen from the beginning of her stay on the ranch, and then broadened again, to include her father and Arminda and her mother.

She could not sleep, she could not write a letter, she could not draw. Gracelyn walked the dark hillside, stumbling until she had learned its contours. When the moon was up, her questions were angry. How can you punish us with pointless beauty?

How can you expect us to preserve life when death is all around? How could you give me a child to care for and give me no control, no power? What do you want from me? What else have I to give?

And gradually, as the summer passed, and there were no answers except for the orderly passing of the night, the owls crying as they hunted, the stars in regular patterns against the blue-black sky, and the cool air that wafted from the scrubby bushes in the draw beyond the wagon, Gracelyn began to give up the questions.

She learned, like the sheep, to protect herself against the darkness. Bunching her emotions, pulling herself together when her grief descended, Gracelyn waited for the light. When the inner darkness eased, she spread herself out as the sheep did, seeking sustenance in the morning.

When she saddled Soot each day and rode back to the ranch, Zandy met her at the barn, looking tired. "Any predators?" he asked.

"Only the owls," she said. *Only the questions,* she thought. "Just the owls," she repeated as he began to unsaddle the horse.

Zandy had an accident. "I don't know what happened," he told Gracelyn. "I must have spaced out for a minute. I woke up in a ditch with the nose of the truck against a fence post. I'll need money to get it fixed."

"Thank God you weren't hurt," she said, and for the first time in the seven months since Emmy's death, Gracelyn put her arms around her husband. He did not resist, but he did not respond. She dropped her arms and went to her desk to write the check he wanted.

Josh appeared one day, without crutches, but limping and using a cane. Gracelyn talked to him about Zandy. "I don't think he's getting over Emmy."

"He talks to Maggie about her once in a while," Josh said. "Give him time. Everyone heals at his own rate. Look at me. Those medicos said I'd be all healed by April."

Gracelyn was thinking, *Zandy shouldn't talk to Maggie. Emmy's our baby. He should talk to me.*

But she didn't say anything to Josh, just picked up the tail end of his conversation and remarked, "I hear they've asked you to be rodeo announcer at the fair. You gonna do it?"

Josh flushed. "I dunno. Maybe I ought to stay away from rodeos." He was quiet after that and soon went home.

One morning in mid-August, Gracelyn decided to move her desk into Emmy's room. She could do her books there. But she hesitated before making the move. Maybe Zandy wouldn't want her to work in Emmy's room.

She waited until they had finished lunch. Zandy started to leave the table. Gracelyn swallowed and took a deep breath. "Wait," she said, "I want to ask you something."

Zandy stopped.

"Would you mind if I moved the desk into Emmy's Addition?" Her voice stumbled on the name.

Zandy's face grew very red. His eyes seemed to go slightly out of focus. He swallowed. "Do what you want with the desk," he said, and left the house.

The only way to make room for the desk was to take down the crib. When Gracelyn first realized that, her heart began to pound, and she had to sit down on the little chair. She huddled there until nearly chore time before beginning to take the crib apart.

She put a hook in the ceiling and hung the mobile on it. She dismantled the crib slowly and, when she was finished, slid the crib and the mattress out of sight under the bed in Zandy's room.

She moved the desk and her chair into the space where the crib had been. Then, holding her breath, she lifted the sketch of Emmy from the wall in Zandy's room and took it to Emmy's Addition. She hung it over the desk where she could see it whenever she raised her eyes.

But that's not fair to Zandy. She stepped into the living room and, grasping Zandy's big recliner, scooted it through the door into the baby's room. She pulled the chair into a corner, facing it toward the wall where the sketch of Emmy hung. Her picture of Crybaby and the kittens was on the side wall. *Two pictures. Only two pictures.* She folded her arms around herself until that pain eased, then she put Zandy's sheep magazines in the box and set it next to the chair.

She could not bring herself to empty the drawers of Emmy's toys and clothes. It was chore time anyway.

Zandy never mentioned the changes she had made. Gracelyn found an empty milk glass by the recliner one morning when she returned from sheep camp or she would never have known he had been in the room.

She liked to rest in the recliner while she mended clothes or wrote letters. She was trying to respond to letters now. Annie had been a faithful correspondent, keeping up a steady stream of small cheerful notes. She had asked only once about Gracelyn's art work. Sick with the pain of it, and unable to explain, Gracelyn had answered bluntly, "I no longer draw." Annie had not harried her. She simply wrote every week.

Josh sat in the recliner sometimes while Gracelyn worked on the record books. He had decided to take the rodeo announcer's job. Maggie was pleased. "That will get him out of our hair for a whole week," she told Gracelyn.

Josh grinned at them. "Gracie likes me in her hair, don't you, Gracie?"

"Don't call me Gracie."

The sheep sold well. At Maggie's insistence, Gracelyn drove with her to Brandon and bought new clothes: jeans and shirts and boots for winter. As they passed the little cemetery on the hill, Maggie slowed her truck. "Do you want to stop?"

Gracelyn shook her head. Zandy had gone there with Maggie to clear the weeds around Emmy's grave and plant a rosebush. Josh had told her that. She looked away from the hillside and said nothing. Maggie drove on by.

Everyone on Plum Creek swung into the fall and winter work. Zandy turned the rams in with the ewes, starting a new cycle.

"Would you like to go to Florida and see your mother for Thanksgiving?" he asked one snowy evening. "We can afford a ticket." He was sitting at the table mending Soot's bridle.

Gracelyn turned from the sink. He hadn't suggested that they go together, and he didn't say anything else. Finally, she said, "No, I'll just make dinner for the Plum Creek family." Zandy shrugged and went back to pushing the awl through the leather strap.

When Thanksgiving was over, the year slid steadily toward Christmas, taking Gracelyn and Zandy downhill with it.

Chapter Seventy-One

GRACELYN'S father called and waited while Maggie drove to Gracelyn and Zandy's place to bring her to the phone. "Gracie, we want you to come to Colorado for Christmas."

And see their small son, just now beginning to crawl? She couldn't bear it. "Daddy, I can't get away. Zandy has no help, and we feed every day."

Gracelyn's mother called and asked Maggie to have Gracelyn call back. "Gracelyn dear, why don't you and Zandy come to Florida for Christmas?"

And add her mother's pain to her own? "Mother, Josh's leg isn't healing well. We're still helping Maggie feed sheep."

Zandy's mother called. "Would you and Gracelyn like to come to Oregon for Christmas?"

When Zandy asked her, Gracelyn said, "What do you want to do?"

He said, "Except for my mother, they're all strangers to me." They decided not to go to Oregon.

Suzanne wrote a long letter. "We have a new station wagon, and we're going to Phoenix again for Christmas. There's plenty of room for you and Zandy, even with the baby's crib and playpen."

The baby's crib. She didn't even read the letter to Zandy.

Maggie invited them to have Christmas dinner with her and Josh and Old Daniel. They went to Maggie's after they finished the morning feeding. Gracelyn had closed the door to Emmy's room on Christmas Eve. She never even looked toward it Christmas morning.

During dinner, they talked about the sheep and the weather, and after dinner, Josh played his accordion. Zandy and Gracelyn sat on the couch for a while, but Gracelyn knew that she could not stay and listen to the music. The grey cloud which had returned after Thanksgiving was thickening around her head.

They left early to do chores, and each found extra things to tend to, Gracelyn in the barn, Zandy in his shop. They ate a late cold supper and went to bed. Gracelyn lay awake listening to the rustling of Zandy's bedcovers as he turned restlessly in his room. She was still awake when the grey light touched the kitchen windows, but she went through the days that followed as if she were asleep.

As January and the anniversary of Emmy's death approached, Gracelyn slid into an abyss. Her hearing was muffled, her sight dimmed, her memory faulty.

She would wake up momentarily, standing in the cold near the grinding machine with a bale of hay in her hands, looking at nothing. Or, she would hear Josh's voice and realize that she had not understood his words and could not answer.

Josh seemed to be in her kitchen all the time. He limped around, turning her separator handle, carrying out ashes, disappearing from her mind as she sank into the emptiness.

Zandy was somewhere. She knew that he was grinding Maggie's hay now, too, because she saw her own entries under Cash Paid in the record book. She helped him treat Soot when the horse cut his leg on a barbed-wire gate. Someone brought a flowering plant and set it on her kitchen counter.

She did not remember putting a new calendar on her desk, nor turning its pages. But one morning, she found herself sitting in the desk chair, her mind fully clear as she stared at the date. It could not be February twentieth. The last time she had seen a calendar, it had said December twenty-fourth.

She got up and put on her coat and boots. Climbing the snowy slope behind the house, she went on until her burning lungs made her stop. Then she looked up at the sky. It was a clean, pale blue as far as she could see.

She spoke aloud. "You win. Emmy can't live. And I can't die." For a moment she saw Emmy's face in her mind, shining with laughter and surrounded by golden-red curls.

"You can't take that away," she said. "Emmy will always laugh in my mind."

The next day she went to see Maggie, who welcomed her with a long hug. "I've missed you."

"Where did I go, Maggie?"

"I don't know, Gracelyn, but Josh and I have been plenty worried about you both."

"Did something happen to Zandy, too?"

"He's been sleepwalking ever since Christmas."

She went home and found Zandy in his shop. She looked at her husband. He was gaunt. She reached to caress his pale bony face. He stood still; his eyes a flat blue. He had not returned from his own abyss. She curled her hand away from his rocklike coldness, her nails digging into her palm. *I want him back the way he was. I want him to make a joke.* But Zandy moved to the workbench. He collected his veterinary tools and put them in the sterilizer.

Spring came early on Plum Creek. The family was busy with both ranches. The creek rose bank-high at spring runoff and washed out the old bridge to the barn. The five of them worked together one Sunday to build a new bridge. Old Daniel had hauled the planks from town.

Josh's leg worried them. He took the easier chores on both ranches, but spoke of moving into town, where he could get therapy and find lighter work. He'd been talking to the people on the rodeo circuit about announcing at other rodeos. He came every day to chat with Gracelyn. She saw more of Josh than she did of Zandy.

But she thought constantly of Zandy, remembering his patient way of teaching her in the vet hospital in Marlin Springs, remembering his jokes, remembering the times he hugged her as he lifted her from the pickup, remembering his hands . . . tearing away the membrane from a twin's nose, urging a tiny bum toward life, holding Emmy up to his face. Caressing Gracelyn. She had to push away the thought of his caresses.

As the earth woke around her, her body came alive. She wanted Zandy. She yearned to return to his bed. But Zandy was unapproachable, and she could not move back into the bedroom unless he asked her.

She delayed going to bed, often going out with Pete to climb the hill behind the house, and one night, standing there, she saw that the evergreens were footed in shadow and crowned with moonlight. The shadows were not black, but more a Prussian blue. She began to tremble. She stared into the varying depths of darkness at the roots of the trees and saw the powdery light that sifted through the needles, dusting the black branches with a sheen of pale silver. She looked up into the sky and saw that the moon was ringed. Colors misted around the circle . . . silver, ivory, cream, gold, copper and shimmering blends of them all. She looked at the night until the chill spring air drove her inside.

She went immediately to her desk and began to draw. She could see the tree in her mind as her pencil raced. The moon hung inside her memory, a gauzy glow behind its translucent veil. She sketched until her fingers cramped and she was shivering in the cold room.

In the days that followed, she carried her sketchpad everywhere, sketching anything, everything. She drew the line of tiny ants that trekked to her sugar canister. She drew a mosquito that landed on her arm while she milked cows. She drew the cows, Crybaby, and her grown-up cats and their kittens. She sketched Pete asleep, awake, scratching his belly with his hind leg, urinating against the tractor wheel. She drew the tractor and the hay grinder. She drew the heavy ewes and looked forward to lambing season and all the new babies. Whenever there was a moment for resting, she used it instead to sketch. Crazy with new sight, she sketched frantically, recording all she could while she could see.

Finally, her frenzy passed and she steadied herself with a

study schedule. She began to read the art books again. She worked on her drawing every evening and in every spare moment. She opened her old class notebooks and did the lessons in proper order, never skipping an exercise nor cheating on the number of practice sketches.

And at last she began to draw the land. *I've earned it. I haven't conquered the land, but it hasn't conquered me. I've earned the right to draw the land.*

She chose a view of the snow-clad blue-shadowed valley stretching away toward the west with the trees along the creek—gaunt and black, but rugged, enduring.

As she drew sketch after sketch of the scene and planned a painting, she could feel her command of her subject and her materials. Her mind reached into the expanse of rough country and drew back all of its cruelty and a hint of the gentleness that would come with spring. *I will send these to Dr. Carlson. These are good enough to send to Dr. Carlson.* The thought gave her a moment of pure joy.

But still, sometimes she simply sat, scarred by pain, feeling Emmy's presence and missing Zandy. He worked from dawn to dark outside and stayed in his shop till after midnight, coming to the door of the room only to say, "Goodnight, Gracelyn."

Once in awhile, he stepped closer to look at the sketch she worked on. Gracelyn's fingers trembled on the pencil when he stood so near. She wanted to reach to him, but she only gripped the pencil tightly and said, "Goodnight, Zandy."

One day, Josh helped her to empty Emmy's dresser drawers and pack up the clothes and toys. They put them under the bed with the crib. They divided the dresser drawers between the record books and the art supplies. Afterwards, Josh insisted that she go for a ride with him in his pickup.

"It's almost chore time," she protested.

"You deserve a reward," he said. They drove to The Silos and drank a Coke and drove home again.

The shearing crew came in April and Gracelyn tied fleeces because she wanted to. She liked to see the sheep emerge from their wooly covers. She knew how much better they would care for their lambs without the thick blankets.

Her setting hens hatched their eggs, and she stood in the sun admiring the little puffs of yellow as the chicks scratched in the dirt, turning away when she heard a whispery echo, "Here shickie, shickie."

The morning of her twenty-fifth birthday, she was in the barn milking the holstein when a truck drove up to the corral. In a moment, Josh limped into the barn.

"Happy Birthday," he said. She finished stripping the cow and stood with the bucket and stool in her hand. Josh held a package wrapped in pink and silver paper.

"Oh, Josh, how sweet of you to remember." She set the bucket and stool on the tool bench and reached for the package. Her hand brushed Josh's and their eyes met.

He took her wrist and pulled her to him, clasping her body tightly against his and putting his mouth to her own. He kissed her hungrily and, dropping the birthday package, Gracelyn embraced him and returned his kisses. Her body pressed forward to his and she didn't stop him as he reached to unbutton her shirt. The touch of his hand on her breast sent shivers through her body. He kept kissing her as he slowly moved her backward toward the pile of oat sacks in the corner of the barn. His hand slid toward her belt buckle and she arched her back to let his fingers slip inside of her jeans.

And then suddenly, clearly, as if it were only that morning that it was happening, Gracelyn saw her father and Arminda coming out of the Lazy-J Motel. *Oh my God.* She jerked her mouth away from Josh's and pulled her shirt close around her, trembling.

"Josh, no. This is not what I want."

"Gracelyn, that's a lie. You do want me."

They stood for a long moment, breathing raggedly. Then Gracelyn said, "You're right. I owe you more than a lie. Josh, you're a good friend, and right now I want you as much as I ever wanted anyone. But I love Zandy. I want to be here if he ever gets over Emmy."

"What if he doesn't, Gracelyn? Can you go on like this forever?"

"I can't leave him," she said. "I want to be here."

"I've waited," Josh said, "to see if he was going to change, but he's not changing, and you have a right to a life, and besides, Gracelyn, I love you."

There were the words she had always yearned to hear. But they were from the wrong man in the wrong time and she wished bitterly that they had never been spoken.

She met Josh's eyes. There was so much pain there that she could not bear to end it that way. Murmuring "I'm sorry. God, Josh, I'm sorry," she stepped forward and embraced him again. He held her close, tightly, and silently until a sound from the door of the barn made them turn. Zandy stood there, a bucket in his hand. Josh dropped his arms away from Gracelyn. Zandy looked at them for a moment and then turned and left the barn.

Josh said, "Oh, my God." He turned to Gracelyn, but she held up a hand and said,

"Go away, Josh. Go home. Go now."

She leaned against the milk cow's stall, gripping the rough wood, biting her lip, reliving the moment when she had first seen her father and Arminda—knowing what she had done to Zandy.

When the sound of Josh's truck died away, Gracelyn went looking for her husband. His truck was near the shop. She walked toward the door, but stopped with her hand on the knob. Zandy was inside, and he was crying.

Chapter Seventy-Two

GRACELYN stood absolutely still. She ached with the need to go to him, but after a long moment, she moved slowly, quietly away. Zandy's grief was too private. He would not want her to see him so naked. Besides, she did not know if he would take comfort from her. She had backed away from him on the night of Emmy's death; she had betrayed him today. He might not want anything at all from her now—or ever again. Gritting her teeth, she turned from the loneliness and despair she heard in his weeping. She ran to the barn, saddled Soot, and took the trail to the summer pasture.

Zandy's tears had released her own, and she wept as she rode: for Emmy, for Zandy, for herself—for Josh, whom she had sent spiraling downward again. And finally, understanding him as she never had before, Gracelyn wept for her father.

By the time she had unsaddled Soot and watered him at the stock tank, Gracelyn was cried out. She tethered the horse loosely so that he could graze, and picking her way slowly, she began to climb toward the bluffs.

Step by step as she climbed, reaching for each rocky handhold, Gracelyn let go of the things she had lost. Finally, she pulled herself up onto a large rock ledge and stood in the cold wind, looking at the land. From the top of the bluffs, she could see the sunlit hills, the shadowed valleys, and the wide plains blurring into the lilac haze of the horizon.

The land was greening again. Even if her marriage was dying, the grass would change from green to gold to silver. Spring snows would mound and melt. Summer lightning would etch the sky. The wind would blow. Autumn would bring russet and olive and raw umber. Winter snow would settle, blue-white in the gullies and lavender under the banks.

I want to be part of it. Even if Zandy doesn't want me. The thought was searing . . . She stood straighter. *Even if Zandy doesn't want me, I'll stay in Montana.* She thought briefly of Annie. *The land endures, Annie. I will stay and paint the land.*

A sound below her drew Gracelyn's attention. Zandy was climbing the hill, Pete scrambling along behind him. Her heart began to pound. When Zandy reached the slope below the ledge, she extended her hand to him. He took it and stepped onto the top of the bluff.

He looked down at her and said, "I thought you went with Josh." A shadow crossed his eyes, as quickly as a high, fast cloud dims the sun for a moment and passes on. "But when I found him, he told me I was a damn fool for thinking you'd leave. Then Maggie told me I was a damn fool if I didn't go home and talk to my wife." His eyes were no longer a flat blue. They were alive with anguish and yearning. They were alive! "And when I got back to the ranch," Zandy continued, "Old Daniel told me I was a damn fool to let you take the horse to the high pasture this early." A tiny grin kinked the corner of Zandy's mouth. "Do you want to make it unanimous?"

Gracelyn grinned at him. "Yep. You're a damn fool if you're planning to fire a good lamb-licker the week before lambing season."

Zandy put his arms around her and pulled her close. He held her there until Pete stuck his nose between them. Then he reached in his pocket and brought out a jar of cottage cheese and two spoons. "I think you ran off without breakfast," he said, offering Gracelyn a spoon. "I'm sorry, but we're all out of Brie." Gracelyn glanced down toward the summer pasture and then met Zandy's eyes, and Emmy was there with them as they remembered.

A wonderful novel you will read, cherish, and lock away in your heart forever...The Good Housekeeping "Novel of the Month" that received more reader acclaim than any other!

PERFECT STRANGERS
LouAnn Gaeddert
_____ 91545-4 $3.95 U.S.   _____ 91546-2 $4.95 Can.

Publishers Book and Audio Mailing Service
P.O. Box 120159, Staten Island, NY 10312-0004
Please send me the book(s) I have checked above. I am enclosing $ _____ (please add $1.50 for the first book, and $.50 for each additional book to cover postage and handling. Send check or money order only—no CODs) or charge my VISA, MASTERCARD or AMERICAN EXPRESS card.

Card number _____

Expiration date _____ Signature _____

Name _____

Address _____

City _____ State/Zip_____
Please allow six weeks for delivery. Prices subject to change without notice. Payment in U.S. funds only. New York residents add applicable sales tax.

Meg— a rising star at a high-powered New York law firm, she has a terrific career as an attorney, and a gorgeous, successful fiancé. What more could she ask for?

Rick— he wants only the best in life: a co-op on Fifth Avenue, control of the hottest account at his advertising agency, and Meg. But is she just another status symbol to him?

Piet— Rick's handsome older brother works the land and shuns the fast life. Meg is drawn to him in a way she does not understand…and cannot resist.

Torn between two brothers and two very different worlds, Meg learns to listen to her heart…and realizes that what's been missing in her life is what matters most of all….

Roses After Rain

by

LouAnn Gaeddert

bestselling author of
Perfect Strangers

When the young woman awakens in the hospital, everyone recognizes her as Amanda Farraday, the selfish socialite wife of Dr. Brent Farraday—yet her clouded memory cannot recall her glamorous lifestyle, nor can she understand why her handsome, desirable husband detests her. The secret lies buried in her true past—a past she must now uncover, or lose her heart's deepest desire...

SHATTERED ILLUSIONS

A NOVEL IN THE BESTSELLING TRADITION OF SANDRA BROWN BY

LINDA RENEE DEJONG